To Ann,

God bless,

Stuart

Goin' Home

(the third Brendan Priest journey)

– Stuart Earl –

www.fast-print.net/store.php

GOIN' HOME
(THE THIRD BRENDAN PRIEST JOURNEY)

A catalogue record for this book is available from the British Library

ISBN 978-178035-700-3

First published 2013 by
FASTPRINT PUBLISHING
Peterborough, England.

Dedication

This book is dedicated to the people who have allowed me to be their minister as they have undertaken similar journeys to Brendan's. I am sure they have ministered to me far more fruitfully than I have to them. My hope is that this book serves as a commentary on what such a journey can entail, and a signpost of hope to the way in which the love upon which the Gospel Good News centres can overcome all difficulties.

Alan's Story: June 6th 1944

The assault on Gold Beach started at 7.37am in the "King" sector. Two battalions (A and D companies) of the 6th Green Howards landed first, supported by the DD tanks of the 4th/7th Dragoons and the special tanks of the Westminster Dragoons. The day's first casualties were suffered by A Company, led by Major Frederick Honeyman, because the water they landed in was so deep that a couple of the men drowned. The rest struggled ashore, discovering their good fortune at landing in a sector where the German defences were weakest, and the coastal strong-points were easily overrun before the troops pushed inland to silence the German batteries.

C Company, led by Captain John Linn, was the last of the four companies to arrive, thirteen minutes behind schedule due to atrocious sea conditions. They were sent on their way by a platoon commander shouting: "Get off the beach, off the beach, off the bloody beach and give the buggers hell!" The delay, however, had given one of the enemy positions not yet overrun the time to regroup, and it now poured its fire down onto the high-water line, where C Company was just coming ashore. 23-year-old Lance Corporal George Postgate, 4390270, of the 6th Green Howards, was one of the 25,000 British soldiers who came ashore on Gold Beach on D-Day. He was also one of the 413 who died on the beach[1].

At exactly the same time as the platoon commander was hurling vulgarities at George and his comrades-in-arms to urge them ashore from their landing-craft, his sister Muriel was screaming and swearing in a similar manner but for a completely different reason. She was in bed at 14 Newport Street, a small terraced house in the Foxheads area of Middlesbrough. It was not because of a telepathic solidarity with her brother nor premonition-grief for his imminent death – she wouldn't find out about that for another four weeks – but because she was in the process of giving birth to her first and only child.

---

[1] The scant details of George Postgate and the action on D-Day are historical fact. His sister Muriel, and the rest of the tale, is fiction. Any resemblance to any members of the Postgate family is accidental and unintentional.

Middlesbrough had been the first English town to be bombed by the Luftwaffe, in May 1940, and had taken a battering throughout the early years of the war, but somehow 14 Newport Street had survived unscathed. Muriel probably wouldn't have noticed if a bomb had dropped in the back yard at that moment, because her attention was focused entirely on her need to get rid of the excruciating pain which eventually, after fifteen sweaty, awful, unforgettable hours of torment, became her firstborn.

Muriel's husband, Bill, was a locomotive driver with the LNER, a reserved occupation. At the precise moment when he became a father, and completely unaware of it, he was on his way back from the station in the middle of town after an exhausting night shift, whistling as he walked, looking forward to cleaning and soaking his soot-grimed body in the tin bath in front of the fire.

But little Alan, as he was to be called, had just put paid to any such dream of relaxation...

June 2012

Chapter 1

It was now a historic tradition. Once, they say, is an event; twice makes it a tradition; three times and it's a historic tradition. Brendan's first and second journeys – down the Americas[2], then round every other nation on the planet in a year[3] – had both begun in the bath. Whilst Brendan's third and final journey didn't exactly start there – it had been in motion throughout most of his second journey, if not before that – it was in the bath that he realised that he might be already on it.

But this journey was going to be very different.

The last two years had been an amazing and hectic experience for the Methodist Minister, now in his early fifties, following God's call on both occasions and being encouraged by the signs of transformation that he saw in himself and others as he and they took God seriously. His two daughters, Ruth and Louisa, had gone in different directions, yet their paths had intersected and their relationships flourished over the last two years as they also found deeper faith and happiness. His old church at Jact[4] in North Tyneside had been on a roller-coaster ride too as they took God seriously and engaged in God's mission work. They'd found that God had a mission which ought to involve a church rather than God having a church that ought to involve mission – and the realisation (that mission came first) had transformed them. The Methodist District Chair, Jack Turner, had also been transformed – from a sceptical and rather navel-gazing structure-man, to someone keen to explore new possibilities for outreach and think "outside the

---

[2] EARL, Stuart, "Thule for Christ's Sake", Arima, 2010, available from the author at s.earl@hotmail.co.uk or from Amazon or Arima

[3] EARL, Stuart, "Brendan and the Great Omission", Arima, 2011, available from the author at s.earl@hotmail.co.uk or from Amazon or Arima

[4] The 10.08 Church in Jact is a fictitious church, in a fictional village, in a fictional Methodist Circuit (North Tyneside). Any resemblance to other churches is accidental and unintentional.

box".

Louisa's fiancé, Ben, was working as a lay minister at Jact, with particular responsibility for the church's interaction with the community. The church was now called the 10.08 Church, because that's the odd time they met on a Sunday morning – and that quirky decision had precipitated a revival of interest and faith-discovery unprecedented and unimagined. Things were buzzing at Jact.

Ruth, now three months pregnant, was back working for Watoto[5] in Uganda, specifically as the co-ordinator of the Brendan Priest Trust, set up after his second journey to administer the $200 million it had raised. The money was now boosting Watoto's work not just in Uganda but in other countries. Ruth's Ugandan husband, Paul, was working alongside her in a job-share.

Brendan had finally got back to Cullercoats in North Tyneside a fortnight ago. He'd spent 365 days hurtling around the world by plane, yacht, sail-boat, kayak, bike, train, Hertz hire-cars – and even ran the last kilometre – to finish with one minute to spare. Now he was relaxing in the bath after his seventh interview for various media in a fortnight – this time for BBC Songs of Praise. He'd shot to fame through his appearances on the American chat show "See Esther", the iconic Esther Blanchett's afternoon "siesta" slot which had championed his cause on both journeys and given him publicity and support beyond his wildest dreams.

Brendan had been given up for dead at the end of his first journey when he was lost at sea in the South Atlantic, but found his way to a remote island and was rescued. It'd happened on his second journey too, when his plane was hit by a terrorist missile. They'd discovered his badly-injured body still strapped to his seat on a beach in East Timor, but it didn't put him off or wreck his plans. Each occasion was probably more stressful for his daughters and Esther than for him, but the whole world had shown interest in his plight and his mission. He'd put the Christian Church's mission back on the agenda once more – especially in its work amongst the world's poorest, and awakened the Church to the existence of its persecuted millions around the world.

---

[5] Watoto is a Christian charity working to give new life and hope to children and communities caught up in the civil war in Uganda and the onslaught of HIV/AIDS. Their website is www.watoto.com.

He lay back in the bath and reflected on how his life had changed: instead of feeling a failure he felt now that he was finally making a contribution to the Kingdom; instead of getting more estranged from his daughters he'd grown much closer – and was thrilled at their faith-development; his previously moribund last church at Jact was now a flagship for new ideas about how Church could be; and his previously flabby body was now trim and muscled. But he had a sore throat and a dry, chesty cough. It had plagued him for much of his second journey. He really ought to go to the doctor and see about getting some antibiotics or something.

He stroked his throat as he mused – and furrowed his brow as he felt how swollen his glands were. Yes, he really ought to get himself checked out – because he felt pretty tired too. He'd put this down to the after-effect of his long days of journeying suddenly having come to a juddering halt – giving his body time to draw breath and start yelling. Yet whilst over the last fortnight his muscles had cramped and ached as he would have expected, the tiredness and sore throat had persisted too. He told himself to ring for an appointment.

The steam billowed – he liked his baths hot. And, of course, he fell asleep...

★ ★ ★

He dreamt that he was standing in a garden. There was a white picket fence at the end, leading to another section of the garden, which extended as far as the eye could see. Beautiful flowers grew in clumps on the grass – like on Teletubbies, he thought, bizarrely. And there was a path, like the yellow-brick road, meandering across the grass towards a gate in the wicker fence. That was where he was heading – he knew that – but he didn't seem to be making much progress. All he could see was the gate in the fence – which was beckoning, inviting, drawing him towards it. He was being pulled backwards at the same time, caught as if on a length of elastic – backwards and forwards. But he couldn't look behind him to see what or who was pulling him back, even though he wanted to be released. He knew, in the dream, that everything was going to be all right.

★ ★ ★

When he awoke, the bath-water was lukewarm, but his perspective on everything was instantly different. His dream was obviously about death – and it chilled him yet excited him all at the same time. What did it mean? What was he supposed to do? Was he misinterpreting it? Was he dying?

Now his sore throat became a threat, his tiredness a symptom of illness not just temporary adjustment. Suddenly that doctor's appointment took on huger implications. He jumped out, looking in the mirror at his throat, now red. Initially shocked and alarmed, Brendan calmed down when he remembered that he'd been rubbing it in a hot bath – no wonder then that it was a bit red...

As he dried himself then got dressed, he began to relax a little. He'd always been prone to hypochondria, but his sore throat through the last year had escaped his usual pessimistic scrutiny because he'd had other things to worry about. Now, with plenty of time on his hands (or had he?) he knew that he could so easily regress back into a hypochondriacal spiral. He'd heard a comedian once joke that early-onset hypochondria starts when you eat your Smarties one by one with a sip of water. Brendan knew that he wasn't as bad as that, but he had a vivid imagination and a little knowledge – a potent combination. Now suddenly he could imagine all kinds of noxious ailments, including ones that put him in a box.

Chapter 2

"Glandular fever."

That's what the doctor said when Brendan eventually got an appointment. He'd looked in Brendan's mouth and prodded his back and stomach.

"Liver and spleen, bonny lad! Usually you get swollen glands, inflamed tonsils, and soreness in your liver and spleen. Does this hurt?" And he stuck his finger hard into a particularly soft bit of back which would have hurt anyone who still had feelings below the neck.

"Ow!" yelled Brendan.

The doctor clucked – not in compassion or apology but in the self-congratulation of a successful diagnosis.

"Have you had glandular fever before?"

"Not that I know of," said Brendan.

"Good!" said the doctor. "That makes it even more likely that you've got it now."

Brendan didn't really see the logic in this – but apparently if you've had it once you usually build up a lifelong immunity to it.

"I'll take some blood," said the sadist in the white coat.

"Come back in a week," he added, after the tubes were capped and labelled. Then he said the words all hypochondriacs long to hear. "You'll still feel the same, of course. There's no cure for it..."

As the tingle went up and down Brendan's spine, the doctor quickly spoilt it. "It'll probably take a couple of months to wear off." Oh, so Brendan only had a short time to revel in actually having a diagnosed illness – he'd better make the most of it.

"Is there anything I should stop doing?" asked Brendan, hoping to be told to stay in bed, not lift the kettle or hoover, avoid washing up, that sort of thing.

"Kissing," said the doctor, with a smirk. "It's highly contagious but only through saliva. Do you get much exercise?"

Brendan snorted – which made his throat sore. "I have been exercising quite a bit recently."

"Well, don't overdo it. Have you done much exercise since the symptoms first appeared?"

Brendan thought back. When had the symptoms first appeared? Probably in the Arctic, 15 months ago, when he'd gone back to visit his Inuit friends at Resolute Bay. Since then he'd cycled nearly 40,000km and broken world records for kayaking. "Yes, I have done quite a bit – but my sore throat started over a year ago. Is it likely to have been glandular fever all that time?"

"Hmm. That's a long time." The doctor scratched his head. "It's a peculiarly persistent strand of glandular fever if that's what it is. It's very unusual for it to last more than a couple of months, though its effects can last for ages – especially fatigue. But not the sore throat or swollen glands – they usually clear up more quickly. Have you had swollen glands and a sore throat constantly over the last year?"

"Pretty much," said Brendan.

"Hmm," said the doctor, unconvincingly. "Come back in a week." Brendan's six minutes were up.

★ ★ ★

It was amazing how many references to death or dying Brendan noticed over the next week. From the usual "deadly serious" and "dead centre" idioms to the more obscure TV reference to "corpsing" by an actor describing how he couldn't stop laughing while filming. The situation in Afghanistan was "grave" and a winning quick single was scored "at the death". No-one else batted an eyelid but for Brendan the death imagery couldn't have been more obvious if a policeman had stopped the traffic, sidled over, got him to lower his window and listed them one by one from his notebook. Brendan noticed every graveyard, every funeral director's and every florist's shop, and thought twice about buying long-life batteries for his TV remote.

He went to the library in Whitley Bay and spent an hour and a half browsing through the medical section, scaring himself silly. He took out a book by an American crime-writer who'd survived throat cancer, but didn't read beyond the second chapter where the author described having his vocal cords removed. He took the book back the next day and browsed this time through the fiction, noticing how many titles referred to death and in the end getting out a humorous book on hypochondria[6]. He was attracted by a comment on the back cover: "This book is capable of startling even the most health-confident into fanatical hand washing." This was his sort of book – in a masochistic sort of way.

Hypochondria had always seemed to Brendan to be a perfectly rational reaction to the gloomy statistics about health – and the unlikelihood of the body's wonders keeping going as steadily as they are meant to. On the walk back from the library, he did a bit of mental arithmetic. He reckoned that his heart by the age of 50 had thumped out two billion beats – and started to wonder how much longer it could go on. Over the half-century of his existence, 30 trillion cells would have replicated themselves properly at least 2,500 times each, so why shouldn't some of them be about to clump together inappropriately, inconveniently and fatally? He took 200,000 breaths a year – surely sooner or later he'd breathe in that rogue virus which would spell the beginning of the end? He'd eaten something like 130,000 meals – how fortunate was he that on no occasion *so far* had he ingested anything deadly?

Brendan had always imagined that it would be a heart attack that would finish him off, despite the terrorist missile attack in East Timor and facing death by starvation or drowning in the cold South Atlantic. Ever since he hit 9.7 on the cholesterol scale at a routine medical 20 years ago, he'd been on Simvastatin, but he'd still been subconsciously waiting for that smack in the chest or the grinding pain in the upper arms which signalled the end of chapter 1 (healthy) and the start of chapter 2 (dying). He hadn't quite got to the hypochondriacal zenith of one writer[7] who believed a heart attack to be so imminent that he always left the door unlocked when he had a bath. Accidents happen, of course – but illness creeps up on you. The abbreviated hypochondriacs' charter starts: "You've been ill long before you notice any symptoms", and ends: "Just as being paranoid doesn't mean that they're not out to

---

[6] DICLAUDIO, Dennis, "The Hypochondriac's Pocket Guide to Horrible Diseases You Probably Already Have", Bloomsbury, 2006.

[7] Alan Coren, allegedly.

get you, so hypochondria doesn't mean that you're not ill".

The rest of the world continued on its merry way, of course. Brendan didn't feel very merry so he subconsciously projected merriness on everyone else just to make himself feel even worse.

Chapter 3

Ruth's EDD (estimated due date) was 12th December. It was more accurate than most such calculations because she was absolutely sure of the date of conception. The only time that she and Paul had slept together in the potential conception period was at Diamantino in Brazil, nearly halfway through her husband's epic kayak journey with her Dad from Uruguay to Trinidad. She'd been with him at Fray Bentos on the night of February 7th, then at Diamantino on March 7th, then again at Grenada on April 10th. It didn't take much working out.

She'd announced her pregnancy to Brendan and the rest of the world via Esther Blanchett's "See Esther" TV show on May 15th, when she was 11 weeks pregnant, and was just emerging from some torrid weeks of morning-sickness. Almost as soon as she'd realised that she might be pregnant, at about six weeks, and had the pregnancy confirmed by a home test and a doctor's visit, she'd started feeling dreadful. She'd heard of some women who never had any sickness, and some who were sick all the way through – so maybe her seven weeks of feeling grotty was about average. She was thrilled about the pregnancy, and regarded the morning-sickness as a means to an end – but it'd still felt awful.

She'd been excited to have her first scan at eight weeks. It was done at Kampala's Paragon Hospital, all paid for by Watoto's health insurance plan. The Paragon was a private hospital with many clientele from the international community in Uganda's capital, and boasted a first-class maternity unit in the south-east of the city. The ultrasound technician played the baby's heartbeat out loud to her – though there were so many rumbles and hisses that it sounded like either she or the baby had chronic wind. It was reassuring to have the baby's heartbeat confirmed, and to be told that the pregnancy wasn't ectopic. She couldn't wait to tell Paul, and that wonderful moment had come at the hotel in Ireland on the morning of the final televised interview, and Paul had been absolutely thrilled. She'd thought that he would be, but it was still great to see him bursting with pride and a desire for the whole world to know. It'd been torture not to tell her Dad till the interview, but lovely to see his tears of joy. Now she was 14 weeks pregnant and very excited about her little bump. The unborn child had been called Nyathi by Paul – which was the Luo word for "baby". She was OK with this, but would ensure that she got equal say in what the child was eventually called.

She and Paul were now on their way to North Tyneside General Hospital (or "Rake Lane" as the locals knew it) for another scan to check for any abnormalities and assess progress. This was where she hoped that Nyathi would be born, and had "put her name down" as soon as she could in the week after her Dad finished his journey.

"I'm *so* excited!" declared Paul, jumping up and down in the car seat as they drove along to the hospital. His enthusiasm wasn't dampened by the queue to get into the car park, nor the half-hour wait for their appointment.

"Hello," said the radiologist. "Please follow me." She led them into a small room. She turned to Paul. "I take it you're Dad?" – at which point Paul burst into tears.

"Yes," he sobbed, laughing at the same time. "It's great, isn't it?"

The radiologist smiled. "We quite often get the blokes crying – you wait till you see the pictures..." She got Ruth to lie down on the bed and reveal her tummy. "Right," she said. "Let's have a look at you." She smeared the goo all over Ruth's tummy, adjusted her headphones and pressed the scanner hard into her skin. "Cor blimey!" she said, alarming Ruth and Paul – but then quickly said, "It's OK. I don't usually find the heartbeat straightaway but this little one just happened to be where the scanner was. And the volume was turned up too high so it was like someone playing the drums! Do you want to have a listen?"

She flicked a switch on the machine and they heard the rapid thud of their child's heart, amazingly quick. "Should it be that fast?" asked Paul.

The radiologist laughed. "Yes, that's perfectly normal. At this stage the heartbeat is much faster because there are so many things happening. Let's have a look..." She fiddled with a few knobs on the machine.

"Hmm. This little one's heartbeat is about 160, which is about normal for a boy – girls are usually a bit lower – but we won't know the gender until about 20 weeks."

"A boy!" sighed Paul.

"And is that better than a girl?" snapped Ruth, jokingly.

"No!" stuttered Paul. "A girl would be just as good." They all laughed.

"Let's see if we can see anything..." said the radiologist. She turned the monitor round so that Ruth and Paul could see. It was all a bit blurry, but then she pointed out a shape. "There! See that? That's probably a leg. Oh look, there's its head. Do you see?" She was almost as excited as Paul. Let's see if I can get a good image... There. Let's see what that looks like." And up on the screen was a static image of their baby. "That looks good, doesn't it? I'll print it off for you." And out came a photo of their child. They couldn't believe it.

"Nyathi," murmured Paul, entranced.

"Is that what you're calling him?" asked the radiologist.

"Yes," said Paul.

"No," said Ruth – and they burst out laughing.

"Now then," said the radiologist. "What tests have you asked for?" They looked at her, puzzled. "Ah, here's the blood test results you had done a few weeks ago. Let's have a look." They waited. "Oh, that all seems fine. The doctor hasn't requested tests for anything."

They still looked puzzled. "What sort of tests?" asked Ruth.

"Well, if there are any signs from the blood test that there's a possibility of Downs Syndrome or any chromosomal abnormalities, they usually ask for a further blood test or even something called a nuchal scan – but they haven't asked for anything so presumably your blood tests were fine." Paul gulped and looked at Ruth. They hadn't thought about any of that.

"Oh, and one more thing," said the radiologist. "I can definitely confirm that it isn't twins – or any more than that."

Paul and Ruth burst out laughing. "Praise the Lord!" said Paul, amidst the tears.

★ ★ ★

They flew back to Uganda the next day. They'd had the scan picture copied, and Brendan and Louisa both had a copy. They'd got another copy for Paul's Mum, who lived in Gulu. They were due in Northern Uganda the following week to check how things were progressing at Bulrushes, which was home for the very youngest children being cared for by Watoto.

Ruth and Paul had been instrumental in persuading Watoto to set up a Bulrushes in Gulu after they'd witnessed first-hand in 2009 the appalling need in the camps but even more so in the countryside beyond the camps. There'd been a Bulrushes in Kampala for several years, caring for abandoned or orphaned babies until they were old enough to join one of the "families" in the Watoto villages. In the villages each family had a house-mother and sometimes another adult helper – and this had been Ruth's job at Suubi when she first came to Uganda. But until they were three years old, the children were cared for at Bulrushes, which had medical facilities for the sickest children, and many nurses and assistants to help feed, clothe and play with them. Watoto had considered it too dangerous to commit similar resources to Gulu until the civil unrest had died down, but through Ruth and Paul's advocacy and Brendan's influx of cash, things had happened quickly.

Gulu Bulrushes had been open less than a year, after a massive injection of cash from sponsorship pledges arising out of Brendan's journey. At its official opening on October 5th 2011, there were already 40 children living there, with only another 20 spaces, all of which had been quickly taken up. Building work was taking place to open another "wing" and that should be completed within the next two months, with plans for Brendan to fly down to open it officially. When Brendan finished his journey last month there were nearly 90 children in a space designed for 60, so the sooner the better.

Paul and Ruth arrived in Entebbe and were met by Jules, one of the Watoto drivers who'd driven Ruth into Kampala when she first arrived in 2007. He high-fived them both and hugged Ruth gently. "Mustn't squeeze da little fella," he said, then erupted into a high cackling laugh that had other passengers at the airport looking across the car-park at them.

After the familiar, slow but sentimental journey up to the city, soaking in the African scenes, smells and noises, they were glad to collapse straight into bed at the Watoto guest-house near the American Embassy. Before they were married there'd been some bother when Ruth and Paul had spent one night in a small single room together because there was no other room available – but all that was history now. They were received back with open arms by Dorothy, the housekeeper, who made a big fuss of Ruth because of the baby.

Tomorrow, they would travel on to Gulu – a long and uncomfortable journey by Landrover. They needed a good night's sleep...

Chapter 4

Ben was very excited. He'd only been the lay minister at Jact for four months, but had already seen some remarkable results. His off-the-wall suggestion, that they make their start-time each Sunday memorable and that they advertise themselves as the 10.08 Church, had fascinated the community and brought them back in droves after their rollercoaster relationship with their local Methodist Church. People's interest had been drawn first by the charismatic Cuban minister drafted in after Brendan left for his first Big Adventure. Caridad Diego and his family took Jact by storm and attendances soared. It was during Caridad's time that Ben had been appointed as Schools Worker to the local secondary schools.

After his contracted two years, Caridad left and another minister arrived who'd been in Fiji for a long time. Unfortunately Cecil hadn't settled, adjusted, listened or bonded in any way, and his five months in charge had seen an exodus from church as spectacular in its own way as the Israelites leaving Egypt. Ben, already in post as a schools worker, felt like Moses pleading "Let my people go!" but the Jact people left of their own accord. When Cecil left, however, it seemed as big a Godsend as the Red Sea parting, and the people had come back. Ben tried to develop the Exodus/Promised Land theme one Sunday and got hopelessly muddled trying to adapt the Biblical story to fit Jact's experience, but everyone knew what he meant and smiled at him anyway. Anything was better than Cecil plodding his way laboriously through Romans word by word. In five months he still hadn't reached the seventh verse where Paul says Hello, which seemed an appropriate commentary on Cecil's ministry, really.

Ben had been able to persuade the teenagers to give the Church another try, and the twice-weekly "Chill" after school was gaining numbers quickly and the 15 laptops donated by the high school were always in demand every Monday and Wednesday for homework, and every other room at the church was occupied with teenagers listening to music or playing games. Over half the pupils at the local secondary school now had special memory-sticks with a big cross emblazoned on them, provided by the church. Every Friday there was an open Youth

Club which regularly attracted over 100 young people and Ben had just started a Youth Alpha Course as part of the Friday night programme. It was all going well.

Ben was even more excited because he and Louisa were getting married on August 4th, and they were wading through preparations for The Big Day. The church people too were getting excited. The whole day was going to be a massive party, from the 9am community fancy-dress football match between the lads and the lasses, through the noon wedding service, to the community barbecue afterwards which would extend well into the evening, with outdoor games and dancing and then fireworks at 10pm, before everyone collapsed in a heap. It was going to be the biggest day in recent Jact history – and dozens of people were involved. People had been recruited to organise everything from drawing up the football teams to arranging how many barbecues were needed to feed the crowds, planning the shopping for the bread buns, burgers, sausages, salad etc., ordering the puddings and drinks from wholesalers, arranging outdoor staging and a gazebo covering for the band, sorting out who would look after the fireworks – and Ben and Louisa were putting together the wedding service itself.

They wanted and needed it to be different from the usual wedding liturgy – but also to be recognisable as a proper worshipful occasion. They both agreed that they wanted to incorporate Jools and his Full Voice Orchestra[8] into it somehow. And they wanted a modern worship band rather than the old church keyboard, which had so much tremolo on it that it reminded Louisa of an old TV programme called "Stars on Sunday". She wouldn't have known about it if her Grandma hadn't videoed every episode when she got a VHS video recorder in the late 1970s, and Louisa discovered the recordings in her Grandma's wardrobe when they were clearing the house. Louisa as a teenager had cringed at the old bloke sat in front of a horribly-false stained-glass window, as he played a quivering chord, leaned into the camera, and whispered in a mellow voice, "We've had a lot of letters this week..." It had given her goose-bumps for weeks.

They'd contacted Jools and the rest of the group, and they were now booked for August 4th and were working on a special "call to worship" as well as a special percussion, breakdance and beatbox compilation for

---

[8] This is the fictional beatbox group of which Ben was a member when Louisa first met him at Greenbelt in "Thule for Christ's Sake".

during the signing of the registers.

★ ★ ★

Last Friday, some of the lads in the Youth Club had come up to Ben. "Hey, Ben. We've got a band called Dead to the World, and wonder if you'd like us to play at the wedding."

He hadn't known quite what to say. He'd thought it highly unlikely that they'd be very good, but agreed to go and listen to them.

They held their practices, they said, on Thursday nights at the Community Centre in Cullercoats, and that was where Ben was heading now. He'd been told that the Community Centre was somewhere behind Mama Rosa's, the Italian restaurant, but wasn't sure how to get to it. He needn't have worried, though, because as he walked along from their flat in Beverley Terrace, he could hear the noise from some distance away. By the front door of the Community Centre it was already ridiculously loud, and when he opened the door it was like being physically attacked. It didn't bode well. But when he was eventually spotted by the band, they stopped playing. The silence was loud now, and Ben's ears hummed.

"Sorry about that, Ben. We're trying out for a Battle of the Bands in town and we need to get used to playing with lots of sound – we don't always do it like this!"

"Good," said Ben. "Otherwise you wouldn't have a chance of playing at our wedding. There's going to be some people over the age of 40 there and they wouldn't survive. So, more quietly please, why don't you show us what you can do? Go on, *impress* me!"

So they did. They'd obviously practised for it. After a "1, 2, 3..." they broke into a funky but rather wonderful version of "Praise my soul the King of Heaven", which climaxed with a saxophone descant during the final verse. Then they eased into a similarly-upbeat version of "Love Divine" which blew Ben away. This time it started with a jazz piano intro and the jazz rhythm continued throughout, with a muted trumpet providing the bridge between verses. It was amazing. Ben didn't have a clue that they were so talented, and was amazed that they weren't famous.

"That's... tremendous!" he said. "I'd no idea you could play like that. I'd be thrilled to have you play at our wedding, but I'd better ask Louisa before I can say for definite. Thanks, guys. What else can you do?" They smiled and played various other Christian songs, usually with sax or trumpet taking the melody, but jazzing it up with portamento or syncopation. One particularly poignant piece had an unaccompanied oboe playing the first verse of the old Easter carol "Now the green blade rises". Because the French tune was set in a minor key, the oboe fitted it perfectly and Ben could sense the hairs on the back of his neck quivering. Then the drum kicked in with a slow repetitive beat da-da-da-dum, da-da-da-dum, da-da-da-dum before the other instruments took their turn. Then, before the last verse, the scruffy-looking 17-year-old playing the oboe as brilliantly as he'd played the guitar produced another unaccompanied bridge before the rest of the band sang, again unaccompanied, "When our hearts are wintry, grieving or in pain, Then your touch can call us back to life again..." When they sang "wintry" the oboe soared high again for the rest of the verse. Ben was transfixed.

"Why don't you play at Church?" he asked. And the band looked amused and pleased at the prospect.

"What, you mean, like, every week?" said the sax player.

"Yes, why not?" said Ben. "And why don't you keep your gear there and practice there for free on a Thursday night. It'll save you a bit of money and do us a massive favour..."

The band members looked at each other, and shrugged their shoulders. "Yeah, why not?"

"Great!" said Ben. "It's a deal!" Then he wondered if he ought to have asked the Church Council first.

★ ★ ★

The following Thursday he asked a few of the Church Council to come down to Cullercoats to listen to the band, having warned the lads beforehand to behave themselves and play some of the stuff they'd played the week before. He'd specifically invited Brenda, the lady who usually played the keyboard, who would be redundant under Ben's plan.

He needn't have worried. Brenda grinned all the way through. It was the same with Sarah Lanleigh, one of the church stewards, who'd been involved for decades at the church but had only been introduced to God by Caridad three years ago, transforming her instantly from being a churchgoer to a worshipper. She couldn't get enough of the music, and seemed to be going through different stages of ecstasy the longer they played. Every different tune was met by an ooooh or an aaaah or some other expression of delight. She clapped after every one, and jumped up and down on a chair like in the old black-and-white footage of Beatles concerts. Perhaps she'd been there when the footage was taken, Ben thought. The other women were impressed too, but managed to keep their feelings better in check. They were all agreed, though – it would be great to have them play for worship.

"They're much better than me..." said Brenda.

"Well, they're certainly *different* from you," agreed Ben, tactfully. "But it's the instruments which are so much better than that horrible keyboard aren't they?"

"Oh yes," said Brenda. "And they'll certainly have the young girls flocking in, won't they?"

"And the older ones!" said Sarah, and they all fell about laughing.

★ ★ ★

The following Sunday morning, the congregation were surprised to see a live band setting up as they came into church. Was this another one of Ben's wild ideas? Would it be cringeworthy, or loud, or what? Ben introduced them and he could see a few eyebrows raised at the name painted brightly on the bass drum: "Dead to the World".

"We will now sing "Praise my soul the King of heaven". Please stand."

And the band started, as they had ten days before for Ben. The saxophone rose and fell. The drums kept a pulse going throughout. The singing seemed stronger and more heartfelt than Ben could remember. And as the saxophone descant subsided at the end of the final verse, everyone spontaneously applauded, including the band. This was definitely how worship should be, thought Ben.

★ ★ ★

There was one other reason why Ben was excited. He'd been invited to a conference in Switzerland organised by the World Council of Churches at the beginning of July, drawing together people from around the world interested in the future shape of the Church. The District Chair, Jack Turner, had told him about it some weeks ago, indicating that countries were being asked to send two representatives – one ordained and one lay – to join the conversation and hear some key speakers. Jack himself had been invited, but had to be at Methodist Conference at the same time. He'd suggested that Ben might take Brendan, his future father-in-law, with him, who'd leapt at the chance.

The paperwork had just come through, as the conference was only a fortnight away. It stated that they'd be staying at the Ecumenical Institute at Bossey, near Geneva, and the key speakers included the British Co-ordinator of Fresh Expressions, the Roman Catholic Archbishop Benedict from Nicaragua, an Anglican Bishop from Nigeria, and Brendan! Ben wondered if Brendan *knew* that he was a keynote speaker...

Before he met Louisa, Ben had only been abroad once – with his family to Fuengirola, where everyone was British anyway. Louisa had swept him off to Uganda last year, where they'd got engaged, and then he'd been flown off in a chartered jet to East Timor when Brendan was lying injured in hospital there. Their last foreign trip of 2011 had been in December, when they'd gone off to Poland to meet up with Brendan, Ruth and Paul and spent Christmas together in a little village called Hel. So the prospect of travelling to Switzerland, seeing the Alps and lakes, and meeting lots of people from around the world seemed like a wonderful pre-wedding adventure. It was a shame Louisa couldn't come too, but she was busy at work and had used up all her holiday allowance, apart from the ten days after the wedding when they would be off on honeymoon, though Ben still hadn't told her where they were going.

The paperwork didn't tell Ben much, because the synopsis of the conference seminars and discussions was full of theological language which didn't mean much to him. He looked down the list of attendees and was relieved to see that there were as many laypeople as clergy. Some people had strings of letters after their name, but many (like Ben) had none. Each delegate was being asked to read some papers before they travelled and to prepare a short description of their own experience of new initiatives in the Church.

Chapter 5

Jack Turner came round to see Brendan the week before they both were off on their travels: Jack to Portsmouth for the Methodist Conference and Brendan to Bossey. Previously, their conversations had been somewhat strained. Jack had only recently emerged from being a rules-and-order man, a Conference-animal who believed in Methodism "as it should be" – the familiar, cosy, safe-if-a-bit-dead Methodism he'd cherished, been ordained into and served religiously. Then, at Conference last year, he'd heard an ordination sermon which had revolutionised his outlook, stirred up a passion for risk and mission which had surprised him as much as thrilled him, and kindled a passion for exciting new initiatives from which previously he would have run away.

The visit was good timing, for Brendan had just come back from hospital.

When Brendan went back to the doctor, he was told that the EBV antibody test had come back negative, but the white blood cell count was abnormally high. So there was something wrong, but it wasn't glandular fever. The doctor had then felt, prodded, stroked, gone "Hmm" a few times, and then donned some plastic gloves and slowly inserted an impossibly-long tube into Brendan's nostril. The tube had a fibre-optic camera, and the doctor watched a TV monitor as the tube disappeared.

"There's a lump," the doctor declared, as matter-of-fact as someone spotting a plane in the sky. Brendan's heart-beat suddenly shot up into the 130s. The doctor looked closely, then retracted the tube with the gentleness of Dyno-Rod.

"It looks to me like a genital wart!" the doctor announced grandiosely, which puzzled Brendan even though he only had a rather rudimentary knowledge of anatomy.

"Aren't they supposed to be... er... down below?" he asked.

"Oh, you can get them in your throat too," said the doctor, with a wink and a leer.

Brendan went bright red. "I can assure you that it won't be genital warts," he said, sounding far too pompous.

"Probably a branchial cyst, then..." said the doctor, explaining that this was some sort of blockage in the anatomical anomaly left over from when we had gills and slithered around in the slime. "It's not very common but nor is it rare enough to feature on the front page of the Lancet," he explained with some relish.

But it did mean that Brendan had had to go for a CT scan, and it was from this that Brendan had just returned, and was still recovering.

Brendan knew the science. A CT scanner was a rotating X-ray machine looking for bumps, lumps and, (let's be honest) tumours from every angle – but he hadn't appreciated just how scary it was. He'd been escorted into a white, clean room that looked like a lab if you're an optimist, like a morgue if you're a hypochondriac – which Brendan was. In the middle was The Monster, sitting there like a huge washing machine which didn't clean your laundry but instead told you how dirty it was. All you had to do was stick your head inside, having been injected with foul gunk which made your tongue feel like it'd been dipped in Dettol. The scan itself might have seemed to some people like a few minutes' restful time while the omniscient machine found out what was wrong. But for Brendan it was half an hour of torture clamped into a white enamel coffin, thinking Cancer and Death (with capital letters).

Afterwards, amazed that he'd survived but feeling like he glowed with radiation like the characters on the Ready Brek advert, he kept getting flashes of panic, with loud noises going off inside his head like the dive alarm on a submarine. There must be several types of hypochondria, he reflected as he gradually calmed down. Some might relish the thought of being inserted into machines and probed by invisible rays, or being opened up and cut apart. But Brendan's hypochondria was the sort which wanted attention but in a *reassuring* way which fondly laughed at how silly and unrealistic such thoughts of illness were.

It was in this context that his conversation with Jack took place.

After the initial polite small talk, and the medical history and descriptions, Jack brought up a different topic. "You know, Brendan, I never really liked you."

"I know," said Brendan with a smile. "You thought I was escaping on a jolly, leaving you in the lurch, running away from my responsibilities. And, you know what? In a way you were right."

"Really?" said Jack. "I'm not sure I was. I was too trapped in my tight little theological box."

"But I *did* want to get away from circuit ministry. I was jaded, fed up, demoralised. When the call came, I was thrilled to have a reason for doing something different, for some excitement. If God hadn't taken me off on that first journey, I'd probably have moved to a different Circuit and been just as useless as I'd been up to that point, if not worse."

"I think I know what you mean. I realise now that I was part of that sausage machine that puts you in at one end, squeezes you tight, and out you pop at the other end – in exactly the expected shape and flavour, because that's the way the system makes you. Thankfully God rescued me from that sort of institutional blandness too."

"Yes," said Brendan. "I've heard that you've had quite a year too. Tell me about it."

"It was at Conference, believe it or not, at the ordination service, and the preacher was our old tutor Richard from Hartley. Somehow, as he told us about the church in Antioch, God whacked me over the head, knocked me flat and picked me up again – and I was changed."

"Good old Richard," said Brendan. "It was Richard who helped me understand my call, through that Study Day he led in the District a few years ago. He seems to make a habit of stirring things up, doesn't he?"

"Yes," said Jack. "He certainly does." They sat back and thought their own private thoughts, companions in silence.

"So what are you going to do now?" asked Jack, after well over a minute.

"I don't know," said Brendan. "I can't really go into Circuit because I don't know what I'm up against medically. It wouldn't be fair for me to be landed on some poor Circuit who might not get value for money. And I don't need a stipend because I've got pots of money..."

"What about helping out at Jact?" suggested Jack. "Ben's doing a grand job, and the Super's helping out when he can, as I am. But having another Minister on hand locally would really help – with Church

Councils, funerals, weddings..."

Brendan sat up with a start. Of course! He could help out without getting in Ben's way – and he could be the one to marry Ben and Louisa! "What an excellent idea! Do you think I could? That'd be wonderful. Would they let me?"

"Well, why don't we ask them? I can swing it at Stationing Committee next week – the medical stuff will clinch it, I'm sure. Then we'll get the Super to call a special Church Council and get the wedding authorisation papers off to the registrars. We should be in time for August 4th. You live in the Circuit anyway, so there's nothing unconstitutional about you being stationed "without appointment" in your home Circuit and "authorised" to conduct weddings. You've been "without appointment" for the last four years anyway."

★ ★ ★

A few days later, surprisingly quickly, Brendan got a phone call from the doctor's. Immediately he feared the worst. They only act with such speed when it was bad news. But it wasn't. It wasn't a tumour the size of a water-melon. It wasn't a tumour at all. It was a branchial cyst. It was good news – but the cyst needed aspirating.

It didn't sound bad when the person on the other end of the phone said it like that. "It needs aspirating." It sounded quite jolly till Brendan realised that it meant stabbing and popping, needles and knives, hospitals and treatment. All of a sudden, it was serious again. It meant going to some place horribly called a cytology clinic. And he heard that he'd been booked in for the following Monday morning, three hours before he was flying off to Switzerland.

★ ★ ★

Brendan turned up at the cytology clinic half an hour early. He'd been a bag of nerves all weekend, and hadn't slept a wink. He'd been on the Internet and learnt that if the centre of the swelling was liquid it was good news. If not, it was bad news. He'd also found some leathery, rough skin at the back of his tongue, which made him think the worst.

He was eventually shown in to a small room containing a kind-looking man in a white coat. "Hello," said the monster, the wolf in sheep's clothing, the conman purporting to be on Brendan's side. "I'm just going to pop this lump you have and see what we've got. OK?" Yes, of course it was OK. Take a knife to my throat, don't mind me.

Brendan shut his eyes while the torturer gave him the local anaesthetic, chatting to Brendan about seeing him on telly, following his progress on both his journeys. If he wasn't wielding a knife, about to cut my throat, thought Brendan, I might think he was quite pleasant.

Then it was over. No pain or discomfort – and Doctor Mengele was waving a small bottle quarter-filled with bright yellowy-green liquid. "Wow, that was a good one!" he exclaimed, as if he was describing a shot at football or a beautiful sunset. "Look at that!"

Brendan didn't really want to, but his attention was drawn to the liquid sloshing around. And it was, clearly, liquid. And that was usually good news, wasn't it? "What happens now?"

"We send this off to the lab and they tell us what it means. We should have the answer in a few days. We'll let you know..."

And that was that. Was it good news? He'd have to wait and see, but right now he had a plane to catch.

Alan's Story:
September 6th 1949

It was a Tuesday, and it was Alan's second day at St. Patrick's Infant School on Lawson Street[9]. He'd been excited in the lead-up to going to school for the first time yesterday but had taken some persuading to do it again. He'd been a bit taken aback yesterday when he encountered the headmistress, who was a nun. He'd never seen one of them before, and had to be hushed when he asked (too loudly) what it was. He'd been further surprised, but not particularly frightened, when one of the first things that happened was assembly, in which one older boy was caned in front of them all for being cheeky. On the whole, it'd been quite good fun. He knew most of his classmates from the rough-and-tumble games they played on the streets. But he'd been surprised when he was told by his Mam at bedtime that he had to go back again the following day. He hadn't realised that this was an ongoing adventure rather than a one-off.

So, on the second day of what would not become an illustrious academic career, Alan was given his usual breakfast of porridge and then sent off to school on his own. His Mam had taken him the first morning, and even come to collect him at home-time, but now he was on his own. As he wandered along the pavements, kicking stones and trying to perfect his whistling, he reflected on Life, like all budding philosophers. The first thing that came to mind was that the family ate a lot of porridge. It was something to do with what his Mam called "rationing", but having never known anything else, the word meant nothing to Alan. He wondered if tea tonight would be that broth again that she made out of bacon bones and pulses. He often felt hungry and wished that he could have a bit more to eat, but he never went without

---

[9] There was indeed a St. Patrick's Infants School on Lawson Street, Foxheads, with a nun as its headmistress. The history and stories of the area have largely been lost due to community fragmentation and housing changes, but much of the details contained in these early parts of Alan's Story are as a result of the research put in by others to gather and record reminiscences from the people of the Foxheads area, and especially those involved in the Northern Echo's "This is the North East" Communigate Project, at www.communigate.co.uk/ne.

a meal of some sort, even if it was only bread. There weren't any fat kids in his street; they were all skinny like him.

Alan's Dad was an engine driver and Alan, though small, was sufficiently street-wise to know that their family was better off than most not only because his Dad was in work but also because he always handed over his wage-packet straight to Alan's Mam. In spite of this, money was always in short supply and often on a Wednesday his Mam would wink at Alan, take him with one hand and his Dad's only suit with the other, and they'd go along to Ernest Hush's Pawn Shop[10] for a ten shilling pledge. It cost ten shillings and sixpence to redeem it on pay day which was Friday. When his Dad got ready to go to the pub on Saturday night he never even knew that his suit had been out of the wardrobe.

The summer of 1949 had been long and hot, and the highlight had been the day they'd gone by train to Saltburn. It was the first time he could remember that he'd seen the sea, even though his Mam insisted that they'd gone last year too. Even though his Dad worked on the railway, it still cost three shillings for two adults' return rail ticket, and ninepence for Alan, so they could only afford to go as a very special treat. His Dad had tried to teach Alan to fish off the pier with hand-lines. After well over two hours, they finally caught one mackerel and thought that they were the best fishermen in the world. His Mam smiled, patted Alan on his cap in congratulation, wrapped the mackerel in a piece of newspaper, and said that they could have it for their tea. They'd gone down to the rocks when the tide went out and found some winkles and mussels. It was the best day ever.

Over the summer, there'd been great excitement in Foxheads[11], because electricity finally arrived[12]. It was all lost on Alan, but he'd enjoyed watching the big Irishmen digging up the pavements and making the deep trench which went right up to their (and everyone else's) front door. He was fascinated by the fact that every room in their

---

[10] There was indeed a shop by that name, as reported in www.kmbro.org/Remember_When_p03.

[11] Foxheads was the name given to a small group of streets in the west part of Middlesbrough town centre, bounded on the east by Marsh Street, on the north by Newport Street, on the south by Cannon Street and on the west by the Gas Tank wall. It got its name from the firm of Fox, Head and Co, established in 1868, which built the nearby Newport Rolling Mills for the manufacture of iron plates.

[12] Electricity indeed didn't arrive in Foxheads till 1949.

two-up, two-down terraced house had one light-fitting – and the light was so much brighter than the old gas-lights. Better still, the kitchen also had an electric socket, into which, yesterday, their first wireless radio was plugged.

After coming back from school, Alan had walked with his parents to Rogers' "Wireless Dealer" shop at 337 Newport Road[13], opposite Parliament Road. They walked back more slowly because his Dad had to keep stopping for a rest. Alan had asked, on one such rest-stop, "Dad, why is it called a wireless if it's got a wire?" He didn't get an answer but he did get a cuff round the ear before they set off again. The wireless weighed a ton and was bigger than Alan. But once they got home, they rushed into the kitchen, plugged it in, and fiddled with all the knobs until the whistle and fuzz suddenly turned into a jazz band! It had been a wonderful evening – only soured by Alan being told that he had to go to bed early because he had school tomorrow. What, again?

He played off-groundy at play-time with his mates, but Sister Agnes, the Big Black Nun, shouted at them when they climbed onto the wall. In afternoon play-time they played tee-mac[14] instead, but again they got told off by Sister when Tommy Greenwood started crying after being smacked on the head. One kid dropped a marble from his pocket, and Alan picked it up quickly and walked off without anybody noticing. It was a really good marble too, a big one with silver flecks. It was another good day.

As he walked home with one of his mates, it was another opportunity for Alan to reflect on Life again.

"D'yer have a good day, Billy?"

"Yeah. You?"

"Yeah."

They walked on in companionable silence, kicking a can.

Alan had, however, already come to some important conclusions

---

[13] This shop really was at that address, according to one correspondent (known only as Frank) in the Communigate local history project.

[14] Tee-mac or tee-allio, was a chasing game with two teams, in which the catchers caught the other team's members by tapping them on the head and shouting "tee-mac". The catchers had a "bay" to put their prisoners in and at least one catcher had to stand guard, in case one of the other team got into the bay without being tee-macked and freed them all.

about Life. The aim of school, he'd decided, was to avoid punishment by not being caught infringing any of the rules. That meant not dozing off, not shouting out, not asking questions in case you should already know the answer, not drawing attention to yourself, and not getting into fights. The aim of Life, though, was to get more (or better) marbles than anyone else.

July 2012

Chapter 6

Brendan hadn't really studied the paperwork sent by the organisers of the conference, but he'd scanned the list of delegates and been thrilled to see Archbishop Benedict's name on the list. He'd met him in Managua during his first journey down the Americas, and been invited by him to speak at an archdiocesan council in front of nearly a thousand priests. It was Benedict who'd rallied the Central American Catholics to support Brendan on his journey, and even persuaded his fellow archbishops to make Brendan a "special envoy" to assist his passage through border controls. It would be wonderful to meet up with Benedict again.

When Brendan and Ben landed in Geneva, they caught the local train out to Nyon, and then a taxi to the 18th century Château de Bossey, set in the countryside 25km outside the city. The first two people Brendan saw were two faces he recognised immediately with amazement.

"Ah, Brendan," said the priest, shaking his hand. "It is really good to see you alive and well."

"Brendan, es bueno verte de nuevo", said the woman, clutching Brendan to her bosom like a long-lost son. She didn't let him go easily. She took his face in her hands and kissed him loudly. Ben stood bemusedly, like an unknowing observer in a filmed street scene.

Brendan released himself with some difficulty from his female admirer, and remembered that Ben was there, looking on. Brendan introduced Ben to them. "And these two people, Ben, are from the bottom of the world. I met them right at the end of my first journey, on Tierra del Fuego in a little village called Puerto Toro which is the southernmost village in the world. Father Segundo here lives in Puerto Williams, and Maria is the lady in Puerto Toro whose house is used for worship and for accommodating strange visitors like myself." He turned back to them. "I can't believe that you are here. It's wonderful to see you again. But *why* are you here?"

"We are here for the conference, of course," said Segundo. "On Isla Navarino, we are experimenting with a different way of doing Church. As the only priest on the island, it is impossible for me to get round to all the villages so we are developing a different pattern which is taking hold throughout Latin America. It is called Basic Church Communities, and Maria here is the leader of the BCC in Puerto Toro. There are twelve of us from Latin America speaking about BCCs."

"That's amazing!" said Brendan. "We're doing something similar in Britain, and Ben here, my future son-in-law, is leader of our version of the BCC. It'll be good for us to compare our stories."

★ ★ ★

Brendan discovered that he was to speak to everyone on the fourth and last evening of the conference, but he didn't really know what he was going to say. His journeys had not really been about new ways of being Church – they were about the primacy of mission, about a global sense of the family of God (recognising the Persecuted Church as brothers and sisters in Christ), and about the need to highlight the plight of the world's disadvantaged majority. But maybe if the Church took all of that seriously, it could change from the moribund and inward-looking institution which it had become in many parts of the Western World.

Maybe he could persuade Ben to join him in the speaking-slot and they could dialogue together about what the Church might look like if it became more mission-minded... As he was working this out in his mind over dinner, he was clapped on the shoulder and heard a loud voice say, "Ah, my special envoy!" He turned in his seat, and saw the beaming face of Archbishop Benedict, whose grin displayed teeth like piano keys, as many black as white. They embraced, and again Brendan introduced Ben and explained who Benedict was.

"It's great to see you again! Are you still watching "See Esther"?" asked Brendan.

"Of course," said the Archbishop. "Otherwise I wouldn't know what my priests are talking about."

"So, you're one of the key speakers here?" Brendan knew that, but he was fishing for some clues as to what Benedict was going to say.

"Yes, apparently I'm regarded as one of the experts on the ecclesiology of Vatican 2 – can you believe it?"

Brendan could believe it, but he didn't have much clue what it meant. "I know a bit about Vatican 2, but not much. Anything I need to know to help me make sense of your talk tonight?"

"It's very simple, really," said Benedict. "The first Vatican Council in 1870 emphasised the Roman bit of Roman Catholic, and the Second Vatican Council in the early 1960s emphasised the Catholic bit. And we're caught in the tension between the two. Vatican 1 wanted to bolster up the Church as a strong institution, properly ordered and tightly controlled, and Vatican 2 wanted to open things up, become much more missional, ecumenical, charismatic. So the priesthood has sometimes over-emphasised the bit about order, and the laity have sometimes felt inhibited and unaffirmed, which is why Clodovis Boff estimates that every year in Latin America 3.5 million Catholics are joining the Pentecostals[15]. What we're trying to do is find a balance between old ways and new ways to keep everybody happy."

★ ★ ★

Brendan found the talk that evening very illuminating. Benedict explained to the Protestant delegates the Catholic background to his talk, using the same explanation as he'd given Brendan at dinner, but then moved into deeper territory.

"Christian Duquoc, the Dominican theologian, likened the divided Church to a broken mirror, reflecting Jesus only in fragments, an incomplete picture[16]. Our task, it seems to me, is to bring those broken pieces together. At Vatican 2, the Church declared itself to be an icon of the Trinity. Hans Küng declared that the three images emphasised at Vatican 2: the people of God, the body of Christ, the temple of the Holy Spirit, are the "fundamental structure" of the Church[17].

"It doesn't sound particularly revolutionary, maybe, but it changed the mindset of Roman Catholicism. You see, the people of God is an

---

[15] BOFF. Clodovis, "The Catholic Church and the New Churches in Latin America", in Sedos Bulletin 31 (1999), pp. 197-199.

[16] Quoted in ed. HÜNERMANN, Peter, "Das Neue Europa, Herausforderung für Kirche und Theologie", Herder, 1993, p.105.

[17] KÜNG, Hans, "The Church", Sheed and Ward, 1967, p.107ff.

entity which goes back long before all structures and hierarchies, from the start making everybody equal[18] in the spirit of Galatians 3. Now again at Vatican 2 the laity were affirmed in a way they'd never felt affirmed previously.

"At the same time, Vatican 2 overturned the exclusivist view that the Church was the only channel by which salvation might be found (extra ecclesiam nulla salus[19]), declaring instead that the Church was not the owner, manager nor often even the essence of the Kingdom of God, but called, as a sacrament or sign of the Kingdom of God, to transform the world into the Kingdom of God.

"This provoked much discussion about the new role of the Church, and in 1992 the Asian Bishops declared[20] that the Kingdom of God is "universally present and at work... wherever God is accepted, wherever the Gospel values are lived, wherever the human being is respected."

"During the 1980s and 1990s, it became clear that the statements of Vatican 2 were prophetic. There were fewer priests, who found it increasingly difficult to preserve the traditional regular pattern of Mass-centred devotional life. At the same time, laypeople were experiencing new spiritual gifts of the Holy Spirit which empowered them and gave them a need to express themselves.

"So, new Basic Ecclesial Communities formed, centred round God's word, organised not according to traditional hierarchical structures but according to the spiritual gifts given amongst the people. This has been a real challenge to the Church. What we've learnt in Latin America, is what Barnabas discovered in the church in Antioch, that there was clear "evidence of the grace of God"[21] in these new BECs, emphasising as they do the importance of the Word of God, of everyone participating equally, of being community-minded, caring and celebratory.

---

[18] Galatians 3: 28 "There is no longer Jew nor Greek, nor male nor female, but all are one in Jesus Christ"

[19] The Latin phrase is shorthand for one of the first doctrines contained in the Catholic Catechism. The original saying by St. Cyprian of Carthage (3rd century AD) is found in his Letter LXXII, *Ad Jubajanum de haereticis baptizandis, section 21.*

[20] Quoted in FUELLENBACH, John, "Church: Community for the Kingdom", Orbis, 2002, p.81.

[21] Acts 11:23

"I know that we will be hearing variations on this theme throughout our conference, but I see in all of our stories a real convergence. Something new and vital is happening across the world, counter-balancing but not threatening the institutional model of Church – and I believe that the Church is at a very exciting point in its history."

★ ★ ★

Brendan was buzzing after Benedict's talk. "That was great, wasn't it?" he said to Ben.

"Dunno," said Ben. "I went to sleep. Too many big words and clever stuff for me, especially after a long day and a big dinner."

Chapter 7

The following day established the pattern for the conference. In the morning there were shared stories in six groups, with laity and clergy segregated into their own discussions, in different rooms in the conference centre – all benefiting from the instant translations, spoken through the head-sets worn by all participants. It was very high-tech, and very efficient. Ben enjoyed these sessions, especially as there were no clergy there – and most people were vaguely normal.

The afternoons were free, but various excursions were offered – the first afternoon it was to Geneva. The second afternoon there was a bus trip to Chamonix, through the Mont Blanc tunnel to Italy and back over the Great St. Bernard's Tunnel and Pass, and returning to Bossey via the lakeside route at Montreux. The third afternoon Brendan and Ben pottered about the local countryside, walking through fields to the little village of Céligny, chancing on its tiny cemetery, where curiously Richard Burton and Alistair Maclean were buried almost side by side.

In the evenings, after dinner, were the keynote speakers.

After the second evening, in which a Nigerian Anglican Bishop described their SCCs (Small Christian Communities – which sounded identical to the BECs) and spoke about the "theological and methodological stages of church empowerment", Ben caught Brendan in the bar and said, "We've got to do something different from all this theology-speak, Brendan – or I'll die of boredom. When it's your turn, why don't the two of us just tell the story of Jact – from your time there, through your journeys and their experiences, to my time there now, and our hopes for the future? How does that sound? Why don't we skip the trip to Lausanne tomorrow afternoon and concentrate on planning our evening's entertainment? You're down for the last evening of all, so they'll all be brain-dead by then anyway..."

★ ★ ★

The following morning, Brendan found himself in the next chair to Segundo, and they got chatting about the previous evening's talk, because they'd both found the Nigerian Bishop helpful in defining where their churches were at. The speaker had described five different church power-models[22], starting with what he called the "provided-for" church where the clergy told the laity what to do, a "parish council" church (which to Brendan's ears described the Methodist Church in Britain accurately) in which the clergy were important in leadership but decisions were taken by a council, then two more stages (the "awakening" church in which spiritual gifts were affirmed and responsibility shared, and the "task-group" church in which laity took responsibility for all that needed to be done) before the perfect church in the speaker's view, which was a "communion of communities", which sounded to Brendan like a cell church.

"So where do you think the Isla Navarino communities are at in all this?" asked Brendan.

"You know, I think that we come out of this rather well," said Segundo. "By accident, or God's grace, we've realised that we must set up small communities of the faithful in the villages, who will largely look after their own needs, week by week – but three or four times a year I go round and spend a weekend with each village, and we celebrate Mass. I consecrate hundreds of wafers, so that they can be used on the other Sundays without me needing to be there, but during the week they meet informally for prayer and Bible study rather than for Mass. Most people find it very liberating, highly affirming, and overwhelmingly empowering. Suddenly they find themselves responsible for thinking about their Christian development and pastoral care, and building up their communities. And they have taken to it really well."

"So you're pretty much at the communion of communities bit, are you?"

"Not quite – because they tend to think of themselves as independent and not needing to join with other communities. I suppose that I am the main point of convergence, as a sort of representative figure and parish leader, but it would be even better if they joined together themselves. The trouble is that they're such diverse communities, spread over a huge area, with some settlements only reachable by boat – and it's really difficult to expect much more from them."

---

[22] These five "stages of church growth" were suggested first by the Lumko Institute in South Africa, as described in PRIOR, Anselm, "Towards a Community Church", Gemiston/Lumko, 1991, pp.17-27.

"And what's Maria's role?"

"Maria's great. She's recognised by everyone at Puerto Toro as their community leader. As you know, most things happen at her house, including a worship and prayer group every evening. She started it up when you were lost at sea, and it's become established now. On Sundays Maria leads the village worship and they share the Reserved Sacrament with liturgy from the Roman Rite for Holy Communion outside of Mass, but it's all done in a very informal manner with everyone taking turns. Instead of the homily, they talk about their reflections on the Gospel, then they have a meal together."

"And how come Maria's been invited to this conference?"

"Well, I was invited because of the remoteness of my parish and the developments that have taken place across Isla Navarino over the last few years – and they asked for a lay rep and I instantly thought of Maria. She's only been off the island once, to the hospital in Ushuaia, but she's never been to mainland South America, let alone Europe. Everything is different and bewildering for her, but she seems to be managing well and has struck up a particular friendship with a lady from Zambia. I think she's feeling reassured that what is happening in Puerto Toro is not wrong, but is actually something exciting and forward-thinking."

★ ★ ★

By the fourth evening, everything had been said more than once, and the general feeling was that there many similarities emerging from what had spontaneously happened at the same time across the world, marking it all as Spirit-led – and that everybody now wanted to go home.

Anticipating this, Brendan and Ben had decided to do something a bit different.

Brendan stood and introduced himself. "I'm Brendan Priest. I'm Archbishop Benedict's Special Envoy and I'm the Church's ambassador to Esther Blanchett (*everybody cheered*). "I won't bore you with all the gory details of my two journeys across and around the world (*everybody booed*) – well, maybe some of the best stories (*everybody cheered*) – but Ben and I have come to challenge you to jump in and have a go."

At that point Ben jumped onto the dais and produced his best street-dance moves, ending with him spinning on his head (*everybody cheered).*

Brendan continued. "Well, perhaps some of us need to not have a go at that *(everyone laughed)*. Thankfully God gives us all different gifts. But hasn't that been one of the major themes of our conference – that actually we are called to recognise one another's different gifts and graces and bind them together within Church in order to speak to the world in whatever tongue or idiom the world around us is using? Where I used to minister, in a little village called Jact, it used to be deadly dull. *(Ben snored into his microphone. Everyone laughed.)* The only people who came to church were people who were over 80 or looked as if they were. *(Ben mimed an old person with a zimmer. Everyone laughed.)* It was like a funeral. *(Ben then began a beatbox version of a funeral, starting with Beethoven's Fifth, then the nails being hammered into the coffin lid, then the minister's words of committal interspersed with amazingly realistic sounds of earth being dropped onto the coffin. Everyone was stunned at Ben's performance and the place was hushed.)* I was depressed and demoralised as a Minister in a place that seemed totally unresponsive to the Gospel, and it was at that point that God called me to my first journey."

At that point a powerpoint slide came on tracing his route from the top of Canada to Cape Horn. And Ben started a rap:

"Now listen to my tale, you people of the world / while my journey down the globe gets slowly unfurled / I'm going with the Spirit as in Acts 1: 8 / Don't think you've done God's mission if you've chatted to your mate / See Judea and Samaria, the people near to you / Whose lives are really diff'rent and you haven't got a clue / Then go fulfil your mission, to the ends of the earth / and see how the Kingdom begins to come to birth / I set off from the top and mighty cold it was / with polar bears and blizzards and an all-day frost / I found a friendly Inuit who gave me his boat / his generosity brought a lump to my throat / I paddled past the icebergs and up the Nelson river / the first person known to man to do it that way ever!"

Ben broke into a percussion beatbox interlude and everyone roared their approval.

"I was wet and I was tired when at last I reached the lake / but I then had my backside badly bitten by a snake / I cycled down the USA and into Mexico / by now I'd met with Esther and appeared on her show / so people came to meet me and hear me talk my talk / and gave me lots of money which helped me walk the walk / I took the kayak with me on a trailer on my bike / I got some funny looks from those who'd never seen the like / so I paddled and I cycled the rest of the way / right down South America for day after day / I crossed all the deserts, I climbed all the hills / I got bit by all the insects, I took all the pills / till I came to the end, cycling into Puerto Toro / thinking I'd be finished the day after tomorrow / I rounded Cape Horn and was paddling back / I got hit by a ship and that was that."

Ben broke into Beethoven's Fifth again – and everyone laughed. Then quickly, he pressed on to the climax:

"I floated in the sea, got swept away / thought this was it, it's my last day / they searched the ocean, declared me gone / but I turned up safe, my struggle won / God had brought me safely through / and he'll do the same for you and you and you."

Everybody laughed and clapped enthusiastically. This was much better than a keynote speaker.

Then Brendan took over, describing his second "call" and putting up a second powerpoint slide, which, while Ben gave his rendition of the Benny Hill theme tune, gradually mapped out a route backwards and forwards around the world, turning this way and that, and finally stretching back across the Atlantic to Ireland and then to the North-East of England. Then he told a few stories: the encounter with a Somali pirate; the long kayak journey from Uruguay to Brazil to Trinidad; the last sprint against the clock from the airport to Cullercoats.

"During this year-long journey, I was blown up, locked up, laid up, set up and fed up and met rampant hippos, Presidents, a glamorous terrorist and, of course, Esther, TV icon. I came home exhausted, and with a throat condition that I'm having tests on. But I came home convinced that when we take mission seriously, amazing things can happen. Not only was this shown by the outpouring of generosity which raised $200 million for Watoto's work with the world's most disadvantaged people, it was also shown by what happened to both my daughters as they found God in a very real and powerful way, and by the church back home in Jact.

"While I was away on my first trip, a Cuban minister came and brought God with him. He reached those parts of the people in Jact that I hadn't been able to find, let alone nurture. Suddenly the Church came alive, the community rallied round and it was all going wonderfully. Ben here was employed as a worker in the local schools and young people started flocking in too. The church folk caught the vision and joined in the mission, bringing the community together, and catching people up in the net of the Kingdom.

"Then the wrong minister was put in and it all fell apart. It became once more all about the old institutional Church which I'd struggled with but not been able to break. Now it returned with its stench of death and decay. Ben was sacked. The people voted with their feet; only the elderly were left.

"After a few months, the minister who was killing off the Spirit left, and the church appointed Ben to bring the people back. His mixture of beatbox, percussion and street-dance brought a surge of spiritual refreshing and hordes of young people and families. The church opened up for after-school clubs, and they gave away customised memory-sticks to the teenagers, which became prized possessions. They changed the worship-time to 10.08, signalling that this was *different*. The community was centred once more around this vibrant, open, Fresh Expression of Church – where everybody has a say and everybody gets involved, because it's *their* church.

"So, please, don't think that Christianity in the UK is dying. In many places it is, but not everywhere – and recent statistics tell us that church decline in the UK has levelled off. Many of us believe that we've got rid of the excess and can now concentrate on investing in the vibrant, hope-bringing, people-centred but Gospel-driven work of winning people for Jesus. So please pray for us. And keep pressing ahead, so that we can follow and learn from you. The heartbeat of Christianity is now below the equator, but those of us in the northern extremities still need you, for we are, are we not, all of us, together, the people of God, the body of Christ, the temple of the Holy Spirit. Thanks be to God."

Brendan and Ben sat down to tumultuous clapping and shouts of approval. It had been a good evening.

Chapter 8

For someone like Brendan who was a ticking time-bomb of activity, impatience and hypochondriacal negativity, having to wait was awful. Being unable to influence the outcome of his medical condition was a horrible experience. He didn't like it one bit. While he'd been in Bossey, he'd sometimes forgotten about it for an hour or two, but it was always there. When they got back, time seemed to go dreadfully slowly.

Jack Turner turned up one day with a book which Brendan had read before. It was by a priest called Vanstone and was called "The Stature of Waiting"[23]. Brendan had read it a long time ago, and vaguely remembered that it was about the Passion of Jesus – the short time between Jesus' arrest and death when he was being "done to" rather than doing the doing himself.

Brendan opened it straightaway, and got hooked from the outset. Vanstone's point was that when Jesus was "handed over" in Gethsemane, his ministry changed from working God's agenda to revealing God's glory. And the glory was revealed by Jesus' vulnerability and inactivity – and supremely when he hung on the Cross. It was wonderfully descriptive of how Brendan felt: being "done to", being "handed over" into the hands of surgeons, machines and illness.

He was reminded of the popular misconception of the old version of the Methodist Covenant Prayer. One line said, "Put me to doing; put me to suffering; let me be employed for you or laid aside for you..." Some people stayed away from the annual Covenant Service on the first Sunday of the New Year when everyone joined in this prayer, because they thought wrongly that in saying "Put me to suffering" they were calling down pain and hardship on themselves. Suffering meant not pain but this same idea of passion/passivity, inactivity, being "done to". "Put me to doing, put me to being done to" made marvellous if uncomfortable sense to Brendan at that moment.

Brendan was particularly transfixed with one observation. Vanstone pointed out that when the centurion saw Jesus on the cross and said,

---

[23] VANSTONE, W.H., "The Stature of Waiting", DLT, 1982.

"Truly this is the Son of God"[24], he couldn't possibly have said it because of anything Jesus said or did. He saw only Jesus being "done to" and in this the centurion saw Jesus' divinity. And, Vanstone concluded, Christians can reveal God's glory too by their vulnerability. Brendan puffed out his cheeks. It was all very well in theory – but it was very difficult to put it into practice.

★ ★ ★

Then the results came back from the cytology clinic.

Everything was clear.

It wasn't cancer.

The world suddenly found its colour again after a season of grey drabness. Brendan rediscovered a spring in his step. He was told that he ought still to get the cyst seen to, but he was happy to put that off for later. There was a wedding to get ready for, things to do, people to see.

His hypochondria had proved wrong once again. And yet he didn't feel let down. If anything, his close brush with cancer was as good as the real thing in the sense of getting people's attention and sympathy – yet with the added bonus that he was going to get better as well, able to revel in the heroism of his survival – like when he'd survived in the South Atlantic or in the aircraft hit by the terrorist missile in East Timor.

★ ★ ★

Louisa was waiting too, apprehensively.

Life at the hospital was much better than it had been. Her nemesis, Sister Lilian, had been transformed by God last year from the worst Sister in the world, intent on ruining Louisa's life and vocation, into a conscientious Sister who'd even nominated Louisa for a top nursing accolade. But the Cardiovascular Unit at the Freeman Hospital was still on tenterhooks to see if the transformation would stick[25]. There was a camera memory-card in the Sister's Office, which held a video clip taken by a patient which showed Sister Lilian hitting Louisa and abusing her for being a Christian. It'd been left on show in the Office

---

[24] Matthew 27: 54

[25] cf. EARL, Stuart, "Brendan and the Great Omission". The character of Sister Lilian is fictional, and any resemblance to anyone working at the Freeman Hospital is purely coincidental.

precisely to remind Sister of where she'd come from, and to reassure Louisa that Sister hadn't destroyed it.

Louisa and Sister Lilian had agreed that after six months of Lilian's continuing good nursing, the memory-card would be wiped, and Sister would then transfer to a different ward to continue her nursing career. That conversation had taken place on January 4th, so the six months probation were up in three days' time. Louisa hadn't forgotten – and she suspected Sister hadn't forgotten either. It was one thing to have an agreement, but what would actually happen?

★ ★ ★

Louisa was also anxious about the wedding. It was now less than five weeks away and there was so much still to do. She'd organised her outfit, and told her Mum and Ruth to "wear something nice but don't worry about colour schemes because we haven't got one", and she'd sorted out with Ben, as soon as he'd got back from Switzerland, the liturgy she wanted for the actual wedding service itself. They still had to find out who was going to conduct the service – the Super was being a bit cagey about it, but he assured her that it would be OK. The band were practising hard and had won the Jact congregation over very quickly. Jools had promised Ben that his Orchestra would be up for it on the day. The women at church had refused to allow Louisa to have anything to do with the catering arrangements – they would look after everything, and would club together to pay for it too as their wedding gift.

Ben had got the Youth Club to organise the community football match for the morning of the wedding. The fancy dress was apparently going to be Vicars and Tarts, with the blokes dressed as tarts and the lasses as vicars. Ben was going to referee the first half, before going off to get himself ready for the wedding, and Harry the pub landlord was going to look after the second half. Both of them were going to be dressed as Darth Vader, and Ben was relieved that he was going to wear the costume first – as Harry was a big bloke and would sweat rather a lot.

Louisa still had to find someone to look after the fireworks, but she knew someone who knew someone who knew the person who did it on Whitley Bay Links every November 5th, so she hoped that she'd get that sorted soon too. Time was running out.

★ ★ ★

Ruth and Paul had longer to wait. It was now Week 19. Still four and a half months to go.

Chapter 9

A week after getting back from Bossey, Brendan's throat had become really sore, his voice raspy, the underneath of his chin swollen, and he went back to see the doctor.

"The cyst must be infected after the aspiration," declared the doctor. "You'll have to go and get it seen to as a matter of urgency."

The doctor got on the phone straightaway to the hospital. After a short conversation he turned and asked Brendan, "What are you doing on Friday?"

Brendan gulped – it looked like he'd be in hospital.

★ ★ ★

The surgeon explained beforehand that they'd be taking out not just the cyst itself but "having a look around", which sounded like a police diver about to enter a murky body-ridden canal. They'd be taking some material from around the site of the cyst, "just to check".

The operation, which Brendan had built up to be as serious and complicated as a head transplant, only took about 20 minutes. Brendan's reaction, when he was told this back on the ward after he'd woken up, was to feel a bit disappointed at its brevity but reassured by it too.

---

[26] To write a novel about someone with cancer is a daunting task, especially if the main character's response includes humour. On Friday May 13th 2011, having already written half this novel, I underwent an eye biopsy during which the consultant told me, as she was digging around inside my eye, that she could see through the microscope clear indications that I had lymphoma, or cancer. Even though the results of the biopsy and an MRI scan subsequently confirmed that it was actually an inflammatory condition called reactive lymphoid hyperplasia, having a consultant mention the C word at you is an *interesting* experience, to say the least. As I revised the first draft in January 2012, I was awaiting Rituximab chemotherapy to stop the presently benign lumps in both eyes becoming malignant. As I return to the text for a final read-through after a further 18 months, I am happy to report that things are still OK medically for me. I hope that the reader will not be upset by or dismiss what follows as insensitive or lacking empathy. I am fully aware because of my pastoral ministry (and my own mother's death at 42) of the devastation which cancer brings, and the book is written as a response to that, and in tribute to those who know about cancer all too well, and have even allowed me pastorally to share some of the journey with them.

Next morning, the surgeon came round. The cyst had been the size of a grape and had filled up again with liquid after the previous aspiration. Brendan should now go back home, and then come back to Outpatients the following Tuesday.

★ ★ ★

It was in Outpatients the following Tuesday that he was told that they'd discovered cancer cells. He'd had cancer for 18 months[26].

Chapter 10

It was odd to sit at one side of a desk and have someone say "cancer" to you from across the healthy side of the desk. Once he heard the word, Brendan's mind went into overload, and he heard little else. Dully, he heard the registrar say, "Come back on Thursday and we'll explain what we're going to do," and he was given an appointment card with the details.

He sat in the car and tried to gather his feelings and thoughts. Almost physically, he pushed away the terror which had been his original response. He prided himself on being logical about everything, and he disciplined himself now to think it through. What was he feeling?

He realised immediately that most of the terror was an artificial defensive reflex – and that he wasn't so much frightened as sad, irritated and even curious. Sad that he might not see much of his grandchildren, that he was too young to die and that he might cause any suffering for Ruth and Louisa; irritated at not knowing how to respond; curious as to what it would be like – not now with the thrill of a hypochondriac but with the genuine fascination of someone entering a new experience. He kept saying "I've got cancer" as he drove home, but didn't feel as if he was dying or even particularly ill. It wasn't that he was being brave – it was just the way he was. If screaming would have helped, he would have screamed.

When he got home, there was no-one there and he went straight onto the Internet. He realised that he didn't know much about cancer, so he looked it up, and was surprised to discover that it wasn't a "word not a sentence" as the old cliché glibly described it, so much as a process. Cancer was a general description of cellular activity, rather than a specific illness like mumps or syphilis.

Brendan tried to get his head round the medical terminology. It appeared that life for a cell from the start (conception) is a pretty boring and predictable routine of dividing and replicating. There's a bit of excitement when the cells get the early chance to "differentiate" – a technical word for specialising into different cells for different parts of body. But it isn't that exciting because they don't have any choice – they're predestined like Edwardian aristocracy to become what their genetic information tells them it's their duty to be.

So life continues to be dull for the drone-like cells, "doing their thing" – whether it's being a kidney cell or a gut cell or whatever – reproducing themselves, then dying when telomeres tell them to. Telomeres seemed to be the genetic equivalent of the man who hires out the rowing-boats, keeping everything in order and then telling you when your time's up.

But some cells become cancerous, which is much more glamorous and exciting. Like the Prodigal Son, cancer cells go off to seek their fortune, with no sense of duty or propriety, thinking that they can do anything they like, the future's endless and they're immortal. The only condition to their immortality is that they don't kill off their host, of course, but they don't consider this. They have no sense of what they are supposed to be or do, so they go off and indulge in wild living. The medical consequence of this is that they form useless and undifferentiated tissue – which wouldn't be so bad except that they keep dividing, and the lump of uselessness (tumour) gets bigger. It's still only a speck, of course, and can sometimes be doing this for years before it becomes noticeable by either the host or a doctor.

Even so, it's still OK as long as the cancerous cells are content to stay where they are (a benign tumour) and not wander off sprinkling and dividing into other bits (metastasis or malignancy). This usually happens because they notice an opening into the enchantingly forbidden territory of nearby lymph glands, which, of course, attracts them, so they go wandering round the lymphatic system or along the arterial highways far away, to share the secrets of eternal cellular life like an itinerant preacher on a demonic evangelistic campaign, invading organs, then growing, clumping and compromising the organs and diverting the body's energies to its own needs.

At that point, Louisa walked in. "How did the results go, Dad?"

"Don't you want to wait and watch Match of the Day?" quipped Brendan.

"Very funny, Dad. Go on, how did you get on?"

"I've got cancer. I'm going to die."

★ ★ ★

Louisa insisted on coming with him to Outpatients on the Thursday. As they waited to be called, Brendan felt as if there was a big flashing arrow pointing down at him shouting "Unclean! Cancer victim! Red alert!" When they were finally ushered in, the phrase that came to Brendan's mind was "like lambs to the slaughter" but then he was inside the execution chamber and the registrar was explaining exactly what Brendan had.

"It's called squamous cell carcinoma, or SCCA."

"What does the A stand for," said Brendan, out loud. Louisa elbowed him to shut up.

"Pardon?" said the registrar.

"Squalid cell carcinoma, you said, or SCCA. But it's only three words, so shouldn't it be SCC?" The registrar looked amusedly at Brendan, as if he were talking backwards or had trained a parrot to speak on his behalf. "Sorry. Carry on," added Brendan, embarrassed.

The registrar looked at him. "Right," he said. "Squamous cell carcinoma is a cancer of the scaly cells in the skin and linings in various bits of your body, in your case your throat – and specifically at the base of your tongue. It can come in different forms: either indolent or aggressive, and either in situ or invasive. Unfortunately yours is aggressive (in other words, it's quick-growing) and it's invasive (in other words, it's already quick-spreading). It seems that it's been there some time before being diagnosed?"

"Yes," said Brendan, weakly. "I was away at the time. I didn't think it was anything important." Even to his own ears, he seemed pathetic, whining, not so much shaking a fist as slapping at the air with a limp wrist.

Louisa gulped too, and butted in. "So what can you do?"

"Ah, yes. What are we going to do? Well, we're going to get a specialist to conduct an extended endoscopy."

"What does that mean?" asked Brendan. Wasn't that a camera? He'd already had one of those.

"It's a tube with a camera, Dad," said Louisa.

"Yes, it is. Quite right," said the registrar. "But this one will have a pair of scissors on the end as well as a camera, and the specialist will use it to cut tissue out to test for cancer as he goes down." It sounded like drilling for oil. "Then we'll probably give you some radiotherapy, and Bob's your uncle!"

No he isn't, thought Brendan, still unable to focus. He couldn't think straight at all. It was like they were talking about someone else.

Louisa, the nurse in the family, asked more questions. What had they taken out the first time? What density of cancerous cells was there? How much did they think the cancer had spread? Were there secondaries? Would there be chemo as well?

The registrar revealed that during the cyst removal they'd also removed a lymph gland because it had been touching the cyst. The cancer had been spread throughout the liquid and walls of the cyst but they wouldn't know the extent of any metastasis until the endoscopy. The radiotherapy regime would be calculated when they knew what they were dealing with. Brendan would probably have a CT scan too.

Brendan asked what he thought was a clever question: "Have I got cyst cancer or tongue cancer, or what?"

"Good question!" said the registrar. Brendan felt temporarily a bit better. "Cysts don't get cancer. They're always secondary. The primary cancer is somewhere nearby, probably in the tongue. That's what we've got to find." Brendan didn't like the sound of that. He wished that he'd kept his mouth shut.

Chapter 11

When he got back home, Brendan phoned Ruth in Uganda. When he'd phoned on Tuesday with the initial verdict, she'd been quite calm and matter-of-fact. Not surprising, really – she'd always been the level-headed member of the family. By now she'd had more time to think things through and came back with all kinds of practical questions: What about the wedding? Should she come over immediately, or hang on till her scheduled flight just before the wedding? Had they said when the radiotherapy would happen, or how long it would last?

Brendan didn't know any of the answers, except to tell her not to come over straightaway – there was no need. He assured her that he was OK – a bit shell-shocked and a bit sore inside and outside his throat, but he didn't feel too poorly. They engaged in a bit of light-hearted banter. It finished with Brendan saying, "It's never easy to hear someone say that you've got invasive, aggressive cancer – but it's growing on me..." There was a pause and then both he and Ruth spontaneously burst out laughing as they realised what he'd accidentally said, then they went silent again as they realised the poignancy and truth of it. Cancer *was* growing on him – that was the trouble.

"So what are you going to do with the time you've got left, Dad? Swim with dolphins – they say that's what everyone has to do while they have the chance? Visit Antarctica? Write your memoirs?" Ruth laughed, and so did Brendan.

But it got him thinking. How much time did he have left? What should he do with it? Not dolphins – he didn't like swimming. Nor Antarctica – it was too cold. Should he write his life-story? What would the title be? Maybe, and he smiled at his wit, they should be called: "Here lies Brendan Priest" – because he'd often said that all memoirs contained exaggeration, wishful thinking and lies. Perhaps he should include a wistful list of all the things he'd never learnt – like how to ride a unicycle or how to burp – or all the things he'd never done, like publish his impossible pub quiz[27]?

---

[27] Throughout both his journeys, Brendan had amused himself by making a mental list of questions to which nobody else could possibly know the answers.

The more he thought about it after the phone call, the more the thought of doing something cerebral gripped him. He'd been given a brain, so maybe he ought to keep it active. He couldn't face the thought of writing his memoirs – who'd want to read them anyway? He hadn't really done anything exciting until three years ago, but he couldn't face the thought of rehashing his journeys.

He decided in the end that he'd try to construct the most bizarre anagram in the world. He loved anagrams, especially long and complicated ones. He'd once won a prize on the Internet for constructing the best anagram of the following story:

> *A teacher was talking to her class of six-year-olds about whales. She insisted it was impossible for whales to swallow humans because, although they are very large, their throats are very small. One young girl in front, Penny Dwyer, put her hand up to say that Jonah was swallowed by a whale.*

> *Irritated, the teacher reiterated to Penny that it is physically impossible for whales to swallow humans. Undeterred, Penny retorted, "When I get to Heaven I'm gonna ask poor Mr. Jonah myself." "Really, Penny?" responded the teacher. "So... what if Jonah went to Hell?" The little girl replied, "Then you ask him."*

It'd taken him weeks of trial and error, but he'd eventually made this into:

> *Leroy Williams gets in the line, and when it's his turn, the preacher says: "Hello, Leroy Williams, what do you want me to pray about for you?" Leroy replies: "Well, Preacher James, I just want you to pray for my hearing." At that, the preacher puts a finger to Leroy's left ear, and places the other hand atop his head. Then he tilts his own head to the heavens and begins praying with great gusto. A few moments later, the preacher removes both hands, steps back, bellows, "Hallelujah!" and asks, "Well, Leroy Williams – how's that hearing of yours now?" Leroy says, "I don't know, Reverend, it ain't till next Wednesday."*

It'd taken Brendan three weeks to work it out – and he'd won £50 for it in the Anagrammy Awards[28].

He turned his attention now, for inspiration, to the library book

---

[28] The website www.anagrammy.com records a similar winning anagram by Tony Crafter in November 2010.

he'd still got, having renewed it several times. He decided he'd attempt an anagram of the blurb on the back[29]:

Dennis DiClaudio: "The Hypochondriac's Pocket Guide to Horrible Diseases You Probably Already Have": Hypochondriacs can now fret appropriately and factually with this pocket guide to forty-five disgusting, horrible diseases. All entries include symptoms, a diagnosis guide, treatment suggestions, a prognosis, and – if you are not yet infected – prevention tips. Because it's ultra-portable, you can (and probably should) have it with you at all times so at the slightest onset of an unmistakably fatal-feeling itchy rash, you can simply whip out your trusty guide, conveniently diagnose yourself, and then let the worrying begin.

After a couple of hours, he'd come up with a grid of 512 letters and a few key words:

A	B	C	D	E	F	G	H	I	J	K	L	M
41	10	16	22	49	10	15	20	43	0	3	25	6

N	O	P	Q	R	S	T	U	V	W	X	Y	Z
34	39	16	0	26	37	45	22	5	5	0	23	0

Funnily enough, the key words included: tumour, cancer, lump, carcinoma, biopsy, scan, radiotherapy, headache, throat, sore, ill, corpse, funeral and death.

He didn't get much further.

---

[29] This blurb is a work of fiction, different from the one on the real book – but utilises several phrases from the original. It has been changed to suit the purposes and story-line of this book, as will become clearer later.

Alan's Story: July 17ᵗʰ 1954

Alan had progressed to the top end of St. Pat's, and then at the age of nine had moved school to another St. Pat's, the Junior School, where the boys played in the playground on the flat roof. The girls were in the yard below. They had different floors too – the boys on the top floor, the girls on the bottom floor – and Alan was very happy with this arrangement. He was pretty good at football, a nippy winger who could run fast and skip out of trouble, but as one of the smallest boys it was often Alan who was sent downstairs to get the ball back when it went over the fence. Within a week, he'd be finishing his first year there.

He didn't have too many memories of the Infants. He remembered, of course, the fierce nun who was the headteacher. And he remembered one of his teachers announcing to the class, with tears in her eyes, that the King had died. He'd been quite upset even though he had no idea what a King was.

Juniors was much better, except for Fridays. Alan hated Fridays, except after lunch. Every Friday lunchtime the whole school was marched to St Pat's Catholic Church for Benediction, with the school choir assembled in the choir stalls to lead the singing of the hymns. One week, because Alan had a couple of mates who sang in the choir, he decided to join them but the music teacher soon singled him out and banned him from ever singing in the choir again.

The Catholic Church was a huge, imposing, dark building with a brighter but cavernous interior. Attending Sunday Mass was compulsory and on Monday morning the teacher always quizzed the class as to which Mass they'd attended and if it was discovered anyone had missed Mass they were caned. Alan hated Mass and was caned frequently until he learned to say that he'd stayed at his cousin's house and attended Mass at another church. The fact that he didn't have a cousin was beside the point.

It was about this time that he began to realise that there was a stigma attached to being a Foxheader. Some teachers spoke disparagingly about the area and the people who lived there, and wherever Alan went in the town people seemed to hold Foxheaders in low esteem, not that Alan particularly cared what others thought.

Alan revelled in his life outside school. In his first few months at Juniors, he'd contented himself with the pagging-out races which many of the first-years joined immediately after school. It involved a group of lads setting off at the same time and just running till, one by one, they "pagged out" until only the winner was left. Alan often did well, but there was always one tall, long-legged boy called Edward who would keep going longer than him.

So he joined in what he considered a more grown-up form of entertainment. At the junction of Marsh Street and Frederick Street was a road bridge which led to the steel works, spanning the end of Newport Street and the railway lines. Lads from St Pat's collected, after school, under the bridge to settle their differences. Alan joined the others, forming a circle around the combatants and then urging on whoever seemed to have the most friends. If it seemed even, he shouted, "Go on the winner!"

Into his life a few weeks ago, along with the onset of summer heat, had come an Italian woman called Angie who sold ice cream from a handcart which she pushed around the streets. If it was warm in the late afternoon, she came into Foxheads and parked her cart smack in the middle of the junction of Prince Charles Street and Frederick Street. Nobody owned a car in those days and Foxheads saw very little traffic, so her cart was not a problem to traffic. Alan spent most afternoons at school lusting after the ice-cream which awaited him. Days when he didn't have any money were hard to bear. Tuppence or, even better, threepence would get him either a sandwich (ice cream spread between two wafers) or a cornet.

Angie's family ran a shop on Cannon Street. It was a busy shop and the bread and milk were kept on the customers' side of the counter, so whenever Alan was sent to buy bread and milk he bypassed the nearest shops and went to Angie's where he'd steal the bread and milk and keep the money. After closing time, Angie would post one of her grown-up sons on the shop doorway whose job it was to let people in and out so she could carry on trading after hours – and warn her if a bobby was coming.

As well as his ill-gotten gains, Alan had quite a lucrative side-line in a gambling game called spanny. It involved a player slammed a penny against a wall. It would rebound and land some distance away from the wall. The next player would do the same but try to land his coin within a hands-span of his opponent's coin. If he could span the distance between the two coins, he won both coins. If he couldn't, his opponent took both coins. Alan may have been short but he had pianist's hands. He couldn't play the piano, but he had the fingers for it. And, for some quirky reason, he could land a coin like his cricketing hero Johnny Wardle, the Yorkshire left-arm wrist-spinner, who could land the cricket-ball in the same spot in the rough, ball after ball after ball.

Alan's wealth was only limited by the poverty of his playmates.

August 2012

Chapter 12

The papers from the Registrar General in Southport had come through on time – and Brendan was now officially an Authorised Person to conduct marriages in the 10.08 Church – and any other Methodist Church in the North Tyneside Registration District. The Church Council had welcomed Brendan's unofficial role as "ordained helper" and he'd already presided at Holy Communion on the last Sunday in July while a Local Preacher preached and Ben led worship. Brendan's throat wasn't up to preaching – his voice had got scratchy and any increase in volume from a husky whisper was agony. He was saving himself for The Big Day.

Brendan was going to be doubling up both as Louisa's Dad – to bring her into church – and as Minister, and he was adamant that he wanted to preach at the wedding service "even if it kills me", though he was rather hoping that it wouldn't.

★ ★ ★

The Big Day dawned bright and cloudless – though there was still a bit of a nip in the air. There was a huge cheer from the dozens of spectators at 8.50am when Ben appeared in his Darth Vader costume, and the assembled vicars and tarts ambled onto the football pitch for a leisurely kick-about. Paul, Ruth's husband, had come along without understanding beforehand what a bizarre and entertaining spectacle it was going to be. He'd felt a bit of a spare part at home anyway, and this looked as if it was going to be much better fun. Some of the tarts had obviously been on the ale the night before, and seemed to be still feeling the effect. Some of them looked so ugly that they wouldn't get a date even if the Elephant Man was on the lookout. The vicars looked very... well, very... *unspiritual* – if the amount of female flesh they were showing was anything to go by.

Ben looked rather dashing in the Darth Vader outfit – though he found the helmet got in the way. He whirled his light sabre round his head and blew his whistle. "Gather round, earthlings!" he shouted. "I can't do the voice, but let the battle commence – and may the force be with you. Vicars will kick off."

"Aren't we supposed to toss for it?" said one of the tarts – it could have been Niall, but Ben wasn't sure.

"Too many tossers as it is!" yelled one of the vicars, in decidedly unecclesiastical language.

"Too right," agreed Ben, and blew his whistle.

The vicars kicked off, booted it upfield, and everyone, including Ben jogged after it. Unfortunately Ben tripped himself up with his light sabre, fell in a heap, and started rolling round in agony. Everyone laughed uproariously until someone realised that Ben really had hurt himself. They gathered round and watched as Ben sat up and said, through clenched teeth, "I think I've busted my ankle."

★ ★ ★

Four of the tarts carried Ben off the pitch, and Paul and another spectator took him to A & E at Rake Lane. Fortunately, at 9.15 on a Saturday morning, it was very quiet – but it caused a bit of a scene when two blokes helped Darth Vader hop into the triage area. "He's getting married at noon, so please try and hurry it up," said Paul.

"Who to – Natalie Portman?" asked the doctor.

"Eh?"

"Natalie Portman. She was the actress who played Luke Skywalker's mother in Star Wars One. Can't remember her film name though... Mind you, if you were marrying her you'd be doing all right."

"Princess Amidala, wasn't it?" said the spectator who'd brought Ben in.

"Yes, it was. Well done!" said the doctor, before Ben interrupted their film buff challenge and asked them to hurry up.

"It's very swollen," said the doctor, finally examining the ankle. "We'll get you into X-ray – but I think you've only sprained it. Are you really getting married at noon?"

When Ben nodded and looked as if he was about to burst into tears, the doctor took command. They were whisked into X-ray, seen immediately, then the doctor had them straight in and confirmed that it was a bad sprain and that the only thing he could give him was a support brace and painkillers.

"The price is right," said the doctor, enigmatically. Was he into TV as well as film?

"We have a checklist for looking after sprained ankles: PRICE: Protection is the P, Rest is the R, Ice is the I, Compression is the C and Elevate is the E. If it's still agony in a week, come back and we'll have another look at it. Meanwhile don't put your weight on it if you can help it. Do you want some crutches?"

Ben nodded. He'd need the crutches to prove that he wasn't having a laugh – especially to convince Louisa.

★ ★ ★

Ben arrived, suitably attired, at the church at 11.30. Brendan met him as he hobbled to the church door. "What was the result?" asked Brendan.

"3-1 to the tarts, apparently," Ben joked, then answered Brendan's forced smile with one of his own. "It's a bad sprain."

"You OK?" asked Brendan. "Does Louisa know?"

"So far – and not yet," said Ben. "She'll kill me."

"Don't you think you'd better warn her?"

"Can you do it?" asked Ben, "Please?" – handing his phone to Brendan.

★ ★ ★

Louisa already knew.

She'd been kept updated by Ruth who'd been updated by Paul. She was worried for Ben, but also thought that it was hilarious. There weren't that many bridegrooms who'd been hospitalised on their wedding day – but Ben was almost certainly the first ever to have injured himself tripping over his light sabre.

When Louisa, Ruth and their Mum Jenna arrived at the church, Brendan gave the nod to Jools, who came to the front, and as everyone hushed, he started a drum-roll – without a drum, of course. Everyone stood. The rest of the Full Voice Orchestra became a fanfare of trumpets, and then Jools gave a sound-only commentary of the car drawing up, the doors opening and shutting, the photographer taking pictures, before he and the Orchestra gave an extremely realistic orchestral rendition of "Here Comes the Bride" – without any instruments, of course. Brendan and Louisa walked down the aisle, with Ruth and Jenna behind.

After Brendan's welcome, the packed congregation joined in enthusiastically with the band's version of "Praise my soul the King of Heaven", then settled as a husky Brendan, aided by the mike, took everyone through the first legal bits.

Paul read, first in Luo then in English, a short extract about love from the "Song of Lawino" a poem by his hero, the Ugandan poet Okot p'Bitek. Then Ruth read 1 Corinthians 13, after which Brendan got up to give the address.

"This is possibly the first wedding in human history where the groom has been taken to hospital in a Darth Vader costume – but then with Louisa and Ben nothing was going to be conventional, was it?

"Ben is not, of course, the only one present who's been spending time in the care of the NHS recently, as many of you will know. After my biopsy a few weeks ago, I woke up the following morning feeling really rough to find myself in a two-bed side ward with a guy who had an oxygen mask over his face. When he saw I was awake, he pulled his mask to the side and croaked Hello.

""Brendan," I said, pointing at myself. That was all I had the strength for.

"Bill," he said, similarly weak.

"Cullercoats," I said.

"Wallsend," said Bill.

"Cancer," I said, pointing at my throat.

"Bill turned to me, lifted his oxygen mask again, pointed to his chest and said "Sagittarius.""

Everyone fell about laughing. It was a relief that the word was out in the open, and Brendan went on to talk about how precious life was. He reminisced a little about the terrorist attack on his plane in East Timor, and how he'd felt as he was recovering from that about the need to witness to the power of love over evil rather than the power of evil over love. He drew the link with the Okot poem and with 1 Corinthians 13, and got quite emotional when he wished Louisa and Ben the very best for their life together, adding, "I hope I get to see quite a bit of it."

He paused, wiped away a tear, and then said, "I was going to say that that gave me a lump in my throat, but I've already got one of those – so instead I'll say that I'm chuffed to bits!"

The congregation aaahed, applauded and cheered.

Everyone sang "Love Divine", before Brendan took Ben and Louisa through the vows. When they got to what used to be the "giving away" bit, Brendan asked the question in the surprisingly modern Methodist liturgy: "Who presents Louisa to be married to Ben?" and at that point Jenna stepped forward and said, "I do." Everyone cheered – they'd been wondering how Brendan would do that. The same question was asked about Ben – and his Mum gave the answer, to another cheer.

When Brendan declared them to be "husband and wife", the loudest cheer of all went up, and Brendan said the prayer which follows the vows and asked everyone to sit down.

Jools and the Orchestra then took over, for an amazing eight minutes of human percussion, with a young man and woman performing some eye-boggling synchronised street-dance – ending up with them "falling in love" and dancing off down the aisle (hip-hop style) – all to the percussion rhythms of the Orchestra and Jools' versions of other musical instruments – a muted trumpet for a slow jazz part of the dance, a violin for the love scene, an organ for the Wedding March and even a set of bagpipes playing "Amazing Grace" for the finale. The congregation were blown away.

Brendan led the final prayers and did the signing of the registers, while Dead to the World played some of their own "wedding variations" before striking up with the Wedding March for real, and Ben and Louisa smiled, laughed and limped their way down the aisle.

It had all gone swimmingly.

★ ★ ★

The catering teams got to work during the photographs, and food was ready and kept being made ready for the rest of the afternoon. Ben sat in a white plastic garden chair, his foot up on a stool with bags of ice to stop the swelling. Louisa wandered round the groups, chatting and laughing, too excited to eat.

Mid-afternoon became early evening, and still the food kept coming. Groups came and groups went – and it seemed that the whole of Jact must have come along at some point. Kids came from the schools, dragging their parents along. Someone had organised a bouncy castle, and the shrieks from the children all added to the fun. The band set up outside under the gazebo and started playing dance music, and soon over a hundred people were dancing the evening away.

At 10pm the fireworks marked the end of the dancing, and the day. Everyone was shattered, exhilarated. Most went to their beds. Large numbers went down the pub. Ben and Louisa were driven to the Grand at Tynemouth for the first night of their honeymoon.

It had been a wonderful day.

Chapter 13

Brendan was told, by someone trying to be helpful, that the Times journalist John Diamond, married to Nigella Lawson, had contracted the same cancer as he had.

"Oh really?" said Brendan. "What happened to him?"

"Oh. Er. I think he died."

Despite this, Brendan got Diamond's book out of the library[30]. He liked one bit in particular, about the fact that once you've got cancer, it changes everything: "Even if somehow it seems to go away, it doesn't – it stays there like a lapsed religion, somewhere in the background waiting for its chance to reappear and claim that it is what defines who you are and that you are a part of its community." Spot on, thought Brendan.

He forced himself through every procedure, treatment and agony of Diamond's rollercoaster ride on the cancer funfair, and was impressed with the way in which Diamond had been able to write so fluently and wittily about something so serious. Tumour and humour usually were found side by side only in a rhyming dictionary, but Diamond had done his best.

He'd still died, though.

★ ★ ★

Towards the end of the month, Brendan went back in for another biopsy. The hospital was depressingly familiar. He knew already where the machine was for the car-park payment. He knew when the hospital shop was open and what they sold. He knew how to get himself registered on the TV/phone machine which dangled like a car-factory robot over each bed. He was no longer afraid of the operation – he'd achieved the higher degrees of hypochondria now, in which it was understood that there was no point fearing an anaesthetic when he had the cancer to worry about, or, at an even higher degree: why should he die in the operating theatre when there was the cancer to wake up to?

---

[30] DIAMOND, John, "C: Because Cowards Get Cancer Too", Vermillion, 1998.

He was a bit irritated by the ridiculous cheerfulness of the porter dragging his bed down the corridor to the butcher's shop. The porter seemed to know everyone and want to make their day brighter with his chirpiness and downright good-heartedness. Brendan wasn't in the mood. It was all right for the porter, he'd be sleeping in his own bed that night...

Brendan woke up to be told that seven strips had been sliced off his throat, tongue and tonsilar stub (whatever that was). It instantly hurt and he demanded painkillers, and remained dosed up for the next three days. The registrar came round on the morning of the third day, like the angel of resurrection – at least, that's what Brendan *hoped* he was going to be like.

Brendan – ever the pessimist – had mused on the best way of conveying bad news. How do you tell someone that they've got cancer? "Now, Mrs. Smith, let's play a little game. You name as many star signs as you can, and I'll tell you when you get to the right one"...?

The registrar smiled, which filled Brendan with a sense of doom. "Well, Mister Priest – I think it might be good news. It's certainly not dreadfully bad news, anyway."

Brendan wished that the registrar could be a bit clearer. He didn't seem to have a very good way with patients. Perhaps that was why he'd chosen a career where most of his encounters were with people under general anaesthetic.

The registar continued. "We had a good look around and didn't see anything resembling a tumour." Was that good news – that there wasn't one – or bad news – that there probably was but that they were too inept to find it?

"Nor has anything significant popped up from the samples taken." The registar stopped. Was that it?

"So what does that mean?"

"Well, we can't do anything else surgical at the moment because we haven't found anything to cut out. Chemotherapy's not really on because it's a bit of a blunt instrument to use at this stage – too many healthy cells would be affected. So our best option, I reckon, is good old radiotherapy!"

Brendan wanted to pick him up on both the "good" and the "old".

He wasn't convinced that there was much good to be drawn from being strapped next to fizzing radioactive isotopes while the radiographers ran for cover behind lead screens. He didn't like the sound of "old" either, it sounded like he didn't merit using the up-to-date stuff.

But the registrar was already explaining – or, at least, trying to. "We're pretty good at it now. In the past we were quite pleased that we knew how to do all this radiation stuff without killing ourselves, but we didn't have a clue what difference it would make to the patients. Now the ray is precision-fired at exactly where the nasty cancer cells are meant to be. The trouble, of course, is that cancer cells cleverly hide in the middle of healthy cells, so we have to zap all of them. The cancer cells get zapped worst but the healthy cells suffer a bit, even though we usually expect them to recover. So we'll have a bash at that then, shall we? OK?"

As if he had any choice... Perhaps he should investigate some of those complimentary health regimes, where you eat broccoli and have coffee enemas – or was it that you drink coffee and have broccoli enemas...? He didn't even like broccoli – not orally anyway, and he suspected that he wouldn't get a lot of pleasure out of broccoli in any other orifice either.

★ ★ ★

Brendan awaited the arrangements for him to start his radiotherapy. Meanwhile further symptoms made his morale dip further. He started to get blinding headaches – not like the migraines that he'd had as a teenager, which had necessitated lying down in a dark room until the pounding pain went away – but curious buzzing pains across his forehead and red flashes across his eyesight. And the buzzing irritation seemed to get worse in waves of pain, until he clenched his teeth and shut his eyes in an attempt at blocking it out.

And his feet got all white and scaly, like athlete's foot. Was this normal for his abnormal condition? Or was foot fungus just one more sign of advancing decrepitude?

He decided to put a few more key words into the anagram he was working on: broccoli diet; headaches between the eyes; fungous feet. In fact, he started again – crossing out the initial words he'd come up with and deciding to make the anagram about hypochondria (reflecting the book) rather than cancer (reflecting him). He quickly added other phrases: "Oh God!", "virus", "is it all psychological?", "whatever's that?", "obscure parasite", "an odd spot for a polyp", "it isn't very funny".

Despite it not being very funny, he was rather enjoying the mental exercise.

Chapter 14

The trouble with pain was that it hurt. And because it hurt, Brendan couldn't easily concentrate on anything else. Even though he knew that pain was part of God's clever alarm system to indicate that something needed attention, he was still surprised and a bit put-out that pain was now a constant disruption to the smooth flow which he'd assumed would be his daily path through life.

But then there was pain – and there was Pain. A sore spot of raw skin between the toes was one thing, but this grinding pain was in a different category altogether.

Jack Turner came along at the worst, or maybe the best of times.

Brendan gritted his teeth. Jack looked embarrassed and hovered in the doorway. "Come in, Jack. It's not you, it's this bloomin' headache which flashes across my eyes. Along with wasps, pain must be the worst bit of God's creation."

"What about jellyfish? They get my vote," offered Jack.

"Yes, they do seem pretty pointless, don't they?" But Brendan still gritted his teeth. "So why did God put so much pain into his story of redemption, then, Jack?"

Jack blew out his cheeks. "Well, I suppose there is quite a bit of it, isn't there? Adam and Eve get thrown out the garden, lots of slaughter in the Old Testament, the torture and execution of Jesus, the martyrs of the Church through the ages, and even in Revelation the suffering saints weep their way to glory. I suppose it's part of what it means for us to live in a suffering world."

"Yeah," said Brendan, clenching his eyes shut. "I suppose it is. But why, when we've got the message that something needs attention, doesn't the pain stop?"

"Don't know," said Jack. "We're told that God can work even our worst suffering into something that's good and wholesome, but it wouldn't win many votes."

"I never did reckon much to that bit in James[31] about greeting your trials with joy," said Brendan.

"Me neither," said Jack. "But you don't need me here to make it worse. How about I say a prayer and then scoot?" Brendan nodded. "Dear God," Jack started, "We don't understand why there's so much pain but we pray that you'll take away this pain from Brendan. We know that there's medical stuff that needs attending to, but he could do without this pain as well. Please take it away. We know that you want the best for us, so we don't understand when bad things happen. Help us with that, Lord. And help us to keep trusting, no matter what. In Jesus' name. Amen."

"Thanks," said Brendan. "That was a good prayer. Real."

★ ★ ★

But it still hurt, for a few hours. Then, as if someone had changed the screen from black and white to colour, the pain was gone, and the world looked brighter again.

Ben was upstairs, cooking dinner, as Brendan knocked at the open door.

"You're a church leader, Ben – why did God create pain?" he said, as he entered their new flat. They'd done a bit of redecorating and the flat was now much brighter and warmer.

"Blimey," said Ben. "Is that your attempt at small talk? Louisa and I usually talk about football or Corrie or the weather. Actually, it's funny you should mention suffering because we're looking at that on Sunday. The passage is 1 Peter 1: 3-7 – which no doubt you know off by heart."

Brendan shrugged and smiled. "Oh, yes, that passage... Of course, I've only studied it in the original Greek..."

They both laughed. Ben said, "You'll have to come and see what we make of it. You can join in, if you want..."

"Who else have you got taking part?" asked Brendan, interested in this new way of getting the people interested in exploring the Bible.

"There's a woman from the pub whose husband's just been laid off, who's worried about paying her mortgage. Then there's old Mrs.

---

[31] James 1:2

Edwards, whose back's playing up again. And me. And you, if you want to join in."

★ ★ ★

On Sunday, after Ben had introduced everyone, he read the passage:

"Praise be to the God and Father of our Lord Jesus Christ! In his great mercy he has given us new birth into a living hope through the resurrection of Jesus Christ from the dead, and into an inheritance that can never perish, spoil or fade. This inheritance is kept in heaven for you, who through faith are shielded by God's power until the coming of the salvation that is ready to be revealed in the last time. In all this you greatly rejoice, though now for a little while you may have had to suffer grief in all kinds of trials. These have come so that the proven genuineness of your faith – of greater worth than gold, which perishes even though refined by fire – may result in praise, glory and honour when Jesus Christ is revealed."

Then he asked the three participants what they thought it meant. Beryl put her hand up, and Ben nodded for her to go first.

"As many of you know, my Len's just been laid off, and wor Tracey and her bairns are living with us too, so money's a bit tight, to say the least. What I want to hear from God is that people who are doing their best will get a fair deal from Him, but this passage seems to say that it'll be even harder for Christians. Not much of a vote-winner, that!"

Mrs. Edwards butted in. She loved the chance to discuss her faith. "Ah but it doesn't really say that, does it? It doesn't say that that anything different will happen to you if you're a Christian, as if God'll wave a magic wand over you and send the bad stuff away, but it does say that he can make something good out of your suffering."

Brendan put his two-pennyworth in. "But it seems to depend on whether you think faith is more important than the other things people strive for."

"I don't ask for much," said Beryl. "But it doesn't seem right for me to be doing my best to keep things going at home while God's mucking us about by making it harder."

"But that's Len's firm's fault, isn't it – not God's?" asked Ben, which made everyone pause.

"But you can't blame people for cancer, can you?" said Brendan, quietly. The congregation hushed. Now it was getting serious.

"Well, Brendan, I'm sure you know what the answer to that is!" It was Mrs. Edwards who'd spoken. She sat up, then winced as her back spasmed. "This passage says it all for me," she smiled. "Firstly we're told about the way in which God has saved his people through Jesus' victory at the resurrection, then we're told about a spiritual trust fund that's been set up for us by Jesus that nothing can touch – unlike our money in Northern Rock! This inheritance is going to be cashed in at the final days, but it's utterly safe till then. Then we're told that we're "shielded by God's power" which sounds pretty good to me. It means that whatever happens to us, nothing can disturb our place with God."

"But what about your back, Mrs. Edwards?" asked Brendan quietly. "And what about my cancer? I don't feel particularly shielded!"

"But the things that really matter are safe, aren't they, Brendan?" came the immediate reply.

Beryl spoke up. "So, if I'm getting this right, God's saying that whatever life throws at you it's not going to matter that much, if we stick with Him. Is that right?"

"Yes, I think that's it," said Brendan, suddenly inspired. "They can take Len's job. They might even take your house. You can even get horrible diseases like I have, or have a lifetime of back pain, like Mrs. Edwards. But the best things in life are untouchable. And if we know that they're the most important things, and that they're guaranteed, why shouldn't we be joyful? It's about us applying faith in every situation."

Ben broke in. "So we can't allow our present troubles, whatever they are, to loom so large that they block out our vision of God's love in the past and in the future. God has done amazing things in history – and especially in Jesus – to ensure our eternal place with him. So we should say, "This is not what defines me. My true safety is guaranteed. That's all that ultimately matters.""

"But what about all this talk about refining metal?" interrupted Mrs. Edwards. "That does sound a bit like God experimenting with us to see how much testing we can take, even though I'm sure that it doesn't mean that..."

"No, I know about metalworking," said Beryl. "My Len does that, or rather *did* that down at the shipyards. His job was in the furnace, where the ore got put in with all its impurities and then my Len made it all white hot so that the rubbish was boiled out, and the metal that was left was stronger and purer than it was before. It's a good thing, otherwise the metal is weaker and could fail under pressure."

"So you apply pressure to make it stronger in order for it to withstand pressure," said Brendan.

"Yes, but you have to know just how much pressure to apply otherwise the metal can burn up in the furnace," said Beryl.

"And that's exactly what I've been saying all along," said Mrs. Edwards. "God, in order to make us perfect, because he loves us, puts us under pressure not because of his unfaithfulness and lack of attention, but precisely because he *cares*. We're not yet what we're meant to be, which is to be like Him. Quite often, I reckon, when we're wondering where God's grace is and crying out for it, it's precisely then that we're actually receiving it. The problem is that we want the easier grace of release, at the very times when God knows that what we actually need is the more uncomfortable grace of refining."

"I suppose Peter knew all about being tested, if it's the same Peter who ran away, denied Jesus but then was trusted with carrying on Jesus' ministry afterwards," said Brendan.

"So, to conclude..." said Ben, smiling at how well the discussion had gone, "It may be that we're too attached to some parts of what God gives us in life, rather than focussing on God who gives us life in the first place. And God wants the very best for us, which means that sometimes, like childbirth itself, we have to fight our way through difficulties in order to enjoy life in all its fullness. Does that make sense?"

"So, I suppose, me and Len and wor Tracey and the bairns'll be OK, won't we – as long as we count our blessings?" added Beryl.

"And even though my back's killing me, it helps me to understand what the pain of others means so that I can show some care for them," said Mrs. Edwards.

"And even though, literally, my cancer may indeed be killing me, none of us are going to be remembered for what happens to us but on how we *respond* to what happens to us," said Brendan. Then he had to go out for a drink of water, as the conversation had made his throat throb.

★ ★ ★

Everyone seemed happy with the outcome. Ben, particularly, was overjoyed with Brendan's contribution.

Brendan had enjoyed it. He knew that he knew the right answers to all this.

The question was whether he actually believed them.

Chapter 15

"Your Dad was on good form today," Ben told Louisa when she got back from work. "But I wish there was something we could do to help."

"What sort of thing did you have in mind?"

"Well, I was thinking on the way back from Church, and I wondered if we could do something to raise some cash for Cancer Research, to show some sort of solidarity with your Dad. He raised loads of money for Watoto, so maybe if people got to know about his cancer, they'd cough up again – and it would give him something positive to take his mind off how lousy he's feeling."

"What sort of thing?"

"I don't know – but I was toying with one idea as I cycled back – what about getting people to sponsor me every week to go to Church?

"But that's daft – you have to go anyway. It's your job!"

"I know that, you dope. I was wondering if maybe they'd sponsor me to come to Church by weird and wacky forms of transport – like on a pogo-stick or by helicopter."

"Helicopter?" spluttered Louisa. "How are you going to organise one of those?"

"I don't know," said Ben, "It's just an idea..."

"Well, it sounds more exciting than a sponsored walk – but do you think people will be interested in it? And how will you get people on board?"

"I suppose I could try and get the local press interested," suggested Ben. It sounded a bit lame to him, and he wished he hadn't mentioned it – but, to his surprise, Louisa started to think out loud.

"What if you got the paper to run a competition – with people suggesting weird and wonderful ways for you to get to Church – and then the paper got celebrities to pull the winning suggestion out of a hat – and you had only a few days to set it up and make it work?"

"But what if they pick something outrageous – like a space rocket?"

"Well, we'd have to specify that it has to be possible, otherwise their suggestion doesn't count."

"But how do I raise money?"

"You charge people to enter the competition – and you get people to sponsor you for how many Sundays you can fulfil the challenge before somebody sets you a feasible challenge which you fail to fulfil."

"Hmmm," said Ben. "It could work, I suppose."

Little did he know what he'd set in motion.

Alan's Story:
September 12th 1959

The last year had been particularly tough for Alan. The only bright spots in his life were football and capitalism. He was still slightly built but had retained his natural speed and stamina, and had a regular place not only in the school football team but also for St Pat's Boys' Club, who usually played on Hustlers playing field. The Parish Priest, Father Shanahan, was a personal friend of Arthur Fitzsimmons[32] who was an Irish international and Boro inside-right, and he arranged for Arthur to put the lads through their paces. Training was held on the flat roof of St Pat's school which had tall railings round it, so that Arthur Fitzsimmons would be away from the prying eyes and autograph hunters of the Cannon Street kids.

The highlight, though, had been when one training session was arranged for Ayresome Park a few weeks ago, just before the season kicked off. Alan and the lads had all looked forward to it as they had visions of running out onto the hallowed turf and having a kick-about. Unfortunately Arthur had other ideas and just ran them around the perimeter track, but they did get to use the communal bath which the Boro players used. Unfortunately none of it improved the team's performance, and that very morning they'd just managed to continue their record run of (now) 24 straight defeats – so Alan at lunchtime had taken the snap decision to retire.

Having reached the grand old age of 15 at the start of the summer, Alan had left school. He'd never been a promising scholar and when Sister Agnes made him sit the "Scholarship" he'd sat fruitlessly through the morning exam but never went back in the afternoon. By the age of 11 he'd already given up on academia as a potential future career. The four years since then hadn't changed his mind.

He'd devoted himself instead to the pursuit of wealth. Money was still tight at home, and became significantly tighter when his Dad had to

---

[32] Arthur Fitzsimmons played for Middlesbrough from 1949 to 1958, but was then transferred to Lincoln City – so I've taken some liberties here with the chronology.

pack in work a year ago. He'd collapsed one day at work and it was discovered that he had TB, which was a common ailment among footplatemen. Being an engine driver and breathing in smoke and coal dust for a number of years had brought it on. He'd finished up in Poole Sanatorium in Nunthorpe[33], where he'd spent many months during the previous year, but was now making a slow recovery. They'd told him that he'd never be allowed on the footplate again, and there was very little money coming in.

This last winter had been bitterly cold, and they often couldn't afford to buy coal for the fire. One Saturday afternoon, after football in the morning, Alan had pushed an old pram all the way to Redcar and filled it up with sea coal from the beach and pushed it all the way home again. He'd also made a bob or two, or more, delivering coal. There was a black man on Marsh Street who sold coal from his house. People would buy a quarter or half a hundredweight of coal and push it home in a wheelbarrow. Alternatively, Alan was paid a penny by the black man to deliver it for them, and then he'd often get another penny from the grateful recipient.

His Mam had got into the habit of sending Alan out with a sixpence or even a shilling after school to exchange for pennies for the gas meter. Alan used to go to a shop and change it but then wander along to the bridge to ask the men passing to and from work if they had any bait[34] left, or any pennies "for the gas". The gas man would call periodically to empty the meter. He counted all the pennies and often gave some back to Alan's Mam as a rebate because she hadn't fiddled the meter. Inevitably, in Foxheads, when people were short of money, they often broke into the gas meter and stole the contents. Alan's Mam was scrupulously honest, and would never dream of such a thing. Alan would have done it at the drop of a hat if he could've thought how to do it without getting found out. He was clever enough to realise that those who pinched from the gas finished up paying far more than they stole when they were taken to court. A standing joke in those days was

---

[33] The mansion Grey Towers and its 77 acre grounds, one mile from Nunthorpe Station and six miles from Middlesbrough, were purchased and presented to the town of Middlesbrough in 1931 specifically to be converted into a sanatorium for the treatment of tuberculosis.

[34] Bait is north-east-speak for packed lunch.

"He's done more meters than Zatopek[35]."

That same bridge, under which he'd urged on young fighters, against which he'd played numerous games of spanny, was now his route to work – along with virtually every other man in Foxheads. At the northern end of the bridge the road turned right down the Forty Foot Road and to the left there was a narrow slip-road that led down to "The Prairie", across which were the two rolling mills of the Dorman Long Steel Works. There was also the Fish Plant (which made fishplates for railway lines), the Wire Works and Teesside Bridge and Engineering Works. In those days these works were all in full production and worked a three-shift system. Alan had picked his job at the Fish Plant from many, but none of them had really appealed to him.

There wasn't a lot that could be said about a fishplate. It was a metal bar, the top and bottom edges of which were machined to taper inwards. Its function was to join two rails together to form the track. The tapered edges meant that the fishplate wedged itself between the top and bottom of the rail when it was bolted into place. Alan had a job in the machining section, operating a four-headed drill which drilled four bolt-holes into every fishplate. It was more tedious than school, but Alan got paid for it, which made all the difference.

He'd also discovered a taste for beer, but never went out on Saturdays unless he was with a crowd of the big lads from work. Beer and pubs played a large part in the lives of most Foxheads men and some of the women. From the age of ten, Alan had been friendly with an old woman who ran a second-hand shop on Cannon Street, and was often paid a penny by her to go to the County Public House on Newport Road to fetch a jug of beer. Even though he was only little, he was always served at the Off Licence at the back of the pub. As a teenager Alan would also walk along with his Dad to The Vine which was on the next block to the County – though he'd never gone in, except one night recently when his Dad had decided to drink his TB-ridden sorrows away and needed carrying home.

Saturday night was fight night in Foxheads. The pubs closed at 10 pm and by about 10.30 there'd be a fight going on somewhere. It might be between individuals or families or even groups, with crowds

---

[35] Emil Zatopek was the Olympic 1948 10,000m champion, and won 5,000, 10,000 and marathon gold medals in 1952. He was injured in 1956 and retired in 1957, but remained the most famous athlete in the world for many years.

gathering to watch. No-one ever interfered unless it was too one-sided, in which case the spectators stepped in and broke it up. The police never got involved. Then the following Saturday night the argument would be dragged up again, and could go on for months.

He also started noticing girls.

September 2012

Chapter 16

Ruth was on Week 26 of the pregnancy now, two-thirds through, but the thought of going through half again of what she'd already endured was devastating – except for the prospect of the end result, of course. No wonder they called it Meternity, she joked, without laughing, to anyone who asked. She'd not enjoyed the first few months because of feeling sick every morning. Then she'd ballooned quickly into someone who looked like they'd been on the pies, so she'd felt that people were staring at her and thinking "fat". Now she was at the stage where it was obvious that the cause of her shape was pregnancy rather than over-eating, but she felt like a beached whale.

They were back in Gulu, checking on the schedule for the finishing touches to the extension at Bulrushes. The new wing of the centre for babies and toddlers was just about ready for the official opening – but they were waiting to see when Brendan may be able to fly out to be the guest of honour. He was the Honorary President of the Brendan Priest Trust, under whose name the wing was being built, and everyone was anxious that he came in person, if at all possible, to perform the official opening. The ward was not yet completely finished, but already accommodated 40 children, with space for another 30 or so.

Ruth found it strange to be surrounded by tiny children, with her own pregnancy getting sufficiently advanced that virtually all her thoughts were about childbirth and motherhood. The helpers at Bulrushes were all mothers, used to children of their own as well as other people's abandoned children. They winked at Ruth, made eyebrow-wiggling suggestive comments about Paul, and insisted on telling Ruth their horror stories about childbirth. There seemed to be some sort of competition as to who had the scariest story and the most horrible experience.

When Paul got back from Watoto HQ that afternoon, she told him some of the stories, and he laughed.

"What are you laughing at?" she complained. "It's OK for you men."

"Well, women exaggerate so much about childbirth, to make it worse than it actually is," said Paul.

"Oh, and you're the expert on childbirth, now, are you?"

"I've been to one," said Paul.

"Have you? I didn't realise," said Ruth. "What was it like?"

"Well, first of all it was very dark. Then it was very bright," laughed Paul – and Ruth hit him on the arm.

★ ★ ★

Brendan phoned. "I've got a date to start my radiotherapy," he said. "Monday September 16th. Can we possibly squeeze in something before then?"

"How about we try to do the opening ceremony sometime around the 12th?" suggested Ruth. "That'd be fine with the people here at Gulu – the sooner the better, really. Why don't you come down a few days beforehand, so that you can go straight back and get ready for your treatment?"

"OK," said Brendan. "Will do – are you still doing all right with What's-his name?"

"You mean Paul?" she asked, wondering whether her Dad had suddenly gone senile.

"No, you dafto, I mean Naffi, or whatever it is your calling the bairn!"

"Nyathi, Dad," she replied. "And we're not going to actually call the baby that – it's just a pet name for him, or her."

"Still don't know whether it's a boy or a girl, then?" asked Brendan.

"No, and we don't want to know either until the birth itself. It makes it more exciting." She changed tack. "Are you sure that you're up for it, Dad?"

"Wouldn't miss it for the world!" said Brendan, brightly.

★ ★ ★

But he wasn't feeling particularly bright. In fact, he was feeling pretty grotty. The headaches continued, banging right between his eyes – not sufficient for him to need to lie down, but making life unpleasant.

He'd also had three of his teeth pulled out a few days previously by the dentist. When he'd gone along for his pre-treatment briefing in the radiology department, they'd told him what they were planning to do. "We're going to irradiate the right-hand side of the neck from the side of your ear to the middle of your chin, and continue down to the right-hand side of your throat." The radiologist said it matter-of-fact, as if they were going to paint the conservatory.

"What side-effects are there going to be?" asked Brendan, fearful of the worst sort of side-effect but rather hoping that there would be a few minor inconveniences of the sort that hypochondriacs need to share with everyone.

"There could well be heightened skin sensitivity and a sore throat for a while, and there will almost certainly be no saliva glands on that side permanently." It didn't seem too bad. He could (he hoped) live with that – spitting out of only one side of his mouth wasn't the worst disability.

"Oh, and you'll lose hair around that area." Not having to shave wasn't bad either – but it'd be odd to have to shave off his little goatee beard after so many years. He'd grown it in the first place because he'd tried a full beard and discovered that he had symmetrical bald patches on his jaw as well as on the top of his head. His ex-wife Jenna had suggested that he looked less boring with some facial hair – a comment which still made him wince. Since then, he'd got quite fond of his little goatee. "It's growing on me..." he used to joke, but now, looking back, Brendan remembered that he'd said the same about his cancer – and the humour paled a little. But he was curious to see what he looked like without it.

"It'll grow back, of course," the radiologist continued. "Well, usually it does. Have you been booked in for dental treatment yet?"

"No," said Brendan, getting a bit annoyed now by the nonchalance of the radiologist. "Why do I need a dentist?"

"Because irradiated teeth don't receive as much oxygen because the small blood vessels tend to collapse, so we advise patients to have any potentially dodgy teeth pulled out before we start the treatment. They're only going to need taking out later on, when you'll feel much less keen on going to the dentists. Plus, if you have them done now, you can get them taken out for free!" He smiled as if he'd just delivered the sales-patter of the century. Brendan wondered if he was on commission from the tooth fairy.

★ ★ ★

Ben had been to see the editor of the Whitley Bay News Guardian – who'd been quite enthusiastic about the idea of the challenge. "We do quite a bit to support charity," he boasted. "Especially cancer. When they painted the town pink to raise awareness of breast cancer, we even changed the colour of our logo."

"Wow," said Ben. Hardly revolutionary, he thought. But he smiled nonetheless. "So, when do you think we can start?"

"Well, it's Wednesday today – so how about we get it in next week's edition, which goes to press on Monday. Can you write something out before the weekend so that one of our journalists can run an article? We all know Brendan's exploits, so it should get a good response."

And that was that. The die was cast. He couldn't back out now. But he didn't know what he'd initiated – or how much attention it would attract...

Chapter 17

On September 9th, Louisa drove Brendan through the Monday rush-hour traffic for his 9.00am appointment at the Freeman. A new Northern Centre for Cancer Care had opened in 2009 at the opposite end of the site from her own Unit, but she knew several of the staff. That week she was on the 2-10 shift, so hadn't needed to take time off. They were there for a CT scan and were directed to the pink area of the waiting room, from which Brendan was led off into the action area, which consisted of a bench and a large hollow ring. He lay on the bench and the bench moved him slowly through the ring. The idea was to plan the angles of attack for the radiotherapy treatment. They got pens out and marked his head and neck, and then he got whisked off to the mould room to get his mask made. The purpose of the mask was to ensure that the area being treated got the maximum amount of radiation that the healthy cells could withstand, and that the beams were fired into exactly the same area every time. Precision was crucial, so the patients had individualised Perspex masks made, to hold the head absolutely still on the bench under the gun, with marks on the mask to line the gun up to the exact "points of entry".

It wasn't exactly spa treatment, not that Brendan had ever been to a spa. They washed his face thoroughly, sponging away with a little pad on a stick for several minutes, dried his face with sterile wipes and covered his face and throat with what looked like putty. Then they slapped hot Plaster of Paris onto the putty, leaving him with two nostril holes but covering everywhere else, including his eyes. It was a good job that he wasn't claustrophobic, but it did seem a bit unnecessary when the beams should be a lot lower than eye-level.

He was told to come back the next day for verification, which, of course, was the trial run – giving Brendan the impression that they didn't really know what they were doing and were hoping that they could get a last bit of practice in before they killed him. Louisa explained that verification was in fact the process whereby the technicians ensured that the beams would not only hit at the right angle at the right place but would also penetrate to the right depth. Perhaps it was good for them to practice, thought Brendan, if it meant that they'd have a better chance of avoiding his spinal column and not making him paralysed.

It involved two sessions of 45 minutes inside the Machine, strapped into his mask and onto the bench, utterly immobile from the shoulders up, while the radiology technicians fiddled about and shouted numbers at each other. Brendan had only once been measured for a posh suit – at John Colliers, now long gone – and it reminded him of that. But then an evil thought about being measured for a coffin came to mind, so he thought about something else instead, or at least tried to.

★ ★ ★

On Thursday September 11th, the Whitley Bay News Guardian carried the story on page 5, under the gripping headline: "How are you getting to Church, Ben?" They knew how to write at the News Guardian. They used one of Ben's wedding photos, showing him with his crutches.

"Brendan Priest, world-famous Methodist Minister at Jact and global explorer, has contracted cancer. To raise money for Cancer Research, his son-in-law Ben, seen here on crutches on his wedding day after dressing up as Darth Vader to referee a Jact community football match and tripping over his light sabre, is inviting News Guardian readers to suggest and sponsor zany ways in which he can get to Church on Sunday mornings. He's taken over from Brendan as minister at Jact. The Church has become known locally as the 10.08 Church, because that's the time when the service begins. There's nothing boring about Jact Methodists!

So get your thinking caps on, you creative people of the area. It only costs 50p per suggestion – and each week we'll get a local celebrity to come and draw the winning entry, then Ben has until Sunday to arrange his transport. We will be there to photograph his journey to Church, and at the same time more of you will catch the idea and put in your suggestions for the following week.

We know how generous our readers are, so let's raise some cash for Cancer Research and show people how daft we Geordies can be! All you need to do is call into our Park View office, with your 50p and your suggestion – and if your suggestion is picked, that's Ben's Challenge for the following Sunday.

We would also love you to sign up to sponsor Ben for every week that he survives the challenge. Just pop into the office and sign a sponsorship form, or you can do it online at the News Guardian website."

★ ★ ★

On Monday September 16th, Ben was asked to come to the newspaper office, where he met the Whitley Bay Chamber of Trade Chairman, who'd been chosen as the local celebrity to draw the winning suggestion. The photographer was ready to capture the moment. "We've had a lot of entries," said the editor. "Over 200. And over 50 sponsors so far."

Ben didn't know whether that was good or not. £100 wasn't bad; 50 sponsors in a few days was pretty good. But it wasn't going to change the world, was it? Still, it was early days.

"And the winner is... Charlie Menzies, aged 7, from St. Mary's School, Cullercoats, who's challenged Ben to go to Church... in a tank!"

They all fell about laughing. That was that, then. Ben wouldn't even make one week.

"Oh well," he said. "That's that, then. Sorry, folks."

"What do you mean?" said the editor. "That shouldn't be a problem. Just get on to the Territorials at Tynemouth – they'll be happy to help, I'm sure. They did a similar thing a while ago for one of those programmes about making someone's dream come true."

Ben was sceptical, to say the least – but he'd give it a try. That was the least he could do.

Chapter 18

The flight to Entebbe seemed very long, even though Brendan slept a little as they crossed over Libya, waking up as the captain announced that they were crossing Darfur. Brendan looked out of the window as the sun rose over the plains of Eastern Darfur, seeing only the wide empty expanse of land and not the hardship caused by the conflicts still being waged to wrest control of the land from others. The world looked much more peaceful from 30,000ft. It had no walls, ramparts, fences or borders, or people...

When Brendan got off the plane at Entebbe he was delighted to be met by Paul, who was flying up with Brendan to Gulu in a special plane arranged by the Government as a sign of their support for Watoto. It wasn't as luxurious as Esther's Learjet, but it certainly beat the usual rattling local flight where you could usually see the rivets popping up and down on the unpainted wings and where your fellow-passengers could well include live chickens or goats.

Brendan only had one day to recover from the flights before the Opening Ceremony, and then would have only one night's rest before the flight back down to Entebbe and the long flight home. He felt pretty tired as they were driven up to the familiar pink hotel in Gulu, but he put a brave and cheery face on as he met Ruth, marvelling at her size ("Thanks, Dad") and her bloom ("Sweat, actually, Dad") and her energy ("Haven't got any, Dad – I'm about to drop"). They agreed that each was more tired than the other, and went in for a long, relaxed dinner – though only Paul seemed to have much of an appetite.

The following day Brendan enjoyed being driven around by Paul to see some of the other work that the Brendan Priest Trust was initiating, principally through the wisdom, creativity and sheer drive of Ruth and Paul. They went first of all to an ex-camp east of Gulu, which was being transformed into a trauma rehabilitation centre for former child soldiers. The idea was to build on Watoto's past work in the area of trauma counselling and rehabilitation, and particularly the programmes which had first brought Paul and Ruth together. This was now being extended from the mothers and children who'd been displaced by the conflict to the boys, now young men, who'd been drawn into the fighting – many of whom were so traumatised by what they'd witnessed and participated in that they were incapable of moving on from it.

The centre was being designed to integrate with the programmes of a new agricultural and technical college so that the former child soldiers could come out at the other end with both the psychosocial and practical skills necessary for them to have a hope of becoming productive citizens in society. This combined centre was going to be a training base for the whole of Northern Uganda.

Paul drove Brendan to another site in the northern suburbs of Gulu, which had been acquired for a brand-new Surgical Hospital. There were still thousands of victims requiring surgical intervention in Northern Uganda, and not just those suffering from war wounds and burns. There were also many women who'd been mutilated and facially disfigured, who required reconstructive surgery before they could begin to recover any sense of self-confidence or self-worth. This small surgical unit would enable this work to grow, and more lives to be transformed. And it was all being made possible only because of him, Brendan! It was incredible. He'd had no idea that his crazy adventures could produce such fruitfulness. But then, he thought, none of us knows what will result from our efforts. This was amazing, though! At the moment there was only a plot of land and some foundations being dug, but by the end of the year, Paul said, they hoped to begin equipping the hospital, and by Easter 2013 it should be open for business.

Brendan smiled. Easter was a good season to start restoring lives...

Paul then took him out of Gulu, eastwards towards Kitgum, to a hillside where Gulu's next Watoto village was being planned. In addition to the existing three villages in the Gulu area, Watoto through the Brendan Priest Trust was aiming to continue building to keep on track with their vision to rescue all orphaned children in Uganda. An optimum size village, Paul explained, required 150 acres of land and would care for 1,000 children. This site had been identified by surveyors as ideal, so the land had been bought and was in the process of being mapped out before building began.

Essential for every village was an elaborate infrastructure that had to be developed before the homes could be fit to inhabit. The requirements included access to water, landscaping, provision of septic systems and electricity. All the Watoto villages had homes with running water and a bathroom, which was rare in rural Africa. This particular village was being planned in collaboration with a new eco-friendly team of planners, who were investigating better ways of constructing the villages so that they were cost-effective, eco-friendly and sustainable for future development.

A little further on, Paul stopped the Landrover and pointed to the horizon. "And that," he said expansively, "is where the Watoto Farms Project is going to be started." Brendan stared, but couldn't see anything but rough ground. "I know it doesn't look very productive at the moment, but we are in the process of buying the land from the Government and have a team of agricultural planners working on how to use the land most effectively."

Paul explained that Uganda's fertile land and climate provided an excellent environment to develop self-sustainability through agricultural and livestock farming – and this was what the Farms Project was aimed at developing for the Watoto children, as they grew older and needed to find employment and become fully independent. The plans were to open three small-scale training farms with various agricultural crops and two more which would concentrate on livestock.

The farms would provide the children with opportunities to learn new skills through the apprentice schemes envisaged, while at the same time helping the villages become self-sustainable with agricultural, meat, dairy and poultry products. Any surplus would then be sold to the market. It was a good plan, carefully thought through.

Paul drove Brendan back into Gulu, and into a run-down part of the town. In an industrial estate with very few active businesses, Paul pointed out one warehouse that seemed to be a hive of activity. "And this is the best of the lot, in my opinion," he said, proudly. "Because this one was *my* idea!" Paul laughed a big, hearty, Ugandan laugh. "Come, I'll show you."

They clambered out of the Landrover, and Brendan saw the sign above the door: The Brendan Priest Trust Production Unit. "Like it?" asked Paul.

"Hmmm," said Brendan, reserving judgement, unsure what it was all about.

Inside they were met by a bedlam of noise – heavy machinery, shouts, bangs, whistles, and above it all, pulsating Ugandan music. It was a factory. More accurately, the Production Unit was a two-part operation designed to provide training for vocational students in carpentry and metalwork. One side of the building was for teaching metalwork skills. Brendan could see doors, windows, and shutters being made – and students learning how to weld and model. The other side had a carpentry section where tables, chairs, chalkboards, and cabinets were created.

"Are these for the villages?" asked Brendan.

"You've got it," said Paul, smiling. This is another part of the grand design – we get cheap materials for the village schools, houses and chapels – and the older children get trained as craftsmen and learn skills which they can take with them into adult life. Everybody wins. There's a programme for developing this Production Unit to make furniture and metalwork for selling at the markets as well."

Brendan was impressed – and said so. Paul beamed. Brendan was introduced to some of the young apprentices, who looked awe-struck at Brendan when they heard his name as if he was the most famous man in the world. It was all a bit unnerving.

From there they drove to Bulrushes, for Brendan to see for the first time the finished new wing which had been built with money donated by sponsors during his second journey round the world. It was modelled on the original Bulrushes in Kampala, as the original Gulu Bulrushes had been – but with its own neonatal section with incubators and a larger dormitory space – unlike the original Kampala Bulrushes where all the children were accommodated in one small room crammed with cots, with only a tiny space between cots for the staff to cross the room. The paintwork was bright and colourful, with murals of children playing – as in any Western hospital children's ward. It was a happy environment even though the children had suffered so much in their short lives so far.

As usual the children looked angelic – with huge white eyes in tiny black faces, all of them eager for a hug. Ruth couldn't lift some of them, but cradled one small child who was nearly two years old, but small enough to be taken for a newborn. Visiting Bulrushes was always the most wonderful and also most difficult of experiences.

The Opening Ceremony itself was the usual parading of dignitaries in their best suits and biggest smiles, anxious to reap kudos from being associated with a successful project, but only when its success was guaranteed. Then Brendan stood up and made a short speech, embarrassed but quietly proud too. Photos followed, then it was all over, everybody left, and life at Gulu Bulrushes resumed its normal routines.

"This is amazing," said Brendan to Ruth over dinner. "You've done so much in such a short space of time. It doesn't seem possible that so much could result from what I did." Ruth beamed. It *was* pretty impressive – and she and Paul had put it all together. It was all going beautifully.

Chapter 19

Ben had had no success with the Territorials, but the man he spoke to suggested that he looked on the Internet.

"What under?" asked Ben. "Tank hire?"

"Yes," said the man from the TA, icily – as if Ben was stupid. "There's a place in Newcastle with quite a business selling tank-driving experiences."

"Oh," said Ben, chastened. "Thanks," he added, lamely.

He got the details from the Internet, and contacted Turboventure[36], who said that they only really ran the tanks on their own land near Belsay. Ben spun the emotional blackmail story about Brendan, laid it on thick, and promised lots of publicity through the local news – and won the boss over.

On Sunday morning, Ben woke up at 8am, had a quick shower, then looked out of the window to see a large military transporter parked outside the house, with a tank sitting on its back. There were two men just getting ready to lower the tank off onto the tarmac, and Ben rushed down to say Hello.

After they'd parked the tank on the side street running to the back of the houses and Beverley Gardens, they came back to the house for a coffee and some breakfast. The men introduced themselves to Louisa, and explained to Ben what they thought would be best.

"It's only an FV432," the boss explained – which wasn't much of an explanation because Ben hadn't got a clue what that meant. "FV is a fighting vehicle – and what you'll actually be in is an Armoured Personnel Carrier, the lightest form of tank at only 15 tons. We're not allowed to let you drive it on the roads, but you can have a quick go if you want when we get off-road at the Church – though it might make a bit of a mess of the grass after last night's rain."

"What do I do?" asked Ben, thrilled to bits that it was going to happen. And it had only cost him £50 for the petrol down from Belsay.

---

[36] www.turboventures.co.uk/tank-experience

Turboventure were donating their time and vehicles for free.

"You sit there in the hot seat."

★ ★ ★

They set off at 9.30am. It was surprisingly smooth as the caterpillar tracks trundled along the road, past St. George's and the Aquarium to the Park Hotel, up to the Sainsbury's shop at the Broadway, and along Beach Road to Tynemouth Pool. Then they turned right past Morrisons to the Foxhunters Roundabout, up past Rake Lane to Jacksons Farm and along the New York road before turning right down Jact Lane into the village.

They were rumbling along at about 10mph – and the whole journey only took about 20 minutes. Heads certainly turned, even that early on a Sunday morning. People walking to get their Sunday papers, or out with the dog, or driving to the shops at Silverlink – all were flabbergasted to see a small tank sharing the road with them. The smiling, waving, figure of Ben standing up in the front seat reassured them that they weren't being invaded, and several cars honked a greeting. People looked out of their windows as some sort of jungle telegraph alerted the residents to the strange creature passing through.

As they entered Jact, dozens of people lined the kerb, cheering and waving as if it were royalty or at least a celebrity, rather than Ben and his two new friends from Turboventure. Grinding round the corner to the Methodist Church, the crowds grew, and there was even a TV crew as well as several photographers. Ben leapt out as they came to a halt, and posed for the cameras.

"Mission accomplished!" he yelled, and everyone cheered. "With many thanks to my new friends at Turboventure, who've let me have the use of their tank for the morning. If you fancy having a go, they offer Tank Driving Gift Vouchers! The camera crews bustled round, asking questions and pointing microphones. The Whitley Bay News Guardian photographer looked a bit put out. "Hope they don't steal our story."

★ ★ ★

During the service, which was even more packed than usual, the men from Turboventure wangled a lift back to Beverley Terrace, drove the transporter back to Jact and finished loading the tank onto the back just in time to grab a coffee with Ben and the congregation at the end of the worship.

That evening, they were one of the first stories on Look North – and both Turboventure and Ben's Challenge – as it was now being called – got a good half-minute of publicity.

The following morning, the News Guardian editor was cock-a-hoop. That morning alone, they'd had over 200 entries handed in, on top of the 200 from the previous week. They'd collected an extra £350 on top of the initial £100 – and they'd lined up a local actor who'd played the vicar on a TV soap to draw the winning entry for the following Sunday. The number of sponsors was now over 250, amounting to an estimated £300 extra income per week. The paper was getting valuable publicity too.

The actor picked an entry from the sackful. "It's from Eric Smith, of Shiremoor, who challenges Ben to go to Church by... unicycle! What about that, Ben?"

Ben smiled. He knew how to ride a unicycle – if he could get hold of one before Sunday. It was a few years since he'd had a go, though – and he'd never ridden one for 3½ miles.

Chapter 20

On the flight back to Newcastle from Schiphol, Brendan was flipping through the Daily Express which the flight attendant had given him, wondering why it was called a newspaper when it was mainly full of either opinion about news, speculation about news coming up or photographs of celebrities doing nothing. One such photograph was of various sporting has-beens gathering for a golf tournament to raise money for the Sir Bobby Robson Foundation. The brief text reminded people that Robson had "lost his brave battle with cancer in July 2009". It got Brendan thinking.

Why did everyone use warfare vocabulary about cancer? Why was it always "brave" when most of the time cancer victims were scared stiff? And hadn't Bobby Robson had four bouts of cancer which he'd seen off before the fifth lot saw *him* off – so shouldn't it have said that he won the fight against cancer 4-1?

Brendan wasn't an ardent pacifist or holy-war advocate, but it wasn't for that reason that the talk about fighting didn't seem to fit. There seemed to be an implicit judgement that if you died of cancer somehow you hadn't been good enough, brave enough or lucky enough and had let the side down and given in. Some people only died after they'd reached 100, but nobody accused them of "losing their battle with the ageing process". Cancer *happened,* like old age did – if nothing killed you off first.

The suggestion that you would fail yourself and your loved ones if you didn't want to use all your dwindling energy to fight the inevitable, brought into play a moral dimension. Acceptance was painted as cowardly. Any remission was undeserved if you hadn't bravely *fought* – and smiled a lot at your visitors through gritted teeth.

And what was all that bravery talk about? Bravery implied a choice, which cancer victims didn't get. It wasn't as if Brendan had willingly taken on cancer to save someone else from it, like one of his distant relatives in World War Two who'd chosen to seal the flooding engine-room from the inside when the ship had been hit by a U-boat torpedo, enabling the others to survive while he perished. Being a cancer victim wasn't like choosing a career in bomb-disposal or selflessly going to the aid of an old lady being mugged.

Brendan turned the page in the "newspaper" and was confronted with another photograph – of a little girl, "brave Kiana", who was going to America for a revolutionary leukemia treatment. The poor kid looked terrified – what choice did she have? She was being dragged off by her distraught parents who'd found another improbable lifeline to which their hope could cling. What was brave about it?

Brendan was reminded of his great-uncle Nat, blown up at Arras in 1916[37]. He'd probably been terrified, not brave – and he'd almost certainly have leapt at the chance to return home if it'd been offered. Brendan lowered the paper and tried to marshal his thoughts. Is it brave if you find yourself in a situation you haven't really chosen but find yourself in – as long as you don't take the easiest way out?

And yet... Brendan's Grandad had gone through the grief of losing his daughter (Brendan's Mum) to cancer when she was in her forties, losing his wife three years later after nearly 50 years of marriage, then losing his second wife after only two years' marriage. He'd decided that he'd had enough and walked into the Marine Lake at Southport and drowned[38]. Was that brave? Or cowardly?

And what should Brendan do, in the face of cancer? He knew that he wasn't brave enough to commit suicide. Yet he knew that the alternative could well be a long process of pain and deterioration, and he didn't feel particularly brave about facing that either. Maybe his approach should be one of resolute acceptance – putting up with the medical indignities or lifestyle deprivations as if it were an inconvenience, like the boiler playing up or tiles coming off the roof.

His resoluteness would be tested straightaway. His first radiotherapy session was due in two days' time.

★ ★ ★

Louisa accompanied him for his treatment. Everyone, of course, was there for the same thing. Unlike the wide spectrum of injuries and situations reflected in the waiting areas in A & E or even the general

---

[37] A story, based on my own great-uncle Nat, blown up at Arras in 1914, told in "Brendan and the Great Omission", p.67.

[38] The description is of my own maternal Grandad.

medical or surgical wards, the collection of humanity assembled in the design-winning Northern Centre for Cancer Care were sadly similar. No little kids howling or sobbing with the smart of a wound, but who'd be boasting about it tomorrow at school. No young men in football strip gloomily contemplating the end of their season but already composing their gory account for workmates. Instead, rows of silent, vacant faces – some with bits missing or misshapen, many gaunt and chemo-bald – already contemplating inactivity on a more long-term (or, from another perspective, a more short-term) scale.

Intensity Modulated Radiation Therapy or IMRT was the state-of-the-art name-of-the-game – supposed to deliver different intensities of radiation in order to protect adjoining healthy tissue and zap the cancer cells. Unlike the more conventional radiotherapy regimes, the Tomotherapy machine required daily, longer visits for only 10 days – but, from the drawn faces of those waiting, it obviously took its toll. Brendan wondered whether the silence was that peculiarly British reticence which rendered its citizens incapable of complaining about poor service in a restaurant or selfish parking by white-van drivers, or whether it was that other peculiarly British characteristic – the stoic London-Blitz solidarity shown in the face of a common but invisible enemy. No-one here, though, was cracking jokes, singing Vera Lynn songs or knitting socks for the troops.

When Brendan entered the hushed sanctuary of the Tomotherapy machine, he got exactly the same impression as on the first occasion when he'd come for "verification". The atmosphere was reverent, as in a mortuary chapel of rest – not a helpful association. Of similar unhelpfulness was the Machine itself, looking like the catafalque on which coffins rest at the crematorium.

He was guided through a routine which he'd get used to over the next ten days. This first day it was a frightening novelty but by the third day it would already be a dull rhythm. It involved sitting around in the waiting area with the others, then being called into The Room with The Machine. He engaged in sparkling conversation with the staff.

"How are you?"

"I've got cancer."

"That's what they all say."

"Really?"

After further similar banalities, he was weighed and told to get onto the bench.

The mask and upper chest restraint were fitted onto him, pressing his head back onto a padded metal plate, reminding him of a documentary he'd once seen about an execution by electric chair. He was slowly taken into the heart of The Machine, briefly wondering whether on the inside it was shiny silver like a rotisserie or matt black like an oven, but he couldn't see because the mask completely covered everything but his nostrils. It felt instantly like one of those torture machines where you were deprived of every sensation and quickly went mad, and he had to concentrate to feel the bench underneath him.

His face was clamped so tightly that he had no feeling of the mask or of his head inside it. It was as if his head had ceased to exist. Then he heard, dimly, the whirr of machinery and a warning buzzer – buzz, silence, buzz, silence, buzz, silence... He lost count, and then there was silence, then one long continuous buzz, then silence. He heard voices and instructions, as presumably they realigned everything, then the whole buzzing process began again. Once more he lost count – was it the same number before the silence, then the long buzz? And so it went on, time and time again.

And all he could think was: I'm going to die.

Afterwards he asked them what all the buzzing was about. "It's for us to clear the room before the radiation happens," said one of the technicians. "Otherwise we wouldn't have a long career."

Everyone laughed, except Brendan.

He prided himself on his logical brain, but he couldn't work radiation out. At various places inside The Room where The Machine lived, and in its antechamber, were those frightening yellow and magenta danger signs with the three propellers. All he knew about radiation was what he'd read about Hiroshima and Chernobyl.

He'd actually visited Hiroshima with Ruth some years before when they'd been en route from Nepal to New Zealand, taking advantage of the mileage allowance available on their "Round the World" air ticket. Their visit, in the stifling heat of an August day, chilled them both – as they wandered through the Memorial Park from the Dome to the eternal flame, past the Children's Peace monument with its displays of paper cranes. They even shared a pizza in a street café built virtually exactly at Ground Zero, and were given a paper crane each as they paid the bill.

Brendan knew that radiation caused cancer and killed people, so how could it cure cancer and save people? He knew the answer, of course – radiation kills cells. The hope in his case was that it was only the nasty ones being zapped.

On the way out of The Room, Brendan was given a tube of fluoride gel to rub into his gums every night. He was about to lose half his saliva glands, which helped food slide down the throat but also helped to neutralise the acidifying effect of food. The gel would stop infections and a build-up of plaque, he was told. But he would find it increasingly hard work to swallow food.

He actually found that he struggled to eat straightaway. And within two days he'd virtually given up eating as his throat was so sore, relying on milk to keep him alive as even orange juice was too painful. When they weighed him on the tenth day, Brendan was nearly a stone lighter. And it didn't change much after the radiotherapy had finished. Brendan was sure that he could feel the cancer at the back of his throat, blocking the passage of food and making him gag just thinking about eating.

Chapter 21

Ben's unicycle ride to Church was a great success – though his thigh muscles ached dreadfully the next day. He only fell off four times. The crowds came out to cheer him along the way – well, "crowds" was a bit of an exaggeration. A few women waved at him as he wobbled past Curves, the ladies' gym on Farringdon Road. Others too by Rake Lane Hospital, then little huddles of spectators along Jact Lane and into the village itself – with a gathering at the church of a hundred people or so, along with the TV crew and photographers. The congregation swelled too, and they decided that for the following Sunday's service they'd set up a sound-relay into the church hall.

So it was a sore Ben who dragged himself to the News Guardian office on Monday, to have a photograph taken of him shaking hands with a local boy who'd made good through playing in Duran Duran. The office had over 1,500 entries for that week's draw – and the amount in the kitty was over £1,000. The following Sunday's challenge involved a canoe – which seemed at first impossible in that there was no water-course through Jact. But then Ben thought of Brendan's long cycle ride down the Americas towing his Inuit kayak and made the decision to re-create it. It would be a useful link with Brendan – and an opportunity to reinforce the reason why he was doing the challenge.

Brendan volunteered to sit in the kayak while Ben rode the bike. Brendan had lost a lot of weight and looked different. He took ages getting out of the kayak at the Church, and he seemed all of a sudden to have become an old person. This realisation of the change in Brendan took Ben by surprise, and he found himself welling up as he spoke in front of the cameras. Ben himself was a bit sore and stiff – though he sensed that he was getting a bit fitter each week. He decided to join a gym – and even took Brendan along to see if he was up for a bit of gentle exercise. But it was all too much for Brendan, and he didn't last long walking on the treadmill before he had to go off to shower and change. He'd felt, he said, as if everyone was laughing at him – even though they weren't.

★ ★ ★

On the last day of September, Brendan went for a walk along Longsands, even though he felt ill. He bumped into someone he'd met before but didn't really know, who remarked on how slim he looked. "I wish I could lose weight like you!" they said.

"Yes, cancer's a great diet," snapped Brendan, too tired and poorly to remain tactful. It wasn't his best moment. Nor theirs.

Alan's Story: March 16th 1964

Alan had only been at the Fish Plant a few months when his Dad had collapsed in The Vine again, and never recovered consciousness. His Mam took this latest blow very hard, and took to her bed. Alan was left to his own devices, usually nefarious, and soon got himself into a load of trouble. His skill at spanny didn't extend to other gambling, and he kept trying to win back his losses, but succeeded only in compounding his debts.

Gambling was prominent among Foxheaders. Even though (perhaps *because*) gambling was illegal, it flourished. Alan's debt was largely to Fred Whitehouse[39], a bookmaker who operated from a back alley between Prince Charles Street and Queen Mary Street. He had a runner who used to warn him when the police were in the area, whereupon Fred's escape route was to disappear into a back yard, go through the house across the street, through another house and he'd be several streets away in no time at all.

By mid-1962, Alan was several hundred pounds adrift, and walked into the local Army Recruiting Office, which was why he was now in Tripoli.

He'd joined up for an initial three years with the Green Howards[40], unaware of the links with his Uncle George who'd died on the day Alan was born. After the horrors of initial training he'd been posted to Mons Barracks in Iserlohn, West Germany, as part of the British Army on the Rhine (BAOR). Alan enjoyed the camaraderie of the army, and took up football again, but found himself up against men much bigger and dirtier who seemed to play out their desire for killing on the football pitch because they never got the chance against the Soviets.

In February 1963, the 1st Battalion had been shipped out to North Africa, first to Benghazi for desert training, then to Tripoli itself. Again there was no fighting to be done, and life was generally pretty dull:

---

[39] Local folk history affirms the existence of a local bookmaker of this name and "turf".

[40] The deployment of the Green Howards, by then known officially as the Alexandra Princess of Wales's Own Yorkshire Regiment, is accurate.

pulling a Wombat up one sand dune, then down the other side; driving a jeep along a dusty track, then back again; digging latrines here, then somewhere else. One highlight was to parade in white dress uniform with polished bayonets for the visit of General Officer Commanding Malta and Libya, Major General the Lord Thurlow[41] – but the Big Man never spoke to him. He occasionally went out with the lads sightseeing, to places like the Roman ruins at Sabratha, but mostly he stayed in barracks, sunbathing. It was too hot for anything else. He'd got himself a wonderful tan, a deep walnut sort of shade on a body that previously had looked pasty-white.

He'd got a scam going with a local shopkeeper, which netted him a few pounds each week. He'd met the man in July last year, on a rare sortie out of camp, attracted by the roadside sign[42]: "FROM REFREGERATOR DRINK PENAPLE COLD AND SWEET". It struck the would-be entrepreneurial Alan that there could be a lucrative trade if he undercut the NAAFI and became the middleman between Abdul and the soldiers. It was highly illegal, of course, and he knew that he'd be up before a court-martial if found out. It worked really well for eight months, but a week ago he had indeed been found out.

He'd already been up before a preliminary hearing and faced the wrath of Lt. Colonel J B Scott (CO 1st Battalion). The lanky officer had paced up and down, banging his stick against his thigh, as Alan stood at attention. He knew that he didn't have a chance, and was summarily carted back to detention, pending court-martial in front of Brigadier Ramsey, the Area Commander.

Alan had plenty of time to review where his life was heading, and his answer was: nowhere. Which made it all the more providential that the padre had come round to see him that morning, March 16th 1964.

Alan had always hung loose from the Catholic priests of his boyhood, mainly because he despised having to go to Mass. He couldn't understand or see the relevance of all the fancy clothes, the bowing and genuflecting, the bells and smells. The only priest he'd liked was Father Shanahan because of his involvement with the football team.

---

[41] Inspired by the photograph at www.greenhowards.org.uk/oldsite/gh-museum-photos/libya/libya-1963-photo-0019.htm

[42] Inspired by the photograph at www.greenhowards.org.uk/oldsite/gh-museum-photos/libya/libya-1963-photo-0017.htm

The padre, however, was different. First of all, he was Church of England; second, he simply wore a clerical collar under his officer uniform; third, he treated Alan like a man; fourth, he talked sense; fifth, he came back and showed an interest in Alan which no-one really had ever done before, except his Mam and Dad.

"What's it all about, do you think, Alan?"

"What, my scam, you mean?"

"No, I know what that was about – making money. I meant *Life*."

"Oh, that... I don't know, Padre, *you* tell *me*!"

So he did.

Over the next three weeks, the padre came in every afternoon and spent an hour with Alan, and by the time his dishonourable discharge was authorised at the court-martial, and Alan was shipped back home, he was a changed man.

Sort of.

October 2012

Chapter 22

Brendan was working on his anagram. He added "I even used a fancy gym recently, but I felt an idiot - everyone laughed" to his list of phrases to get into it. It was looking quite good so far, but the test with an anagram was always nearer the end with whatever was left over after the good phrases had been used. So far he had the following:

Broccoli diet;
Headaches between the eyes;
Fungous feet;
Oh God;
Virus;
Is it all psychological;
Whatever's that;
Obscure parasite;
An odd spot for a polyp;
It isn't very funny;
I even used a fancy gym recently, but I felt an idiot - everyone laughed.

But there was a long way to go. He amended the letter-chart, knocking off 193 letters – leaving 319 letters to rearrange. Maybe his story over the next few weeks would throw up a few other notable phrases...

The radiotherapy had come to an end – and he felt wretched. The weight had fallen off him dramatically. The vague six-pack that he'd had when he returned from his second journey just four months ago was now looking more like a keg, for his chest had disintegrated from chunky pecs to wobbly moobs and there was no deviation in his body-shape from his shoulders until the start of a big, floppy pot-belly. He looked like the exact opposite of an hour-glass figure. He decided to add "big floppy pot-belly" and "really sad waistline" to the list for the anagram, and ticked off the letters: 37 more accounted for, only 282 left.

★ ★ ★

Ben received a phone call from America. It was Esther Blanchett, in person. Now this was a *real* celebrity. He sat up in his chair when he realised who it was.

"Hi Ben," she drawled. "How's it going?"

"OK, thanks. But Brendan's not so well, as you may have heard."

"I know. It's awful. My P.A. spotted something on the Internet and I've just seen a Youtube clip of Brendan on your Look North news, and he looks *awful.*"

Not the most tactful description, but Ben didn't dare say so. He explained about the radiotherapy, its side-effects on Brendan and passed on the uncertainty about the prognosis. "There seems to be a good survival rate, but everybody's cancer is different so statistics don't count for much."

"But that's *dreadful,*" Esther replied. "So what can I do to help?"

That rather took the wind out of Ben's sails. "Well, I'm not sure, really. Brendan's in the best hands at the Freeman. They've got all the most modern technology there and they're doing everything they can."

"But surely they could do with more machines, couldn't they? Can I buy some? Surely they can speed things up, can't they?"

Ben was flabbergasted. It was beyond his imagination for someone to have so much wealth at their disposal that they can talk of "buying more machines". He'd flown in Esther's Learjet and the chartered Gulfstream she'd arranged when Brendan's plane was blown up, but he still couldn't get his head round it. "Well, I don't know what to say. I'm trying to organise some fundraising for Cancer Research but it's peanuts really – though anything is better than nothing."

"Well, how about I boost your fundraising by an immediate donation of half a million dollars, and then we try to generate some fundraising through my TV show. It worked pretty well for Watoto, didn't it?"

Ben was speechless. Half a million dollars! And it certainly *had* worked well before – they'd raised $200 million through Brendan's second journey. He searched for something to say.

"That's amazing, Esther. Thank you ever so much. Brendan will be absolutely thrilled when I tell him – but how do you want to organise this? It's beyond our ability here to cope with the sort of campaign half a million dollars will demand."

"Tell you what, Ben. Why don't I come across at the weekend, and we'll do a show from England, explaining the situation and launching the campaign? And we can get a team from here across there to sort out the campaign and work out how to play it. How does that sound?"

It sounded amazing.

What a woman.

★ ★ ★

Ben phoned the editor of the News Guardian to tell him that he didn't need a celebrity for the following Monday – he'd be bringing his own. When the editor heard who it was, he paused, and then sounded suddenly very humble. "Do you think, maybe, she would come to the office and do the draw here? And we could meet her?"

Ben assured him that that was the plan. He could almost hear a "Hold the front page!" emerging from the other end, as the editor tried to work out the implications for the paper. This would be the biggest thing *ever*.

It rather made his latest challenge – to arrive at church on a donkey – pale into insignificance. He used the same animal which they'd borrowed on Palm Sunday, but Ben walked most of the way because he thought the poor beast wouldn't cope with his weight. It took them a good while, because the donkey kept stopping to eat flowers hanging over garden walls, but they made it in time, with Ben riding along Jact Lane – to be greeted by hundreds and hundreds of people, keen to applaud Ben but even keener to see who'd just arrived in the big limo. When Esther emerged, the crowds went wild and it was 10.05 before they were able to get into church. Brendan was already there, sat at the front on his own, and Esther ignored everyone else and went straight to him, embracing him and shedding a few tears in the process.

Ben found it a bit daunting leading the worship with a celebrity and a film crew in the congregation, but Ben and the musicians in Dead to the World were up for it and the songs and prayers were powerful. The worship theme was Identity, centred around the David and Goliath story. Ben had the passage from 1 Samuel 17 read out loud, and then asked the congregation to write down on a piece of paper who they were. They had a good laugh as people shouted out what they'd written, especially when one young lad said "Zitty".

"That's what my mates call me," he explained.

Most, of course, had written their name – and stopped. Some had written their name and what they did for a living (Esther was in this category). Others again had written their name plus their relationships (many women had done this: mother of..., wife of...). Brendan, tellingly, had written "Brendan, cancer victim".

Then Ben got people to look again at the story, and introduced the idea of identity amnesia, or forgetting who you really were. He said that the Israelites had been cowed by the Philistines and especially their champion Goliath, and had forgotten that they were the children of Almighty God. David triumphed only because he knew that he came from the people who'd been promised victory by God. He asked people to write down again who they thought they were, in the light of this discussion. And he reminded them of his travel arrangements that day and that Jesus had chosen to enter Jerusalem humbly on a donkey.

While they were writing down their own version of their true identity in Christ, he introduced another reading: 2 Peter 1: 8-9, which described Christians as those who are not "ineffective and unproductive in their knowledge of our Lord Jesus Christ", or who have not "forgotten that they have been cleansed from their past sins."

He then introduced another idea: identity replacement, saying that this was the result of the amnesia: that we often take on false identities because we forget our real identities. "It's a bit like Adam and Eve," he said, "Who forgot that they were "made to worship God" and instead became people "trying to be God."

Esther put her hand up. "Can I say something, Ben?" He nodded, and everybody hushed as she turned to the congregation (and the cameras). "I think you've got a remarkable young man to lead you here, folks. He's certainly made me think – because when you're famous like me you sometimes get lulled into thinking you're bigger and better than you really are – and that you're better than everybody else. So I thank you, Ben, for reminding me that we are all, as we Americans say[43], "created equal under God", and that that relationship with God defines us and gives us more significance than anything else."

"I want also to say that you've got a remarkable man in your midst with dear Brendan, who's suffering so dreadfully at the moment. I want you all to rally round these people over the next weeks and months, praying with me for Brendan's recovery, and raising funds for the Brendan Priest Cancer Care Trust. I don't want any of us to be, what was it, "ineffective and unproductive"? So I've arranged a special charity with that name, and have started it off with half a million dollars..." (there was a gasp) "...And I'll be hoping that together we can raise far more than that with your efforts here and the worldwide publicity generated by my TV show. So we're going to put Jact on the map once again – and I hope that you relish being at the centre of such an exciting project!" She sat down, and the congregation roared their approval.

They prayed and sang a song to finish with, but everyone had lost interest in worship and the whole assembly was buzzing with the news of the Trust and what it might mean.

Esther stayed at the Grand Hotel in Tynemouth with her entourage, and breezed into the News Guardian Office in Whitley Bay at 9.30am on the Monday morning, to draw the winning entry that week (Simon Hodges from North Shields; hovercraft), before leaving for the airport and her Learjet.

---

[43] Esther mistakenly quotes two different sections of Lincoln's Gettsyburg address, bringing them together into one phrase.

Chapter 23

The News Guardian produced a five-page spread on Esther's visit, with photos of her in the office with the editor, full photo coverage of the Sunday morning and a press release issued by Oracle (Esther's company) about the Trust. It was the biggest day in the paper's history, and they printed twice as many copies as usual. The number of sponsors grew to over 1,500 – raising over £4,000 per week for as long as Ben kept fulfilling his challenges.

★ ★ ★

After the excitement of the visit by Esther, and the amazing boost she'd given to the fundraising, life seemed a bit dull again for Brendan. He retreated back into the world of anagrams, and got thinking about all the countries he'd visited over the last few years. Then he just happened to see that "Mali and Qatar" was an anagram of "Iraq and Malta", and he was away for the next two days playing with the names of countries.

At the end of the afternoon, "Gabon and Italy" had become "Libya and Tonga"; "Belarus and India" became "Liberia and Sudan" and "Algeria and Sudan" became "Israel and Uganda".

The following day, he had a go at four nations at once, and by the end of the morning "Argentina, Belarus, Guinea and Somalia" had become "Guatemala, Lebanon, Nigeria and Russia" – and by the end of the afternoon he was very proud to have transformed the seven nations of "Ireland, Micronesia, Oman, Papua New Guinea, San Marino, Uganda and Zambia" into the nine nations of "Armenia, Gabon, Guinea, India, Monaco, Panama, Peru, Suriname and Swaziland".

But then Louisa came home and told him he was sad. So he returned to the hypochondria anagram – without much progress.

Chapter 24

Ben received another phone call from Esther on the following Thursday afternoon, just as he was putting a pizza in the oven. "Hi Ben!" said the now-familiar American drawl, "How're y'all doing? How's the hovercraft-driving?"

He laughed. "We're good, thanks. Louisa's out at work. Brendan's struggling a bit at the moment but he thoroughly enjoyed seeing you again – it bucked him up a bit. And the good news on the hovercraft is that, well, I've found one. There's a London company called Chillisauce[44] that runs hovercraft events in the North-East and with the lure of free publicity and a mention on "See Esther", they couldn't say Yes fast enough."

Now Esther laughed. "I'm sure we can manage that. I'm sending a team over to find an office from which we can co-ordinate the fundraising, and we need a UK co-ordinator who can hold everything together and raise the profile of the campaign. That's why I'm phoning. Hopefully it can be someone with an established link to both Brendan and the NHS, who's used to the finances of successful campaigns, somebody bright and enthusiastic rather than some dull old guy in a suit. Can you think of anyone?"

"No," said Ben. "I can't think of anyone right this minute. I don't really move in those sorts of circles."

"Oh, c'mon, Ben. You know who I'm thinking of!"

Ben was puzzled. What was she on about?

"I mean Louisa, you clutz! Your wife, for cryin' out loud! She's bright; she's good with money stuff – as she showed with the proceeds from Brendan's first journey; she's good with people, as her nursing career shows; she's good with the NHS – she's just won that award from the Royal College or whatever it's called, hasn't she?"

Ben was stunned. "But she's already got a job," he said, weakly.

"But this is an amazing opportunity to stamp her mark on the

---

[44] www.chillisauce.co.uk/activity-weekends/newcastle/hovercraft/

world. She'd be employed as part of my organisation, answerable to me and my managers, but making a name for herself in the North-East of England – and she'd be able to work closely with you and her Dad. And if she wanted, at any point she could go back to nursing – if that's what she really wants to do. But I don't want to appoint her without your say-so – not because she's married to you but because it's your idea we're building on and I think you should be involved in deciding how it develops."

"But... I'd *love* Louisa to do this. She loves nursing because it helps her feel that she's doing something worthwhile – but this would be even better. It'd be an amazing opportunity for her – but how do you know she'd do a good job?"

"Hey, Ben. I'm a pretty good judge of character – and I think you've got one helluva woman there. Let *me* take the risk on this one, OK? When does Louisa finish work? Can I call her later on and talk to her about it?"

"That'd be wonderful. She finishes at 10pm and is usually home by 10.45 – but she's usually pretty drained and goes to bed pretty soon afterwards."

"OK. There's five hours difference so that would make it 5.45, say 6pm here. That'll work for me. Don't say anything about it to her – I'd like it to be a surprise."

★ ★ ★

Ben couldn't relax at all. He phoned Louisa up at work – much to her surprise and worry.

"Is everything OK?" she blurted. "Is it Dad?"

"Don't panic, there's nothing wrong. I just thought I'd phone up to see how you're doing."

"Oh, OK. Are you sure everything's OK?"

"Of course I'm sure. Anyway, how are you doing?"

"I'm doing OK. But, if you must know, it's not one of my best shifts. We've just had one of the transplant patients die rather suddenly, so everyone's a bit stunned and upset. I'm just having a quick coffee before sorting out the body before the relatives get here, so I can't really chat."

"Oh dear, sorry about that," said Ben. "Will you be able to get away on time at the end of your shift?"

"Yes, I should think so. Why, Ben? What's going on? If you're planning anything, unplan it – I'm jiggered. Unless, of course, it involves..." She giggled, and turned the phone off, saving him the embarrassment of having to reply.

★ ★ ★

When Louisa got home, she found Ben watching some footie highlights on the TV, but he instantly and uncharacteristically switched it off, sped off to the kitchen and came back with a cold glass of dry white wine for her, got her to sit down on the sofa, and asked her how she was.

"Suspicious – that's what I am. What've you done? What've you broken?"

"Nothing!" he laughed, playing the innocent. "I love you, that's all!" – which, apparently, was the right answer. Louisa leapt on him, tickled and kissed him and managed to do all of that without spilling her wine. Then the phone went – and she groaned.

"Who can that be at this hour?" she moaned. "Just leave it, Ben. I'm not in." But he was already out of his seat and across to the phone.

"It's for you!" he announced, with a big grin on his face.

★ ★ ★

After the phone call, Louisa was stunned. Amazed. Bewildered. She couldn't get her mind in gear to think through the implications of Esther's amazing offer. It was... remarkable.

They stayed up ages trying to talk it through.

"But I'm a nurse – not a project manager."

"So far you are – but who knows what sort of a difference you could make if you got involved in providing cancer care to the North-East through your leadership of this?"

"But how can I? What do I know about business and corporate management? Nothing!"

"But that isn't what Esther wants! She wants someone who'll breathe a bit of fresh air into the stuffy world of NHS politics."

"Well, I certainly know a bit about systems and how they go wrong. Sister Lilian taught me plenty about that!"

"And you're good with money. And you obviously have a close link with Brendan – which will be important for whoever does the job. And you've got loads of contacts at the Freeman, which is where all the cancer stuff happens, isn't it?"

"Well, quite a bit of it. But they also do plenty at the RVI."

"You see, you know how it all maps out on the ground. And I bet you can easily see what's missing and what would really benefit cancer victims."

"Well, I might, I suppose. But I'm not really trained in specialised cancer work, even though I've seen a fair bit of it."

They argued themselves round in circles. It was only as they finally dragged themselves off to bed, well past midnight, that Ben realised neither of them had mentioned money. "How much is she offering you?"

"Twice as much as I'm on now – with loads of benefits. Plus a productivity bonus of an extra 0.5% of whatever's raised."

"Wow. That could be a lot! Shame she didn't make the offer before she stumped up half a million dollars..." Ben laughed.

"Oh, it includes that. I'd get $2,500 as a signing-on fee."

That shut him up.

Chapter 25

Brendan had already had the full range of reactions to his cancer from friends and acquaintances.

The people at Church were mostly older than him, and some seemed to see Brendan's cancer as a threat to their own morale – as if the one whom they'd expected to do their own funeral was now cheating them by threatening to peg out first. They tended to minimise the seriousness of Brendan's illness, which meant that Brendan often reacted by over-egging the likelihood of his own death before theirs – almost to spite them. So it'd become a bit of a negative cycle.

Then there were those who seemed to lap up any morbid detail they could. Really? That big? These people seemed to thrive on being in the know – as if knowledge was power. So Brendan tried to feed them as little information as possible. He seemed to have developed a sense of discernment about whether they were genuinely interested or were just after gossip-fodder.

Another group of people projected their own fears onto Brendan. They either proclaimed that they were sure Brendan would get better – as if they had a hotline to God or believed that Brendan was curiously immortal. Brendan couldn't be bothered to indulge their fear, so he usually just shrugged off their false optimism. Or they made out that Brendan was ruining their happiness by creating a problem. How dare he be ill because it was ruining their cosy life. It became a sort of cancer-by-proxy, whereby they had an awful time and made sure that Brendan knew how awful it was for them.

Some people forgot that Brendan was ill, and phoned up asking him to do this or that, a baptism or a talk. When he pointed out that he couldn't easily commit himself and why, they then apologised for troubling him. He then said that he'd like to help if he could, so they went ahead and pressed him to put it in his diary. If he stressed that it had to be provisional they got uppity again. So Brendan apologised for making them feel guilty and booked the baptism or talk into his diary anyway. It was a ridiculous merry-go-round of trying not to step on people's toes but managing to stamp on them instead.

The truth was that he did feel a little brighter, though he couldn't stomach much in the way of food. The worst side-effect was not the curious lack of saliva which left him dry-mouthed and with a dry-chested cough, nor was it the sore throat, which was rough but endurable. He could cope with the all-pervading nausea which necessitated anti-emetic pills. He endured relatively lightly the constipation caused by all his medication. Worst of all was the effect on his taste-buds, not that he was very epicurean. He'd never been one for the gourmet pretentiousness which stuck out for pink beef and al-dente vegetables or pasta. He never bothered much if it was a bit soggy, sunk in the middle or wasn't quite the right colour. He'd avoided the eighties' obsession with the avocado, the nineties' fad for sun-dried tomatoes and the noughties' taste for pesto or couscous. He didn't much care for little portions on huge plates. But now he didn't have *any* taste for *anything*. Not even the hot curries with which he'd tried in the past to show that he was made of strong stuff. Everything still smelled wonderful, but now tasted insipid.

At College a long time ago he'd once been given a persimmon to eat, which had sucked all the moisture out of his mouth and rendered the fruit inedible. Now everything he ate had that same property. His mouth dried up instantly and the food became like candle-wax if solid or wallpaper paste if runny.

The weight, unsurprisingly, continued to fall off him.

He remembered that when this had happened to John Diamond, the journalist, another self-acclaimed "food Philistine", he'd interpreted his loss of taste as the compassion of God, who "causes the raddled nose of the tertiary syphilitic to drop off... (so that) the dying wretch avoids smelling his own putrefying flesh."[45] It was wonderful use of language, but was that how God worked? Even though Brendan was similarly undiscerning in the field of gastronomy, what was the point of God denying him the ability to taste good food?

Brendan was assigned a dietician, who encouraged him to eat everything that they usually told people not to eat – especially food containing great globs of fat or sugar, in the hope that some of the food would somehow get through and provide nutrition before the body recognised that it was eating something and protested.

---

[45] Ibid. p.114, in which Diamond quotes a sermon by John Donne.

Yet, despite all this and the fact that he was sure with some sixth-sense that the cancer was not only still there but spreading, Brendan felt brighter. He took to listening to classical music, and found distraction with anagrams of composers until Louisa caught him at it and told him off again.

He'd managed, however, to transform "Bernstein, Handel, Pachelbel, Prokofiev, Ravel, Scarlatti, Schumann, Sousa and Stamitz" into "Beethoven, Brahms, Casals, Dvorak, Faure, Holst, Liszt, Palestrina, Puccini and Telemann" before she made him stop. It was nine into ten – his best yet.

He tried to get out for a walk each day, but often couldn't manage the steps down to Longsands so had to potter along the top pavement until the wind or rain sent him home again. He started to get pins and needles across his back, and tried all kinds of liniments to take away the tingling.

He added "pins and needles across my back. I did try using a liniment on it the other day" to his other phrases for the long anagram, which consumed another 62 letters and took him well over halfway.

But alongside this brightness was a deep sense that time was running out for him.

★ ★ ★

Time was passing all too slowly for Ruth too. It was now, in mid-October, Week 32. The baby was moving around like a prisoner in the exercise yard, round and round and round. Often, to Paul's delight but her bemusement, a knee or an elbow would bulge out from the dome of her belly or, to her discomfort, jab something inside her and make her wince.

The two of them were still in Kampala most of the time, though Paul went off for two days each week up to Gulu to check on the building work in the various projects. He made sure that he took one of Watoto's satellite phones with him at all times, so that he was never out of touch if something changed for Ruth. They knew now that the baby was viable and that even if Ruth went into labour suddenly, there shouldn't be any risk to the child or to her – as long as she stayed close to the hospital. But Ruth was anxious to come back to Britain – to see her Dad and to receive a better standard of hospital care. So, in consultation with Paul and Watoto, she'd arranged to fly back in three weeks' time. She tried meanwhile to keep herself going – looking over contracts, schedules, inventories, accounts – but it was getting more of a struggle both to concentrate and to summon up any energy.

★ ★ ★

Louisa had spoken to the management at the Freeman, who readily agreed to release her with immediate effect but encouraged her not to turn her back on nursing completely because, they told her, she was a "very capable" nurse. They waived her notice on condition that the team from Detroit under her management set up their base at the Freeman, so that they could not only keep an eye on what happened but also bask in any kudos that might be going. This suited Louisa and the team perfectly – for it gave them the use of offices now and, potentially, laboratory space later.

So Louisa found herself at the forefront of a team of Americans, all of them younger than her but with a lot more knowledge about business and procedures. And yet she felt curiously unthreatened by them, and they responded respectfully to her leadership. Most of the team were from marketing backgrounds, and set off immediately into the networks, advertising their new product (the Trust), with Esther Blanchett always hovering in the background as an invisible fairy godmother.

Go-ahead moguls of industry and business quickly jumped on the bandwagon with sponsorship and resources. The media beat a path to their door, offering space on TV chat shows, news programmes, and advertising slots in cinema and across the broad swathe of the Internet.

Within a week, Louisa's diary was filled with appointments, and she learnt quickly that the best way of approaching these exposures was to be herself. The fact that she was raw and unaffected was part of the sales pitch. The fact that she was Brendan's daughter was a bigger selling-point. The link with Esther, however, was the biggest draw of all.

By the end of the month, she'd raised over £35 million in corporate sponsorship deals, and been offered all kinds of help with the project. She couldn't ignore the fact that according to the terms of her contract she'd already earned $175,000 in productivity bonus. She'd earned more in two weeks than she would have earned in five years as a nurse.

When she told Ben about the sort of money she was earning, he nearly had a fit. "But that's ridiculous!" he protested.

"I know," Louisa agreed. "So what shall we do with it?"

"Well, we don't need anything, do we? We've got a lovely flat which you already own. We could do with a car maybe, so that you can drive to work rather than carry on catching the bus – but we don't really need anything else, do we? Why don't we just give it back to the Trust?"

"Yes, that'd be good. But I'll have to work out the most tax-efficient way of doing it. How about I keep the salary and give the productivity money away?"

"Sounds good to me," said Ben. "I've never had any money, so I've never really felt the need for it."

Louisa gave him a big kiss. "You're a good man, you are, you know. I'm glad I picked you."

At this, Ben hooted with laughter and jumped on top of her. "Oh, so you picked me, did you?" It dissolved into squeals and giggles and then turned into something even more enjoyable.

Chapter 26

Ben had managed over the previous weeks to acquire and get the hang of driving a hovercraft, a dustbin-lorry and a dog-sled. The most recent challenge was a sky-dive, weather-permitting, or a pram if not. He rather hoped it would be cloudy, but Sunday dawned fair and bright, and Louisa drove him in their new shiny red Beetle to Shotton Airfield near Peterlee. The training and flight had been arranged privately, but the Peterlee Parachute Centre were going to do a freefall display whilst Ben and his instructor did a tandem skydive[46].

They took off at 9am in a Cessna Grand Caravan turbine parachuting aircraft, which was probably older than Ben and the instructor if you put their ages together, and took 20 minutes to circle up into the wispy clouds and head north. It gave the instructor time to coach Ben on what order things happened in – not helped by the jokes of the display team who were taking the mickey out of the instructor all the way through. One extra instructor was going to take a video of Ben on the way down.

There were 15 freefallers crammed into the seat-less Cessna, sitting between each other's legs like some sort of stag party drinking game. 12 of them were jumping first, from 15,000 feet – which would only give them about a minute freefalling time to attempt a "ring", then the plane would drop to 13,000 feet and Brendan, strapped to the front of the instructor, would freefall for about half a minute before the parachute opened and he came down rather more slowly, hopefully. The photographer would climb out first onto the wing and shoot them preparing to jump, then follow them down immediately and manoeuvre himself to get shots close up, before breaking away as their parachute was deployed and freefalling a few seconds longer to get ahead of them, parachuting down to land first and taking some footage of them landing, hopefully, in the grassy front of the Church.

As the door was opened, the wind whistled past and the display team leapt out in a continuous stream of limbs and shouts, suddenly the

---

[46] What follows is loosely based on a tandem skydive I did at Shotton Airfield to raise funds for Action Aid in May 2009.

enormity of the challenge hit Ben. Why was he doing this? Then, all too soon, the plane was empty and he was being shuffled forwards, there was one last check of the fastenings, one last reminder of the procedures, then he was dangling over the edge of the plane, not touching it because he was sitting on the instructor's knee, arms crossed on his chest. Then he was suddenly somersaulting forwards and downwards, seeing the ground below then the plane then the ground again, but not taking it in, searching quickly for the display team but not seeing them. He did remember to open his arms wide. Quickly, amazingly, someone floated in front of him – the photographer pointing the video camera at him, encouraging him to do a thumbs-up before waving and flying off to the left. The instructor tapped Ben on the shoulder and he crossed his arms again and suddenly was yanked skywards as the parachute opened.

It felt like he'd gone upwards, but actually he'd decelerated from 150mph to about 25 mph and was still descending earthwards. The instructor now was yelling in his ear, congratulating him on getting everything right, and pointing out the display team, now parachuting close to the ground off to the left. Brendan could make out features in the landscape: Whitley Bay lighthouse to the right, the newly-refurbished dome of Spanish City underneath, and Earsdon church tower to the left. That was the direction into which they now turned, with a swirl that made Ben feel a bit sick, but suddenly he scanned across to recognise Jact coming towards them, with the big white cross on the grass outside the church, created the previous night by the lads from the Youth Club out of old fibreglass panels.

They seemed to be missing their target, but then the instructor swooped them round – at which point Ben nearly lost his breakfast. They came in over the houses and landed just a few metres away from the centre of the cross. The crowd cheered and Ben waved. The instructor unclipped the fastenings and Ben was able to stagger into the arms of Louisa, who gave him a big hug. "Not too tight, he whispered, "Or I'll chuck up."

The first song that morning was "Lord, I come to you"[47], with its chorus reference to the passage in Isaiah 40: "And as I wait, I'll rise up like an eagle, and I will soar with you, Your Spirit leads me on in the

---

[47] By Geoff Bullock, lyrics quoted from
www.lyricsmania.com/power_of_your_love_lyrics_hillsong_united.html

power of Your love."

Now that he was once again on terra firma, Ben could appreciate the words better. Up there he'd been exhilarated during the freefall but hadn't really had time to enjoy it before it was over, and the parachuting had made him feel sick. Perhaps being an eagle wasn't all it was cracked up to be.

But the last three weeks of challenges had brought in £900, £3,200 and £12,150 respectively. Publicity was growing, as was nationwide interest in the fundraising project. The sponsors were flocking on board as well – now there were over 12,000 offering more than £30,000 for every week Ben fulfilled the challenge. At the same time, Esther had given the project a huge boost on her shows – and the Oracle team under Louisa had received over $12 million already, mainly from the US, but unsurprisingly from further afield too. Esther was a worldwide celebrity – and so was her fan-base.

Within three weeks of starting the job, Louisa was suddenly responsible for nearly $50 million. What was she supposed to do with it?

Alan's story: July 21st 1969

The morning after watching Neil Armstrong walk on the moon, Alan could hardly walk to the bathroom. He and his mates had had a few beers, and he was suffering now. They'd had a great time, though, and the air down at the Wheatsheaf was full of speculation about progress, and what mankind would achieve next.

Tom had reckoned they were going to Mars, but Jim put his money on colonising the moon and sending ordinary people to live there, "a bit like them new flats they're going to build at Byker, which no-one'll want to live in. They're bound to send somebody there – and I reckon the moon'll be the same." Everyone'd laughed at that point, comparing the moon to Byker – mind you, it was a bit of a wasteland both before and after they'd pulled down all the old slums.

Alan didn't often get a hangover, because he didn't often go out with the lads, especially since his marriage to Pauline last year. He kept getting ribbed about that, because most of his mates at work were single. He'd discovered in himself, though, an old-fashioned streak that cherished old traditions, and the idea of marriage and settling down had been rather attractive.

Despite his army record, he'd managed to get a job at the Ministry at Benton, on the eastern outskirts of Newcastle. His Mam had died, so he had no ties now with Middlesbrough. He was still wary of the place, conscious still of his debt to Fred Whitehouse, though he was probably dead too by now. Alan had got digs in Shiremoor, and felt that he was making something of himself at long last. He'd secretly been visiting a new sunbed parlour in Wallsend, which kept his Libyan tan going. It was his one bit of vanity, he thought, comparing himself favourable with the whiteness of his mates. He knew it got the attention of the girls as well.

He'd not exactly been "converted" by the padre, but he'd been "impressed" by him into a duty-bound, rules-and-obedience model of Christianity which at least provided a framework on which Alan could hang his future. God became for him a sort of benign CO, who gave regulations and expected him to comply, with rewards if he did and jankers[48] if he didn't.

He'd turned his back on illegal money-making schemes but was on the lookout for his Big Chance, which hadn't yet happened. The Ministry was definitely not going to be his path to fame and fortune. The Civil Service was steady and unremarkable, but it was safe and he and the rest of the drones were constantly being reminded by the hierarchy that one of the Ministry's main attractions was the civil service pension at the end of it. But Alan felt like a small fish in a very big aquarium, swimming round and round under the scrutiny (and protection) of others, but never achieving anything or doing anything differently.

It would do for now.

The highlight of his week had become the Rex or the Plaza on a Saturday night. He wasn't really into the dancing, but that was the place where blokes went to find a girlfriend, and often a wife. Two years ago he'd met Pauline, one of a group of girls from Jact on a night out to celebrate someone's 21st. It hadn't been love at first sight, but they'd liked each other and had a laugh, and agreed to meet up again the following Saturday, and things had progressed gradually from that point, culminating in their marriage at Jact Methodist Church on September 1st 1968.

Pauline's parents attended the church every Sunday, but Pauline herself had voted with her feet some years before. Yet she wanted to go back there for the wedding, and the Minister said that he wanted them to come regularly to prove that they were committed both to each other and to God. This fitted in well with Alan's view of God, and he didn't have a problem with the services, which were much more understandable than anything he remembered from his past. The singing was lively, to some good stomping tunes belted out by young Brenda on the old harmonium, and the Minister himself was young and lively and the sermons usually were peppered with funny stories and illustrations. Pauline wasn't particularly impressed, but Alan decided that he might give it a go after the wedding as well as beforehand.

After the honeymoon in Llandudno, they returned to their new

---

[48] An Army term for withdrawal of privileges or the imposition of light punishment or extra duties.

council house in Jact, near enough to Pauline's parents that Alan could borrow her Dad's lawnmower, but far enough away that her Mam didn't keep popping round. They didn't have much, but they were happy. Pauline indulged him with his little trips to Wallsend to top up his tan, even though it seemed to her a bit unnecessary. It kept him happy. It did make Pauline feel a bit white in comparison when they walked out together, though.

And in the last year, he'd gradually got more involved at the Methodist Church. He went along most Sunday mornings and had even been invited to join the Finance Committee. The Committee had only met three times but Alan had proposed various ideas about bringing in extra income, even though the old fogies had vetoed most of them. Pauline's Dad had been really pleased that Alan had kept going. Pauline herself usually stayed in bed and had a lie-in, before cooking Sunday lunch ready for Alan when he came home. The arrangement seemed to be working fine all round.

Now, though, he had to get himself ready for work. It was Monday, and another five days of processing forms lay ahead of him. He made himself some toast, but couldn't face it – and staggered off to the Metro.

November 2012

Chapter 27

Brendan's quality of life was being blighted by his difficulty eating. Whatever he managed to con his body into taking down into itself usually re-emerged in protest within a few seconds. It made the whole exercise futile, and caused coughing, retching (both of which hurt his throat dreadfully) and, oddly, earache.

He went to the oncologist who seemed baffled by it, but suggested that perhaps a surgeon should take a look. Brendan wasn't stupid – he knew that this meant more knife-work, but before that he had to endure another naso-endoscope. It felt like a pencil was being rammed up his nose and was deeply unpleasant. What made it worse was that it revealed nothing. There was no obvious reason why food was continuing to come back up.

They sent him for another CT scan, blood tests and X rays. Whilst they had him in their clutches, they also sent him down for a barium swallow.

"Don't I get the full meal?" he asked the nurse.

"Believe me, you don't want all three courses, just stick with the starter," she replied, handing him a plastic cup of poison.

Brendan tried to gulp it down – but his throat objected and most of it came back down his nose. As he wiped himself down, he was reminded of the joke which he'd told against himself many times. Throat cancer *was* hard to swallow, but especially when they made him drink foul concoctions. For the first time, he was glad that his taste buds were shot. It *looked* disgusting – couldn't they make it at least *look* like cherryade?

"I won't be returning to this restaurant in a hurry," he joked to the nurse.

She looked at him pitifully, but he wasn't sure whether it was at his pathetic joke or his pathetic condition. There were so many different tests and procedures they were trying on him, as if they had to prove to him that they weren't skimping because of the NHS cuts. But it seemed like they were just going down a list of possibilities, ticking off items in turn, rather than having much clue about what was happening inside him.

On November 5th, he went in to face the fireworks. The blood tests were fine – no problem. The barium swallow revealed no problems either in the oesophagus or lower down. The X rays were inconclusive. But the CT scan showed two suspicious shadows where there shouldn't be anything – one (as expected) at the stem of his tongue, the other (unexpectedly) at the site of his tonsils which had been surgically removed when he was a lad. The good news, however, was that there was no apparent enlargement of his lymph glands.

He was booked in the following Thursday for a double biopsy.

★ ★ ★

Ben and Louisa were finding life stressful but exciting. Louisa was determined not to get suckered into spending any of the Trust's money until the consultative group had formed a strategy about how it could be used most effectively and appropriately. She was particularly keen to see if there was anything that arose out of her Dad's treatment that needed extra equipment or research. Until they knew what he was facing, they couldn't make much progress.

Ben was trying to maintain a sense of equilibrium. His wife was now the CEO of a leading-edge cancer charity, and he was bumbling along as a lay minister, with help from an increasingly incapacitated Brendan, and trying to meet increasingly more complicated challenges week by week. In recent weeks he'd been able to find, hire or arrange, and arrive at Church in a pram (the week after the sky-dive), a JCB and a lifeboat.

The latter proved quite easy, as they had good contacts with the Cullercoats Lifeboat Station. RNLI HQ in Poole confirmed that they were happy for Cullercoats to loan Ben their retired inflatable lifeboat, and to launch the official lifeboat for a training exercise so that Ben could borrow their boat-carrier and vehicle for the morning.

On the following Monday morning, he'd turned up at the News Guardian office to be photographed with a Newcastle United footballer, who drew out of the enormous sack of entries the most puzzling challenge yet: crowd-surfing. The editor looked at Ben in puzzlement – what did it mean? Ben thought that he knew, but hoped that he was wrong. They phoned up the "winner" who was a young guy who'd been down for a stag weekend, and actually lived in Glasgow.

"What exactly do you have in mind?" asked the editor.

"Crowd-surfing like in a mosh pit," came the reply.

The editor was glad that his expression couldn't be seen by the person on the end of the phone. Crowd surfing? Mosh pit? "Oh, yes... that!" he said, "Thanks ever so much."

"That's cool," said the man on the other end. "That's what I meant, I think. I dunno, really. I was drunk at the time."

The editor put the phone down and shook his head. "Apparently he meant surfing in a crowd with a moss-pit, whatever that means."

Ben laughed. "No, it's a *mosh* pit!" he said. "It's the standing-up part of a gig which is jam-packed with young people. Crowd-surfing is when they pass people backwards and forwards over the heads of the crowd."

The editor looked confused, but Ben wanted to consider the options. Was it possible? He was about 13 stone, so there was no way a single line of people could carry him over their heads, but maybe a *double* row of people could? Was it possible to challenge people back – for them to get involved themselves in a mass exercise? How many people would he need?

He set about doing some calculations in the News Guardian office. He already knew that it was exactly three miles from his front door to the Jact Church, as long as they took the pedestrian route which cut the corner through the Marden Estate. He'd need to be supported, he reckoned, by eight people at a time. He was six feet tall, which was, he calculated, 0.001136364 of a mile. So the number of people needed for the full three miles was 21,120.

"Are there that many people in Whitley Bay?" he asked.

"Oh yes," said the editor. "We circulate 21,000 copies each week house to house and have over 56,000 copies printed each week in total. The official population over 15 years of age is about 39,000, I seem to remember. I've got the latest demographics in a file somewhere – let me have a look for it..." He scrabbled around in a filing cabinet...

"Here we are. The number of people between the ages of 15 and 54 is 23,279; the number of people over 55, 15,634 – and that's just in Whitley Bay. When the news gets out, people may well come from miles away."

"But will sufficient numbers turn out early on a Sunday morning?" asked Ben.

"Well, that'll be the challenge, won't it? And if they don't, those at the start who've passed you onwards will have to run on ahead and have a second go, won't they?"

★ ★ ★

Brendan turned up at the Freeman on the Thursday morning for his biopsy. He was taken up to the ward, changed into a surgical gown, then prepped for the short op by the surgeon, who explained what she was going to do (take a sliver of skin here, a sliver there, here a sliver, there a sliver, everywhere a sliver, sliver...). Old Macdonald not only had a farm but could make a set of suitcases out of the skin Brendan was donating.

Then the anaesthetist came along and asked Brendan the same questions they always asked. He was given a pre-med and wheeled down shortly after 2pm. And he was back on the ward just over an hour later. When he woke up he could instantly feel his throat on fire, and was given the sort of painkillers they give horses. He kept asking for more painkillers throughout the evening and kept waking up in the night and demanding more.

The following morning, he was beside himself – and when the surgeon appeared mid-morning he went for her. "I've never known agony like this. I can hardly talk it hurts so much. What on earth have you done to me?" She smiled at him sweetly and said, "Well, Mr. Priest, if talking causes you such agony, I suggest you don't talk then. But it won't hurt to listen, will it?"

Brendan wanted to say a whole load more, but she did have a point. He nodded for her to continue.

"OK. This is what we did. We took tiny slivers of tissue from all your tonsilar area. I don't know if you know much about tonsils – you probably thought you'd got shot of them when you had your tonsillectomy, but even when you've had what we call the palatine tonsils taken out, there's still a tonsilar stub, which is what we took biopsies from yesterday. The tonsils are made of lymphoid tissue, which contains cells of the immune system that are involved in fighting infection. There's also a patch of lymphoid tissue at the base of the tongue, called the lingual tonsil. We took biopsy material from there too, and were surprised at how rough the skin of the tongue was. Other lymphoid tissue occurs in the adenoid area which is the highest part of the pharynx behind the nasal passages, and we took samples from there too. So it's not surprising that you feel a bit sore, because that area is very sensitive."

"We sent the tissue samples straight down to histopathology. And the results are mixed. The adenoids are clear. But I'm sorry to say that there are signs of cancer in both the other areas: the tonsilar stub and the stem of your tongue, and some of the lymph nodes seem to contain secondaries too. So I'm afraid it means a more major operation, to remove the tumours on the stub and the tongue and see how many lymph nodes we have to remove in your neck before we catch up with its spread."

"Can I go home now?" croaked Brendan, concluding that he was going to die and he'd rather do it at home.

"Of course you can. But we'll give you plenty of painkillers and have you back on Tuesday afternoon for the operation on Wednesday morning. That OK?

Brendan gulped. Of course it was OK. He was going to die anyway, so why bother?

Chapter 28

On that same Thursday, the News Guardian was distributed, with its big headlines challenging the people of North Tyneside to turn out in force along the route – with maps attached and rough timings, starting at 7.00 and finishing at 10.00am, if all went to plan. "BE PART OF A WORLD RECORD ATTEMPT THIS SUNDAY" shouted the headline. The paper explained that officials from Guinness World Records were going to be there, counting the number of participants and timing the whole event.

The present world record for crowd surfing, it reported, was held by a Dutch DJ and radio presenter, Giel Beelen, who spent two hours, three minutes and 30 seconds aloft being passed around 250 helpers in Hilversum while his show went out on radio[49]. "But the people of the North-East can do better, can't we?" came the challenge. "Not only are we going to smash the number of participants, but we are also going to break the duration record. Come and join in!"

Big posters went up in Whitley Bay and North Shields town centres, advertising the "Community Event in aid of Cancer Research", with big pictures of Ben and Brendan, and, of course, Esther Blanchett. A4 posters were taken round for display in every shop, every pub, every church, and wrapped around lampposts. It was the talk of the town. It was on Look North and all the local radio programmes, and a massive Facebook campaign was initiated to encourage people to take part. A pipe band was organised to march along the route ahead of Ben, and the police and St. John's Ambulance were forewarned about the plans and timings.

★ ★ ★

Ben woke when his alarm clock went off on Sunday morning at 5.30am, and went out in their car to check the route. Already there were hundreds of people taking up their positions on the pavements along the route, which had been spray-painted by the police the night before,

---

[49] www.metro.co.uk/weird/859543-crowd-surfing-world-record-smashed-by-dj-giel-beelen#ixzz1NMxqDZIJ

like the white line put down for the London Marathon. The roads were busy, with people trying to find parking places even at that early hour, and causing traffic mayhem, particularly on the side-roads of the Marden Estate and Preston Grange.

By 6.30, the roads were gridlocked and the police were going frantic. Cars were told to park illegally on the sides of the main roads in order to free up through-traffic, not that anyone wanted to go anywhere. Helicopters flew overhead. At 6.45, Ben stepped out through the front door to a huge cheer from the crowds gathered on the opposite side of the road, who immediately surged forwards blocking the road entirely. A policeman with a megaphone told them to get back but they ignored him completely.

Ben took the megaphone and spoke to the crowd.

"It's great to see you all, but we do need to make sure that everybody's safe. So can those of you who are hoping to be part of the world record come onto this pavement, and those of you who aren't that bothered stay on the other side? At least then the traffic can get through and nobody will get knocked down. Thank you. We'll be starting on time at 7am."

He then had a conversation with the man from Guinness World Records, who had a hand-clicker and was intending walking the route and counting everyone who touched Ben in the human chain. He wasn't relishing the task. "We'll do our best," he said. "There are three of us, actually, so we'll average out our calculations and come up with a total that'll be near enough. We also require you to wear a bike helmet in case you get dropped. Health and Safety, you know…"

The pipe band assembled and tuned up, then set off with two minutes to go. Ben donned his bike helmet, feeling rather silly, and stood on the wall outside the house so that he'd be in position. A siren went off at 7am precisely, and Ben lowered himself gingerly onto the sea of hands in front of him, and was alarmed when he was launched northwards at a much greater pace than he'd anticipated. "Hang on, guys!" he yelled. "Not so quick or we'll be there in an hour. Take your time and I might not throw up over you!" The crowd laughed and his pace grew more sedate. It was a very strange feeling, having people grabbing his backside and his legs. The two men and a woman from Guinness walked at the side, watching and clicking carefully.

Ben had wisely elected to go feet-first, which meant that he could look up and see where he was going. When he reached the Metro bridge on Mast Lane, he was amazed to see the line of participants/spectators stretching way beyond the roundabout. It did seem as if the seemingly outlandish challenge might be fulfilled after all. Many of those who'd passed him forwards followed his progress, forming an increasingly lengthy street-wide phalanx of supporters.

It wasn't a comfortable mode of transport. He got prodded and jabbed and went up and down like on a rollercoaster and his head jolted up and down. He discovered that the best approach was to dig his head stiffly into his shoulders and try to keep his body pretty stiff as well. He was accompanied by a police car and the cars of photographers. The Oracle team had organised for schoolchildren from Marden High to collect money in buckets before and after Ben, and the buckets were deposited in the team's minibus as they got filled.

The line continued unbroken all the way up Farringdon Road, and across the playing-fields to the Foxhunters Roundabout. It was amazing. Parked or gridlocked cars hooted. Residents waved from upstairs windows. The pipe band played the same tune over and over again – well, it might have been a different tune but it certainly sounded the same to Ben. On and on the line continued, passing Ben hand over hand in an unbroken chain. He nearly fell when a group of young teenagers near the bus-stop outside Rake Lane Hospital couldn't carry his weight, but the guy from Guinness stepped in and held Ben up while others clustered round. Whenever the line had to cross a road, the police kept the road open till the very last minute, then assembled the spectators across the road while Ben was passed across, then dispersed the line and waved the traffic through after the column of supporters following Ben had passed too. It was a smooth operation – even though one particular lorry driver wasn't too impressed at the delay and sounded his horn in protest. The crowd waved back cheerily, which only made him more exasperated.

The waiting column conveyed Ben along Jact Lane – a good ten minutes earlier than the schedule – and round the bends into the heart of the village, finally reaching the Methodist Church, virtually submerged by the crowd. Ben was passed hand over hand right to the front door of the church, where he was let down gently by none other than Jack Turner himself, the District Chair. "Hope you're not going to claim this on your travel expenses," Jack said, with a chuckle.

The Bible reading they were looking at that morning was the healing miracle where four friends lower a sick man through a hole in the roof into the presence of Jesus[50]. It seemed appropriate, but the crowd packed outside the church weren't that bothered. They enjoyed the music which they could hear through the tannoy system set up on the church roof, but most people drifted away when they realised that the media show was over.

The man from Guinness came up to Ben at the end of the service. "I enjoyed that," he said. "The church I go to in London is much more traditional than that. By the way, I can confirm that you've set two new Guinness World Records for the longest and biggest crowd surfing event, at two hours, 51 minutes and 38 seconds and 31,483 participants."

It got onto the national news this time. The BBC even conducted an interview with Ben and with Brendan, and the donations the following week poured in. When they finished counting the money in the buckets there was over £20,000. The whole campaign was really taking off.

---

[50] Mark 2: 3-5

Chapter 29

Brendan was thrilled with the way that the campaign was going – and especially delighted that Louisa was relishing the challenge of her exciting new position. The weekend had dragged for him – everyone else was very busy organising the crowd-surf, whereas he had nothing to do. His throat and mouth were agony, and he took the painkillers as soon as the label allowed. Some of the pills he was taking had amazingly complicated chemical names.

He decided to have a go at anagrams of chemical elements but struggled with it. He'd only managed one by the end of the Sunday, and even though he'd been interrupted by the BBC demanding an interview, he couldn't really blame his poor results on that. The truth was that he was too tired to concentrate. So he sat staring at "Barium + Boron + Curium + Neon + Platinum = Bromine + Carbon + Plutonium + Uranium" without really knowing why. Five into four wasn't too impressive. Perhaps it was the mention of uranium which threw his concentration.

He had another look at the hypochondria anagram too, adding "unusual rough skin on my tongue", "a dry chest", and (remembering the genital wart hypothesis) "it's a particularly big wart, mind..." He counted off the letters against his grid, and had 157 letters left:

A	B	C	D	E	F	G	H	I	J	K	L	M
11	2	4	6	12	3	5	8	15	0	1	5	1

N	O	P	Q	R	S	T	U	V	W	X	Y	Z
10	17	5	0	8	14	17	7	0	1	0	5	0

But he didn't have the energy for it now. The only two new words he could see were CANCER and DEATH...

★ ★ ★

A waddling and exhausted Ruth arrived with her husband Paul on November 11th, the day Brendan went in for his op. Louisa was glad of the distraction from worrying about her Dad and went to meet them at Newcastle Airport, doubling up with hysterical laughter when she saw how round and ungainly her sister was. "Bloomin' eck!" she cried, "It's like the Ark Royal coming into port."

Ruth burst into tears.

Louisa instantly snapped into compassion-mode. "I'm sorry, Ruthie. I was only having a laugh. Are you OK?"

"Yes!" wailed Ruth. "But I feel so enormous. It's like my life's over. I've just become an incubator for the baby and I don't exist as me any more." And she burst into tears again. They went for a coffee – except that Ruth had water. She hadn't been able to bear the smell or taste of coffee for 8½ months now.

Afterwards, Louisa ushered them both to her waiting Beetle. "Sorry it doesn't come with double doors," she said. And this time Ruth sniffed and smiled.

The bottom flat at Beverley Terrace had been unoccupied since Ben moved up to the top floor, so Ruth and Paul moved into the rather rudimentary accommodation. At least she didn't have to manage the stairs.

"Sorry, it's a bit... basic," said Louisa. "Ben wasn't much into interior decor, or furniture, come to that. But there's a bed and a bathroom and a kitchenette, so you've probably got everything you need. Now what can I get you?"

"Nothing," said Ruth immediately. "I just want to crawl into bed."

★ ★ ★

Brendan had gone into hospital with Louisa the day before, and Louisa had sat with him as the surgeon explained what she was going to do.

"The aim of the operation is to identify and eliminate the primary tumours, and also to get rid of secondaries in your lymphatic system. That's what we're going to start with, as it involves liaising with the histopathology lab downstairs. So we dissect your neck and remove the lymph glands two by two from the top downwards."

Dissect didn't sound good – that's what Brendan had done at school to dead rats. But he liked the two by two bit, imagining the lymph glands going into the Noah's Ark of histopathology hand-in-hand.

"Each time we excise a pair of lymph glands, we send them down to the lab and they phone back and say if they're cancerous. And we keep doing that until they say that there isn't any trace of cancer. Then we take another couple out just to make sure – and when that comes back negative we've stopped the rot, as it were. Are you following me so far?"

Brendan nodded. It reminded him of when he had tried to level up the legs of a small coffee table and kept sawing bits off until all he had left was a new bread board.

"Then we turn our attention to the primaries. I'll probably start on the tongue, cutting along the centre of it until I get to the tumour. I'll cut round that and get rid of it, along with as much of the healthy tissue round it as I need to, to ensure that we get all the cancerous stuff out. Then I'll have a similar go at the tonsilar stub and probably get rid of it altogether and a bit of the oropharyngeal wall to ensure we've sorted that part out too. Any questions?"

Brendan had lots of questions flying around in his head. He didn't want to sound stupid, but in the end he just spoke his fears: "Is there a danger that you'll take my whole tongue out? Will I be able to talk again? What are my chances?" They sounded like inept questions to Brendan – cowardly even, but the surgeon didn't bat an eyelid.

"It is unlikely that you will wake up without a tongue, but we may have to take more of it away than we anticipate. If that happens, we'll then arrange for a plastic surgeon to come in and fashion a replacement section out of a chunk of your forearm whilst you're still in theatre. You should be able to talk perfectly well after a few days, except that if your tongue is shortened you may need some speech therapy to get the hang of making the right sounds again. I don't know what to say about your chances. Of surviving the operation, 95%. Of being free of cancer after the op, 50%. Of surviving for three years or more, 60%. Will that do?"

Louisa squeezed his hand. He wished that he hadn't asked, really. For Brendan it was 50-50 – he'd either die or he wouldn't. He'd either be cured or he wouldn't. But the surgeon hadn't finished.

"When you come round afterwards you'll have a breathing tube and a feeding tube inserted into your nostril, which will be a little uncomfortable. There's a very strong possibility that you'll also have a temporary tracheotomy tube to allow you to breathe more easily. There may also be a direct feeding tube into your stomach. You'll be unable to move your lower jaw because we will probably have had to saw it in half to get in to do the work, so the stitches will be underneath your chin down to your Adam's Apple – that's why we'll be trying to divert everything else away from your mouth."

Brendan was a bit shocked by this. Sawing his jaw in half? He tried to picture it, opening his jaw up like a book, it seemed, to get to the base of his tongue from underneath. Like mechanics changing a car's catalytic convertor by going down into the inspection pit rather than crawling through the bonnet, maybe... It still didn't seem natural, but then surgery wasn't, was it?

★ ★ ★

He was glad that he was first on the list in the morning, as he hadn't slept well and couldn't cope with the worry of waiting any longer. Everything happened in a relaxed and light-hearted way, the nurses laughing and joking as they washed him and shaved him, then the anaesthetist coming in and giving him the pre-med and telling him a weak joke about the Dalai Lama refusing anaesthetics for a tooth extraction because he wanted to transcend dental medication. Then the porters laughed and joked as they wheeled him off to be mutilated.

Eight and a half hours later he came round briefly in High Dependency, aware only that he was still alive, before sleeping all night, and waking in the morning unable to speak or feel anything inside his mouth. Panicking, he signalled to the nurse for a pad so that he could write a question.

"Do I still have a tongue?" he wrote.

The nurse drew the curtains around the bed and gently opened his mouth. She smiled and nodded. "Yes, Brendan, you do still have a tongue, but it looks a bit battered. Do you want to have a look?"

He nodded, and she went to get a mirror. He looked, and, yes, there was a very pink, very bloated, stitched-up tongue, that looked dead in his mouth, like a lump of meat on a butcher's slab. He had a neat line of black stitches under his chin, running down to his Adam's Apple and there was a small tube sticking out of his windpipe. He had two other tubes sticking out the sides of his neck, draining fluid away from where they'd taken lymph nodes away. He had another tube into his windpipe via a nostril so that air could pass past his tongue, plus another tube in the other nostril through which he would eventually be fed liquid gunk. He had a tube in his arm for antibiotics, another two in the other arm for glucose and for morphine. There was a catheter too. He felt like he should be renamed You Tube.

But he was alive...

★ ★ ★

The surgeon came round to see him, but didn't say very much. She explained that the lymph glands hadn't been too bad, and they'd only had to remove down to about halfway, so at least the cancer hadn't spread throughout his lymphatic system – "or at least not by that route". Thanks, thought Brendan. Very comforting.

"I cut out a tumour at the base of your tongue which was about the size and shape of a computer mouse," she said, unemotionally. Brendan's eyebrows shot up. He couldn't imagine that he had sufficient tongue for a piece that size to be cut out – and yet he'd seen what looked like a normal tongue. "We reconstructed the tongue from a flap of muscle in your leg."

And instantly he felt it – a sharp, raw wound on the outside of his thigh. Agony. Or was he just imagining it? Yes, maybe it was a shock reaction – imagining that he ought to feel pain, so he did. Was he cracking up?

"The trouble was that I still couldn't get much of the surrounding tissue because there just wasn't room – so I can't be absolutely positive that we've got it all, I'm afraid. I'm hopeful that we have, but we'll put you forward for a bit more radiotherapy to make sure. But you need to take time to get over this first. You'll be here for three days probably, then back onto a general ward. Any questions? Oh, no, you can't talk, can you? Well, write any questions down on your notepad and I'll do my best to answer it tomorrow."

And with that, she was off. Proper little ray of sunshine she was. Brendan remembered a quotation from Oscar Wilde: "Some cause happiness wherever they go; others, *whenever* they go."

★ ★ ★

Ben arrived at church the following Sunday in a Formula 1 racing car. Esther had arranged it. She knew someone on the Board of Directors at Indianapolis.

Detroit's street circuit had been the venue for the US Grand Prix in the 1980s, and some of the fervour of motor racing lived on in the city. Not too far down the road was Indianapolis, the home of American motor sport and the location of the Hall of Fame Museum, which included in its exhibits a Stewart-Ford SF-2 Formula One car once driven by Jos Verstappen in 1998[51]. Somehow Esther had persuaded or paid the museum authorities to fly the exhibit across to Britain, and Ben was allowed to sit in it while it was driven on the back of a flat-bed lorry from Cullercoats to Jact – as long as he didn't touch anything. Then it was flown back again to Indianapolis and resumed its place in the museum.

Maybe it was cheating – but Ben reckoned that it was OK. So did the editor, keen to keep the attention of the media on his little paper. And the money kept pouring in – over 5,000 entries the following day, from which the winning entry was picked out by the local newsreader: Hot-air balloon (weather-permitting), otherwise, hopping.

---

[51] The museum does have this car, but I doubt whether it loans it out.

Chapter 30

Brendan was hopping mad, as he lay there flat on his back. He was a preacher, and now he couldn't talk – what was God playing at? And yet, in a way, he was curiously calm. He couldn't see any point arguing with God – what good would that do? More positively, he felt OK about leaving God to sort him out. He was just cross at everything, frustrated at his helplessness.

After two days back on the general ward, the drainage tubes and the tracheotomy tube were removed, and his catheter taken out. Constant morphine became occasional morphine and analgesics. The breathing tube flattening his tongue got taken out and he tried to talk – but all that came out were noises like a caveman and streams of dribble sluicing out of the side of his mouth. His tongue was still a dead piece of meat blocking the bottom of his mouth. The nurses had to lift it gently out of the way to clean underneath, when they checked the major wound at the back of his throat. Despite only having half of his saliva glands operational, he seemed to be producing enough spit to fill a swimming pool – not that anybody would want to swim in it, because it was bubbly and flecked with bits of clotted blood. Because he couldn't control his jaw muscles, he couldn't keep his mouth shut, so it leaked out whenever he moved his head. They gave him a suction tube like dental assistants use, but even at reduced power he still usually got it stuck onto the inside of his cheek or his tongue, which was agony. His tongue may have been dormant but it obviously had nerves running through it. It tended to flop back when he lay on his back and he frequently woke up with an attack of coughing because it had blocked his airway.

The oncologist confided in Brendan that they were puzzled about his condition.

"SCCA is usually found in people who are heavy smokers and drinkers. You don't fit in either category, and, actually you're remarkably fit for your age, with a strong heart and perfect blood pressure. So we're mystified as to why you have SCCA at all. On top of that, we've discovered traces of something called Human Papilloma Virus or HPV in the tonsilar tumour, but not in the tongue tumour, which is a rare combination that I've not come across before. Nor from my quick research has anyone else. I wonder whether this is an area that your Trust might investigate."

"What's Human Whatever Virus?" wrote Brendan on his bedside pad.

"HPV, we call it, because even we find it a bit of a mouthful, if you'll pardon the pun in your case. It's a DNA virus, which has various strains and variations, some of which most people get at some point in their lives. It causes verrucas and warts, and in a third of the strains it's transmitted sexually..."

Brendan shuddered – genital warts again...

"...Cervical cancer, for example, is commonly caused by HPV. It's only rarely that it occurs in the throat or even higher. So we're left with a mystery. The most obvious explanation is that you have two simultaneous but completely unrelated primary cancers, which need treating in different ways."

Brendan couldn't get his head round it. He wrote on the pad: "Getting cancer once is regarded as unlucky. What is it called if you get two cancers at the same time?"

The oncologist shrugged. "Perhaps somebody doesn't like you?"

Brendan smiled. He knew that God wanted the best for him, abundantly. What he hadn't realised was that God's abundance might extend to giving out a double dose of cancer, though. Joking aside, it was just one of those things – or two of those things in his case. He'd just have to deal with it. He changed tack, and wrote on the pad: "So, this HPV thing – what does it do? Is it that the one tumour's a diseased wart, and the other's a proper cancer?"

The oncologist shook his head. "No, it doesn't really work like that. Both of your SCCA tumours are similar in their form and shape – it's the reason they're there which is different. The strain of HPV which we've detected in the tonsilar stub is not one of the STD strains, but it's one which deactivates the retinoblastoma protein which suppresses tumours. We usually counteract that through chemotherapy. The other tumour, however, is HPV negative, which means that it has to be treated more specifically with either a different form of chemotherapy – which we can't do in this case because of the more specific needs of the *other* tumour – or with radiotherapy. So I'm afraid we're going to have to do both. Chemoradiotherapy isn't a new invention, but it's usually only used in the UK in complicated cases, like yours, where we have to try and do two things at once. In America they use it more frequently in HNC."

Brendan looked blank. The oncologist apologised for the jargon. "Sorry, HNC stands for head and neck cancer. It does mean that there's a danger that the two treatments counteract rather than complement each other, so it may be a bit of a rocky ride, I'm afraid."

"What are my chances?" wrote Brendan, his usual question. He felt that he needed to know what he was up against.

The oncologist shrugged. "I don't know. As I said, there's no research on this rare combination, as far as I'm aware. And they're only statistics anyway. Even a 95% survival rate means that 5% die – and you might be in either group, mightn't you?" And on that happy thought, he left.

* * *

After Ben had put in hours sorting out a hot-air-balloonist willing to come to the coast, he was phoned up on the Saturday to say that the weather forecast was poor and he would have to postpone it. Hopping it was, then. He made a provisional booking for the following week, and began to think about hopping.

The trouble with hopping was that it was fine for about 20m, maybe 50m at a push, but three miles, even alternating legs every 20m, would be impossible. The strain on the thigh muscles was immense, and he just wasn't physically up to it. He had a go outside the house, and couldn't do more than 30m before having to swap legs. When he tried the next lot of hopping on his preferred leg, he hardly made 10m before collapsing in a heap. The world record, apparently, was seven minutes – by a 12-year-old called Liam. So how could Ben do three miles? He only had Saturday evening to think about it, so he couldn't be too choosy or intricate in his plans – not that he had *any* possible solutions at that point.

Then he remembered that he still had his crutches from his wedding day. He looked up "hopping" and the dictionary definition was "to move by jumping on one foot", which didn't say anything about assistance. If he rigged up a strap from his waist to rest his free foot in, he reckoned that swinging himself along on his crutches, one-footed, would technically count as hopping. And if either leg got cramp, he could change legs. Not literally, of course – he was stuck with the ones he had.

He reckoned that he could nearly reach walking speed, and gave himself an hour and a quarter to complete the three miles. Everything went smoothly – although some people seemed to grumble that he wasn't in a balloon, even when he explained that they don't fly in 30mph winds, and one or two others seemed to think that using crutches was cheating. Did it really matter?

The next Sunday too was overcast and windy and the balloon flight got cancelled again. That week the alternative was a bit easier to organise: a yacht. Brendan had laughed when that was drawn out as the winner – the editor looked askance at him, knowing that Jact wasn't on a navigable stretch of water.

"But not all yachts are water-borne. What about sand-yachting, or whiking?" Ben asked.

The editor looked strangely at him. "I've heard of sand-yachting, but what on earth is whiking?"

Brendan explained that he'd seen it at Greenbelt – and even had a go there. "A whike is a tricycle you lie back on, which has a sail. It has handbrakes on the double back wheels when the sail is up, to stop it blowing away before you get on it, then when you're using the sail to boost your speed you can decelerate too by using a foot-brake on the single front wheel and the handbrakes to keep it level. You steer with levers at the side and pedal with your feet like on a normal bike. It was great fun, but I expect that it could get interesting on a windy day."

"How fast does it go?"

"About 30mph, I think – not that I'd dare go that fast. With a nice breeze you don't have to pedal much. And apparently it's legal to go on the roads and use cycle lanes."

In fact, it turned out to be a lot of fun – especially when he overturned as he swept round triumphantly into the church car park, too cocky for his own good. The cameras caught it all, and Esther made a point a few days later of telling him that it had been seen by about 35 million people throughout the world. But it generated more interest.

Now there were over a quarter of a million sponsors, mostly abroad – netting £450,000 for every week's successful challenge. The Whike was Ben's 15th challenge, which meant £6,750,000 if the people joining the sponsorship later on coughed up for the weeks they'd missed too. The number of entries each week was increasing too. The News Guardian hired a covered skip into which they emptied all the entries as they arrived – making a photo-opportunity each week out of the celebrity either dangling over the side to reach the entries, or jumping in and wafting the entries around before choosing one. They co-opted two of the Americans from Louisa's team just to open the envelopes and record the 50p from each one. Then the money had to be counted, bagged and banked by arrangement with Securicor. The total was now surpassing 25,000 entries each week, which was a lot of 50p pieces.

Chapter 31

Louisa was able to take the oncologist's suggestion of an area for potential research to the consultative board she'd set up a few weeks before. There was some scepticism expressed about the usefulness of the research, in that the occurrence of two simultaneous but independent primary oropharyngeal cancers with different aetiologies and treatments was so incredibly rare. They wondered whether there would be sufficient data to warrant even trying to set up a clinical research programme. It would involve a team trawling through lists of oncologists all over the world, but especially in the USA, where chemoradiotherapy was most commonly used, and contacting them for likely case studies. The research would only be fruitful if they could find sufficient data to make the "sample size" large enough to validate conclusions.

The corporate sponsorship of the Trust was growing quickly. The financial world hadn't had much to cheer about for several years, and those with capital had failed, it seemed, to find much to invest in. But the venture capitalists were now eager to find worthwhile investments, and seemed to judge that the Trust was, indeed, trustworthy. The total raised was now approaching £120 million.

"What can you buy with that sort of money?" asked Louisa.

"Well," said one NHS regional manager, "The latest figures we've got are for 2011. A new cancer care unit in Bracknell serving a population of 120,000 cost about £20 million two years ago, including £1 million for a new LINAC machine. You'd have to factor in the on-costs for staff and utilities, of course – and inflation, but you could probably have five more towns in the UK providing local radiotherapy treatments."

Another NHS financial wizard joined in. "If you wanted to focus on the research side of medicine, Cambridge Breast Cancer Research Unit cost only £2 million to set-up in 2011 with on-costs each year of less than half a million. You could have loads of those."

The local NHS director piped up, "Hopefully we can centre our projects on the North-East, but we're aware that with the Sir Bobby

Robson Cancer Trials Research Centre here at the Freeman we already have a regional centre of excellence. Similarly people do seem to be able to access the Newcastle hospitals relatively easily, so maybe we ought to be looking at something entirely different."

Everybody looked blankly at each other.

"Brendan's oncologist is absolutely right," said one of the oncologists on the group. "Chemoradiotherapy is the only way in which Brendan's rather special case can be treated. But unfortunately chemoradiotherapy is associated with systemic toxicities that often get in the way of a successful outcome, and isn't really the direction that most oncologists would want the research to take."

Louisa gulped. This was her Dad whom they were discussing.

But the oncologist hadn't finished. "Most HNC research is now focussing on the molecular biology of SCCA in an attempt to target and attack the process by which tumours form and grow."

"So is that the area our research money ought to home in on?" asked the NHS regional director.

"Well, that's where nearly every other cancer research unit is concentrating its efforts at the moment, so it would be a matter of finding an area which isn't being covered. I'm not really up to speed on what's happening in that field but I'm sure we can have a look at that as well."

They agreed to employ a team of postgraduates specialising in oncology to "research the research", and to give six members of the American team a crash course in head and neck oncology and then direct them to try to gather data on cases like Brendan's: simultaneous but unrelated oropharyngeal cancers.

Louisa was content with where they'd reached. She knew that she was way out of her depth, but at least she could follow things so far and hadn't embarrassed herself too much. She liked the idea of both the actions they'd initiated, and hoped that the American team in particular would uncover sufficient cases to warrant further research and draw together the evidence into some sort of pattern which might make things clearer for those treating her Dad.

* * *

It was now nearly the end of November. Ruth had become virtually housebound, except for the major excursion of going in to see her Dad. Paul was flapping around the flat helplessly, like a penguin at a flying competition. Louisa and Ben caught the air of tension whenever they entered or left Beverley Terrace. The next fortnight was going to be tough.

Ben, however, was still negotiating a hot-air balloon for the following Sunday. It was that or being towed in a bath, which he thought was relatively straight-forward to organise. If he could find a bath – and a trailer to put it on – and someone to tow him...

★ ★ ★

Brendan was still on the post-surgery recovery ward. His only source of nutrition was being pumped straight into his stomach via the tube. His tongue still didn't function, necessitating this by-pass route, but looking at what he was being fed, Brendan was quite pleased it didn't have to go through his mouth. It was called Jevity, and came in half-litre bottles. Worst of all, it was beige. Brendan had always had a thing about beige ever since their first manse had been decorated throughout in beige and magnolia. This pale, diarrhoea-looking, fat-soaked food was pumped into Brendan over the course of two hours every time everyone else was enjoying proper food. To make it worse, the pump kept getting blocked by chewier bits of Jevity, so the nurses had to come and unblock it manually, picking the gloopy, clumpy bits out. He was told that he needed 2,000 calories a day to recover, so because each Jevity bottle contained 500 calories, he needed four bottles a day which meant that the ordeal took eight hours of each day.

On the last day of November he was finally discharged, not just because he was going stir-crazy but also because Louisa's nursing experience meant that there would be someone on hand at home if anything untoward happened. Brendan felt a bit of a fraud, as he was wheeled out to Louisa's Beetle for the trip home. He was still hooked up to the Jevity, and the car-boot got filled with crates of the wretched stuff. He hoped fervently that the little movement he was beginning to achieve now with his tongue might improve rapidly, so that he could at least try something different.

He hadn't really appreciated his tongue before this. Of course there was its role in language, and the acquired skill of placing it in just the right place to make the right sound. These previously-taken-for-granted subtleties were still way beyond him, so the noises were those of an idiot who in earlier times would have been patted on the head and sidelined. The problem was that he had different bits of muscle from different bits of him trying to achieve co-ordination, and at the moment it was more Keystone Kops than SAS. He also found that he couldn't reach his teeth at the front so several consonant sounds eluded him completely. It was a bit worrying for a preacher...

When he tried eating through his mouth for the first time after the operation, he discovered that the tongue is used to push food to the back of the throat ready for swallowing, and is needed for the swallow itself. He couldn't manage any such movement, so he had to let the first mouthful sit on his tongue, then push it as far back as he could with his next mouthful, without gagging on it, then tilt his head back, hoping that it went down smoothly. At first he couldn't get this right and kept choking, which was agony. The last mouthful had to be pushed back with a spoon, which he couldn't get the hang of at all, and eventually resorted to fishing most of the food back out again and throwing it away. Drinking similarly was problematic – he could tip his head back and let it flow to the back, hoping it might go down the right hole, but usually a fair bit ran out of his mouth too. Again, the last drop of liquid usually crept underneath his tongue and he sometimes had to lean forwards and let it dribble out.

He wasn't ready to be taken to a restaurant yet...

Alan's Story: April 6ᵗʰ 1974

Alan was snuggled down on the sofa with Pauline, watching the Eurovision Song Contest in colour. They'd only bought the TV the previous week, and still hadn't got tired of how good it was compared to the old walnut-surround black-and-white they'd had previously – a massive piece of furniture with a ridiculously tiny screen. This TV was far better, and Pauline was in her element.

"Ooh, I like this one. It's Sweden. They're supposed to be one of the favourites."

Alan had drawn France in the office sweepstake, which was also supposed to have a good chance, so he was quite keen to see how they'd do. He'd been happy with the pick, because he rather liked France. They tried to get there every summer so that he could improve and show off his tan. He still kept going to the tanning shop in Wallsend, but was thinking of buying his own sunbed if they came down a bit in price.

He'd read that the French entry was someone called Dani, but he didn't know any more than that, except that the song was something to do with life at 25, or so he'd heard. He'd instantly thought back to what *he'd* been doing at the age of 25, and it hadn't been too bad. He'd just got married and moved in to their home in Jact. So maybe the song would do well.

He listened while Abba belted out "Waterloo", and grudgingly admitted that they were good. Much better than that Australian woman who'd already been on for the United Kingdom[52].

"You wait till France comes on, they'll knock your socks off," he predicted.

"No, France aren't singing," said Pauline. "They've dropped out."

"What do you mean?" shouted Alan. "They can't drop out. I've got them in the sweepstake."

"That's a quid wasted, then," said Pauline. "They've dropped out.

---

[52] Olivia Newton-John sang second, with "Long Live Love", and came fourth.

It's their President's funeral today so they've withdrawn out of respect[53]."

Alan slumped back in despair. What was the world coming to? He kept watching but his heart wasn't in it. Even Katie Boyle, the presenter, didn't perk him up, as she usually did. When the Wombles came on as the interval entertainment, he got up and grabbed his coat[54].

"I can't stand any more of this," he declared. "I'm going down the Farmer's Arms."

★ ★ ★

When he got back, several pints and hours later, Pauline was snoring gently in front of the TV. He woke her up and asked who'd won.

"Can't remember," she replied, sleepily, climbing the stairs. "I think it was Sweden."

"Ah well. I didn't think much to it. Anyway, I need to go to bed too because I'm on duty in the morning."

He was a Church Trustee and Steward now at Jact Methodist Church, and he and a woman called Sarah were pretty much in charge of everything. The old fogies seemed to have all died off, and left everything for the two of them to arrange. Alan rather enjoyed the power and prestige that it gave him. He was still in a low-level position at the Ministry in Benton, constantly at the beck and call of his superiors, so church was an oasis of responsibility and authority.

Sarah and he got on well together. Her husband, like Pauline, didn't go – so they were in similar situations, though Sarah was about five years older than him. She was a southerner who'd come up here from Essex, he thought, but had been on the scene at the Methodist Church much longer than he had. The two of them spent at least one evening a week at some meeting or other. They didn't bother with the Bible Study, but nearly everything else meant that Alan and Sarah would be there, making sure that nothing went amiss.

---

[53] France had been going to enter this Eurovision with the song "La vie à vingt-cinq ans" by Dani, but they withdrew after the French President, Georges Pompidou, died in the week of the contest. Since his funeral was held on the day of the contest, it was deemed inappropriate for the French to take part. Dani was televised sitting in the audience at the point the French song should have been performed, after the Irish and before the German entry.

[54] The Wombles really did provide the half-time entertainment.

Alan was also in charge of Property (exterior), with Sarah running Property (interior), and he'd had a bit of work to do over the last few weeks with a leaking roof in the men's toilets. Sarah had agreed that it only became Property (interior) at the point where redecoration had to be done, so it was up to Alan not just to get the roof fixed but to check that the ceiling was sound. He'd gone up into the roof space a few days ago and discovered that the water which had come in through the gap where the slates had come off had all disappeared, but the ceiling itself seemed to have dried out without any long-term damage.

He'd have to check it out again in the morning, he sighed, as he climbed the stairs after Pauline. Still, that was what a Steward was for, wasn't it?

December 2012

Chapter 32

Advent Sunday dawned, December 1ˢᵗ, with a clear, still sky, as promised by the weather forecast – ideal for hot-air ballooning. The team from Morpeth arrived and set up their equipment on the Boat Field, just opposite Beverley Terrace on the flat area of grass where a long time ago the fishing boats, normally kept in the harbour, were brought when the weather closed in. No storms today, though – and the balloon flight was definitely on.

It was never the start of a balloon flight that was the problem in good weather – it was the landing. Basically a balloon goes where the wind takes it, though an experienced balloonist will ascend and descend to catch whichever wind current at a particular altitude suits their purpose best, because winds vary in direction and speed at different heights, apparently.

The balloon itself was unfolded and laid out on the grass, with a large crowd of on-lookers watching avidly, including a rather nervous Ben. The fragile-looking wicker basket was propped sideways and the burner mechanism attached to it. Then the team brought out a huge fan, connected it to a generator and started to inflate the balloon. When there was enough air in the balloon, the crew lit the pilot-light, opened the propane cylinder valve and blasted the burner flame into the envelope mouth. This heated the air, building the pressure until the balloon inflated more fully and started to lift off the ground.

The ground crew members held the basket down until the pilot and a well-wrapped-up Ben were on board. The balloon basket was also attached to the ground crew vehicle until the last minute, so the balloon wouldn't be blown away before it was ready to launch. When everything was set, the ground crew released the balloon and the pilot fired a steady flame from the burner. As the air heated up, the balloon lifted right off the ground, while the crowd cheered and Ben nervously waved, holding onto the rope tightly.

Amazingly, this entire process took less than 15 minutes. The flight itself, with a gentle 5mph breeze at 500ft, took just forty minutes, but as they soared over Rake Lane Hospital, the pilot explained that the landing could be interesting.

"It's impossible for us to land near the church as there are too many houses and not enough room, so we're aiming for a field between the northern end of the village and the Metro line. There are a few sheep in there but nothing else that's dangerous, such as power lines. The team will already be there, so they can help us land and hopefully will have cleared the sheep out of the way. It's nice and flat, and with so little wind it should be easy. Are you OK with that?"

Ben nodded. Anywhere on earth would be OK. It was pleasant, but 500ft was rather... high. They gently descended over Jacksons Farm, with the horses neighing and jumping in the field as the balloon's shadow fell on them. Ben admired the skill with which the pilot opened and closed the little parachute valve, as the pilot called it, letting hot air out of the top of the balloon to control their descent.

They came in very low over the village, at less than 100ft, but clearing the power lines easily, swooping down on the field a few hundred yards away. The ground crew was already in place, nearer the village than the Metro line to ease their exit and minimise any risk. The pilot yelled at Ben to hold on tight as the ground gently came towards them. The landing itself involved a few little bumps to stop the balloon gradually, and the ground crew grabbed hold of the basket while the pilot shut off the flame and the pilot-light, helped Ben out, and joined the ground crew to tilt the basket over so the balloon dropped slowly to earth.

"Perfect!" said the pilot, shaking Ben's hand.

"Perfect!" agreed Ben, in that he was still alive.

★ ★ ★

Dead to the World struck up at the start of the service with the Advent hymn "Lo, he comes with clouds descending", but their jazzed-up version of the traditional Charles Wesley hymn brought the old tune to life. The drummer, in particular, seemed to be enjoying himself.

The theme for the service was not the First Coming, but the Second Coming, which was the traditional pattern for Advent. Many churches avoided it and projected forward to Christmas, the First Coming, because they didn't know what to do with the second one. Ben, typically, had decided to tackle it full on.

The service didn't, however, dwell exclusively on end-of-the-world stuff, but was rooted in the small transformations happening in Jact. After telling some inspiring stories, Ben closed his reflections with a summary of what he thought the real issues were.

"The old word for Second Coming literally meant "presence". Between now and then, Jesus is sort-of absent but sort-of half-present, isn't he? He's gone in that he's not walking the earth like he once did. But he's also here through the Spirit of Jesus, as Paul calls the Holy Spirit, helping us to carry on his work of transforming the world like he's told us to do.

"But when he's present again, fully present at the end of time, he will take from us our work of transforming the world, and judge us all on the basis of what we've done or not done to help the cause..

"That's why the stuff we're doing to raise funds for cancer research is so important. That's why Brendan's journeys to raise awareness of mission and the suffering of the Third World made such an impact, not just financially but also spiritually. We are part of something much bigger than our own puny efforts, for God is with us, and God will triumph when all things are made new in Him.

"Judgement isn't the loveliest thought, but it's fashionable again as society has become more intolerant of injustice and wants to see things put right. We're promised, however, that God's mercy will prevail, and that those who've trusted in him and done their best won't be condemned."

They sang And Can It Be, jazzed-up and at some pace. When they came to "No condemnation now I dread; Jesus, and all in him is mine!" Ben thought of Brendan, just out of hospital, still so weak, uncertain of what lay ahead. And when they came to the final lines: "Bold I approach the eternal throne, and claim the crown through Christ, my own," tears streamed down Ben's cheeks.

Chapter 33

Louisa opened up the discussion. "Thanks, all of you, for coming today. We're here to begin to pinpoint how best we can spend the money that's been raised. First of all, we need to work out in what direction our research might go. I've asked Bill Winterton, our chief oncologist here at the Freeman, to give us an overview. This may be dead boring for the scientists amongst us, but it'll be really important for the rest of us. So, can you tell us, Bill, how molecular biology works when it comes to cancer research? But please remember that some of us aren't scientists, so you'll have to explain it in phrases we can all understand."

Bill smiled as if this was a challenge he'd been looking forward to all his life. He even licked his lips, took off his jacket and rolled up his shirtsleeves. "OK, I'll give it a go. Please interrupt if there's something you don't understand."[55]

They all nodded.

"I know two jokes about cancer research. The first is: "Cancer Research is my favourite charity, because when you need a pen you can always find one of theirs.""

Some people smiled; most didn't.

"Actually, there's a lot of truth in that. I've got hundreds of them. The other joke is: "Isn't Cancer Research making good progress? Every day they discover something else that causes it.""

Everyone smiled this time, ruefully.

"But actually, it's true. We've identified six steps in the progressive stages of cancer from nothing to massive tumours. All six steps have to happen for a tumour to be formed, and each step offers a potential target for molecular therapy. So cancer research tends to split into these

---

[55] The detail in what follows is my own interpretation of complicated academic research. Most of this overview comes from an American research paper: BAYON, Rodrigo, "Targeted Molecular Therapy in Head and Neck Squamous Cell Carcinoma", 2011, at www.emedicine.medscape.com/article/854971-overview#a30. I *think* that I understand it and have described it all correctly – and hope that you can follow it too. It's not, however, essential to the story-line...

six areas of interest, although obviously there are some research programmes which try to bridge across different areas so that everybody is kept in touch with what everybody else is doing. Are you following me so far?"

They nodded.

"OK. Let's go a bit deeper. We've discovered that there are some significant differences between cancer cells and normal cells. So, obviously, we target anything which is unique to cancer cells and not found in normal cells, so that whatever we then do won't affect normal cells. Failing that, we target anything which is found much *more* in cancer cells than normal ones, so that the damage to the normal cells is less significant. This frankly is why surgery, chemotherapy and radiotherapy are all a bit of a broad-brush approach, because they tend to kill off not just cancer cells but surrounding normal cells too, and this is why *molecular* therapy may well end up being the one that works best. Back to the six stages then, OK?"

They nodded. Louisa smiled. Bill was good at this.

"The first stage is when proto-oncogenes are activated into becoming oncogenes. Now..." He held up his hand. "I know that's probably gobbledygook, so I'll try to explain what that means."

They smiled.

"Proto-oncogenes are really important in regulating both the size of cells and what *sort* of cells they become. If we didn't have proto-oncogenes, cells would grow wrongly and could all grow into the wrong sort of cell, so inside us would be a whole mess of gloop which would be no good for anything. But thankfully, we all have proto-oncogenes. The trouble comes when they mutate into oncogenes. If we could stop that happening, bingo, we'd have prevented cancer. But we can't – yet. But lots of research is going into this area."

He had a sip of water.

"Step two is the inhibition of growth inhibition, which sounds double-dutch, I know. Basically, it's good for things to grow, and then to die. It's the way life's designed. But if growth gets out of control, it messes everything up – as the weeds in my garden will testify. So there are clever bits inside us which inhibit growth and keep everything hunky-dory. If those inhibitors, however, are themselves inhibited, then growth can get out of control – which is what happens next in the cancer process. If we can get rid of these inhibitor-inhibitors, then the normal healthy cycle of cell growth and cell death will resume, and nothing will come of the oncogenes. People are working on that too."

He had another sip of water.

"The two cancers which Brendan has, are, as I'm sure you're aware, different forms of head and neck squamous cell carcinomas – called HNSCCAs for short, not that that's very short!"

Everybody laughed, on cue. Bill smiled. It was going well.

"Now, this growth problem at step two is the cause of over 90% of HNSCAAs. So that's where a wide array of research is concentrating. That brings us on to the third of the six stages. Are you still up for this?"

They all nodded. The financial experts were fascinated. The oncologists seemed to be marking Bill out of ten for content and presentation. Louisa was amazed. Even with her nursing studies, she'd never understood how complicated it all was.

Bill continued. "OK. The third stage in the progress of cancer is what I call the Jesus stage."

Everybody looked up, a bit shocked that Bill put cancer and Jesus together. He hastily explained.

"I'm not, I hope, being offensive to the Christians amongst us. The resurrection of Jesus is believed by Christians to put death, as it were, to death, to wipe out its significance. That's what happens next in the cancer process. Stage Three is when the natural cycle of cell death is destroyed, and cells which should die instead keep living, growing and getting increasingly harmful to the rest of the body, invading space that they shouldn't invade, blocking pathways and infecting different cells nearby. Which leads us into the fourth stage, which is immortality."

Everybody smiled. He was good at this.

"Normal cells can only replicate a finite number of times. There are things in our DNA called telomeres which regulate this process. Every time the cell replicates itself, some of the telomeres get lost so in the end there aren't any left and the chromosomes become unstable and die. In cancer cells, the telomeres don't get lost with every cycle, so the cells keep replicating. There's a nasty enzyme called telomerase, which prevents the loss of the telomeres, and this enzyme is found in almost all HNSCCAs. So there's a whole host of researchers trying to see if they can nobble telomerase."

Louisa could tell that she was struggling to concentrate. A few other people's eyes were glazing over.

"OK. Fifth stage in the process: angiogenesis, which is the clever word for growing blood vessels. This is critical if tumours are to grow and metastasize, for blood vessels are necessary for the cancer cells to get the nutrients they need. So, if we could stop this process, or severely limit it, the tumours wouldn't grow. There's something called VEGF – which stands for vascular endothelial growth factor – which seems to be reported in about 40% of HNSCCAs, so some research programmes are targeting that. Control that, and we may have it cracked."

Some smiled. Others nodded. Bill kept going, as if it were important, like a big zit, to get it all out in one go.

"And the last stage, you'll be happy to know, is tissue invasion or metastasis. The cancer cell wants to take over the world, and the way it does it is to sprout blood vessel shoots out through the various outer coatings of its own cell, then migrate across to an adjoining cell and drill through its coatings and attach itself to its next location, and then keep doing that forever unless checked. There are various complicated techniques to stop this happening at each stage, especially in attempting to suppress a glycoprotein called EpCAM, but none of them so far has made much impact."

He clapped his hands together, and everyone shot up in their seats. "All we have to do now is decide which bit of the enemy forces we're going to attack, and the best way of doing it. I think our best way forward is for the scientists amongst us to go away and have a look at the breadth of research projects that are happening, and then when we meet again next week, we'll ask for their conclusions, argue them out and maybe get a clearer picture where the best use of our resources can be made."

It was definitely "Battle On."

Chapter 34

Five days after coming out of hospital, Brendan woke up choking. He couldn't breathe at all, and nor could he move or shout for help. He felt like he was drowning. Fortunately Louisa had had the foresight to give him a hand-bell to ring if he needed anything, and it happened to be lying on his pillow, and he managed to ring it once before passing out.

Louisa heard, got up and found Brendan unconscious and turning blue. She did everything that was necessary, not panicking but clicking into nurse-mode immediately, clearing his flaccid tongue from his airway into which it had rolled when Brendan had rolled over onto his back as he slept, and putting him in the recovery position, having checked that he was breathing and his pulse was settling, even though he was still unconscious.

Then she phoned for an ambulance, and Brendan found himself back in the hospital when he woke up, with another tracheotomy tube poking out of his throat, an oxygen mask over his face, and hooked up to a heart monitor because an EEG reading when he'd been brought in had shown worrying results, as if his oxygen-starved heart had been struggling to stave off a heart attack.

"You had a lucky escape there," said the nurse. "Apparently if your daughter hadn't found you, you'd have been dead within another half a minute."

Brendan wasn't sure what to do with that information. Should he be happy? Thankful? Annoyed at how dependent he was? Frustrated at his vulnerability and helplessness? He was all of those things. He couldn't in fact say anything at all, because with the tube in place he was mute once more.

★ ★ ★

Two days later, Ben rigged up an old metal bath on the same trailer which Brendan had used for the kayak all the way down the Americas. He fitted a tow-bar to the back of the Beetle, and Louisa drove him to church. It was a very easy challenge to fulfil, relatively speaking. Ben had filled the bath with bubble bath and hot water before he got in, and then donned his wetsuit for the ride. There was still some water in the bath when he got out at Jact, but not much. The crowd still loved it, and the donations kept rolling in.

The following day, Ben strolled into the newspaper office to meet Sting, who picked the winning entry out of the back of a lorry. They reckoned that there were now over 150,000 entries in the back of the lorry, and nearly 600,000 sponsors worldwide, which could well net over £1.2 million for each week successfully completed.

★ ★ ★

Ruth had been having Braxton-Hicks contractions for a few months, once or twice a day, as if her insides were just testing themselves for The Big Event. But during the last few days they'd been getting more intense and had started to hurt. When she sat down, they quickly subsided, so she knew that they weren't real contractions.

When the midwife came round, Ruth asked her the question. "When will I know? What's the difference between them and *real* contractions?"

The midwife smiled. "You'll *know*," she said. "They're longer, more regular, more frequent and more painful. Believe me, you'll *know*."

And she was right. For this, Ruth knew, was it.

★ ★ ★

Paul rushed round the flat like Corporal Jones on Dad's Army, telling everyone not to panic with his voice but not his demeanour, but fortunately for everyone, Ben was back from work and supervised the 5.30pm evacuation to the hospital, driving Ruth and Paul in the Beetle, leaving them at the door of the Maternity Unit, and coming home to wait.

He phoned Louisa, who rushed home to monitor Ruth's progress through the hourly bulletins from Paul. Louisa phoned her Mum, who made immediate arrangements to come up by plane from Exeter. Because it was by now mid-evening on Friday, she phoned back to say that she'd be catching the 7.10am flight the following morning, getting into Newcastle Airport at 8.25am.

"Can you come and get me?" she asked.

"Of course Ben can," said Louisa. "I'll be waiting for a phone call, if it hasn't happened by then."

★ ★ ★

Paul phoned regularly all through the night, telling them each time that nothing had happened, but that the midwives were assuring him that Ruth was doing well and that babies don't tend to rush out, especially a first one.

★ ★ ★

At 8am, Paul phoned again, to say excitedly that he had seen the baby's head but it had gone back in again. Ben left for the airport.

He returned with Jenna at 9.10am, but there was still no news.

★ ★ ★

At 9.30, Paul phoned to say that Ruth was getting tired, and they were talking of a Caesarian. He rushed back into the Unit to be with her. The others were left to pace the room.

"Should we get in touch with Dad?" asked Louisa, suddenly.

They all felt guilty. They'd forgotten all about him.

"I'll do it," said Jenna.

★ ★ ★

"What did you say?" asked Louisa, when her Mum returned.

"I told him what was happening, and told him to pray hard."

"What did he say?"

"Aaargh, nnnnnh, tfutfutfu, or something like that," said Jenna, and they all burst into laughter.

★ ★ ★

They waited, and waited.

Then, finally, at 10.40am, the phone rang. Louisa leapt to it.

"Yes?" she shouted.

"It's a boy!" whispered a weary but ecstatic Paul, ignoring Louisa's instant shriek of joy. "A beautiful baby boy. Ruth had to have a Caesarean but she's OK. They've just brought her back to the Unit and she's still knocked out so they've just got me to feed my little baby boy with a bottle. It's just wonderful..."

★ ★ ★

After the initial euphoria, and a bit more information had been pried out of Paul, they made arrangements to visit in a couple of hours, then Jenna said that she was going to phone Brendan.

★ ★ ★

"What did he say this time?" asked Louisa.

"Aaargh, nnnnnh, tfutfutfu, once again," said Jenna. "But this time he was sobbing. Daft old stick – he was always the emotional one."

But then everybody burst into tears as well. Friday December 13th had been not an unlucky/lucky day but a *blessed* day. It had also been a long day already, and it was still only 11am.

Chapter 35

Brendan was overjoyed to hear about the birth of his grandson, Matthew. He'd felt utterly helpless after receiving the first phone call from Jenna, but was pleased that they'd rung to let him know what was happening. In this waiting game at least they were as helpless as him, and they, like him, would have been sending up some pretty focussed prayers to God that everything would proceed smoothly.

When Jenna phoned the second time, after such an impossibly long wait, he was beside himself with worry and so he just collapsed with emotion as she told him that all was well. He lay back, his pillow drenched, utterly spent, but so thrilled. Matthew, he knew, meant "gift of God".

How true.

★ ★ ★

Ben had to ride a camel to Church on the Sunday. It was being delivered from Ashbourne in Derbyshire, and arrived at 8.30am.

When it arrived, it was getting a bit fed up of having been in a horse-box for nearly four hours, and immediately spat at everyone as soon as it was led out. It had definitely got the hump. In fact, Olly had *two* humps, with rugs between them for Ben to sit on. He wasn't sure about it and expected a bit more spitting, especially because Olly seemed to snarl at him and showed his teeth, looking at him a bit suspiciously. Once Ben was up in the saddle, however, everything went well. The owner walked at the side all the way, holding a rein, so all Ben had to do was hang on and enjoy the view.

They'd decided to do the Nativity service that week, before the schools broke up. So they had a few sheep from the farm at the end of the village to accompany the shepherds, and Olly the camel got led into church briefly to accompany Ben and the visitors from the East. As usual there was an abundance of dressing-gowns and tea-towels for those playing humans and tinsel haloes and pretty white dresses for those pretending to be angels. The parents, as usual, were thrilled and the Story got told. It was a bit chaotic, and Olly didn't seem to enjoy the band and kept grunting and blowing, so he got led out and ate some grass outside, before the horse-box arrived to pick him up for the long journey back to Derbyshire.

★ ★ ★

Louisa went into work on the Monday morning with a big smile on her face. "I'm an auntie!" she announced, and showed everyone the photos of her holding little Matthew.

But then it was down to business. The consultative group met at 10am, and it was obvious right from the start that it wasn't going to be easy.

Five of the scientists spent the first 45 minutes arguing for their particular pet project. Difficult technical language was bandied about, and the non-scientists were struggling to understand where the discussion was going. Some of them had hijacked the findings of the post-grads who'd been tracking the current research, but others had gone with their own particular hobby-horse.

Louisa butted in eventually. "OK, folks, I'm getting lost in the debate here, and I'm sure that I'm not on my own. Let's backtrack for a moment to think what we're looking for. The important criteria seem to me to be as follows: firstly, a project which no-one yet has had the ingenuity to spot or the technique or resources to pursue; secondly, a project which is innovative, not jumping on the back of or playing a bit-part in another research programme; thirdly, a project which captures non-scientists' imaginations and gets them excited about something they can identify with; and fourthly, something which can directly relate to my Dad's situation. Anyone got any objections to that?"

There was a stunned silence. They hadn't seen this side of Louisa before. Decisive, incisive, persuasive. No-one could see any reason to add anything, or change anything.

"So let's start again and look at some of the suggestions you've been making in the light of those agreed criteria. Who wants to go first?"

But no-one did. None of the projects they'd been championing seemed to be of much consequence in the light of Louisa's clear-thinking. Then Bill spoke up. He hadn't made any suggestion up to that point, but had had plenty to say about each of the suggestions which the others had made.

"I want to introduce one possibility. It's a bit technical, but I think it might fit the criteria. It concerns a variation on a drug called Celecoxib[56], which you may have heard of. The variation itself isn't exactly a household name – but it could become one, if my idea comes to fruition. Celecoxib hasn't really figured much in the world of cancer research for nine years or so, and I'll explain why not.

"Celecoxib was created in the early 1990s by Pfizer, the largest pharmaceutical company in the world. It's had a huge success in treating inflammatory conditions such as osteoarthritis, and as a general analgesic for period pains and conditions such as ankylosing spondylitis, where long-term pain relief is required. It's relatively inexpensive but has netted Pfizer over \$50 million.

"It's known in the cancer business as a selective COX-2 inhibitor, which I'll explain in a moment. And that's why it's got a bit of a bad name. Some other COX-2 inhibitors (but *not* Celecoxib) were the subject of intense concern nine years ago about a possible increased risk of heart attacks and strokes, and our drug got tarred – unjustifiably, in my opinion – with the same brush. The links were never proven anyway.

"So, folks, we're dealing with a controversial but well-known drug. Its use in cancer treatment, however, has been limited by that old rumour that it might increase the risk of a heart attack. But, I repeat, these rumours have never been substantiated for Celecoxib.

"Its use in cancer research, however, was originally linked principally to its inhibition of COX-2. I ought to explain now what that means. Cyclooxygenase-2 (COX-2) is a nasty enzyme, both cancer-enhancing and cancer-indicating. In other words, it's one of those flashing lights which draw our attention to the presence of cancer cells. COX-2 is seen in increased amounts in several cancers but especially in the head and neck, including SCCA, which is, of course, what Brendan has unfortunately contracted. So the fourth of Louisa's criteria, the link with Brendan, is definitely met.

"But curiously, recent research[57] indicates that it's actually some

---

[56] The drug's history and general usage is as described.

[57] cf. CHUANG, Huan-Ching; KARDOSH, A; GAFFNEY, KJ; PETASIS, NA; SCHONTHAL, AH (2008), "COX-2 inhibition is neither necessary nor sufficient for celecoxib to suppress tumor cell proliferation and focus formation in vitro", article in *Molecular Cancer* 7:38.

other property of the drug which inhibits malignant tumour cells, rather than its anti-COX-2 effect. Some researchers have produced another version of the drug, without any anti-COX-2 element at all, which actually has *stronger* anti-cancer activity than Celecoxib itself. It is this variation in which I'm interested.

"I hope that you're following this. Now I get to the meaty part. This particular variation, which is called 2.5-dimethyl-celecoxib (or DMC for short), has already been shown to be helpful in other areas of medicine, such as stopping abdominal adhesions, but it has not yet been tried as an anti-HNSSCA drug. In other words, this is a new area, ripe for research, and the results I spoke of a moment ago indicate that it might well be very fruitful.

"But there's another reason why I've chosen it. Celecoxib was trialled in the early 2000s specifically as an accompanying drug for CRT, chemoradiotherapy, in the treatment of, wait for it, locally advanced or recurrent HNC, head and neck cancer. Does that fit the bill, or what? And, what's more, it had some really good results in the early 2000s reinforcing the multi-agent cisplatin/paclitaxel CRT package[58]. But then the clinical trials were suspended because of those rumours, and haven't as yet been resumed. That's what I'm suggesting we do.

"But remember that the trials stopped only because of those unfounded rumours. Remember too that it's not the COX-2 inhibiting function we're interested in but some other unknown quality which the drug has, but which its variation has even more abundantly. I want us to use this variation, and go for clinical trials with it alongside the already tried and tested best CRT package of cisplatin/paclitaxel. It's even possible that this could have an effect on Brendan. What do you think?"

There was a long silence. Then Louisa spoke. "It obviously meets the fourth criterion. It seems to meet the first and the second, but I don't know how revolutionary it is. Whether we can get it into the minds of non-scientists may be a bigger challenge. What do the rest of you think?"

One of the other oncologists immediately got rather excited.

---

[58] cf. PRELLOP P, PETERS G, CARROLL W, NABELL L, SPENCER S, OVE R, "Radiosensitization with a COX2 inhibitor with chemoradiation for head and neck cancer", an article in *Proceedings of the American Society of Clinical Oncology*, 2006;24:300s. Abstract 5582.

"Celecoxib certainly hasn't got a good name in cancer research, but maybe that's undeserved. A variation of it would definitely be seen as excitingly controversial and "on the edge". We may be able to piggy-back onto the research being done about this other significant property of Celecoxib, but the idea of using this variation sounds like a brilliant innovation to me."

"I like the idea of its specificity to Brendan. That'll sway the undecided," said the regional head of NHS finance.

No-one else spoke, but as Louisa looked around the table, there was a lot of nodding, pursed lips, raised eyebrows and scratching of chins.

"OK then. Give me more information on this variation, and we'll focus on that for the next week. Give me all you can on it and on any trials in which it's been used so far. I want one of you, (Phil, maybe?) to analyse the variation biologically and tell me in language I can understand what's different about it, and what the precise ingredient is which seems to have such an effect on cancer cells. Well done, folks. Same time next week, which will be our last meeting before Christmas. Hopefully we can wrap it up then."

Some people got the joke – wrapping it up before Christmas... Others were already in the corridor, busy and focussed. They had something to go on now. And they wanted to please Louisa and do it well.

Chapter 36

On December 21st, a proud Paul and an exhausted but radiant Ruth came home to Beverley Terrace. It was wonderful for Ruth to have someone to see to Matthew when he cried, because in the hospital they'd expected her to do it, even though the act of bending over and picking him up was painful. Now Paul, the proud father, leapt up at the slightest murmur, and all Ruth had to do was receive the baby for breast-feeding.

★ ★ ★

That same morning, Ben went off to the News Guardian office to be told that because there wouldn't be a paper coming out between Christmas and the New Year, he could probably have the week off. But he didn't think that that was in the spirit of the challenges, and asked the editor to pick an entry out of the container anyway. They'd had a big freight container delivered a few weeks ago, and it was full of tiny bits of paper. The editor reckoned that the surge in entries had levelled off at about 20,000 per week, but each week's were in addition to the ones already received. The number of sponsors too had plateaued in the UK, but internationally there were still tens of thousands coming in each week. The American team monitoring it all estimated about 900,000 sponsors, which could amount to about £1.7 million for each week's successful challenge. Beside this, the 400,000 or so challenge entries didn't seem much, but at 50p a time it added up to another £200,000.

The editor clambered into the container and fished around on the floor, emerging with a piece of paper on which was written "Hearse".

"I don't think we'll go with that one," he said. "Bad taste."

He drew another one, this time from the top of the pile, which suggested "being shot out of a cannon."

"I'm not very good at this, am I?" he said, clambering back in.

"Hang on," said Ben. "What's wrong with that one? I've always fancied being a human cannonball."

"Are you serious?" asked the editor.

★ ★ ★

Louisa's consultative group met that same morning with a sense of triumph in the air. There was a confidence in the room, as if they were on the brink of a successful project.

"OK, Phil, you're the chief molecular biologist. Tell us about our variation."

"Right, well, first of all, it's referred to by those who've used it as DMC[59], which is a bit easier to remember than 2.5-dimethyl-celecoxib. So that's what we're calling it from now on, OK?"

Everyone nodded. DMC sounded good.

"It's a variation, you remember, of a well-known drug called Celecoxib, which seems to have the ability to inhibit cell proliferation and stimulate apoptopic cell death at much lower concentrations. So it operates not just at step two of Bill's six steps, but also at steps three and six. Do you remember what they are?"

Everyone nodded quickly. Louisa *thought* that she remembered all six steps but didn't want to seem silly in front of all the others. She suspected that she wasn't on her own. Phil was a bit more professorial than Bill had been, using clever words like "apoptopic" when he didn't need to. "Normal cell death" would have done just as well.

"I don't want to bore you with the biology of it, but these two functions are mediated by different parts of the Celecoxib molecule and can be separated. Not only that, variations can be generated, like DMC, which retain only one of the functions. The clever thing about DMC is that it mimics faithfully all the numerous anti-tumour effects of Celecoxib, but without the increased risk of anti-COX-2 complications which Celecoxib was rumoured to induce.

"The result is that DMC might well have a marked effect in reducing tumour neovascularisation (which is the production of red blood cells) and stopping angiogenesis (which, you will remember, is the production of new blood vessels), both of which would dramatically

---

[59] The research project being proposed is a variation of that conducted by Axel Schonthal and others in the University of South California in the late 2000s, described in SCHONTHAL, Alex, "Antitumor properties of dimethyl-celecoxib, a derivative of celecoxib that does not inhibit cyclooxygenase-2: implications for glioma therapy", an article in the Journal of Neurosurgery, April 2006, vol. 20, no. 4.

inhibit tumour growth. I think we ought to go for it."

Louisa nodded, but looked puzzled. "But what is it that makes it more potent against HNC than Celecoxib? So far all you're telling us is that it does the same thing without the side-effects. What's the added-value?"

Phil nodded in recognition of Louisa's point. Then he shrugged his shoulders. "You've hit the nail on the head, Louisa. And the answer is that I just don't know. But when we find out, that could be the Nobel Prize winner."

The group discussed the process of setting up the clinical trials. It would be some months before it would launch, with many processes to go through before they were allowed to proceed, but at least they could make a start.

Louisa reported that the other section of the American team, trawling oncologists across the world for cases of simultaneous but unrelated HNSSCAs, hadn't reported much progress. It suggested that Brendan's condition was rarer than they'd thought, and that this part of the research possibilities was unlikely to be viable.

They outlined a programme of meetings and targets for the next few months, and wished each other Happy Christmas. Louisa wondered how happy it would be for her – wonderful with regards to little Matthew, but anxious about the state of her Dad.

★ ★ ★

The following day, Brendan returned home, wary now of everything and a little daunted at being set free, but thrilled to meet his grandson for the first time.

He still had the tracheotomy, because he was very nervous about sleeping and having his tongue choke him again. They said that he could keep it in over Christmas, but that he had to keep manually exercising his tongue, which became part of the Christmas fun and games: "Have you done your exercises, Dad?"

The tracheotomy-technician at the hospital had fitted Brendan with a tube which allowed him to speak, a clever device with a valve which blocked off the airway when he breathed out, allowing air to pass through his vocal cords. It made Brendan sound like a cross between Darth Vader and the Terminator, and he didn't really like it. It certainly wouldn't enhance his preaching. He'd also been given something called a Buchanan Bib which was a bit like little Matthew's bib but made out of foam and cotton. It was designed to fit over the tracheotomy tube so that the general public wouldn't gawp at the hole in his neck, but it also filtered out impurities and humidified the tube. It came with its own little bag of tricks, including brushes, sponge-pads, and spare tapes.

And, of course, he was back on the Jevity. Happy Bloody Christmas.

★ ★ ★

Ben was having a bit of a problem with the human cannonball challenge – and not just the logistics of finding someone to lend him the right sort of cannon.

He discovered that the current world record for the furthest human cannonball flight was just over 61m, which meant a discharge speed of over 70mph. That sounded scary. He definitely wouldn't be attempting a world record on this challenge. But he also discovered that there were at least 30 deaths recorded due to this circus act, one as recent as 2011 in Kent when a safety net failed. His main problem, therefore, was fear.

He didn't know whether it was good or bad when he discovered that they didn't use gunpowder to propel the human cannonball, but either a spring mechanism or, in the more sophisticated acts, a jet of compressed air. Ben didn't know which sounded worst. Then, to his enormous relief, he read that it took months to train someone to do the act, so Ben could justifiably claim that it was too dangerous, too stupid and practically impossible for him to attempt it.

He phoned up the editor's mobile immediately and explained his dilemma. The editor agreed with Ben and told him that he'd be at the office in the morning and they'd pick another challenge. "It'd better be an easy one, mind, because you won't have long to prepare."

★ ★ ★

"Walking backwards" was the next paper drawn out of the container. Technologically uncomplicated, but it proved exhausting and very difficult. He had a practice on the Saturday night and could only manage about 50m before he fell over, complaining of cramp.

"It's all wrong," he complained. "My feet just don't naturally go down that way round and it's killing my calves."

"Wimp!" cried Louisa, laughing – but then Ben reminded her that there was over £1.9 million riding on it, and, once he failed, that was it – no more challenges, no more sponsorship, no more income to the Trust.

That shut her up.

They decided that they would take their time on the Sunday morning, so that he wouldn't feel that he had to over-exert his calf muscles. He set off at 7.30am, allowing himself 2½ hours to do the three miles. But he walked very gingerly and put his feet down "like money", as his Dad would've said. It took ages, but Louisa walked with him (the correct way round, in her case) so at least he had someone to talk to.

They finally got onto the subject of Brendan.

"What do you think of his chances?" asked Louisa.

"What do you mean?" asked Ben, perplexed by the way she'd phrased it.

"He's not going to make it, is he?"

She paused. Ben wondered whether he was supposed to give an answer. But then she spoke again. "I'm not very optimistic. His throat's a real mess and I'm not confident that they've got rid of the primary, let alone the secondaries."

"I don't know," said Ben, helplessly flinging his arms up. "How would I know? But we can't do any more than we're doing, and nor can he."

Then he fell over, Louisa laughed, and the moment had passed.

★ ★ ★

It was odd them all being together for Christmas, especially with Jenna as well. There was no reason to be awkward, however, and Jenna flitted around helping as if she was an established family member, especially caring for Ruth and making meals, though everyone else mucked in. But little Matthew made it an especially significant Christmas.

Brendan had a reprise of his dream about the garden with the gate. But, like the first time, he didn't tell anyone. This time, ominously, he was much closer to the gate...

Chapter 37

Brendan was getting sick of his monotonous diet, and went back on the 27th to have the tube removed. He'd decided that he'd rather choke in his sleep than have any more of the Beige Bilge, as he called it. His throat was still dreadfully sore, and he could only really cope with liquids and mashed up solids which would slip down easily. It wasn't a lot of laughs.

While everyone else was running round after the baby's needs or watching inane repeats on television, Brendan decided to have another go at the hypochondria anagram. He checked out all the letters which he still had left, and started playing with them. He quickly put together "griping, churning pains" and added a few small connecting words to make the phrases into abbreviated sentences.

By 8pm on New Year's Eve, he'd come up with:

Oh God, a dry chest, unusual rough skin on my tongue! A virus? Or is it all psychological? Whatever's that? If it's a particularly big wart, it's odd, isn't it? See that? It's a really sad waistline, a big, floppy pot-belly! Pains are griping, churning, mind... Oh, no! Bloody headaches play between the eyes. It isn't very funny.
I try a broccoli diet to get fit. I even used a fancy gym recently, but I felt an idiot - everyone laughed.
Fungous feet! Face it? Sure. But suppose it's an obscure parasite? And pins and needles across my back! Curious, that... I did try using a liniment on it the other day.
Goodness, look! An odd spot for a polyp!

And he was left with the following letters:

A C D E E E E H H H H H I L L M N
O O O O P R S S T T U W Y Y

From which, at just before 9pm, after much tinkering, he made:

"Where's my phone? Hello? Is that you, Doc?"

He added it as a last line, and felt a sense of satisfaction[60]. It wasn't as fluent as his prize-winner, but he was still rather pleased with himself as he went to bed.

---

[60] The website www.anagrammy.com records a similar winning anagram by Ellie Dent in September 2006.

Alan's Story: May 4th 1979

Alan stayed up till the early hours, but then went to bed as soon as it became obvious that Margaret Thatcher had won. It was depressing living in such a Labour stronghold as North Tyneside, but at least nationally there could be an exciting new start after the Winter of Discontent. The country had been stymied as a result of widespread strikes by trade unions demanding larger pay rises for their members, because the Labour government of James Callaghan had tried to hold a pay freeze to control inflation. To make it worse, the weather turned very cold in the early months of 1979 with blizzards and deep snow, and it became the coldest winter since 1962–63, which added to people's misery.

Alan kept his views very much to himself at work, even though the over-riding sense at the Ministry was frustration that public sector pay and conditions had lagged behind the wage settlements in the private sector, and there'd been a Day of Action on January 22nd when the four main public service unions called out their 1.5 million members in protest at the Government's attempt to impose a 5% pay ceiling. Alan was quiet not because he sensed he was swimming against a strong Labour tide but mainly because he didn't have much to do with anyone else at work.

Others climbed the ladder towards civil service mediocrity, whereas Alan still languished at the lower end of the hierarchy. He hadn't done anything to earn rebuke; he just hadn't done anything to impress either. He turned up, did what needed to be done, clocked in at the right time, clocked out at the right time, and that was that. He refused to go on courses, training opportunities or anything extra, citing his responsibilities at home and church as reasons for his work to rule. Actually, that was what he was doing now: working, and *living*, to rule.

The spark had gone out of his marriage. They still liked each other and *depended* upon one another – maybe that was the problem. Alan made sufficient sarcastic comments for Pauline to feel obliged to fit into Alan's timetables and expectations. She left him to his life at Church, while she went out with her friends, but they met up at breakfast (8.00am prompt, so he could catch the 8.32 Metro) and dinner (6.05pm prompt, so he could watch the news headlines first) and sometimes spoke at bedtime and weekends. He was happy to have his meals and washing done for him, and to let her do what she liked the rest of the time. That was the unspoken rule. Alan was quite happy with that, and believed that Pauline was too.

The bright spot in his life was Jact Methodist Church, where he believed that he was The Man. Sarah Lanleigh was The Woman, and between them they ran the show. Ministers occasionally fluttered around thinking that they had an important role but Alan and Sarah usually managed to put them straight, and everything continued like clockwork. The rule here was local tradition, not the edicts of the Methodist Connexion, though Alan and Sarah studied them as they came out to make sure that they could answer back if anyone quoted a Standing Order at them. And Alan's attitude to Church was as conservative as his attitude to politics. The rule in fact was: what Alan and Sarah say, goes.

Sunday was the highlight of Alan's week. He liked to walk to the church, as long as it wasn't raining, with his attaché case tucked underneath his arm, having sorted out on the Saturday whom he needed to see and to whom he needed to delegate some minor task. He looked after the finances, so there were usually forms to be filled in and papers to be signed. During the sermon, he usually looked at his checklist to make sure that he'd managed to get everything done, and started making his checklist for what needed doing during the week, checking his diary to see what nights he was out at a meeting.

He liked going to Circuit Meeting, as it was now called. It used to be the Quarterly Meeting, though part of the fun had gone out of it as Ministers were now paid centrally rather than having to queue up to be paid at the Meeting to remind them to whom they were accountable and dependent. Still, it gave him and Sarah a chance to ensure that nothing was done at Circuit level which would impinge on life at Jact, and to remind the Circuit how hard the two of them were working in service to their beloved church.

Jact had a vibrant community and church-going still featured in many people's lives. Attendances had peaked in the 1960s and had slid downhill since then, but at the end of the 1970s they were still one of the biggest churches in the Circuit, having about 150 members and some good children's groups. They shared their Minister with Trinity,

Earsdon and West Allotment, so the Minister's presence was sufficiently in demand in all four villages for him not to get anything innovative done in any of them – which, of course, suited Alan and Sarah perfectly.

As Alan settled into his armchair at the end of another day ticked off towards The Day when he could draw his (wonderful) pension, he switched on the news. There she was, the Blessed Margaret, quoting the words of some saint or other: "Where there is discord, may we bring harmony; where there is error, may we bring truth; where there is doubt, may we bring faith; where there is despair, may we bring hope." That's the spirit, he said to himself, unaware that she was quoting the version used by Alcoholics Anonymous rather than the Church[61]. The future was safe, he thought.

All the talk about a grocer's daughter making it to Number Ten got him thinking about his own origins. He reckoned that he'd actually done quite well for himself – a Foxheads lad who'd got a proper job and was a fine, upstanding figure in the community. The fact that he fiddled his taxes was beside the point.

He smiled to himself as he climbed the stairs for the customary half-hour on his sunbed.

---

[61] This alternative version of the Prayer of St. Francis of Assisi is to be found in Chapter 11 of the "Twelve Steps and Twelve Traditions", 2002, AA World Services.

January 2013

Chapter 38

The phone calls began at 11am on January 3rd.

"I think it's in bad taste!"

"I thought it was brilliant, and I've phoned him up to let him know that."

"Funniest card I've had in ages. What a guy!"

"It had me in tears..."

After the first call, Louisa asked her Dad what it was all about.

"Ah," he said, still not talking well. "I hahone hay ean a aaah..."

He pointed to the writing pad.

"I suppose they mean the cards," he wrote.

"What cards?"

And he showed Louisa the card that he'd sent to everyone he knew. He gave her a list of recipients. It ran to several pages: all the church people; the District Chair; Esther and Arnold in America; people he'd met on his journeys; the medical team involved in his treatment, even including the surgeon who'd been a bit curt with him – everyone. He'd even sent one to Fahada al-Yazid, the terrorist ex-PA of Esther, addressed to her "c/o CIA, Washington".

On the front of the card was a cartoon of a Brendan-like character storming furiously out of a Cancer Research shop, and below it was: "I've just been in for my 2013 calendar, but it only goes up to June!" Inside the card it said, "They said they could only give me 6 months at the most." And underneath, was printed: "Happy New Year from Brendan", and underneath that, a big smiley face.

Louisa turned to him, tears welling in her eyes. He grinned and winked. She gave him a big hug, sobbing uncontrollably.

★ ★ ★

"It's been a good thing for this paper," said the editor. "And for the town of Whitley Bay. It's put Jact on the map and it's definitely raised a whole pile of cash for the Trust. You should be proud of yourself, Ben!"

Ben shrugged modestly. He had to admit, though – it had been brilliant. "Long way to go yet," he said.

"That's what I want to talk to you about," said the editor. "I think we're coming to the end of the road."

"What do you mean?" said Ben. Did he know something about Brendan's condition that no-one else did?

"I mean Ben's Challenge. I've had a long think about it over Christmas and I think it's just about run its course."

Ben was shocked. "How come?"

"The entries are going down each week now. The sponsors have dried up completely in the UK. It's only Esther keeping it going. I think you'd be better going out with a bang."

For a horrible moment, Ben thought he was referring to the human cannonball challenge, but then it dawned on him what he meant. "I don't see why it shouldn't keep going. Every week it nets another £2 million."

"But only if the sponsors stay in touch. You might have a whole load of them telling you to get stuffed if you're either asking too much or it goes on forever – and remember that you've still got to get them to cough up."

Ben sighed. He could see his point.

"OK. I'll have a think about it. Let's do the draw."

It was another actor who was the celebrity this week. He stepped into the container and picked an entry. "Helicopter," he read.

"That'll be good," said Ben. "I've never been in a helicopter. Where can I get one of them from?"

"You can borrow mine, if you like," said the actor. He was obviously more successful than Ben had imagined.

★ ★ ★

Ben thought long and hard about what the editor had suggested. He made a list of all the challenges he'd fulfilled so far:

1.	Tank	11.	Lifeboat
2.	Unicycle	12.	Crowd-surf
3.	Canoe	13.	Formula 1 car
4.	Donkey	14.	Hopping
5.	Hovercraft	15.	Yachting whike
6.	Dustbin lorry	16.	Hot-air balloon
7.	Dog-sled	17.	Bath
8.	Sky-dive	18.	Camel
9.	Pram	19.	Walking backwards
10.	JCB	20.	Helicopter

Maybe he should stop when he'd done 25 challenges – it seemed a good round number. He'd announce to all the sponsors and entrants that that was what he was going to do, and that for the last four weeks *he'd* choose the mode of transport – and they'd be the most spectacular he could find...

He floated the idea with Louisa, who was a bit shocked at first, as he had been – but then saw the wisdom in it. It seemed a bit daft to kill the goose that was laying the golden eggs, but maybe the goose *was* getting a bit past it. She hoped that Brendan wouldn't be upset or feel that they were giving up on him, or anything daft like that, nor that the Trust would object at the sudden loss of income. They had plenty to be going on with.

★ ★ ★

The first meeting of the New Year found the consultative group ready for action.

Bill had written up a draft clinical trials protocol for them to study. It described the scientific rationale, objectives, design, methodology, statistical considerations, and organization of the planned trial. It contained a precise study plan for executing the clinical trial, not only to assure the safety and health of the trial subjects, but also to provide an exact template for trial conduct so that those taking part at the twenty locations would administer the treatment in exactly the same way. It was carefully written to conform to the ICH guidelines[62].

The trial was to consist of a strict dose of DMC, at one of five dose levels (from 200mg to 600mg) given orally twice daily. The variation was to determine maximum tolerated dose (MTD). For each of the various combinations there were ten SCCA patients, making a trial size of 200 patients. This was about right for a major clinical trial and would probably give recognisable and approved conclusions. But, if accepted, the trial would take at least 18 months. The treatments themselves would only span 15 weeks, but the effects would have to be observed over a long period.

Currently, the most widely used standard CRT regimen was 3 bursts of 100 mg/m^2 cisplatin every 3 weeks, with 3 weeks recuperation between bursts, combined with 70 Gy radiation delivered in 1.8 – 2.0 Gy daily fractions. But Bill wanted to make the trial a randomised phase 3 trial, in which various CRT regimens would be administered in a double-blind project (i.e. neither the patient nor the oncologist knew which precise drug or combination was being administered alongside the standardised radiotherapy). The fact that DMC had already gone safely through Phase 1 and 2 trials and was being used in other areas helped them to justify going straight to the final phase 3 stage.

So in addition to the single-agent CRT regimen with cisplatin on its own, Bill was also suggesting several multi-agent CRT regimens: cisplatin and paclitaxel; cisplatin and 5-FU; and 5-FU and hydroxyurea. These, Bill explained, were the agents most widely used in CRT currently, because they'd produced the best results in previous trials. The dosages for each were in line with current guidelines.

It looked wonderfully comprehensive. The conclusions should then be comparable to similar trials with Celecoxib.

"And how much might this cost?" asked Louisa.

"Ah," said the NHS regional manager. "I might be able to help you there. I was recently involved in setting up a multi-centre trial involving patients in the UK, Germany, Brazil, Mexico and the US. The cost in each country varied considerably, but the average cost per patient per treatment day was about $5,000. For 200 patients that would be $1

---

[62] "Good Clinical Practice" guidance is issued by the International Conference on Harmonization of Technical Requirements for Registration of Pharmaceuticals for Human Use (ICH).

million. The length of the treatment involved in the trial would be forty days, so we're talking about $40 million for the treatment trial, plus an on-cost of about $8 million to $10 million for the observational and analytical period which followed. So we're probably looking at $50 million altogether. Which at today's exchange rate of $1.64 to the pound equates to just over £31 million."

"And how much have we got?" asked Louisa, looking to the fund manager, who was one of the Oracle team.

"As of January 4, not counting the unquantifiable sponsorship pledges of individuals across the world on the basis of Ben's Challenge, which on the latest projection could amount to a further £38 million, we still had total assets of just over £186.7 million."

Louisa puffed out her cheeks. "We can afford it then."

Chapter 39

Brendan felt awful.

His weight-loss continued. He still couldn't bear solids, so he was on a liquid diet of porridge, soup and high-energy drinks. He couldn't be bothered with the pain and slowness involved in trying anything more solid – and he couldn't taste it anyway, so what was the point? He refused Jevity, and the result was that he wasn't imbibing sufficient calories to maintain (let alone increase) his weight.

In the mirror Brendan looked like someone else. It wasn't him. This person was too thin, a little old man who should have been called Albert or Sid. His watch kept swivelling round his wrist. His wedding ring fell off, and got lost. His usual clothes now were the cancer-victim uniform of draw-string trousers and baggy jumper.

On average his bowel movements were fine, but in fact they alternated violently between extreme constipation and extreme diarrhoea, with very little time spent in the comfortable middle ground.

His back ached constantly, probably as a result of the loss of cushioning his weight loss had caused. His usual day-time position was lying down till he coughed, which made him jerk upright to clear his airways. This was his usual night-time position too, so he didn't sleep very well.

He still couldn't talk properly. His taste buds had been obliterated. He had mouth ulcers on one side of his mouth because of the radiotherapy. He'd lost half his saliva glands but oddly produced so much saliva that he dribbled a lot.

He had constant earache, apparently because of pain referred from the wounds in his throat (how did that work?) and his lower jaw ached where it had been sawn in half. He also had a frozen shoulder as a result of the neck dissection having sliced through a nerve.

His throat was very sore. Very, very sore.

Apart from that, he was fine.

But the worst bit of all was the nagging feeling that the cancer hadn't all been eradicated, and that he was dying.

★ ★ ★

The letter arrived, out of the blue, on a cold, wintry morning when everything seemed grey. Brendan was looking out of the window across the road to the sea, trying to work out where the grey of the sky finished and the grey of the sea started, and saw the postman coming – not that he was particularly bothered by mail, or anything else for that matter.

Ruth brought the letter in, and handed it over. "It's got a postmark from Austin, Texas. Isn't that where your cyclist friend came from?"

Brendan sat forward in his chair. "Carol? Quick – let me see!" It actually came out differently, but Ruth knew what he meant.

On his first journey down the Americas he'd cycled some of the way with an American widow called Carol. He'd first met her as he passed through a Kansas village called El Dorado, and rode with her all the way to her son's in Austin. There'd been a bit more than a friendship formed, and Carol had definitely been up for more still, but Brendan had eventually decided that he needed to pursue his journey, and nothing had come of it. He hadn't forgotten her, though, and wondered once or twice on his second journey how she was and what she was doing.

He ripped the airmail letter open, only to find that it was from someone whose name meant nothing to him: Sandra. Who was she? "It's not from Carol," he announced to Ruth, disappointedly.

But when he started to read, with Ruth looking on, his eyes widened in surprise, then tears began to run down his cheeks. "Fahada!" he whispered. "I don't believe it!"

Fahada had been Esther's personal assistant and lover, but had been secretly plotting all through Brendan's second journey to make sure that he'd fail. She'd been born into an Egyptian family steeped in terrorism, and had been smuggled into America as a "sleeper" long before 9/11, ready to strike a blow for the Islamist cause at the right time. Her father and her "controller" took over and blew up Brendan's plane in East Timor, but Brendan survived, Fahada was arrested and had been detained by the CIA.

Brendan handed the letter to Ruth, who read:

Dear Brendan,

I know this letter will come as a shock to you, but I used to be known as Fahada. I wanted to write and say Thank You – not only for refusing to testify against me but for introducing me to Jesus. I want to tell you how it happened.

When I was detained by the CIA, for some reason they gleefully showed me a recording of your interview in East Timor, in which you spoke of forgiveness. I couldn't believe that you could forgive me, and I read the Bible in my cell, and decided that Jesus offered the world far more love and hope than I'd ever encountered in Islam, so I converted and have found great joy in Him. I know that I've done terrible things, but that God still loves me.

Esther too refused to testify against me, and the men in suits realised that putting me on trial would be counter-productive, for it would show up their immigration shortfalls and make people more anxious of Islamist infiltration. So they offered me a deal: If I told them everything I knew about my father and his friends, my brother and Saeed, they'd put me in a witness-protection program with a new name and identity – and a new face and shape, which don't stand out as much as the ones God gave me. I cannot see or meet anyone I've known before, including you – but I'm allowed one letter to you and one to Esther, and then you will hear from me no more. I'm presently in Texas but will be moving to a quiet place somewhere else and trying to begin a new life. I sign this letter with my temporary name, but that's not what my new name will be.

I've heard that you are now ill, and will be praying for your recovery.

Best wishes,

Sandra

"Dad, that's wonderful! Fancy Fahada turning to Jesus, after all that she did to thwart your mission. You must be thrilled..."

"Yes," said Brendan, wiping his eyes. "God is good." He actually said, "Ga ib goo" but Ruth knew exactly what he meant. To anyone else, though, Brendan's words sounded like the droolings of a drunk. Would he ever speak properly again?

Chapter 40

Brendan's speech therapy had been running for a few weeks, but there weren't many signs of improvement, which for a preacher was utterly depressing. Most of Melanie's therapy was geared to training his tongue to move on its own, and especially to help him eat properly.

Each session was like a gym session for his tongue. It was like trying to get a TV-watching couch-potato to do push-ups and star-jumps, but in Brendan's case the reluctant exerciser was a lump of muscle which was criss-crossed like a map of the London Underground and far happier lying dormant on the bottom of his mouth.

An additional problem with Brendan's speech was that even when he physically stretched out his tongue by hand it didn't quite extend to his teeth, making most sounds impossible anyway. He'd never previously appreciated how clever speech was, and how many movements had to be precise before words came out right. He could do vowels brilliantly because he merely held his mouth open in the right shape and made a noise, but consonants were more problematic. He could do "ph/f" by blowing hard, and "c/k" by half-spitting in the back of his throat. "M" was fine too, and "p" and "w", because they relied on lips rather than the tongue, but everything else was tricky.

Melanie had been trying the usually weaponry in the speech therapy – stimulation techniques such as brushing (pressure massage), icing (thermal stimulation), quick stretch (tapping), and vibration (manual and mechanical), in order to prepare Brendan's tongue for movement. They'd shared a few laughs as Melanie produced various vibrators or gadgets, but none of them seemed to produce anything except more frustration. It became apparent that these strategies couldn't change the range of movement or the strength of the tongue without additional muscle movement, which Brendan didn't possess. So she'd just started a different technique which attempted to stimulate initial tongue movement and contraction and to provide movement against resistance so that the tongue became stronger.

"You're a real challenge, you are, Brendan!" said Melanie.

He smiled and winked.

"There are six normal patterns of tongue movements and you haven't got any of them. You can't cup your tongue for the basic suckling shape; you can't stick your tongue out; you can't lift your tongue to press on the top of your mouth to suck; you can't raise the tip of your tongue to help suck or form consonant sounds against your teeth or palate; you can't lift your tongue to move food along the palate and you can't do lateral tongue movements which manoeuvre food between your molars for chewing and then enable swallowing to take place. It's no wonder you're having such difficulty eating or talking. You're a real challenge. But I... am... not... going... to... give... up... on... you." She said each word separately as she tapped on Brendan's flaccid tongue with her forefinger.

★ ★ ★

Melanie had sent Brendan along the previous week for further neuro-imagery at the RVI, and he'd come back with the news that the scan had found a structural lesion located at the crossing-point of the vagal and hypoglossal nerves. It didn't mean anything to him, but Melanie nodded.

"It still doesn't explain *how* this happened. It could be a result of the operation, because they cut something they shouldn't have – but it's more likely to be some kind of neuropathy because of something else, like the tracheotomy tube. There's something called Tapia's Syndrome resulting from that sort of indirect damage to the nerves."

Brendan instantly thought of the dead tapir he'd seen being eaten by a majestic jaguar as they kayaked up the Paraguay River the previous February, nearly a year ago[63].

When he wrote this on his pad, Melanie explained that this was Tapia's Syndrome, and had nothing to do with South American animals.

"It's named after the Spanish neurologist[64] who in 1905 located the neural damage causing paralysis of the tongue to a bullfighter who'd been silly enough to get gored in the neck by a bull."

"Is it permanent?" wrote Brendan.

"Oh no," said Melanie. "They thought so at the time, but it was all a

---

[63] Described in "Brendan and the Great Omission", p. 366.

[64] A.G. Tapia, "Un caso de parálisis..." in El Siglo Médico, Madrid, 1905, 52: 211-213.

load of bull." They both erupted in laughter, with Brendan dissolving into painful coughing.

"Sorry!" said Melanie. "If they managed to recover the bullfighter's speech a century ago, I'm sure we can do something for you. Speech therapy today's much more sophisticated, so I'm sure we can achieve good results – even in a difficult patient like you!" She prodded Brendan in the ribs, and he smiled.

He liked Melanie a lot.

★ ★ ★

Ruth was feeling increasingly useless, except as a food-production system for little Matthew. She was proving extremely efficient at this, though she was getting a bit sore. He seemed to have the suction strength of an industrial hoover and gums with the grip of a bulldog clip. She could sense herself "filling up" between feeds and when she was woken for a feed in the night she sometimes felt on the verge of exploding. Matthew didn't seem to mind and took life as it came: feed, burp, smile, sleep, scream, feed, burp, etc.

Paul had had to fly back to Uganda during the first week of 2013, his paternity leave complete. He needed to keep tabs on the projects in Gulu, and was particularly keen to chase up the bureaucratic procedures which otherwise would stop any activity for months. He knew well that speed was not a part of the African psyche except in athletics. But Watoto was now, thanks to Brendan, a high-profile motivator for change in Northern Uganda, and Paul, the charity's up-front man, carried considerable clout.

Uganda was still suffering, however, from the blight of corruption. Even though Watoto was now a huge influence in establishing good practice in commerce and local government, Paul still had to battle against expectations of payments for smoothing the processes. He'd challenged every official who'd openly asked for payment – and even seen some officials dismissed – but there was always someone else trying to supplement their meagre income by extorting money from those wanting something from them.

The national leadership wasn't setting the best example – misappropriating aid money or using it extravagantly themselves to reinforce already-inflated salaries, luxuriate their official residences, or buy ridiculously ornate office furnishings and luxury 4x4s for their own use. Watoto refused to go along with any such practice, and had a sufficiently high national profile to make a difference, and for that and other reasons usually preferred to work through their own projects independently of national bodies. When planning permission or sale-of-land contracts were needed, however, Paul had to assert Watoto's unequivocal Christian policies against any level of corruption.

The bureaucracy of planning and land purchase was handled by the district council, which subsisted on whatever money trickled down after the national officials had taken their cut. Unfortunately the local government salaries were meagre, with an inbuilt expectation that most of their revenue would come from backhanders. Tenders for work in construction usually went to the campaign managers of the district councillors, who often authorised the use of sub-standard materials to save more money for themselves and to pay their own bribes further down the work-scale. Corruption had become so endemic in Uganda and was such an accepted way of life that when someone was appointed or elected to a public office they were expected to exploit their opportunity to make significant money. It was this sub-culture of corruption that Uganda needed to eradicate if it was ever to develop properly for the good of all – and Paul was doing his best.

The head of state was supposed to preside over the eradication of corruption at the centre. When he failed at that task, he also lost any moral ground to enforce any such discipline at the local government level. In fact, as long as corrupt district officials remained loyal to the president and the ruling party, there was very little chance of concrete action ever being taken against them – except, perhaps, if donors such as Paul and Watoto demanded it.

Paul's access to the Brendan Priest Trust funds meant that he could cut through some of the red tape, but he was still up against opposition from some local officials who seemed to be concerned more about ensuring their own income-channels than in developing the Gulu economy and services.

The world might be changing very quickly, but the wheels of progress in Uganda turned rather too slowly for Paul's tastes – and he was having to fight the same battle over and over again with one particular bureaucrat in Gulu, who seemed to gain huge satisfaction from opposing or delaying anything that passed across his desk.

Paul wondered what he could do, and then had an inspiration.

Chapter 41

The briefcase arrived at Watoto HQ in Gulu a few weeks later, sent from an obscure Internet-based business in London. It was at the bottom of a large crate marked "Office Supplies", full of boxes of envelopes, clipboard pads, staplers, dictation machines, printers and CCTV cameras. All the rest was needed (though not necessarily from London) but was camouflage for the briefcase, which contained a hidden camera and tape-recorder of the highest quality available[65].

Paul had no idea about whether such an eavesdropping device was available in Uganda, but didn't want to alert anyone in the country to his anti-corruption activities – hence his trawling of the Internet and purchase from Advanced Intelligence. It had cost $1,800, but would be well worth it if he could get the evidence he needed to bring down Nelson Amandla[66], a second cousin of Usuru Amandla, who'd been the Northern Uganda Transition Initiative (NUTI) chairman until its official closing in May 2011[67], but was still hugely influential. His second cousin thus believed himself unassailable in Northern Uganda.

The application for the land purchase for the Watoto Farms Project was being held up by Mr. Amandla, just as he'd held up the previous purchases of land for the Production Unit, Surgical Hospital and the Watoto villages around Gulu. He was the land man – and he'd made it clear that he'd only move on any transaction once he'd received sufficient reward. He'd had to give in on the other deals due to pressure from the national government in Kampala who needed to avoid Esther Blanchett telling the world how corrupt Uganda was. But now, the

---

[65] The briefcase is based on one advertised at www.advanced-intelligence.com/product_video_vid088.html

[66] Usuru Amandla was given this role and briefly quoted in "Thule for Christ's Sake", but the character here is unrelated to anyone, and any resemblance to anyone in local government in Uganda is unintentional. The caricature and story is included to make a stereotype more concrete.

[67] NUTI was wound up by the USAID contractors DynCorp International on May 15th 2011 – who decided that it had done its job of easing Northern Uganda through the instability of the immediate post-war period.

media spotlight was elsewhere – on certain Eurozone countries after the second credit crunch hit, on Afghanistan after the removal of American troops, and on renewed tensions in the Middle East after various Arab countries had erupted in internal conflict. So Amandla believed that he could use his position to challenge Paul into paying him to smooth a passage for the land purchase.

Paul had had a dummy run with the briefcase, taking it with him down to Kampala for a Watoto board meeting. He'd put the briefcase down on a table in the corner, and it'd not only recorded every sentence spoken for more than two hours, but had recorded a video through a 60° pinhole camera hidden behind a one-way mirror in the side of the case. It started recording as soon as Paul put it down on the table, and turned the lock of the case – and it kept going throughout. The video and audio playback were of excellent quality.

Paul filled the case with bundles of banknotes amounting to five million shillings (about $2,000) and set off for his private meeting with Mr. Amandla at Gulu District Administration HQ, a plush new office complex constructed in 2008 with development money at the time when the camps were overflowing with thousands of people needing urgent basic assistance.

He was kept sitting in the outer office for 35 minutes beyond the agreed meeting time before the door opened. Paul shut the case, which he'd kept open on his knee, locked it, stood up, and was escorted into the office of Mr. Amandla, which was the corner office at the top of the building, looking out over the countryside to the north and west of the town. He'd got the best office in the complex, of course.

"Come in, my friend," said the beaming Nelson. "I assume we'll be achieving progress in that very difficult land purchase I've been working so hard on. Unfortunately it has required a *lot* of my time and energy..."

None of the usual small-talk, then. It was straight down to business.

"Mr. Amandla," said Paul. "I've come to see if there is anything I can do to help the purchase through."

"Ah, you're finally understanding the way in which the Gulu District Administration works. I've always struggled to understand your reluctance to use traditional ways of strengthening deals, and am pleased to see that you've now seen the error of your ways."

Paul's stomach turned at the gall and arrogance of the man. "This is difficult for me, but I need to ensure that the programme of development set out by the Brendan Priest Trust doesn't get stalled by local bureaucracy – and I think I now understand what I have to do to ensure that everything proceeds properly."

"Oh good. So let's get down to business. The purchase price was negotiated last year to a base price of 500 million shillings, was it not? Well, I would imagine that if we made that 600 million shillings we could have the transaction completed by next week." He smiled.

"Do you mean that everything is complete except for your supervision of the final signing of the deal, and that there will be a fee for your expertise in achieving that?"

"I suppose you could say that. I prefer myself to call it a consultancy fee – equivalent to 15% of the total sale price."

Paul did the sums. The extra 100 million ($40,000) was all going to Amandla, with 15% on top of that.

"So what do I need to do to secure the deal?"

"Have you got the money with you?" asked Amandla.

Paul spluttered. "Of course not! I'm not going to carry that much money around with me. I do have five million shillings, however, which I could put down as a deposit."

He unlocked and opened the case, and lifted out the money, then put it back on top of the case as he re-locked it, re-activating the recording equipment.

"Maybe you could write me a receipt?"

Amandla sniffed, as if to say "Is that all?", then laughed as he reached forward and grabbed the money in a big fist. "People like me don't issue receipts. You'll just have to take my word for it." And he laughed again.

"So you'll have the documentation drawn up and signed by the end of next week, will you?" asked Paul, affecting the wheedling tone of someone who knew that they're the underdog.

"If you make sure the 100 million shillings has been transferred into my bank account – the account number on this piece of paper – then I'll sign the papers. You must come back next week and transfer the 500 million to the government land registry account, which is the account number below. Make sure you don't get them mixed up!" He laughed loudly.

"Ah, but it'll be 100 million minus the five million I just gave you, won't it?" whined Paul.

"What five million?" Amandla smiled. "It's always good when gentlemen finalise deals with honour, isn't it?"

And he laughed for the fourth time, stood up, and showed Paul out.

★ ★ ★

Paul caught a plane down to Entebbe, and went straight into the Watoto CEO's office. He and Alan Tomlinson had had a few run-ins when Paul and Ruth had been working for Watoto three years ago, at the start of their relationship, but that was all ancient history now.

He'd called Alan from Watoto HQ in Gulu, which is where the Brendan Priest Trust had their office. "I need to speak to you on a matter of some urgency and importance, and ask your advice."

He'd flown down straightaway and Jules the driver was waiting for him at Entebbe. They chatted about Ruth and the baby as Jules negotiated the streets of southern Kampala, finally drawing up with a lurch outside the old cinema which housed Watoto HQ in the centre of the city.

"You're looking quite the businessman now, Paul, with your shiny new briefcase and smart suit," was Jules cheery farewell as the Landrover chugged off into the traffic.

Indeed I am, thought Paul, as he waved at the receptionist and climbed up to Alan's office.

★ ★ ★

The scandal hit the very next morning. The recording had gone out on a late-night news show, missing most Ugandans but not the vigilant eyes of the scandal-happy media. The morning TV news bulletins and front pages were full of it. "SHAME!" yelled the headline of the Kampala Times, with a picture of a smiling Amandla clutching the wad of dollars. "Will nothing ever change?" asked the Uganda Mail, with a similar photograph but with a more philosophical piece about the inevitability of corruption. The Gulu Times was more forthright:

"AMANDLA CAUGHT WITH HIS FINGERS IN THE MONEY-BAG!" it shouted, with the same picture, and a word-for-word transcript of the conversation.

Paul didn't get the Trust's five million shillings back. But he did save the Trust the extra 95 million shillings, and the embarrassed government ensured that the land purchase went through quickly at the start of the following week.

He stayed for a week to make sure that everyone knew what they were doing, then headed home – into a further storm...

Chapter 42

Louisa had started the year with her usual go-ahead enthusiasm, but the edge was taken off that quickly when the clinical trials for DMC seemed to flounder immediately. The Government was wary of fast-tracking anything, let alone something as contentious as a once-vilified drug. The facts that Celecoxib was not being used in the trial, that it was still being administered to thousands of people under appropriate conditions, and that the DMC variant was such an exciting new prospect in all kinds of research already sanctioned, were irrelevant, it seemed. The clinical trials were put on indefinite hold "until further research is undertaken", said the fax which came through to Louisa's office at the Freeman.

They'd hit a brick wall. Louisa wanted to hit lots of people. Paul walked back into a simmering cauldron of a seething Louisa and the rest of the household trying to avoid her and terrified of saying the wrong thing.

Louisa decided to contact Esther, to see if her miracle-worker employer could produce one more. She could get private planes to land on aircraft carriers[68], but could she do anything about UK health politics?

"Hi, sweetie. What can I help you with?" Esther's greetings were always so cloyingly *American.*

Louisa explained the situation as quickly and dispassionately as she could.

"Well, you could always get everyone to come to America. I'm sure I could persuade an American university to co-ordinate the programme..."

Louisa gulped. It was very generous of Esther to use her influence in that way – but she didn't want to leave her Dad, and she didn't really fancy moving to America at all. She'd never lived anywhere other than Britain, and wasn't keen on the idea. She tried to explain her reluctance, but it was the separation from Brendan that clinched it.

---

[68] It happened in "Brendan and the Great Omission" p. 345

"OK sweetie, I'll see what I can do."

★ ★ ★

Four days later, the Prime Minister made the following announcement in Prime Minister's Questions in the House of Commons, to a planted question by a junior minister in the Health Department:

"I am proud to announce that the Government's partnership with private trusts continues with the announcement of a bold clinical trials programme to undertake an exciting new development in cancer research. The Brendan Priest Cancer Care Trust is putting up £40 million and this country is enabling this work to be co-ordinated here by making facilities available in our hospitals, and requiring our oncology departments to co-operate in this new venture. This is one further sign of this government's commitment to the National Health Service and our aim to make the United Kingdom a centre of medical excellence!"

He sat down to cheers from his own side and groans from the Opposition. But it didn't matter, because the more important consideration was that the green light had been given for the clinical trials to proceed. Furthermore, they were now public knowledge, and the Trust had been given massive publicity.

Louisa didn't know how Esther had done it, but she'd proved once again that her influence extended much further than it should.

★ ★ ★

Brendan's name was all over the newspapers the following day, not that he was that interested. But he'd been thrilled to discover the day before that his tongue did have some movement. He'd lifted his tongue up from the bottom of his mouth right up to the top. This was after Melanie had challenged him to press upwards onto her finger as it lay on the top of his tongue. Patiently, untiringly, she'd kept going, day after day, reaching into Brendan's mouth and rolling up his tongue, grabbing hold of it and yanking it from side to side, pushing it up with her finger to the top of his mouth and trying to get him to keep it there.

She'd put small vibrating machines onto his tongue which sent out thudding pulses, which Brendan felt more and more – and not just because his whole mouth shook. He could feel the pulses through his tongue. Melanie was thrilled when he told her, and redoubled her efforts manually to get the tongue muscle used to moving, in the hope that it would somehow catch the idea and do it by itself.

The breakthrough had been the previous afternoon when he'd kept his tongue up at the top of his mouth for a second before it flopped down again.

"Up, up!" cried Melanie, hoisting it again with her finger, and squealing with delight when it stayed up there again. Brendan smiled, but then he was required to repeat it again and again and again, until he could do it every time for at least ten seconds.

"Now lift it on your own!" ordered Melanie. "It's the same muscle you've already been using, so there's no reason why you shouldn't do it yourself!"

And slowly, inexorably slowly, he'd lifted his tongue upwards, flat as a pancake still but that bending movement should come later, and kept it at the top of his mouth before slowly lowering it to the bottom of his mouth again.

Melanie shrieked. "You're showing off now!" she yelled, then threw her arms around his neck and gave him a big kiss. Ruth and Matthew happened to come in at that point, much to everyone's embarrassment, but that was quickly forgotten when Melanie demanded that Brendan show them his latest achievement. Ruth clapped her hands in appreciation, but then Matthew started crying so she had to attend to him.

"Well done, Dad!" she shouted as she bustled down the stairs. "I'm proud of you – and you, Melanie!"

★ ★ ★

Ben and Louisa were treated to a similar demonstration when they got in from work, and they decided to send out for a Chinese takeaway to celebrate, but it was spoilt somewhat when Brendan choked on his first bit of char siu and had to content himself with the soup while the others made short work of the main dishes.

Ben told the others of his progress with the Challenge. He was now into the final weeks, having chosen and completed the first of the two special forms of transport – a yellow submarine and the Goodies' trandem.

The yellow submarine was a small lightweight bright-yellow submersible designed for the new and expanding trade in leisure submersibles. Apparently the next thing for "the man who has everything" was to own his own submarine, and most super-yachts now had an internal underwater dock and store facility designed to house at least one submersible. Through some of Esther's contacts, he'd arranged with a UK company in Essex for the hire of a Subeo Gemini[69], which arrived on the back of a big lorry, and looked like something out of science fiction, with its two bulbous Perspex domes and little "wings" for buoyancy. The domes opened which meant that Ben could sit waving to people all the way to church. It was clever of Subeo to have painted it yellow, and the Beatles song was amplified through a loudspeaker on the front of the lorry all the way, calling people enjoying a leisurely read of their newspapers to get outside and view this unique vehicle coming along their road.

A similar thing happened the following Sunday when Ben, Louisa and its owner rode the official second-series red trandem up to Jact. When the Goodies had left the BBC to join ITV, they had to leave it behind, but LWT made a blue version for their series. The red one was sold in a BBC props auction, and ended up being ridden across Africa for charity[70], but Ben had managed to track the owner down and arrange for the trandem bike to be brought up to the North East. The Goodies theme tune brought the residents of Cullercoats, the Marden estate, Preston Grange, New York and Jact out of their homes for the second Sunday in a row.

Ben was in the process of getting a Tardis for the following Sunday but was struggling with the final two weeks.

"It has to be really unique," he kept saying. "What do you think?"

The current favourites were a Popemobile and an elephant. Ben was sure that His Holiness would be happy to do without wheels for the weekend, but how could they get it to Jact – and was it worth the expense and worry? They'd managed to ferry a Formula 1 car across from America, but that was in conjunction with She Who Can Do Anything...

---

[69] www.nautica.it/superyacht/513/service/geminieng.htm has the Gemini's specifications and photographs. It is advertised as "the world's first recreational submarine".

[70] cf. SPOWERS, Rory, "Three Men on a Bike", Canongate Books, 1995 (with a foreword by Bill Oddie)

Alan's Story: February 3rd 1984

Nine months ago, Dr. John Buster of the Los Angeles School of Medicine had performed the first ever embryo transfer from one woman to another which was to result in a live birth. And that birth had just been reported that morning in the New York Times, though it had happened a fortnight ago[71]. In the procedure, an embryo that was just beginning to develop was transferred from one woman, in whom it had been conceived by artificial insemination, to another woman who gave birth to the infant 38 weeks later. The sperm used in the artificial insemination came from the husband of the woman who bore the baby.

This scientific breakthrough was to establish standards and become an agent of change for women throughout the world who suffered from infertility or genetic disorders which could otherwise be passed on to their children. This donor embryo transfer was the first of innumerable such procedures to enable such women to become pregnant and give birth to a child who contained their husband's genetic make-up.

Alan's attention, however, back in Jact, was diverted by the overwhelming event of his own son's birth that morning.

They'd not needed any such scientific process, of course. But how on earth it had happened was a mystery to Alan. Well, of course he knew *how* it had happened, and he could even remember *when* conception must have taken place, because there hadn't been more than three or four times when it *could* have happened. But why now? They'd never been particularly bothered when pregnancy didn't happen during the first years of their marriage, and they'd assumed that one of them must be infertile, but they'd not been bothered enough to have it checked out. But a week in Marbella last May Day must have somehow done the trick.

Pauline had kept the news to herself for half the pregnancy, unsure about her own reaction and apprehensive about what Alan's might be. When he found out 4 months ago, he hadn't been sure quite how he felt about it, from the initial shock of the news to the onset of Pauline's contractions yesterday. He'd had 4 months to get used to the idea, but

---

[71] www.nytimes.com/1984/02/04/us/infertile-woman-has-baby-through-embryo-transfer

when the squirming, wailing purple and red thing had emerged from Pauline after half a day of Alan dutifully holding her hand, he'd found himself flooding instantly with paternal feelings, which not only surprised him but worried him. What sort of a Dad would he be? He was nearly 40, for goodness' sake – was he going to be able to cope?

Pauline and his son were still in the hospital. She'd done well, because she was no spring chicken either, and they'd been telling her throughout the pregnancy that it wasn't straightforward becoming a mother for the first time at the age of 38, nearly 39. She was pretty tired and sore, so they'd suggested that she stayed in, and she'd joked that Alan would have to make his own tea. Alan didn't find it as funny as everyone else obviously did, and went down the Farmer's Arms for a pie and a pint.

Now, as he reflected on a Friday utterly different from the usual dreariness of the Ministry, he looked forward to a different weekend from usual, before going back to work on the Monday. He'd have to take Pauline's parents to see her, he supposed, because her Dad had suffered a heart attack a few months ago and wasn't allowed to drive. Then he'd have to check that they'd got everything in place for their son to come home. They already had a cot and nappies and all that stuff, but he wanted to make sure that he knew how to disconnect the baby carrier bit from the pram chassis and how it fitted into the car. And he'd have to do something about food as well. And he was on duty, of course, at Church on the Sunday. He'd have to work out when he wanted the baptism and tell the Minister. There was a lot to do.

The Minister had only been there since last September, another in a long line of probationer ministers sent to learn their trade at Jact. The trouble was that youthful enthusiasm sometimes got in the way of good sense. This one had dared to suggest a few weeks earlier that two younger people who'd only been coming to the Methodist Church for a couple of years should become Church Stewards. How ridiculous was that! Of course he'd been told that he was well out of order, and Sarah, bless her, had told him that he risked splitting the church. Hopefully, he'd now shut up and concentrate on what he was supposed to be there for, rather than introducing schism and undermining all that was good at Jact. That was the trouble with these young Ministers they kept sending them, straight out of College. They always thought that they knew best, when it was patently obvious that he and Sarah knew what was right for Jact. They'd had to get rid of one Minister a few years ago who'd had similar revolutionary leanings. This one wouldn't last long either if he didn't toe the line...

He sighed, and reflected on how strange and different his life was now going to be. He nodded to himself, as he sat there in front of the fire watching late-night TV, confirming to himself that he indeed was quite proud of becoming a father. He was actually looking forward to seeing his son again tomorrow. He'd have to stop referring to his son as just his son, of course. Pauline had been going on about names for weeks and had a short-list of favourites, but none of them had really got him excited.

Then, it struck him. The perfect name: Alan (Junior), a chip off the old block. Perfect.

He couldn't wait to tell Pauline.

February 2013

Chapter 43

The Tardis lookalike on the back of a lorry provided the third Sunday morning in a row when the residents of Ben's route were disturbed with a blaring theme-tune, but the people flocked out of their houses to see the Doctor Who mode of transport, and waved at Ben as he sat on its roof waving to the crowds.

When they got to the church in Jact, Ben led worship with the Superintendent on the subject of travelling through time – not in the Doctor Who sense but as people on a journey through time – as Ben put it, "between a garden and a city, between a couple and a crowd, between a tree with the knowledge of good and evil and a tree for the healing of the nations."

They encouraged the congregation to see that the world was in the in-between bit of the Biblical story – a long way on from Genesis (garden/couple/Eden tree) but an unknown period before Revelation (city/crowd/healing tree).

"So what happens when we die?" asked Ben. "Do we go into some sort of spiritual hibernation till we zip off to heaven in the final chapter?"

"Certainly not," said the Super. People sat forward. What *did* happen, then?

"Well we don't go to some other place like Purgatory, do we?" asked Ben.

"No, we don't. The Catholics made that up. It's not in the Bible at all."

The congregation was hooked now – what *did* happen?

The Super carried on regardless. "And we certainly don't go to heaven on the Last Day!"

Someone in the congregation gasped – it might have been Mrs.

Edwards, faithful Mrs. Edwards, having apoplexy at the Super's heresy.

"Isn't that a bit, sort of, heretical?" asked Ben.

"No, it's very biblical. You see, in Revelation, it makes it quite clear that heaven comes to earth. "Then I saw the Holy City, the new Jerusalem, coming down out of heaven from God." Revelation 21 verse 2. Verse 3 says, "Now the dwelling of God is with men, and he will live with them." You see, the description of the Holy City is full of human activity: kings, commerce, streets, treasures, a tree which has leaves for the healing of the nations. At the end of time, heaven comes to earth and eternity is *here*."

There was a collective sigh of relief. It wasn't heresy, then.

"OK," said Ben. "I can cope with the novel idea that we don't go to heaven, it comes to us. But what happens between now and then?"

"We have a lovely sleep in Paradise."

"So Paradise isn't the same as heaven, then?"

"I don't think so," said the Super. "When Jesus dies on the Cross he definitely doesn't go to heaven – that comes at the resurrection when he shows us what will happen on the Last Day when the general resurrection takes place. The only difference is that then heaven will come to us. So where does he go? He goes to Paradise, and we know that because he says to the thief, "Today you will be with me in Paradise.""

"So is Paradise where the harp-playing and sitting on clouds happens?"

"No, that's fiction as well. In Paradise we sleep, awaiting the Last Day's resurrection. But it is a good place to be, and all is well. Then, the Bible says, we "awake"."

"So is that what it means when Jesus says, "In my Father's house are many rooms and I go to prepare a place for you"[72]?"

"Sort of. Bishop Tom Wright says that the Greek word used for "place" in John 14 actually means "temporary staging-post" rather than "final destination", which would make sense, wouldn't it?"

★ ★ ★

---

[72] John 14: 2

The worship had gone well, and Ben, as always, took the recording of the service back to Brendan, so that he could enjoy the worship and the teaching without having to be there. Ben didn't think much about it until later that Sunday afternoon, when he got a text from Brendan asking him to pop downstairs and have a chat.

Brendan pushed a piece of paper at him.

Ben scanned the handwritten script, which seemed to be a sermon about resurrection, based on Romans 8:38: "Nothing can separate us from the love of God in Christ Jesus our Lord." It was headed "Brendan's Last Sermon" and picked up on the Bible teaching of the morning, making four points:

1. God is with us at all times, even when we're frightened about dying;

2. The earth matters (heaven will be here) so we should look after it;

3. What we do on earth matters (we should work hard at the process of transformation which will be made complete by God on the Last Day);

4. Jesus is in charge (Matthew 28:20: "I have been given all authority in heaven *and on earth*"), so all will be well.

Brendan wrote another sentence on his pad, and pushed it over to Ben. It read, "To be preached at my funeral."

Ben looked up, his eyes watering.

Brendan smiled, through his own tears, and raised his thumb.

Ben raised his thumb in response. No words had been said, but they didn't need to be. All *would* be well.

Chapter 44

Louisa was feeling rather superfluous. Much of the essential work was now being undertaken by others. The clinical trials were due to start within a few weeks. There were 20 hospitals across the world whichhad been lured into participating both by the publicity that the trials had already received due to the Prime Minister's announcement in the House of Commons and by the money which was being made available up-front by the Brendan Priest Cancer Care Trust. One of the 20 hospitals was Newcastle's Freeman. So Louisa decided, on a gloomy, wet and otherwise meeting-less and meaningless February afternoon, to go along to see the clinician overseeing the Newcastle trials.

Dr. Hanif Aggarwal greeted her warmly. "I'm very pleased to meet you, Louisa, because I have heard such a lot about you over the last few weeks."

Louisa raised an eyebrow. "Really? What are they saying? It's probably completely untrue..."

Dr. Aggarwal laughed. "All good, I assure you. They say that you're breathing a bit of much-needed fresh air into the stuffy bureaucracy of health care."

Now it was Louisa's turn to laugh. "I only hope that I can keep bluffing them into thinking that I know what I'm doing!"

They both smiled, instantly warming to each other. Dr. Aggarwal then explained what the trials were going to involve.

"We've identified ten SCCA patients already connected with the Northern Centre for Cancer Care, at various early pre-radiotherapy stages in their treatment, but now awaiting the next stage. They've all agreed to enter these trials, and I've personally chatted with all ten and can say that they're actually rather excited to be able to participate in such a high-profile research project – especially because it is linked with your father. It's a shame that this comes too late for him to participate personally, as more radiotherapy is out of the question for him. But at least he'll know that something good's coming out of his illness."

Louisa gulped. She didn't like the sound of that "too late for him" comment, but knew that it was true, in the sense that only so much radiotherapy can be endured before it starts doing far more harm than good.

Dr. Aggarwal then explained how the "double-blind" aspect of the trials would be conducted.

"Of course I can't tell you which patients are involved, for it's totally confidential. Nor can I tell you officially which of the four drug regimens of chemotherapy they're on, except to say that the regimen is the same for all ten patients here – and they've been randomly paired off to receive the five different dosages, but no-one except me knows which dosage goes with which pair of patients."

Louisa was puzzled. "Won't those administering the dosages be able to tell whether they're giving 200mg or 600mg?"

Dr. Aggarwal smiled. "You'd think so, wouldn't you? But the dosages are pre-prepared and delivered to each patient in individualised vials with their name clearly labelled, and the dosage is mixed with a placebo to the same volume of 700mg in every vial. The various vials are being prepared right now in my lab under strict controls, and the labels will be attached by me personally when each batch is ready. We expect to have all the vials prepared by the end of this month, ready to start on March 1st."

They continued chatting about the trials, then Dr. Aggarwal turned to more personal matters.

"I hope you don't mind me saying this, Louisa, but I think what you're doing is wonderful. The world of medical research does tend to be very competitive and cut-throat, but these trials seem to be shot through with a sense of generosity and charity which is why most of us came into health care in the first place."

Louisa nodded. She too had been inspired into nursing by a desire to help people, and it had somehow kept her going through all the hassles she'd endured. But there were too many nurses, like the pre-conversion Sister Lillian, who'd lost that sense of vocation altogether.

"And, if I may say so, though I've never met your father, I've great respect for him. In my faith, Hinduism, we're taught to pursue dharma, which is the calling to fit in with the unity of all things through our own personal duty of integrity. I recognise that in your father and find him an inspiration. Do pass on my good wishes to him and assure him of my prayers."

Louisa was moved by the doctor's sincerity, and promised to convey his message that evening. The afternoon had not been meaningless after all – far from it.

★ ★ ★

Brendan had had a good afternoon too. Melanie had been round again, and had enabled him to bend his tongue upwards rather than just lift it flat to the top of his mouth. She'd achieved this by starting with the lifting movement which Brendan had mastered last time, but then putting one finger on the top of his tongue and pressing upwards with another finger underneath the tip of his tongue, to get Brendan's ravaged tongue muscles used to the idea.

It had been hard work, but after the sort of effort which bulged out the veins in his temple and sent rivulets of sweat coursing down his forehead, Brendan was thrilled to find that he could *feel* his tongue bending. "I haa hee i be-i", he shouted, triumphantly, nearly biting off Melanie's fingers. Then, more slowly, no fingers in the way: "I han hee i benin!"

"YES!" shouted Melanie, high-fiving Brendan. "You can *feel* it bending, now, can't you? Yes!" And she immediately took his cheeks in her hands and landed a big kiss right on his lips. "And did you hear the "n" sound?"

Brendan nodded, red-faced both with his achievement and with the kiss.

"Now try something else. Say Nana for me a few times." Brendan felt a nana as he said it, but he kept saying it till he got really rather good at it. "Now try to feel your way with your tongue a little bit further forward along the top of your mouth towards your front teeth and see if you can make the nana into a dada." And he did. It took a bit of fiddling around with Melanie's fingers inside his mouth, but after a minute or so he was saying Dada like a proud but bemused ten-month-old before adoring parents who suddenly think they've got a budding intellectual in the family. He laughed at the thought of re-learning these basic skills. He and Jenna had taken nine months or so encouraging each of their children to start speaking then had spent the rest of their childhoods hoping that they'd shut up.

"Now a final lesson for today. I want you to try to say your name. You won't be able to say the "r" sound, but see what it sounds like. Brendan has some tricky combinations of "n" and "d", so it won't be easy." Well, Brendan did his best, going through "Bennan" to "Beddad", then "Beddan", and finally managing "Benadan, which, if he tried his best, sort-of became "Bendan" if the listener was aware of what he was trying to say.

"Well done!" enthused Melanie. Now we're going to have a quick practice, and then get the family in so they can listen to you. Are you ready? Repeat after me: My name is Brendan."

"My ame is Benadan."

"My aim will be Brendan too if you don't do better than that, mate. Come on, Brendan, remember the "n"."

"My aname is Benadan."

"Now you've gone all Italian on me. One-a-more-a-time-a: My name is Brendan."

"My name is Benadan." – which got him another kiss.

Melanie shrieked and charged out of the door. "Calling all members of the Priest family," she shouted. "Come to hear the Reverend Brendan Priest give his latest pronouncement!" Doors opened. Ruth poked her head over the banister, little Matthew in her arms, looking upwards to see what was going on. Ben was just coming downstairs.

"Is that everybody?" asked Melanie.

"Well, it'll have to do. Sit down there on the sofa, facing Brendan."

They did what they were told. Melanie may have been only in her early thirties but she was very enthusiastic and compelling.

"Right, Brendan, your audience awaits!"

A rather red-faced Brendan stood up and cleared his throat as if he was going to make the speech of his life. "My name is Benadan," he said, clearly and deliberately, then high-fived Melanie who was shrieking "Yes! Yes!" as she danced round the room.

Ruth and Ben laughed, clapped and joined in the shrieking and dancing, but then Matthew started screaming at the sudden noise so they all sat down and had a breather.

Chapter 45

CBS broke the news story at 2.38pm on February 18th, though it never made it onto the BBC news[73] and quickly disappeared off the American national news too. It was just another appalling American gun tragedy which seemed to most British people who heard about it just one more good reason why American gun laws were ridiculous, and to most American readers just one more good reason why they had to have guns to defend themselves. The headline was "Relative Held in Texas Quintuple Murders":

> *Five family members were found dead at their home in southeast Texas, and a relative is being held by police for questioning. The Austin County Sheriff's Office has said in a statement that deputies found the bodies of three adults and two children on Sunday afternoon at a home in Bellville.*
>
> *Authorities would not release any additional information about the slayings, including the names of the victims, their relationship, or how they were killed. The Texas Rangers are helping with the investigation.*
>
> *Sources later told CBS Affiliate KHOU that the victims were the wife, two children, brother and pregnant sister-in-law of the suspect, who was picked up Sunday on an unrelated charge. KHOU correspondent Courtney Zukowski reports that, according to one source, the bodies were discovered when another relative came to the home to take the children out for the afternoon.*
>
> *The station's sources said four bodies were found inside the home, and a fifth was found in a backyard pond.*
>
> *"It's a devastating loss," Austin County Sgt. Paul Faircloth told KHOU. "Everyone knows everybody here and it reaches through to the hearts of the community."*

Like most violent news stories in America, most people who knew anyone in Austin scanned the subsequent reports to reassure themselves that they didn't know anyone involved, then forgot about it.

★ ★ ★

---

[73] The news report is only slightly changed from an online CBS news story uploaded at 2.38pm on January 18th 2010, found at
www.cbsnews.com/stories/2010/01/18/national/main6111935.shtml

The phone call happened eight days later, and it was Ruth who answered the phone.

"Have I got the right house for Brendan Priest?" asked the soft, American, female voice.

"Yes, that's right," said Ruth. "But he's not able to speak right now."

"Oh," said the voice. "Is he with someone?"

It seemed to Ruth a strange question to ask, and she felt like saying that it was none of her business. Ruth only knew two American women, Esther and Fahada – and she was sure that this mystery caller was neither of them. But she'd also detected a catch in the woman's voice, as if she was close to tears, so she caught herself before telling the woman off.

"No, it isn't that. He's ill and he can't speak at all, to anyone."

The woman promptly gave an anguished cry and burst into tears. Ruth couldn't work out what was happening. Who was this woman, and why was she so upset?

"Can I help you?" she asked. "I'm Ruth, Brendan's daughter."

There was a long silence on the other end, broken only by sobs and jerky breathing. Ruth waited patiently. Finally the woman spoke.

"Hello, Ruth. Brendan told me all about you. My name's Carol. I live *(her voice caught as she said it)* – or rather *lived* – in Texas. I spent a few weeks with your father when he cycled through the States on his first journey. I don't know whether he mentioned me..." Carol broke off, as if she was unsure what else to say.

"Carol? The cyclist? That's great! Dad couldn't stop talking about you for ages when he got back! He'll be thrilled that you've got in touch." Then Ruth paused. "But I'm sad to have to tell you that he's very ill. He's got cancer of the tongue and throat and he's only just learning how to speak again after his operations and treatment."

"Oh no..." said Carol. "That's awful. I seem to bring bad luck on everyone."

There was a pause before Carol continued, "I don't know what to say except that I'm so sorry and I wish him all the best. Please tell him that I was asking after him."

And with that, the phone went dead.

Ruth dialled 1471 but the number was unobtainable. She rushed off upstairs to tell her Dad, who was thrilled to hear who the caller was, but then perplexed as Ruth recounted the conversation. They both speculated on the significance of the "live, or rather lived" detail, and on the bit about her bringing bad luck on everyone. What had happened to her?

Brendan spent the rest of that Tuesday remembering some of the adventures that he and Carol had shared. They'd met in Kansas, when Brendan caught her up on the road from El Dorado to Wichita. When her bike fell to bits, he'd put her and the bike into the kayak on his trailer and ridden her into the centre of Oklahoma City while she whooped and screamed with the hilarity of it all, causing mayhem on the city streets as everyone laughed and pointed.

Over the next few days they'd shared a few kisses and hugs and things could have gone a lot further if Brendan hadn't told Carol that he needed to concentrate on the journey rather than start a relationship. They'd continued cycling together after that, but Carol had clearly been disappointed and the conversation wasn't anywhere near as easy or warm.

It had been a bit of a relief when they'd arrived at Austin and gone their separate ways, only to meet again briefly the following day when Brendan got knocked off his bike and needed her help. That brought a sort of healing to their friendship and their second farewell had been warm and not necessarily final. Despite the fact that they'd lost contact and Brendan's second journey had made it impossible to renew their friendship, he'd thought of her often. Only a few weeks before when the letter from Fahada had arrived with its Texan postmark he'd instantly hoped that it was from Carol.

Now she'd finally made contact, but what was the matter with her? How could he get in touch?

Chapter 46

Louisa and Ben, like Ruth, were delighted and disturbed by the phone call from Carol, but felt unable to help unravel the mystery. Everyone hoped that she'd get in touch again.

Louisa had another job to fulfil, however, and couldn't work out what to do. It was all Esther's fault. She'd phoned up a fortnight earlier with a new project.

"Hi, Louisa!"

She'd instantly known who it was. No-one else whom she knew had Esther's drawl.

"Hi, Esther!" she'd replied. It still felt odd having a media megastar as her employer and friend.

"I've had an idea, sweetie, that I hope you can help me with," declared Esther in her typical cut-to-the-chase fashion, and she'd proceeded to explain her plans. She wanted to do a series on her chat-shows about the clinical trials and wondered if Louisa could set it up in Newcastle. "I'd only need three or four of the patients and access to their families – I'm sure it'll work..."

Louisa had tried to explain about the confidentiality involved in the trials, that no-one except the clinician heading the trials knew which patients were involved, but it'd cut no ice with Esther. "Oh, don't worry about that, sweetie, we can work around little details like that!" She'd laughed, and so had Louisa. This was, after all, She Who Can Do Anything.

"I'll see what I can do," Louisa had promised.

★ ★ ★

Dr. Aggarwal had been immediately very concerned and cautious. "The only way we could do it would be if the patients themselves waived their right to confidentiality. I'll write to all ten of them, explaining what's being planned and asking if they're prepared to get involved."

He'd been true to his word, had contacted those selected for the trials and heard back from them by the end of the week. Five of them were keen to be involved, and were invited, with their families, to a meeting in Dr. Aggarwal's office to meet Louisa and talk it through. It was scheduled for February 27th, only two days before the trials were to begin.

Louisa had contacted Esther. "That's good news," she'd said. "I'll send a film crew over for the meeting, but it's on the clear understanding that if any of the five patients decide not to go through with it, none of the footage from the meeting will be used, and I'll wait till the trials start and only film those who are willing."

It had sounded good to Louisa, so here she was on February 27th, in Dr. Aggarwal's office, with 23 people plus a film crew, waiting for a live link to the Oracle Studios in Detroit to be activated. Esther had insisted on it, so that she could meet with the patients and their families and answer their questions.

The five patients were an interesting bunch: a rather pale and saggy housewife in her fifties from North Shields who looked as if she was here solely to get on the telly and had come with her two pale and saggy daughters and a loud grandchild in a pushchair; a professional-looking thirty-something lady from Durham who looked as if to her cancer was a campaign to be won, who was on her own; a newly-retired headmaster from Carlisle with his rather nervous wife; a Corbridge scaffolder with a finely-tuned physique and tattoos, who'd come with a group of his mates and was trying to act tough even though he looked scared stiff; and a retired civil servant from North Tyneside, who had a mass of scars all down one side of his face and across the top of his head. It looked as if he'd been cajoled into coming by his domineering wife.

Suddenly, the flat-screen monitor crackled and showed the familiar face of Esther Blanchett, media megastar. There was a gasp from someone, probably (Louisa thought) the woman from Shields.

"Hi y'all!" was the greeting from across the Atlantic. "So good to see y'all. How 'bout we introduce ourselves? I'm Esther, as you probably know, and I'm keen to document your progress through the trials, if you're willing. You're gonna be the stars of the show, however, if you wanna be – and you'll be paid the going rate for appearance fees. It'll all be done in accordance with the proper procedures and the contract which I'll ask each of you to sign, before the trials commence. Now, how 'bout the five of you introduce yourselves to me and tell me who you've brought along?"

The introductions followed. It was quite amusing for Louisa to see the five in action. Sharon from Shields almost curtseyed to the screen, so overwhelmed was she to be in the (virtual) company of a celebrity. Dawn, the bank manager from Durham, said very little and seemed unsure why she'd put herself into the position of sharing a room with the family from Shields, and seemed to be treating it like the early rounds of The Apprentice. Eric the headmaster was quite chatty, as was the scaffolder – who was called Darren. His mates seemed to be enjoying the opportunity to chat with Esther too, as if it was a competition to see who could chat her up most effectively. Alan, the retired civil servant, was less hearty, if not truculent.

It was Alan who came up with the first question: "How much are we going to get paid?" His wife dug him in the ribs with her elbow, but the question had been asked before his wince escaped.

"The contract specifies eight interviews in addition to this conversation now, which will only be used on the programme if you're all happy. There'll be an initial interview with you and your families, then one at the start and end of each three-week treatment period, followed by a catch-up interview six months after the last treatment to see how you are. For every programme you appear in, you'll each receive $10,000."

The room was instantly silent, then just as quickly filled with a babble of voices, especially from Sharon and her daughters, who were reacting as if they'd just won the Lottery.

"What if we have to drop out of the trials for any reason?" asked Eric, the headteacher.

"Good question," said Esther. "But I'm afraid the contract is quite clear that you only get paid for the shows you appear on. If you keep going and appear on all eight shows, you get $80,000. If you don't, you don't."

"What if the cancer kills us before the end of the programmes?" asked Dawn – which rather killed the euphoria.

"Same thing, I'm afraid, Dawn. You only get paid for footage shown on the show."

The mood grew a bit sombre, so Esther tried to jack it up again by asking Sharon what she was going to do with the money.

"I'm taking the bairns to Ibiza," she declared – which puzzled Esther who was unfamiliar both with "bairn" and "Ibiza". But it made everyone else smile – especially when she added, "Then I'm gonna buy wor Tommy them drums he's allus wanted."

All five signed up there and then, and received an envelope and a copy of the contract. The envelope contained a signing-on bonus of $10,000 which included their payment for footage of the meeting being shown on the following day's "See Esther" show.

★ ★ ★

"Now here's where you earn your bonus, Louisa," said Esther. "You'll be too busy yourself to do this, but I want you to recruit someone to accompany the patients through the trials. It needs to be a nurse so that they can help explain the treatment, but it'd be really great if it was someone who was a bit of a character, someone you wouldn't expect to see on TV, but someone not afraid to be themselves and be real with the patients and their families on camera, responding to their highs and lows. Does anyone come to mind?"

"No," said Louisa. "How long have I got?"

"Trials start in two days time, don't they? So I need them ready for then."

Then Louisa got a flash of inspiration. She knew *exactly* the right person for the job. But would she do it?

Chapter 47

The final two Sundays of Ben's challenge had come and gone. The Popemobile was a bit of a let-down – the vehicle itself arrived by charter plane courtesy of Esther's conversation on the phone with His Holiness himself, but it just looked like a customised minivan and even the amplified choral music didn't seem to help people understand what it was. Ben had briefly considered getting dressed up in a Pope fancy-dress outfit, but thought that that would be taking things a bit far and might annoy the local Catholics.

The elephant, however, was a fitting climax to the 25 challenges. Ben found it by trawling through various websites offering Indian weddings, and eventually found one in Bradford which hired out its own trained elephant. Only the wealthiest families could afford the full package, which included the elephant decorated in red and gold cloths accompanied by traditional dhol drummers and Bhangra wedding dancers. Cheapskate bridegrooms apparently went on a white horse, or on the bus. But Ben wanted the elephant, and managed to hire it for £2,500 for the weekend. With the dancers and drummers it would have been £8,000, so he convinced himself that he'd got a good deal.

"It'll come with its handler and cloths and the howdah..." said the man on the phone.

"The what?" asked Ben.

"The howdah is the seat and canopy," explained the man on the phone, making Ben feel a bit stupid and insensitive.

"Oh, I see. Sorry about that – I'm not used to riding elephants." Ben had meant it as a joke, but the man on the phone took him seriously.

"Don't worry about that. You'll be accompanied at all times by the elephant's handler. Do you have a bike helmet?"

Ben instantly foresaw a picture of himself wearing his bright yellow bike-helmet, perched precariously on the back of an elephant, doing arm signals to turn right. But then he thought of a good question. "How fast does the elephant go?"

The man on the phone was quiet for a few seconds. "How fast do you want her to go?" he asked, but then, without waiting for an answer, continued, "She can probably safely go about the same pace as a human."

"That sounds perfect," said Ben, which piqued the curiosity of the man on the phone.

"What did you have in mind?"

Ben told him about the Challenge, and the journey from the house to the church, over three miles away. "Will that be a problem for the elephant?" he asked.

"Not at all – but the handler's not used to walking more than 200 yards, so I'll warn him that he'll have a bit more exercise than usual."

★ ★ ★

The elephant arrived on the Saturday afternoon in a huge ex-removal van which had straw on its floor and windows at the front so that the elephant could see where it was going. The handler/driver was from Bradford and spoke in a broad Yorkshire accent, even though he looked Indian. When Ben asked about the window in the van, Kev (the handler) explained that the elephant used to get travel-sick. "And you don't want to clear up after that, I'm telling you."

This final Challenge had been well publicised in the News Guardian, and there were crowds outside the house, who oooh'd, aaah'd and cheered when the elephant, decked out in its cloths and howdah was led out of the van. It was a magnificent sight, and one almost certainly unprecedented for Beverley Terrace. The next cheer came when Kev produced an aluminium ladder which he propped up against the elephant's side, up which he climbed to check the fastenings on the howdah, before descending and beckoning Ben forward. Resplendent in his fluorescent bike helmet, Ben wobbled his way up the ladder and sat gingerly in the howdah, which was surprisingly comfortable. He felt a bit of a wally as the crowd waved them off, some following and dancing round the elephant, who plodded on regardless. At the first corner a huge shout went up when the elephant lifted its tail and deposited an enormous round turd in the middle of the road.

"Treat it as a roundabout!" yelled one joker from the crowd and everyone roared.

The crowds lined the route, and Ben thoroughly enjoyed the view from his elevated position, even though the howdah swayed rather alarmingly from side to side as the elephant trundled on.

Even though it was a cold morning, the elephant seemed oblivious – though Kev started to complain that it was too far on such a cold day. "Not for her, but for me!" he laughed, taking off one of his many layers because he was working up quite a sweat.

By the time they turned into Jact Lane, the crowd following the elephant and lining the pavements was almost as numerous as for the crowd-surf world-record back in November. And when they finally reached the church there was a huge cheer. Kev flopped down against a tree, and Ben had to shout for someone to get a ladder so that he could descend and get ready for leading the worship.

As usual, the crowds were too big to fit into church, but the tannoy relaying the service was now part of the scenery, and hundreds congregated on the lawn outside, enjoying the crispness of the morning and the sight of the elephant lying down next to church, tethered to a tree while Kev went off in a taxi to get the van.

The worship was vibrant. The band had put in extra effort, and produced some fine music to accompany the songs. They'd been practising a new song based on Isaiah's vision of God in the Temple, which spoke of God being high and lifted up, which was a fine worship song but got most people thinking of Ben on the back of the elephant.

Ben used the old Indian story of the blind men and the elephant as the basis for his "reflections". "I want to tell you a story that comes from India and has many different versions. Six blind men were asked to work out what an elephant looked like by feeling different parts of the elephant's body. The blind man who feels a leg says the elephant's like a pillar; the one who feels the tail says the elephant's like a rope; the one who feels the trunk says the elephant's like a tree branch; the one who feels the ear says the elephant's like a hand fan; the one who feels the belly says the elephant's like a wall; and the one who feels the tusk says the elephant's like a solid pipe. A king explains to them: "All of you are right. The reason every one of you is telling it differently is because each one of you touched a different part of the elephant. So, actually the elephant has all the features you mentioned. But your knowledge is incomplete, because you haven't seen the whole of it."

"This story's been used to illustrate all kinds of truths, but I want to ask you to reflect on the elephant you saw this morning. You saw the whole thing, and yet you still don't really understand what an elephant is, do you? I certainly don't and I was riding on top of it all the way! I know what it looks like, but that's all I can really say about it. Others will know different things about elephants, or tell different stories about elephants, but none of us can know *everything* there is to know about elephants. But so what? We don't *need* to know, do we?

"Most of the versions of the story I told are about the principle of living in harmony with people who have different belief systems, and say that no single understanding is complete and perfect. I want to echo that, but also say that I think the Christian view of God as seen in Jesus is the best picture I've found. But life will always only give us part of the experience, part of the understanding, part of the totality which is overseen by God.

"I've now completed the last of my 25 Challenges, but there is so much more to be experienced, so much more to be learnt as we stumble blindly into the future. For Brendan, of course, life has brought its own specific challenge, in which we will continue to support him, even though these Challenges are finished. For us as a human race we're constantly battling to see a bigger picture, to work out what our place and responsibilities should be in this world of ours, and to work together to build a better understanding of what life's all about.

"Jesus never saw an elephant, but he tried to describe something just as indescribable, which he called the Kingdom of God. He said that it's like a net, like a seed, like a feast, like yeast, like a treasure-chest, like a field, like a child. Lots of different pictures – each in its own way helpful, yet no one picture adequate. Yet it's important that we know how important this Kingdom is – for it's the greatest treasure of all.

"It's simple, really, though. The Kingdom is wherever the King rules. So it is wherever and whenever *you* are, *if* you let God rule. It's as simple and uncomplicated as that, but, of course, it'll mean thousands of different things in different situations. Brendan's struggle with cancer is at the forefront of our minds, but we also know that because Brendan puts God first he's already enjoying life in the Kingdom of God. And we can do the same.

"Are *you* at peace? Do you *feel* at peace? No matter what might happen to you? Putting God first, letting him rule *your* life is the Christian answer to the big questions of ultimate meaning. We may not see the whole of the Kingdom, but we've been given in Jesus an insight into the DNA of the Kingdom, which is shot through every part of it. And that, my friends, is all that we need.

"I want to end by telling you how the Sufi Muslim version of the story ends, in which the men are not blind but have been led into a darkened room to examine the elephant. The story ends with the wish that someone had brought a candle with them."

Ben paused at this point. People thought that he'd finished. But then came his one-line conclusion: "But the Gospel says that Jesus is the Light of the World."

The congregation sighed. Ben wasn't supposed to preach, as he hadn't started his formal training – but none of them cared, because God was speaking through him. The prayers, led by a Local Preacher, encouraged the people to own Ben's words, to respond to God's request to rule in their hearts, and to pray for those undergoing particular struggles. There was a silence, in which several people said afterwards they'd felt God's presence in the room, and one lady even said that she felt that she'd been healed of her back pain.

Some remarkable things were happening...

Alan's Story: November 9th 1989

On the day that the Berlin Wall came down, heralding a new era of peace in Europe, the garden wall between Alan's house and the one next door came down too, heralding the start of a war.

It had been leaning over Alan's roses for some years, the cracks in it getting longer and broader, until a huge section of it, some twenty-foot or so, came crashing down in a gale in the middle of the night. Alan rushed out into the front garden in his pyjamas, wondering whether there'd been a plane crash, but could see nothing amiss till the next morning when Pauline alerted him to it over breakfast.

He went to work, fully expecting it all to be sorted when he got home, but Pauline met him with a piece of paper when he got in.

"Thought you might need to look at this," she said, as she took Alan Junior up for his bath. It was a builder's estimate for £2,495 (including VAT) for a new wall, with some photographs of what the wall used to look like, from Alan's garden. There was a letter attached, from a solicitor.

"Dear Sir,
We are instructed by your neighbour, Mr. Arthur Brown, of 14 Murton Close, that you have neglected to care for your side of Mr. Brown's wall, and have allowed it to deteriorate without attention to pointing (as shown in the enclosed photographs) resulting in its collapse. Our client has obtained the enclosed quotation to build a new wall, and is willing to pay half the costs towards it. He accepts that whilst the maintenance of his wall is his responsibility, your planting of impenetrable rosebushes (as shown in the enclosed photographs) immediately in front of the wall rendered the task impossible, and so he believes that the responsibility of paying for the new wall should be shared equally.
We are confident that you will agree and ask that you send a cheque for the amount of £1247.50 to our address by first post on November 30th so that the matter can be settled before it goes to court."

Alan was apoplectic, and stormed round to the neighbour's front door to demand to know what it was all about.

"I've been instructed by my solicitor not to say anything to you," said Mr. Brown, and shut the door.

Alan stormed back round to his house and slammed the door. "Arthur Brown – Arf a brain more like! The cheek of the man! As if we should pay for his bloody wall when it's wrecked my bloody roses!"

Pauline shushed him from the kitchen.

"Don't swear in front of the bairn, dear. And the roses weren't exactly prize blooms were they? I'm glad to get rid of them, to tell you the truth, they were so thick and ugly, and little Alan's pricked his fingers on them several times."

"Oh, that's right!" shouted Alan. "Have a go, why don't you, like you always do? You never take my side, do you? Well, I'm off down the Farmer's!" With that, he hurled himself out the house, banging the door shut behind him, completely ignoring the fact that his dinner was just being served, as always, at 6.05pm by the ever- dutiful Pauline.

March 2013

Chapter 48

It had now been exactly 14 months since Lilian's life-changing religious experience, and she and Louisa had developed a good friendship. When Lilian's six-month "trial period" was over, Louisa had told her to carry on with the good work, her reward for which was to be pulled into and enclosed by Lilian's bosom like a small child on an under-inflated bouncy castle.

When Louisa left in October, Lilian took her and the other nurses out to As You Like It[74], an amazing restaurant and music venue in Jesmond, where someone she knew was appearing in the "Supper Club" – a Friday/Saturday night event with live blues, soul, swing or jazz as a backdrop for the crowds lounging around on unmatching sofas and a random selection of strange chairs.

They'd kept in touch, with Louisa popping into the Unit at the Freeman whenever she was visiting. Invariably Lilian would show Louisa the office cupboard in which the memory card still sat, which held the pictures of Lilian at her lowest point. "It's still there!" Lilian would point out.

Just after the New Year, on the anniversary of the Big God Moment, as Lilian named it, Louisa had gone in to find Lilian strangely subdued. "What's the matter?" she'd asked.

Lilian had looked up from her desk and smiled. "I was just thinking how good God's been to me when I deserved to be punished for what I did – and I'm still here and God's still doing good things in my life. Only yesterday we had one patient going downhill fast who asked me to pray with her! Me! And do you know what happened?"

She cackled, then broke into a big booming laugh. "God only went and healed her, didn't He?" And she collapsed in fits of laughter. "That got the doctors talking, I can tell you!"

---

[74] It is just as described – a fantastic place (www.asyoulikeitjesmond.com)

A month later, Lilian had seemed subdued again. "I don't know what it is but I feel that God's got something else in store for me and I'm unsure what to do about it. I suppose I've got to be patient and keep praying for Him to guide me."

So now, when Louisa walked in and asked her to do a job interviewing patients on the clinical trials, Lilian just threw her hands up in the air. "I knew it!" she shouted. "I *knew* that something special was just around the corner. Of course I'll do it – but what do I have to do?"

Louisa explained that it was meant to be just a short-term secondment from her job in the Unit, which would be kept open for her. It would only be for an initial two months, then for a further week in six months time. "You'll have to accompany the patients to their treatment, explain what is happening, and go to their homes to see how they are coping with it all."

"Sounds good to me," said Lilian. "What's the catch?"

"You'll be being filmed for "See Esther"."

Lilian looked shocked, her mouth open like the entrance to the Tyne Tunnel. She stood there with her hand to her mouth. "Lordy," she whispered. "Me, on television?"

Then she laughed loudly, like the scream on a horror film. "I'll have to have a makeover," she declared. "When do I start?"

"Tomorrow."

★ ★ ★

Lilian turned out to be a natural in front of camera, even without a proper makeover, though she'd managed to get her hair done. Her "screen test" earlier that morning had proved spectacular, when she did a little dance in front of the camera. Despite the fact that her dancing was like watching five people trying to get out of a collapsed three-man tent, her confidence and vitality won the director's thumbs-up, as long as she promised not to dance again. Her rich baritone voice was good for audio and she had a stage-whisper which was as clear as David Attenborough stalking gorillas, which augured well for the in-hospital scenes.

So in the early afternoon, Lilian's TV career began, as she glided like a genial fork-lift truck along the corridors of the Freeman, showing the five patients (and the camera) the lab where the chemotherapy vials had been prepared, then taking them down to the radiotherapy unit where their daily fractions of radiation would be administered. Even though she was a newcomer herself to this branch of nursing, she'd done her homework the night before, remembered her lines and captivated them all by her formidable presence.

Esther phoned Louisa the following day. "She's a Godsend, that Lilian character – where d'you find her?"

"God sent her," said Louisa, and explained their story.

"You really are one amazing lady, you know," said Esther, at the end of the account. "I chose wisely when I employed you, didn't I?"

★ ★ ★

Carol phoned again exactly a week after her first conversation. It happened to be Ruth who answered, as she had last time.

"Hello?" said the same hesitant, soft American voice.

"Carol?" said Ruth. "Is that you? Oh, I'm so pleased that you've called again. We were all really worried about you after last time. How are you?"

There was a long pause. "Not good, really. Can you give me an email address for you, and I'll send you an explanation of what's happened. I can't talk about it yet, but at least you'll know why I'm getting in touch after so long."

Ruth dictated her own email address, and was just about to say "Don't go" when the phone went dead again. She rushed upstairs to tell her Dad about it, before going back downstairs in the hope that the email would come through immediately. Several minutes later, it did, but it was ten minutes or so before she came back upstairs and handed over a print-out to her Dad.

"It's awful," she said, and waited for him to read it.

It was a short message, informing them that Carol's son had been caught embezzling funds from his company and had gone on the run. He'd gone home one morning while the police were looking for him, murdered his wife, his two children, and his brother and pregnant sister-in-law who happened to be staying overnight, then drove off in his car to throw himself off a bridge, only to be caught by the police.

Carol wrote at the bottom, "I've lost everything, and I didn't know what to do or who could help. Then I remembered Brendan and felt that he was the right person to talk to, only for you to tell me that he too had been struck down, and I felt that everything was hopeless. But today I woke up and felt that I needed to talk it out or I'd go mad, and that Brendan was the man who'd listen. If he doesn't feel up to seeing me, I'll understand completely – but if he's able to help me one last time, I'd come running."

Brendan put the message down and stared into space. Tears welled up and ran down his cheeks. He scribbled on his pad: "Tell her to come at once. I'd love to see her." Then he thrust the pad at Ruth, and shooed her to deal with it immediately.

Chapter 49

Jack Turner, District Chair, happened to call the following day. Brendan showed him the email from Carol. "What do I do?" he wrote on his pad.

"You do what you're called by God to do. To listen with the whole of your being. To be yourself. To give yourself as fully as you can to help people in their hour of need. To show God's love."

Brendan scrawled on the pad: "Not much then!"

"Do your best," said Jack, wisely. "That's all any of us can do. And leave the rest to God."

They settled into another comfortable silence. This had been their pattern over the last few months. Jack had popped in roughly once a month, sharing with Brendan news about the District, gossip about what was happening at Methodist HQ, but mostly an hour or so passed sitting together in quietness. But on this occasion, Brendan was keen to converse, even if he could only do it slowly by writing on his pad.

"Have you ever played Cluedo?" he wrote.

Jack smiled. "Oh yes – we used to play it all the time when the kids were growing up. Professor Plum in the ballroom with a candlestick. I was useless at it – and the kids always cheated."

Brendan wrote for several minutes, then passed the pad across to Jack, who read: "Cluedo is a race to see who can get to the end first. It can be very frustrating, as new details emerge which knock your half-baked theories out the window. You often realise that you've been drawn down the wrong path. Like life. We often wish that we knew what was in the envelope, the solution to all our searchings. Yet the Bible tells us, doesn't it?"

Jack thought hard. What did Brendan mean? "Personally, I like the bit in Revelation 5 when the angels gather to worship around the great scroll of Life."

Brendan nodded enthusiastically. They were thinking along the same lines.

Jack continued: "They despair because they wonder who is worthy to open the scroll and read the scroll of Life. Then the Christ figure steps forward – of course, the Lamb of God is worthy. Why? Because He defeated death. He won the victory. Nothing else matters as much as this. That's what gives Life its meaning."

Brendan scribbled away again. "Eavesdropping on eternity. Also Revelation 7."

Jack looked puzzled, then pulled out his Bible and read the chapter. "Ah yes," he said. "I see what you mean. We get a different set of worshippers, this time the faithful redeemed people of God who've come through their suffering, and are now personally comforted by their God who comes down from his throne to wipe away their tears."

Brendan scribbled away some more: "At the end, the envelope reveals the answer to the whodunnit: God did it, in the world, with Jesus. The trouble is, we don't always see the clues."

Jack prayed with Brendan, thanking God that Brendan knew the answers, and asking God to help both of them share the answers with others.

★ ★ ★

Paul arrived back from Uganda the following afternoon. It was three weeks since he'd last seen his wife and son, so there was much rejoicing. Matthew cried when Paul threw him up in the air but then was gurgling with pleasure a few moments later when Paul pushed his nose into his son's tummy and tickled him.

Ruth too was delighted to see Paul again, and gave him a big kiss. She was happy for him to go off to supervise the important work developing in Uganda, but was utterly exhausted by the childcare demands. It was with some relief that she handed Matthew over to his father.

"Your turn," she announced. "I'm off to bed."

★ ★ ★

The following morning, Paul shared with them his excitement at the developing work in Uganda which the Trust was making possible. The trauma rehabilitation centre in one of the old refugee camps was now fully operational, with over 50 former boy-soldiers learning self-sufficiency agriculture skills and 50 more enrolled for the following year. The surgical unit was still on track to open at Easter, in a few weeks time, and the new Watoto village was half-built, with the possibility of opening fully after Christmas. The Farms Project was still a long way off, but the land purchases had been made and experts had been appointed to oversee the planning. The Production Unit was still churning out hundreds of beds and doors and cupboards – and an extra unit in the industrial estate had been rented to store the furniture ready for the new village.

"What about Bulrushes?" asked Ruth, who'd finally emerged from a long sleep interrupted only to feed Matthew, not that she remembered any of it. "Is it full yet?"

"Over-full," said Paul. "We're already looking at buying up the property next-door so that we can extend again."

"Where are they all coming from?" Ruth shook her head. This particular project was her baby. She missed being there, having her finger on the pulse. She'd known all along that Bulrushes was only dealing with the tip of the iceberg – and that there were hundreds, if not thousands more left to die for every one child that Bulrushes found and helped.

"That's the problem we face," said Paul. "The more that Bulrushes does, the more publicity it receives, so the more people hear about it and the more children suddenly arrive on our doorstep – sometimes literally. The matron was telling me that the other week she went to fetch a new-born baby who'd been abandoned, wrapped up in a blanket, in a skip on the building site next door. Pinned to the blanket was a paper which simply said "Watoto". The poor mother knew that workers would arrive early in the morning, so her baby's cries would be heard and he'd be safe."

"What despair the mother must have felt, to abandon her child like that," said Ruth, holding Matthew close to her as she spoke.

"But that's Africa for you, I'm afraid," said Paul. "Every child whom we help at Bulrushes will either have no mother at all because she's died, or a mother so desperate that she gave up her child to be brought up by others who could look after it properly. Nothing we can do will change that."

"But we must keep trying," said Ruth, rocking Matthew in her arms, reflecting how cruel and how wonderful life could be.

★ ★ ★

Carol arrived on March 9th, exhausted and speechless. There was a poignant and rather lovely reunion with Brendan, and they held each other for a long time, saying nothing, but just holding each other close, before Carol broke the embrace and burst into tears. Ruth led her to her room, and that's where she stayed for the next three days, eating whatever Ruth brought but unable to speak.

Chapter 50

Brendan felt both honoured and bewildered by Carol's need of him. He was also confused by the swirl of emotions within himself, some of which absurdly were rather romantic. When they'd embraced, he'd been surprised to find himself getting rather aroused – a part of him that he'd assumed was as lifeless as his tongue.

He knew that he wouldn't be able to do anything to help Carol until she was ready, so he reconciled himself to waiting. It stirred up positive thoughts in him just to have someone needing his ministry once again, because his physical deterioration had inevitably made him feel useless.

He still felt ill all the time. He had morphine patches for the constant pain in his throat and the nagging earache which the oncologist had said was a common after-effect of throat surgery. He was tired most of the time because he still had to go to bed sitting up, which helped him not to choke but meant that he didn't sleep much either. He was getting better at eating, as his tongue movement now helped him swallow, but the swallowing itself was still painful and all food tasted bland.

★ ★ ★

Ruth was exhausted too. Paul's home-coming had relieved her of some of her parental duties, but because she was still breastfeeding Matthew she still had interrupted sleep patterns. Paul was a doting father and an attentive husband, but didn't really have much clue about the needs of babies or mothers. He did, however, cook a few meals and do the shopping, which made it a little easier for her. But Ruth now had another dependent, Carol, for whom she'd taken responsibility despite the other calls on her time and attention.

Louisa and Ben lived on the top floor, and were rarely around or saw one another during the daytime, so liked to spend their evenings together as a recently married couple, rather than wading into the emotional maelstrom downstairs. Ben usually popped in towards the end of the afternoon, to chat with Brendan and play with his nephew for an hour or so, then went upstairs to prepare dinner for Louisa and himself. When Louisa got in, she too popped in for a few minutes to chat to her Dad but then went upstairs for a shower before dinner. Sometimes she popped back down again – and at least twice a week they all ate dinner together – but the onus for keeping the household going seemed to have fallen on Ruth.

She looked after her Dad's medication, made sure that he was settled in bed and had everything he needed for the night, as well as managing the kitchen and the cleaning, and looking after a three-month-old, a husband and a distraught American who wouldn't come out of her room.

★ ★ ★

The high points of Brendan's week had recently become the visits of Melanie, the speech-therapist – especially since the breakthroughs they'd achieved. He'd quickly mastered the synchronised "r" movement but it still came out like a "w" sometimes. He was getting better at the "nd" double-action too, and was beginning to say his name quite fluently. He'd mastered "j" and "l", was getting there with "s" and "t" and was eager to tackle the harder, back-of-the-mouth sounds such as "c/k" and "g".

Melanie had explained that it was these back-of-the-mouth sounds which were hardest of all because the tongue had to stretch upwards from its root, and the flat of the tongue rather than its tip was propelled onto the roof of the mouth. Brendan had tried to anticipate his next lesson by using his own fingers to manipulate his tongue upwards, but he hadn't got anywhere and was a bit downhearted when Melanie arrived the next time.

She noticed straightaway, and asked him what the matter was. He showed her the email from Carol and slowly explained that she'd arrived two days ago and was anxious for him to help her.

Melanie was horrified when she read the email and made Brendan feel much better when she said, "At least she's come to the right person."

When Brendan looked up at her, she explained. "You'd be the person I'd come to if I had a problem."

Brendan wrote on his pad: "I can't believe that you'd have any problems."

Melanie laughed. "It's men who cause all the problems – especially men like you!" She poked him with her finger and made him laugh.

Brendan scribbled away again on his pad. "I've been trying to educate my tongue to do the last set of sounds but all I did was dribble down my chin."

Melanie took the pad, laughed, joked about trying to make her redundant, and threw the pad across the room straight into the wastepaper bin without even hitting the sides. "Slam dunk!" she yelled, high-fiving Brendan and then getting him to say it too. It sounded like "lamb dump" which made them both laugh.

"That's the pad redundant, and soon it'll be me, because we're going for it now. No more writing, everything spoken from now on, OK?"

Brendan nodded obediently.

"Right, down to business – we'll have you saying "successive saggy coccyxes" in no time."

Brendan had a go. "Zuzzedib zaddy dob dizzes," which brought more laughter.

Melanie set to work...

★ ★ ★

Three days after she'd arrived, Carol emerged from her room mid-morning and made herself a cup of tea, before locking herself in the bathroom for a couple of hours. At 2.30pm she re-appeared, still red-eyed but at least with her hair washed and gelled, her make-up on, and a dab of perfume on her wrists and behind her ears. She looked good, Brendan thought, but didn't say so.

She sat down next to Brendan and held his hand. "I'm sorry about all this, Brendan. I don't want to talk about it yet, but I do want to help. Ruth's been so good to me and she's so tired, so I've decided I'm going to make myself useful."

That evening, they all sat down to dinner together: Brendan, Louisa, Ben, Paul, Ruth, Paul – and Carol, who'd cooked a pot roast and made an apple pie. Everyone was thrilled to see Carol re-emerge, and she smiled as she listened to the "safe" conversation about what had happened to everyone that day. At the end of the meal she quietly excused herself and said Good Night, even though it was only 8.30pm.

Ruth went to check on Matthew a few minutes later and reported back that she'd heard Carol crying in her room.

"It's OK," said Brendan, slowly. "She's done well today."

Everyone looked at Brendan and smiled.

"Hey, Dad," said Louisa, "That was a pretty good speech, and you even managed a "k"."

Brendan grinned. "I'm getting cocky." They all applauded. He decided not to push his luck with "successive saggy coccyxes".

Chapter 51

Lilian had taken each of the five patients through their first few days of chemoradiotherapy, accompanying them into the treatment room where they were given the chemo, then down to the radiotherapy suite for their short daily burst from the Big Machine. She calmed their nerves, explained about the clonking noises they'd hear, helped them choose music for the headphones and had a laugh with them about their musical tastes, then reappeared immediately after treatment to soothe them and answer their questions. The film crew accompanied her everywhere, and the hospital staff co-operated magnificently. The RT technician even smiled.

After three days doing that, she'd told the patients that she'd be contacting each of them at home to find an afternoon or evening when she could visit them, find out a bit more about them, and give the TV audience a bigger picture of how the trials and treatment were affecting their daily lives. They all agreed, some more readily than others, and filming arrangements had been made for the following two weeks.

Now Lilian was in the middle of those visits. She'd already been to the Balkwell estate in North Shields to visit Sharon and "the bairns" – her own two unmarried daughters with three children between them, who all lived in the same three-bedroom council house. Her son Tommy, the would-be drummer, lived with his girlfriend in a one-bedroom upstairs flat just across the road. Even Lilian was appalled at their living conditions, and she wondered quite where Tommy would put his drum kit, and what the people in the downstairs flat would think.

She'd also been out to Corbridge to see Darren, who lived with his elderly parents near the Black Bull in the centre of the village. Lilian was shocked this time to see the despair on their faces, which contrasted sharply with the cheeky chirpiness with which Darren confronted his cancer.

"He's my only son," whispered Darren's mother, while his father patted her hand.

Darren took Lilian and the film crew down to Hexham, where he worked, and introduced her to his mates and his boss.

"He's a good lad," said the boss. "I hope you can get him right again."

The most recent visit she'd done was to Eric, the retired headmaster in Carlisle, who actually lived in Bow, a little hamlet to the west of the town. Their large beamed house was a recent barn-conversion, bought the previous year for his retirement. They'd lived in the northern part of Carlisle before that, close to the secondary school where Eric had worked. His wife, Cathy, was a small sparrow of a woman, who hopped about straightening cushions and making tea, and seemed constantly nervous about saying the wrong thing. Eric was much more relaxed, and was very matter-of-fact about his cancer.

"I know the prognosis is pretty bleak, but even if it doesn't work out for me, maybe through the trials some good will come for someone else."

* * *

It was March 19th when Carol got a phone call telling her that her son had managed to commit suicide in his cell, by hanging himself with a strip of plastic torn off his mattress. She sat stunned after putting the phone down, then relayed the news to Brendan and Ruth.

"What should I do, Brendan?"

"Go back and sort out the funeral," he said, slowly but firmly. "Be as strong as you can be, get through the funeral, then, when you're ready, come back here. You're always welcome here. You're not on your own."

It was a long speech for him, but an important one. He felt strong, despite his physical weakness. Carol needed someone to be strong for her, to be there for her.

"Am I a horrible mother for being thankful that my son's dead?" Carol asked.

Brendan and Ruth shook their heads, and smiled at her.

"Not at all," said Brendan. "Maybe now he's at peace."

Carol nodded, and smiled. Ruth stepped forward and gave Carol a hug. "Do you want one of us to come back to the States with you?"

"No, dear – thanks all the same. This is something I have to do on my own. You've got enough to do here. Look after him while I'm gone, won't you? But I promise, Brendan, that I'll be back."

She reached for the phone and made arrangements to fly back to Texas. Then she went to pack.

★ ★ ★

A few days later, Brendan suddenly got a new stabbing pain at the site of the old tumour on the stem of his tongue. Suddenly he and the oncologist remembered their concern that they might not have eradicated the entire tumour the first time round. Brendan was hurried in for a further scan, and was sent home to await the results, which would be available the following day.

Chapter 52

The cancer was back, at the site of the original tumour.

And there was every chance that it had spread down the gullet. The oncologist suggested removing the entire tongue, but with no guarantee that even that would do the trick.

Brendan was instantly more upset for Melanie than he was for himself. She'd tried so hard and done so well with him, so he was really disappointed that her efforts might be in vain. Removing his tongue would be the end of speech therapy because it would be the end of speech. Full stop. For anybody that was massive, but for a preacher it was even worse. He'd still be able to make a noise, but wouldn't have the ability to form words. It would be grunts only – a reversion to teenager-status.

After the tongue removal, a plastic surgeon would take out a lump of muscle in Brendan's back and sew it into his mouth – not as a new tongue but as a flap which would fill the gap. Also his epiglottis would be removed (the little waggly thing that stops food and drink going down the windpipe) along with a mass of sub-lingual folds above the vocal cords. The only way for Brendan to eat and drink would be by tube into his stomach. The oncologist said that Brendan's difficulty with speech therapy was probably a sign that the tongue cancer had been restricting the blood supply to the muscle.

"But I can speak OK again now," protested Brendan.

"Yes, you've done well," agreed the oncologist, "But all to no avail, I'm afraid."

There was a pause, then Brendan asked the question he'd been mulling over for weeks, anticipating a crisis such as this. "What if I don't have the operation?"

"Are you thinking of refusing treatment?" asked the oncologist, peering over his glasses at Brendan.

Brendan nodded.

The oncologist drew up his chair close to Brendan, and cleared his throat. "For the record, I'd have to advise against that, and put that in your notes. But off the record, I'd applaud your decision. To be perfectly frank with you, there's at least a 50-50 chance that we'll end up chasing the cancer down your gullet even if we remove your tongue. The operation's a big one, with severe after-effects, no guarantee that the cancer would be eradicated, and with diminished quality of life for at least four months, even if you last that long."

Brendan gulped. The oncologist was certainly not pulling any punches. He looked him in the eye. "What would you do if it were you with the cancer, not me?"

"I hope I'd be strong enough to do the same as you."

Brendan rose from the chair, shook hands with the oncologist, thanked him, and walked out of the room. He felt curiously at peace with his decision, even though he knew that this pretty much added up to declaring a death sentence on himself. He'd always been an advocate for quality rather than quantity of life, and now that it was not an academic theory but a decision about his own mortality, he knew he'd been right all along.

His only worry was how to tell the family.

★ ★ ★

He didn't get back home till tea-time, as the ambulance had been everywhere in the region dropping patients off one by one. At least it'd given him time to think. He'd insisted that he wanted to go in for the consultation by himself, as he'd had an inkling that the news wouldn't be good. Paul had dropped him off that morning and offered to come back for him, but Brendan said that he'd come back by ambulance.

"Oh, I'm OK," he announced, when asked. "I'll tell you all at dinner."

Fortunately, or providentially, it was one of their family dinners, which Paul and Ruth prepared together in the downstairs flat, bringing it up with a flourish. They put the baby alarm on so that they'd hear Matthew if he woke up crying, then tucked in.

"So," said Ruth, "How did you get on, Dad?"

Brendan put his knife and fork down. "Good and bad," he said.

They looked at him, puzzled.

"The cancer's back with a vengeance, I'm afraid."

They all stopped eating, and looked at him, appalled.

"What do you mean, Dad?" asked Louisa. "What did they say?"

"It's back, at the old site at the root of the tongue, and probably down my throat as well. They say that they could remove the entire tongue but it may well have spread down my throat anyway."

"So what are they going to do?" asked Ruth, her voice trembling..

"Nothing," said Brendan. "I've told them that I don't want any further treatment, and I'll enjoy whatever time remains for me."

The girls both burst into tears, as did Ben. Paul looked as if he might join them.

"But it's not all bad," said Brendan. They looked at him in confusion.

"I get to keep my tongue so at least I can still keep seeing Melanie." And he smiled. Ruth rushed out of the room, sobbing.

Louisa smiled, through her tears. "You're a prat, Dad, but I love you." And she burst out crying, even louder this time and gave him a big hug.

The food went cold. No-one was very hungry anyway.

★ ★ ★

Carol phoned the following morning. After the initial greetings, she asked how everybody was, and Ruth told her about Brendan's scan results. There was a silence at the other end.

"He's quite a guy, your Dad," Carol finally said. "It takes a helluva lot of guts to make that sort of decision."

Ruth agreed, but Carol hadn't finished.

"My husband clung on and on to every little remote possibility, and went through far too many operations in the hope that the next one might cure him. All it did was rob him of the last two years of his life, because he was always in hospital."

Ruth was quiet. "I suppose you're right, but it's very hard to take," she mumbled, afraid that her Dad would hear the conversation.

"I know, dear," said Carol – which brought a flush of shame to

Ruth's cheeks.

"I'm so sorry, Carol, thinking about my own trouble when you've got so much more to deal with. How've you been doing?"

"Pretty good, I think," replied Carol, almost chirpily. "The funeral was difficult but I got through that. Now I've been getting my brother, who's a lawyer, to sort out all the estates. I'm suddenly rather rich, because with both my sons and their families dead I'm the only one left to inherit it all – not that there was much left with my eldest who had such financial difficulties, but my other son was a successful businessman and had quite a lot to his name."

She said it so matter-of-fact. It wasn't that she cared about her bank balance, it was just something to say which wasn't either morbid or maudlin.

"So what are you going to do now?" asked Ruth.

"I'm coming over to help look after your Dad, if that's OK with you. I'd like him to help me get over all this, if he's still willing. I promise I won't get in the way. Is that OK?"

"Of course it is," said Ruth. "I'm sure he'll be glad to see you."

★ ★ ★

Oddly, Melanie took the news worst of all.

She was already unusually subdued when she arrived, but when she heard the news, she was distraught. Ruth had to go and make her a cup of tea before she calmed down.

"It's not fair!" she declared.

"What do you mean?" asked Brendan.

"It's not fair that a really good man like you has to die while other nasty pieces of work get put on fancy trials for new drugs and what not."

"What do you mean?"

"My feller's Dad is horrible, but he's got himself on some fancy new treatment at the Freeman for his cancer."

Brendan was gobsmacked. He didn't even know that Melanie had "a feller", let alone that she knew someone on the clinical trials.

Alan's story: June 6th 1994

Alan, Pauline and Alan (Junior) settled on the sofa to watch Coronation Street. It was Alan's 50th birthday, but he wasn't making a big fuss about it. They'd been down the Farmer's Arms for an early dinner (Happy Hour before 6.30pm) and were settling in for the evening, though Alan (Junior) knew that he'd be packed off to bed at the end of Corrie.

Percy Sugden, Maud Grimes and her daughter Maureen Webster were in France to visit the D-Day cemeteries, on the 50th anniversary of the Normandy landings.

Pauline sniffed as Percy wept at the graves of old comrades. "Must be awful for people like Percy," she said. "Survivor guilt and all that."

"What's that, Mam?" asked Alan (Junior).

"It's when your friends get killed and you don't, but then you feel guilty that you didn't die with them," she explained.

"What's the point of that?" Alan (Junior) replied. "That's daft."

"I don't think you've got any choice about it. It's just the way you feel," chipped in Alan (Senior). "Did I ever tell you about my Uncle George?" he asked, changing the subject. "He was killed on D-Day. He's probably buried in one of them graves."

"Cool," said Alan (Junior). "Was he blown up?"

"Don't know, son," said Alan (Senior), realising that he didn't know anything about the man who'd died as he was being born. Perhaps he ought to find out one day.

Alan (Junior) was taking a closer interest in the TV, as if he'd find out more by listening hard. But the story had moved on. Now it was just Maud and Maureen and they were in an American cemetery. Maud took Maureen to a grave in the American cemetery and pointed out the grave of a Danny Kennedy, saying that he was Maureen's real father. Maureen was stunned at the revelation and Maud told Maureen that she wanted her to know the truth about her father before Maud died.

"Are you my real Dad?" asked Alan (Junior), getting a clip round his ears for his cheek.

★ ★ ★

Later, after Alan (Junior) had been persuaded to go to bed, with more clips round the ear threatened by his father, Pauline handed Alan his mid-evening cuppa and said, "Alan, I don't want to get at you, but I've been meaning to have a word with you for some time now. I do wish you wouldn't smack wor Alan like that."

"What do you mean?" Alan's hackles were rising immediately.

"You know what I mean. One day he's going to be bigger than you and he'll hit you back. You need to show him a bit of love, not all this aggression."

Alan threw down his paper. "I'm not listening to this. I'm off down the Farmer's." And, as she waited to hear the front door slam, like it usually did when they had a row, she heard him yell, "Some bloody birthday this turned out to be!"

★ ★ ★

Pauline sat and wept. It was getting worse, this animosity that Alan bore towards her, Alan (Junior), the people at Church if they didn't do what he wanted, and, come to think of it, just about everyone else. She wondered what had gone wrong.

Was it work? She knew that he wasn't happy at work, and was stuck in a rut, but he didn't seem to have any ambition to do anything else.

Was it Church? Had something gone wrong, which meant that he couldn't play at being head of his little empire, like he usually did? But as soon as she thought it, she dismissed it. She knew that his malaise had been growing for some years, and it was a welcome relief for her that he had Church to go out to, because it gave her a bit of peace, especially when he took their son with him.

Was she the problem? She ran a hand down her body. She wasn't as slim as she'd once been, even though she tried to keep herself looking nice. Not that he seemed to notice. She did everything he seemed to expect, looking after him and their son, washing and ironing, cooking and shopping – what more did he want?

Was it some sort of midlife crisis? She'd heard about those but didn't really understand what they were on about. Was it the male menopause – she'd read about that too but it all sounded a load of cobblers to her. It was just an excuse for men to have it off with some bimbo who didn't care about anyone else. Was that why he kept up his ridiculous love-affair with the sunbed upstairs?

Then it struck her. Perhaps her Alan was having an affair. Was it that Sarah Lanleigh woman from Church? Then she laughed. No, whatever was wrong, it wasn't that. He wasn't really that bothered with sex, she was pretty certain about that.

So what was it?

As she went into the kitchen to pour the cold coffee away and wash up the cup, she shook her head. Some bloody birthday this had turned out to be, that's for certain...

April 2013

Chapter 53

Dawn wanted Lilian to film her at work in the bank, which was on the main street of one of Durham's leafier suburbs. It proved to be quite an adventure, because the whole city seemed to have got to hear what was happening, and turned up to put money in or take money out or arrange an appointment to chat about their mortgage. At one stage there were queues outside the door. Dawn was not averse to a spot of self-publicity, and was doing crowd control as well as demonstrating her prowess at customer service, whilst maintaining a fixed smile for the camera.

Lilian felt a bit out of her depth, but soldiered on regardless, interviewing colleagues who all seemed to assume that this was an audition for The Apprentice too. Cancer never got a mention. She wondered what Dawn had said to them.

When they followed Dawn back to her two-up two-down cottage, she admitted that she hadn't told them what the filming was for, and had let them assume that it was some kind of documentary or new internal monitoring. She hadn't told anyone that she had cancer.

★ ★ ★

Lilian's visit to Alan, the retired civil servant, was similarly bizarre. He lived in one of the suburban villages near the coast, which seemed a sleepy-hollow sort of a place to Lilian, who was used to a more active pace to community life. The most exciting thing in the village seemed to be the Methodist Church – which was a bit of a laugh in itself. It had bunting strung across from the church to a lamppost, and seemed to be a hive of activity, even late on a Wednesday afternoon, with dozens of teenagers milling around outside. She made this her introductory question: "Do you have much to do with the church in the village?"

"Certainly not!" came the curt reply.

They filmed Alan coming out from his house into the garden,

which was in a quiet little cul-de-sac backing onto some farmland.

"You seem to like gardening…" was Lilian's next gambit.

"Hate it," he snapped. "But somebody has to do it, don't they?"

"Nice roses," said Lilian, not that she had a clue. They did seem a bit out of control, though. Alan ignored her anyway.

Alan's wife was out somewhere, so they never did get to meet her. At the end of the afternoon, Lilian wondered whether they'd find anything useful to broadcast. He seemed such a miserable old grouch.

★ ★ ★

Carol returned on April 3rd, the Tuesday after Easter.

It had been a strange and compelling Eastertide for Brendan and his family, due to the news about Brendan's condition which they were all still absorbing. Brendan decided that he wanted to go to Church, but needed it to be quiet and undemanding. He'd walked slowly along the road to St. George's, a large Grade-1 listed edifice with a high churchmanship involving bells and smells. But it had provided what he was after – a solemn service of reflection on Good Friday, followed by a restrained Eucharist on Easter Day. What is more, hardly anyone spoke to him, which was just what he wanted.

Carol breezed in with a flurry of suitcases and bags, having caught a taxi from the airport.

"We'd have come to get you," said Ruth, but Carol hushed her.

"Didn't want to put anyone out," she said. It wasn't in any way a grumble – she was happy to make her own way there. And money, of course, was not a problem…

Carol brought a lightness to the conversation around the dinner-table that evening, making them laugh with her account of her brother trying to give her good advice about property investment when she clearly had no interest in such matters. At one point he'd asked her if she'd ever considered buying a hotel. "Ed", she said, "Hotels are for staying in, not investing in." It wasn't particularly funny, but her accent and the way she told the story made everyone smile. She was quite feisty, was Carol.

Brendan was quiet – not that he could get a word in edgeways anyway. He was happy to see glimpses of the old Carol whom he remembered. He wondered what she was covering up, and what would need to be exposed as they chatted together so that she could deal with it properly.

★ ★ ★

Melanie was now down to one visit a week, trying to help Brendan with complicated sounds like "ch" and "th" and do further exercises to make his tongue more flexible and responsive. He still wasn't very good at "successive saggy coccyxes".

They got talking about Melanie's "feller" who was called Alan. He'd just come out of the Army after a 12-year stint, which had taken him to Iraq and Afghanistan – and left him cynical and angry. "Except with me," she said. "He's lovely with me. But he does fly off the handle a bit too easily, and especially if he's had a few pints. He came back from the pub one night with a long cut across his forehead, but he wouldn't tell me what had happened and told me not to mention it again, which upset me. You're supposed to be able to talk about everything if you love each other, aren't you?"

Brendan nodded. "You're supposed to," he said. "But it's not always as easy as it sounds – especially if there's stuff from the past that hasn't been properly dealt with. If he's been in Iraq and Afghanistan, he'll have seen some pretty horrible stuff, which he may not have had the chance to deal with properly."

Melanie sniffed. "What am I supposed to do, then. Get him to talk about it?"

"Only if he's ready for it. You'll have to take your cue from him. Does he have nightmares?"

"Yes, he does. Bad ones. Sometimes he screams in his sleep and it frightens me."

"Does he ever talk about his time in the army?"

"No, he doesn't. In fact, he told me that he wants to forget all about it. I don't think it was a very good time for him."

Brendan paused. "What's he doing with himself now?"

Melanie brightened. "He's got a job delivering Yellow Pages and stuff like that. He quite likes it because it's out in the open air. He can't stand being inside all the time."

"And what's happening with his Dad? You mentioned that he was having some new treatment?"

"That's what Alan said. But I don't know any more. I've never met his Dad but Alan says he's horrible."

"Does Alan keep in touch with him?" asked Brendan.

"I don't think so. He goes to see his Mam, though. She's nice. I've met her."

"So," said Brendan, leaning back and smiling, "Are you and Alan... "serious"?"

Melanie blushed. "I hope so," she said. "I'm getting a bit old for all this courting malarkey. I need to find a good bloke who'll stick with me – and I reckon it might be Alan. I hope so, anyway..."

Chapter 54

It was the following morning when Carol announced that she was ready to talk about everything. Brendan had no need to be elsewhere and no-one was scheduled to visit, so they agreed to go for it straightaway.

"On one condition, Carol," said Brendan.

"What's that?"

"That you talk to me as Brendan, not as a Minister."

She looked puzzled.

"Aren't you a Minister just as much as you are Brendan?" she asked.

"In a way, yes. But if I'm here as a Minister I can't give you the sort of kiss that I might want to."

Carol laughed, came across and kissed him hard and long. "Brendan it is, then," she murmured in his ear, then went off to put the kettle on, while Brendan tried to collect his thoughts and his emotions.

When she'd settled in a chair at the side of Brendan's – not too close, not too far away, she began. She looked out of the window as she began her tale, fearful of looking straight at Brendan

"I can't understand what I feel about what Carl did. I'm surprised that he had such violence in him, because he was always such a quiet and dependable child, and was never particularly difficult. He went to College, got a good job. He adored Jenny and the children, was in the local country club and was well respected. But it was all a bit of a show. Underneath he was so anxious to please that he over-egged how much he was earning, was over-generous to preserve the image he'd created, and got further and further into debt until the bank threatened to foreclose on the house. That's when he started embezzling money from the firm, and it all spiralled out of control.

"I guess he just snapped and felt that life was not worth living. He left a note to say that he wanted to stop his family from being ashamed of him. That was why he killed them, he said. How crazy is that?

"Anyway, I think he'd flipped and suffered a complete mental breakdown. So I'm not angry with him. I just feel so sorry for him, and wish that I could've helped – but he was too proud to ask for help and covered up his difficulties so well. Not even his wife knew what was really happening. Nor did I. It's so sad. But I am glad in a way that he did kill himself – for at least he was spared living the rest of his life with the knowledge of what he'd done.

"The sad thing is that he took my whole family with him. My other son, Mark, and his pretty wife, who was five months pregnant with their first baby. If I'd been there, it would have been me too. He took everyone with him, leaving me with nobody."

She paused, stifled a sob, and blew her nose.

"Not with nobody, Carol," said Brendan. "You've still got your brother – and me."

Carole smiled. "Oh, I don't really get on that well with Ed. He's too starchy and he's always going on about getting the paperwork straight. That's all he seems to care about. Paperwork, paperwork. No wonder he's never married. But as for you, Brendan..."

She looked at him for the first time. "I don't know what to say. I haven't really had the chance to get to know you properly, but I feel as if I've known you all my life."

Brendan cleared his throat rather painfully, had a sip of his tea, and decided to get back to business. "How do you *feel*, Carol? Numb? Angry? Betrayed? Disappointed?"

Carol thought hard before she answered.

"All of those things and none of those things – if that doesn't sound stupid. I loved my two grandchildren and was really excited that another one was on the way. Now I'll never have the chance to watch them grow up and maybe even have children of their own. That makes me sad, and a bit lost, I suppose. What's there to look forward to, if you've got no-one to be proud of, no-one to fuss over or worry about, and no-one to share any of it with?"

She paused, looked Brendan in the eye, and he looked back at her, without saying a word.

"Anyway, where was I? Oh yes. What do I feel? I hate to admit it, Brendan, but I actually feel curiously free. I've got no reason ever to go to Austin again – in fact, I don't ever want to see the place. No reason even to go back to the States, except that I don't know anywhere else. But for the first time in my life I can just jump on a plane, without worrying about anyone else, and come here to be with you. I can do whatever I want. Is that wrong?"

Brendan reached across and held her hand. "Of course it's not wrong. And I'm flattered that you want to be here with me – even though I'm falling to bits and can't offer you much."

"But I don't want anything from you, Brendan, except to spend my days with you, to have someone to love. Will you let me love you, Brendan, even if it's only for a short time?"

Brendan kept hold of her hand, but said nothing till she looked up, worried that he might be unsure. "Of course I will, Carol. I'd love you to share my journey, but I don't think it'll be very easy."

"I know," Carol said. "My husband died of cancer after three years or more of operations and treatments and he was always having nurses coming in to swap his tubes or change his dressings. I couldn't get near him as he slipped away – he wouldn't let me. I think you and me will do it much better. We may even have a few laughs along the way, what d'you think?"

Brendan smiled. "Sounds good to me."

★ ★ ★

Ruth noticed the difference when she was getting lunch ready. "You two seem quite feisty today," she said.

Carol and Brendan laughed.

"Yeah," said Carol. "We're getting along just fine."

Ruth smiled. It was good to see her Dad smiling. Carol was good for him, she decided. Then she thought, it's such a shame that they won't have long to enjoy their friendship. And she started to cry, and couldn't stop. It was odd – she wasn't crying for herself losing her Dad, or for Matthew not really getting to know his Grandad. She was crying because her Dad wouldn't be able to get the most out of the love that he and Carol obviously shared. The salad she was preparing was soaked by the time she'd finished, but she dried her eyes, took the lunch into the other room, and asked them when they were going to get married.

Brendan and Carol looked at each other in astonishment. They'd only just met one another again, and here was Ruth telling them to get married – after all that Carol had just gone through, and all that lay ahead for Brendan! And yet, within just a few seconds, they realised that it was exactly what they wanted.

"You mean, you wouldn't mind?" spluttered Brendan.

Ruth laughed. "Of course not. You should enjoy life together for as long as you can. Carol obviously makes you happy, and you make her happy, so why wait?"

Brendan and Carol looked at each other again, and then burst into big grins. "Guess we've got no choice, then, have we?" said Carol.

"But I haven't even asked you?" said Brendan.

"Oh we don't need to live in a bygone age. This is 2013, Brendan. Things are different now. Just go with the flow."

The three of them shared a big hug. Dinner-time would be interesting...

★ ★ ★

Louisa and Ben were just as thrilled as Ruth and Paul were. The conversation turned to weddings, and Louisa offered Carol her wedding dress, which nearly made Carol spill her drink.

"Thanks for the offer, dear, but not only would I not fit into it, but I think white is a little inappropriate at my time of life."

Brendan waved them into silence. "No fuss," he said. "I couldn't cope with any fuss. Just something quiet, that's all I want. Anything more would be too much."

"What about what I want, Brendan Priest?" Carol butted in. "Don't I have a say in it?"

Brendan looked guilty for a minute, but then realised that she was pulling his leg. "And what would you like, dear?"

Carol thought for a moment. "Maybe something quiet – no fuss, that sort of thing." And they all laughed and carried on making their plans.

Chapter 55

Melanie burst into the main room the following week with the news that she had a special announcement to make. "Come on, both of you," she said to Carol and Brendan, sitting them down. "Are you ready?" They nodded. "I'm ENGAGED!" she shrieked, holding out her hand to show them her ring. They cooed and sighed dutifully, but were actually thrilled for her, especially because of their own news.

"Actually," said Brendan quietly, "I've got an announcement too."

He paused. Melanie stopped in her tracks, worried about what he was going to say. Brendan extended the pause, before shouting, "WE'RE ENGAGED TOO!"

Melanie looked gobsmacked, then raised her eyebrows and shrieked all the more. They all did a little jig, then sat down in an exhausted heap.

"Go on, tell me," said Melanie. "What's brought all this on? If you don't mind me saying, it's a bit quick, isn't it? And after everything you've been through..." She tailed off, aware that she was probably saying the wrong things.

Brendan and Carol laughed to put her at ease.

"That's why we're getting married quickly, for we probably haven't got long left and want to make the most of it," said Carol, giving Melanie a big theatrical wink. "Know what I mean?"

Everybody went red, including Carol.

"Only joking," she said. "It's not like that at all. We just want to spend every precious moment together, and tell the world about how we feel."

"And tell them that love triumphs over everything," said Brendan, ever the preacher. He paused. "But what about you, Melanie? Sorry for butting in on your big news. What's your story?"

"He asked me last night. We went out to Bruno's, just down the road, and just as we were finishing our starters, he asked me, just like that. I nearly choked on my bruschetta. He'd even got the ring, isn't it nice?"

She showed it to them again, and they looked admiringly at it.

"Have you got a ring too?" asked Melanie.

"No, I haven't," said Carol. "Not yet, anyway... But your story's far more interesting. Did he not go down on one knee?"

"No, he's not that sort," said Melanie.

"Neither's Brendan. Mind you, if he got down on one knee he might not make it back up!"

They all laughed. "But what about all those worries you had?" asked Brendan.

"He talked to me about everything. He explained about his nightmares, but said that he was actually seeing someone from Military Mental Health CIC[75] (whatever that is) to talk about them. They're about a village in Iraq where someone in his platoon shot a child thinking he was a sniper, but I don't know any more than that. That's why he doesn't like being enclosed by walls, because it reminds him how scared they all were of being ambushed."

"It sounds like he's doing the right thing, getting counselling," said Brendan.

"Yes, I'm proud of him. He told me about his Dad too, and how hard he's going to try to be a better husband to me and father to our kids than his Dad ever was to him and his Mam."

"Sounds to me like he's serious and that he loves you," Brendan said. "And that's all you can ask for, isn't it?"

"No, dear," said Carol, patting his knee. "That's all you *need*."

★ ★ ★

Paul went off to London the next day, en route to Gulu for the official opening of the Surgical Hospital, then on to Cape Town for the

---

[75] It's actually a Community Interest Company (CIC), based in Sunderland, set up as a Social Enterprise, founded by veterans for veterans, with the tag "Who Cares Wins". They offer courses in stress awareness, anger management etc. Their website is www.militarymentalhealth.co.uk

official opening of Watoto Church Cape Town[76] on May 1st. Watoto had always been keen to see their model replicated across different parts of Africa, and the strategy was to base their social action, as in Uganda, around the establishment of a life-enriching local church.

Paul had been asked to speak at the opening celebration about the exciting projects which he and Ruth had developed in Gulu, and specifically to commend the three programmes that were being established in Cape Town straightaway: Baby Watoto, a Bulrushes-type programme to rescue orphaned and destitute babies; Living Hope, a programme like Ruth and Paul had led in the camps to restore dignity to vulnerable women; and Watoto 360°, a discipleship course used across the Watoto villages in Uganda to equip young people to change their world with the love of Jesus.

He'd never been to South Africa before, and was excited to be asked to represent Watoto at such a prestigious event, even though it meant that he was separated from Ruth and Matthew and was missing out on the excitement about Brendan and Carol's wedding.

★ ★ ★

Brendan phoned Jack Turner the same day that Paul left for South Africa.

"I've got some news," he said.

"Brendan, I've heard. Your Super phoned me. I'm so sorry to hear that the cancer's returned and that there's nothing much that they can do. Can I come round and visit you?"

"Oh that," said Brendan. "Yes, that's right. Of course you can come round. But that wasn't what I was phoning about."

On the other end of the phone, Jack was mystified. What was he going on about? What could be more important than the awful news about the cancer?

Brendan continued. "The thing is, Jack, I'm getting married, and I wondered if you'd be my best man."

Jack was lost for words. Married? To whom? Why? Why him to be best man? A few years ago they disliked one another intensely. Was

---

[76] The opening of Watoto Church Cape Town actually happened on May 1st 2011, along with the three projects described.

Brendan going mad?

"Well, Brendan, that's a bit of a surprise, to say the least. I'm, er, very happy for you both, whoever she is. Who is she?"

Brendan told him about Carol, and about their perspective on the remaining months or maybe just weeks of Brendan's life.

Jack blew out his cheeks. "Crikey, Brendan, you don't half do things wholeheartedly, I'll give you that. Of course I'll be your best man. When is it?"

"Four weeks on Thursday," said Brendan – which was a bit sooner than Jack had been expecting.

"Blimey, don't hang about, do you?" said Jack, frantically looking for his diary. "What date's that?"

"May 16th – the feast day of St. Brendan. It seemed appropriate, really, the two of us launching out into a new adventure, trusting in God to see us through the storms of life, just like Brendan did in his coracle."

Jack had found his diary. "Of course I'll do it. I was due to go down for a meeting to Church House, but this is far more important. I'd be honoured. Thanks for asking me. Where's it going to be – Jact?"

"Yes, Jact. But there's only going to be a few people invited. We don't want any fuss."

That's what you think, thought Jack. If the news gets out, they'll be lining the streets...

★ ★ ★

Brendan and Carol went to see the Registrar in North Shields that morning, having made a provisional booking with the Superintendent Minister that he'd marry them on May 16th. The Registrar frowned a little at the tightness of the time schedule, but when they explained that Brendan was terminally ill, he rushed through the process as quickly as he could, and promised to expedite the documentation check with America that Carol's nationality required.

"The certificate should be ready on May 15th," he said. "I hope that you'll not have any hiccups and that everything will go smoothly."

They handed over their fee and went off home to study the

documentation which the Registrar had given them. They were required to change Carol's visa status from "tourist" to "marriage". Normally, an American was required to return to the U.S. to apply for a special marriage visa, but the registrar had sat down, written and given them a letter explaining the special circumstances to the visa authorities, which he hoped would be sufficient.

But Brendan knew an even surer way of making sure that the visa complications would be sorted out quickly...

★ ★ ★

"Esther, it's Brendan, Brendan Priest."

"Brendan! What a nice surprise – and you're talking so well. How's it going?"

Brendan explained about his latest diagnosis, and the poor outcome that seemed inevitable. Esther was dreadfully upset, and quizzed him for ages on whether there was anything that she could do – fly him to a specialist back in Detroit, pay for a special hyper-expensive drug – anything.

"No, Esther, there's nothing left except prayer – and there's plenty of that happening. But that's not why I phoned. I wonder if you can help me. I'm planning on getting married..."

Esther was amazed at his news, and thrilled for him. When she heard about the visa complications for Carol, she promised that she'd sort it out. "But there's one condition, Brendan."

"Yes, you can come," he sighed, knowing what she was going to say. "But come incognito – we don't want any fuss. There's only going to be a few of us."

"I understand," Esther replied. "I don't usually do incognito, but I'll try my best. Can I bring a film crew?"

"No you can't!" shouted Brendan, only to hear Esther cackling in the background.

"Got you there, Brendan," she laughed.

★ ★ ★

Three days later, a thick official envelope addressed to Carol landed on the doorstep in Beverley Terrace, from the Embassy of the United

States of America. It contained a new passport, complete with marriage visa, stamped by the U.K. Border Agency, back-dated to her entry into the U.K. on March 9th.

"Hey, this ain't bad. Listen to this: The U.S. Embassy knew we were engaged before I'd even seen you again, Brendan!" shouted Carol.

"Ah well," said Brendan. "They say that the United States knows everything first, don't they?"

Chapter 56

The U.K. Wedding Belles website informed all prospective 2013 brides that the average cost of a 2011 wedding (the latest figures available) was £18,605. Carol showed it to Brendan, who harrumphed. He looked down the run-down, and jabbed his finger at the various entries. "Well, we don't need that one, or that one, or that, or that..."

Carol cleared her throat theatrically. "Excuse me, dearest, but have you not heard that it's the bride's day?"

"Yes," said Brendan, "And what a load of rubbish it is."

"So whose day is it, dearest?"

"Well, the first time I got married it turned out to be the bride's mother's day. She told everyone what to do, who sat where, who said what and what everyone had to wear."

"But whose day is it on May 16th, dearest?" Brendan thought about it for far too long, and got a playful slap on the head. "It's *our* day, dearest, isn't it? Yours, a bit, and mine, a lot. And I'll be paying for it so I can have what I want, get it?"

"Yes, dear."

★ ★ ★

When they looked at it more closely, they realised that most of the items on the Wedding Belles list were indeed unnecessary and undesirable in their case anyway. They'd already decided to dispense with an engagement ring, posh invitations, stag and hen nights, insurance, reception, wedding dress, posh outfits for the men, bridesmaids outfits, limo, photographer, video, entertainment at the reception, wedding cake, honeymoon – all of which, according to the list on the website had already saved them over £15,000.

Instead, they were planning to have only seven guests: Ruth, Paul, Matthew, Louisa, Ben, Jack and Esther. They'd be having a very simple service led by the Superintendent Minister, with no hymns, no music, no sermon – just a reading (1 Corinthians 13) and the vows. Then they'd have a private lunch upstairs at the Grand Hotel, and then go home.

When Esther was told the plans, she immediately hired the best suite at the Grand for herself for the night, and a limo and driver for her entire 26-hour stay. The Learjet was, as ever, on standby.

★ ★ ★

On April 24th, as everyone settled for the night, Brendan had another choking fit, much worse than usual and collapsed across the bed. Carol heard him and realised that something was wrong, rushed in and screamed when she saw that he'd turned blue and was unconscious. Louisa rushed downstairs in her pyjamas and once again managed to get him breathing by poking her finger down his throat which seemed to clear his airway. The blueness faded, but he didn't regain consciousness, so they phoned an ambulance.

Brendan was taken to hospital where they gave him a sedative to keep him unconscious, while they worked out what to do. The Emergency Care Unit doctor told Louisa that a preliminary examination of Brendan's throat indicated that the airway was very narrow, which was giving them cause for concern, so the immediate plan was to give him another tracheotomy to give the swelling in his airway time to go down. They'd keep Brendan in for a few days after waking him up, to enable them to do scans of his neck to see what had happened and what they could do to stop it happening again.

So Brendan woke up the following morning back in hospital, with another tracheotomy tube poking out of his throat, an oxygen mask over his face, feeling bruised and battered but glad to be alive. He remembered that in the instant before he'd lost consciousness, he'd wondered if he'd make it to his wedding or whether that was it. At least, he thought, he'd got something to look forward to now, someone worth surviving a bit longer for – and when Carol came in a little later, he knew that being married to her would be wonderful. When he saw her concerned smile, he was lost for words – but she didn't notice, because, with the tube in place, he couldn't have spoken even if he'd known what to say.

Brendan scribbled a note on a pad, assuring Carol that she should proceed with all the wedding plans, promising that he wasn't going to miss it for the world, and that all would be well. They sat for a while holding hands, then Brendan fell asleep, and she left quietly.

★ ★ ★

Louisa and Ruth had decided that Carol should be at the forefront of their thoughts and care, and that they should take a back-seat when it came to their Dad's care and welfare. They'd explained this to Carol earlier that morning over breakfast, emphasising that it wasn't that they didn't care about their Dad – far from it – but that Carol needed to be by his side more than they did.

Carol was deeply moved by this, and started to cry. "You know, I never really got the chance to get close to my daughters-in-law, and sons are different, aren't they? But I already feel so close to you two. Thanks for receiving me into the family so warmly."

This prompted a "group hug" and a bit of "solidarity weeping", broken when Matthew started screaming, Louisa said that she had to go to work, and Carol left for the hospital.

★ ★ ★

Ruth fielded a phone call from Esther in the afternoon, asking if her right-hand-man Arnold Joseph could come to the wedding as well. "I told him about your Dad's illness at yesterday's board meeting and he was really upset. Then I told him about the wedding and he insisted that he wanted to come, if that was OK..."

"I'll ask Dad as soon as I can," Ruth promised. "But he's been admitted into hospital again after a bit of a do last night. They've rung to say that he's OK, but I won't be seeing him till tonight, so I'll ask him then, and get back to you as soon as I can."

★ ★ ★

Later on, the Super phoned. After Ruth told him about the latest medical update, the Super had a request. "I know it's meant to be a quiet affair, but I wondered if it might be OK for the Circuit Stewards and some of the Ministers to come to the wedding – just to sit in the back row, you understand..."

Ruth promised to ask.

"And Sarah Lanleigh at Jact has asked if she can do the flowers for the wedding, but I rather got the impression that Brendan wasn't wanting any flowers. What do you think?"

"I know my Dad wanted it to be low-key, but I'm sure that if when they come into church there are a few flowers around, he won't chuck a strop and walk out in disgust."

The Super chuckled. "Yes, I get your drift. Mum's the word, eh?"

"And if a few people get to hear about it, and want to come to church, they can't really stop them, can they?" Ruth asked.

"It'd be illegal to stop them," the Super confirmed, conspiratorially.

"We'd better make sure that it's only a few, though, hadn't we?" said Ruth.

"Of course," agreed the Super. "They don't want any fuss, after all, do they?"

Chapter 57

When Lilian went back to see the soon-to-be Famous Five at the start of their second three-week treatment, she could already spot a difference. The three youngest (Dawn, Darren and Sharon) seemed to be dealing with the treatment well, but the two oldest (Eric and Alan) appeared gaunter and more wizened than when they'd started six weeks earlier.

By the time she went back to see them in their homes, a fortnight later, the contrast was even more marked. Sharon had already been to Ibiza with the bairns and both she and her daughters were sporting decent tans – if you prefer a ruddy shade of pink to brown, that is. Lilian got some great soundbites out of them, like "Couldn't understand why they didn't speak English?" and "At least they had chips". Tommy had been threatened with eviction because of his drumming at all hours, but otherwise all was well.

"But what about you, Sharon – how are you feeling?"

"Me, I'm canny, me. I don't know what they're givin' me, but it's doin' the trick, I reckon."

It was a similar story with Dawn and Darren. Dawn was rushing around as usual at work, organising everybody and smiling for the camera, but she revealed that she hadn't been sick at all since the treatment began, and felt much better. Darren was much more confident, and reckoned that he had much more energy.

With the other two, though, it was a very different matter.

Eric was in bed most afternoons and evenings now. Going to the hospital for treatment every morning took it out of him, and he tended to sleep most of the rest of the time, but then be unable to sleep at night because he was frequently dreadfully sick. Even if he didn't actually throw up, he felt horribly nauseous. He'd lost a lot of weight, and, frankly, looked to Lilian as if he might peg out any day. She'd had patients in the Cardiovascular Unit at the Freeman looking better than him after they'd died.

Alan, the retired civil servant who'd started out with skin cancer which had spread to his neck and throat, was almost as bad. He'd had to have another string of little lumps removed from the side of his face during the three weeks of respite from chemoradiotherapy, and had yet more stitches and scars to present to the camera. It was not only his skin which was twisted, however. He gave every impression of being bitter and twisted in character as well.

Lilian finally met Pauline, Alan's wife, who seemed haggard and worn-out by the effort of supporting her husband through it all. She seemed, like many Geordie wives, strong and forthright – yet Lilian reckoned this was largely in her case because she'd had to stand up to Alan all their married life, which couldn't have been easy.

"He doesn't seem very happy with the treatment," whispered Lilian in her David Attenborough voice.

"No, he's never happy. He hasn't been happy for a long time, but the cancer's eating away at him in every way. It's really hard for me to be here at all but he hasn't got anybody else, so it's down to me, isn't it?"

Lilian wondered if they'd be able to use this in the show. It was almost too revealing, too personal. She warmed to Pauline, and didn't want to get her into any more hassles with her husband.

★ ★ ★

The first two "See Esther" shows, incorporating clips from Lilian's interviews and shots of the patients having their treatment, had been well received. Esther had phoned Lilian directly to congratulate her on her work, which had made Lilian's day, if not her year. Esther was running a series on healthcare issues, as this was still a hot potato in America, with Obama's healthcare reforms having been such an important issue in the 2012 elections – and the storm since his re-election when the reforms were beginning to get implemented was still raging across the country. Hearing about advances in medicine – if that's what happened as a result of the trials – would be a positive spin on what had become a fractious issue.

Furthermore, the American audience seemed to have warmed to the five patients – especially, curiously, Sharon. Even though most of the people polled admitted they couldn't understand a word she said, she was going down magnificently, and Esther reported that someone had formed an on-line "We love Sharon" fan-club which already had nearly a thousand members, and there'd been at least one marriage proposal.

She'd also used the shows to bring people up-to-date with Brendan, chronicling his ever-deteriorating prognosis but also the wonderful news of his impending marriage. American audiences loved a good romance, so when Esther told the story of Carol's meeting Brendan on his bike ride down America, their enforced separation, Carol's family's tragic deaths and her subsequent reunion with Brendan, whirlwind courtship and engagement, the show's audience rocketed, the ratings soared to record figures, and Brendan became, yet again, the most asked-after person in America. And the money flooded in.

★ ★ ★

Oblivious to all this, Brendan sat at home, muted by his tracheotomy, being fed through a tube, sick of being an invalid but anxious to get strong for his wedding.

Alan's story: October 12th 1999

It had been another boring day at the Ministry. Across the world, all kinds of exciting headlines were being made, as Alan had just heard on the 6pm news headlines. The UN had been marking the day when the population of the world had supposedly reached six billion. In Pakistan there'd been a bloodless coup, and the head of the army had ousted the Prime Minister. But, till that moment, life was as dreary as ever at 12 Murton Close. It was all, however, about to change.

Alan (Junior) appeared at 6.07pm, two minutes late for dinner.

"And where do you think you've been?" snarled Alan (Senior).

"I *know* where I've been," snarled back Alan (Junior).

Sarcasm and cheek were the usual modes of conversation between the two of them. Pauline sighed. Their son was now a gangly six-footer with no channel down which to discharge the testosterone swilling around his system. She felt like a referee most of the time.

"Well?" pressed Alan (Senior).

"Out with my mates!" spat Alan (Junior), grudgingly. Any answer was a concession, it seemed. "You're only jealous because you haven't got any."

"Less of your lip," warned Alan (Senior). There was an uneasy silence as they ate.

"Had a good day at school, dear?" asked Pauline.

"No. Slob had it in for me again."

Slob was the lovely nickname given to his history teacher, whose approach to teaching was dictation, intimidation and punishment rather than more trendy ideas of "getting alongside" and "making the subject come alive". Because Alan (Junior) hated history even more than he hated every other subject, he'd become a particular target for Slob's wrath and sadism.

"I've got a letter you have to sign."

Alan (Senior) held out his hand. "Give."

"Can't it wait till after dinner?" pleaded Pauline, anxious to avoid conflict at the table.

"Give," insisted Alan (Senior). His son slapped it down on the table.

He read the note, which demanded their attendance at a meeting the following evening to "discuss Alan's lack of progress", warning that he would do very poorly in his GCSEs "unless Alan changes his attitude".

"You're a real disappointment, you are," said Alan (Senior). "You'll never get anywhere in this world if you don't change your ways."

"Oh like you're the big achiever, eh?" goaded Alan (Junior). "Stuck in some crap little job in Benton, with all the other faceless bureaucrats! What have you got to show for all your hard work, eh? A fake tan and a pathetic life..."

And that was the day, and the moment, when Alan (Senior) finally lost it.

He reached across the table, grabbed his son's jumper with one fist and slapped him hard across his face with his other hand – so hard that it stung his hand. Alan (Junior) struggled to get away, but couldn't break his Dad's hold on his jumper. The dinner went flying as they grappled across the table.

Then Alan (Junior) hit his Dad – hard. Not a slap but a real punch, knocking him back and over his chair. As Alan (Senior) tried to clear his head, he heard the door slam.

"Good riddance!" he yelled, not that his son could hear him. "Don't ever come back until you apologise!"

"What do you mean?" yelled Pauline, uncharacteristically raising her voice to her husband. "It's *you* that needs to apologise. You're a brute and I've had enough of you. We'll be round at my Dad's."

And she walked out, picking up her coat. "I'll be back for my things," she yelled before she left.

Alan lay back on the floor, still sprawled in the remains of his dinner.

★ ★ ★

He cleared up the mess, depositing it all in the sink. She could sort it when she came back, he said to himself. He was sure that she *would* be back, when she'd had time to calm down and realise that they'd been too soft on their son. They needed to get him to knuckle down to his studies and make something of his life, instead of hanging around with those losers who dossed around on street corners smoking and intimidating the elderly. No son of his was going to fritter away all the care that'd gone into his upbringing.

He left for the Church Council meeting. It was the first one chaired by their new Minister, Brendan Priest. He looked OK, but Alan was a bit unsure how it would work out, because Brendan was the first Minister in ages not to come to them fresh out of college. He'd been somewhere near Manchester for his first two appointments, so came to them with a potentially dangerous amount of experience and know-how. Alan was keen to be there to check that everything started off on the right foot, and that this Brendan character wouldn't upset the applecart.

★ ★ ★

To his surprise, his home was in darkness when Alan walked back from the Church Council. It'd all gone quite well. This Brendan guy seemed to be OK, not wanting to change anything straightaway but "seeing how it all worked". Reports were circulating that he visited properly. He seemed to know what he was doing with the committee meetings, and his preaching wasn't too bad.

Yes, it'd all gone quite well.

But where was Pauline?

May 2013

Chapter 58

Louisa had a meeting with Dr. Aggarwal to monitor how the trials were going. It was now the start of the second respite period – in other words, the Famous Five had three weeks off before their last three-week burst of treatment. It wasn't so much that she needed to check that everything was going according to plan – but that she was interested in his observations at this relatively early stage in the process, and in his opinion of the Famous Five in particular.

Dr. Aggarwal was happy to reveal some of the details. "The particular chemotherapy regimen we're using in the Newcastle trials is DMC, of course, as with all the trials, but with the single-agent variation, cisplatin on its own.

"The trouble is, as you will recall, that cisplatin when used with radiotherapy causes severe side-effects, such as increased toxicity of the kidney, mouth and nervous system, as well as nausea and vomiting, all of which makes the treatment suitable only for patients who have normal renal function and are generally performing well.

"When cisplatin was combined with Celecoxib years ago, mainly in cervical cancer patients, the toxicity results were even worse, so it was quickly discontinued. The early research on DMC, however, has seemed to indicate that it might be rather different, so what we are hoping for is that we get at least as good, if not better tumour-management results with DMC plus cisplatin plus radiotherapy, but especially that we get far fewer toxic side-effects."

Louisa nodded. She understood most of what he'd said. "And what does it look like so far?"

Dr. Aggarwal blew out his cheeks. "Well, it's still very early days, but I have to say that here in Newcastle we're getting about the same sort of results as we would expect with Celecoxib, with perhaps a little less toxicity, but not much. What is exciting, though, is that three other centres, which share one of the multi-agent drug regimens, are showing a complete across-the-board absence of any toxicity whatsoever – so far. This is very encouraging, but, of course, the bottom line is what the scans reveal at the end of the last treatment. No sickness is fine, but if the tumours grow, then it's not much good."

"The down-side of our Famous Five, who are the only ones I can tell you about, is that the two worse outcomes amongst our group are patients who'd normally not be given cisplatin, because they both have kidney problems. We had hoped that DMC would make the cisplatin better for them, but it doesn't look very good so far. Let's wait and see what the scans say, though."

★ ★ ★

Brendan and Carol's quiet wedding with seven guests was looking ever more improbable – not because of Brendan's health, but because news had leaked out and the whole of North Tyneside, and further afield, seemed to be caught up in the drama of it all.

It was Esther's fault. The shows were proving so riveting that even the BBC national news had reported the next chapter of the Brendan Phenomenon. Somehow Brendan and Carol remained unaware of this, but Ruth had a hard job running to answer the phone before anyone else – to ward off reporters and requests for interviews, and preserve the illusion of the couple's low-key expectations.

Ben was constantly being asked for details of the plans, and was getting increasingly frustrated at the "no comment" response that he'd been told by Brendan to give. But Sarah Lanleigh knew the logistics of the day, and made sure that everybody knew the full timetable and that everybody was sworn to secrecy. So the secret was kept by all the thousands who got to know, most of whom oddly imagined that hardly anyone else knew.

★ ★ ★

Carol and Brendan were enjoying a quiet cup of tea one afternoon, which was about the only drink that Brendan could taste.

"Do you mind that everybody knows about the wedding?" she asked.

"No," said Brendan. "But I do find it funny that the family thinks we don't know."

"Yes, it's funny, isn't it? I haven't the heart to tell dear Ruth that she doesn't have to pretend that it's a wrong number when yet another reporter phones." They chuckled to each other.

"You know this enlargement of the tumour in your throat, Brendan..."

"Yes?"

"Is that the way, you know, that it's going to happen – that one day you just won't be able to breathe, and that'll be that?"

Brendan thought about it, quite interested in the question rather than bothered about it. "I don't think so, because if it got that bad they'd give me another tracheotomy to bypass the throat altogether."

"Oh yes, I hadn't thought of that."

They sipped their tea, contemplating.

"So how *will* it happen, do you think?" Carol asked.

"Well, sooner or later, if it hasn't already, it'll get into my lymph nodes and then it could go anywhere. So it'll probably be one of the major organs shutting down that'll finish me off."

"I see," said Carol, and they continued sipping their tea. "Biscuit?" she asked.

★ ★ ★

The attendance at the 10.08 Church had slipped a little since the end of Ben's Challenges, but they were packed every week all the same. Ben was content to take a bit of a back seat some Sundays, especially if it was a Local Preacher appointed on the Plan, at which services Ben usually led the first part of the worship then went off to help with Young Church. But whenever it was the Super or another of the more creative preachers, Ben preferred to engage in a dialogue with them instead of having them preach a formal sermon. It seemed to go down well whenever this happened, and the numbers swelled for those services.

The Sunday before The Wedding, Ben and the Super were the double-act, and they got the congregation thinking about being in control. It started out with some light-hearted banter about Brendan and Carol's expectation of a quiet wedding. "And we all know how quiet and low-key it's going to be, don't we?" asked Ben, to widespread mirth.

"But what about more serious upheavals..." asked the Super, "...like redundancy, illness or bereavement? What about the cancer which seems to be in control of Brendan now, rather than the other way round? What does the Bible have to say about that feeling of helplessness?"

"But in what way do we ever have control?" asked Ben. "I couldn't control where I was born, or whether I was brought up as a Christian, or a Muslim, or an atheist. Nor could I control who'd offer me a job or who'd fall in love with me or when and how I'll die? What control do any of us have, really?"

"Maybe our desire for control is an idol," said the Super. "Maybe the delusion of our own sovereignty is the greatest delusion of all."

Ben then did a magic trick. He took an A5 sheet, with the clear message printed on it "I AM IN CONTROL", ripped it into four pieces which he crammed into his mouth. He then reached into his mouth, and drew out a string of white paper, which turned yellow, then pink, and kept streaming out of his mouth in an unbroken cascade of paper, traversing all the colours of the rainbow and producing a long streamer which stretched across the church and halfway back again before Ben reached into his mouth and produced a few soggy scraps and threw them in the bin. "You see, you may think that you're in control and you know where possibilities end and where the limits are, but actually, with God, you never know what He'll do next – because a Christian is someone who gives up control of their life – and hands it over to God."

The congregation clapped, bemused by the trick but also captivated by the message.

"But what about Brendan?" asked the Super. "Does that mean that we should expect some sort of miracle to happen? Should we keep praying that God will heal him? If God's in control then surely he won't want Brendan to die so quickly, especially when he's just getting married?"

Ben paused, even though they'd scripted what he would say. He wanted to deliver it powerfully and persuasively. "Of course we should keep praying – but the best prayer of all is not "Do this", "Do that", but "May Your will be done, Lord – even though I don't understand it right now." Brendan's found love in his personal life, which is marvellous – but he's fully aware that he may not enjoy it for very long here – but in the sure and certain knowledge that it will endure forever, because love conquers death and illness, and everything else that life can throw at us. If you turn to Romans chapter 8, you'll see that that is precisely what St. Paul said to those beleaguered Christians in Rome, in the midst of their vulnerability and difficulty. Or turn to 1 Corinthians 13, which, by the way, they're having at their wedding on Thursday, which clearly assures us that "Love never ends"."

The Super took up the theme. "God isn't some sort of divine chess-player who moves pawns like us around at his whim and for his pleasure. Nor is he some sort of divine waiter who's here at our beck and call, to give us precisely what we've ordered. He's a God who is Almighty but never controlling, All-loving but never sentimental, All-powerful but never restricting our free-will. He *is* in control, but we still get to make choices – which is the best of all possibilities."

Ben gave the final flourish, stepping down into the congregation and gathering up the magic streamer. "Don't stay with the boring little "I am in control", which restricts you to the black and white, and the limited imagination we're given. Instead let God's multicolour, eternal stream of possibility go into you and come out of you, making the world a brighter, bigger place, and a place of beauty and wonder, as it's meant to be."

"So," said the Super, "If you were happening to pass by next Thursday, come in and be a part of a celebration of the endless possibility of love – *but don't tell Brendan that I invited you – it's a SECRET!*"

Chapter 59

Paul returned from South Africa excited and overwhelmed by what he'd seen. The opening ceremony of the Surgical Hospital in Gulu had been a grand occasion, even without Brendan, but he was even more excited about Watoto South Africa. The Cape Town church's opening celebration had been tremendous, and the plans were awesome. But so was the problem.

"It's appalling to hear the figures," he told Ruth. "I had no idea. The most recent figures they had were from way back in 2007, but even then the UN said that there were 33.2 million people with HIV/AIDS, and two thirds of them lived in Sub-Saharan Africa. About 3,000 people died of AIDS every day in sub-Saharan Africa in 2007, but there were about 5,000 new HIV infections every day. And the more recent estimates are that it's getting even worse than that. In South Africa alone, they reckon that there are 2.5 million orphaned children. It's like Uganda during the worst years, but so much bigger.

"They took us round some of the poorest areas in Cape Town – and then took us round the bit that all the Western tourists flock to, underneath Table Mountain. It was like two different planets. But the rich part of Cape Town is a cover-up, a distraction from the poverty, crime and disease which ravage the rest of the city and much of the nation."

"So what can Watoto do, realistically?" asked Ruth.

"Well, they've already bought and equipped the site for Bulrushes Cape Town. They reckon that last year alone, 550 babies were abandoned in the city – left outside childcare homes, in dumps, toilets, crèches and even in drains. So at least they're saving a few, even if the scale of the challenge is so vast."

"And what's your involvement going to be?" asked Ruth, thinking that it would become *her* involvement soon too, when Matthew was a bit bigger and was bottle-fed.

"Nothing," said Paul. "After the wedding, I'm due back in Gulu. The South African team will be completely independent. Unless, of course, they want to call in an expert..." Paul started strutting around like some of the goal celebrations he'd seen on Match of the Day. Ruth threw a cushion at him. "Or, maybe, two experts," he finished lamely.

★ ★ ★

The phone went yet again, but this time it was Carol who answered it, as she was just passing on the way to the kitchen. "Hello?" she said.

There was a pause. Then: "Hello, is that Mrs. Priest?"

"Not yet," she said, "But I soon will be! What do you want?"

"Oh," said the man on the other end, somewhat knocked out of his stride. "Is Brendan there?"

"Yes, he is, but he's asleep at the moment, so I don't really want to wake him. He had a bad night last night. Can I take a message?"

"Yes, sure. My name's Eric Tate from Open Doors, and I've got some good news for him. Can you ask him to phone me back?"

"Sure," said Carol, taking down the number.

When Brendan surfaced, at about 11.30, Carol told him about the phone call.

"I wonder what that's about," said Brendan. "He's a good bloke, is Eric. I had quite a lot to do with him in the preparations for my second journey – and he gave me lots of useful advice about the Persecuted Church. I'll give him a ring..."

"Hello, Eric? It's Brendan here."

"Hey, Brendan – how are you, mate? I heard that you were struggling, and we've been praying for you."

"Oh, I'm OK, but the cancer's terminal, so I don't know how long I've got left, but I'm about to get married!"

"Wow, congratulations. That's wonderful! When's the wedding?"

"The day after tomorrow – St. Brendan's Day."

"That's... fascinating," said Eric. "Can I come?"

Brendan was stunned. "Of course you can, my friend. It'd be lovely to see you. Are you sure that you can spare the time? It's a long way from Witney, you know..."

"I know," laughed Eric. "But, to be perfectly honest, I was hoping to come and see you anyway as soon as possible, with a friend."

Brendan now was intrigued. "Go on," he said.

"I've got Alimjan Yimit[77] with me. They've thrown him and his family out of China, and they've found their way to the UK. We're putting them up in a house in Witney for now, but he'd love to come and see you again."

Brendan was speechless. It was rare that any good news came out of China, as far as Christianity was concerned. And this news was both good and bad. To be expelled meant freedom for Alimjan and his family from the religious persecution which had cost them so much, but it left the small group of Christians in Kaxgar even smaller and weaker. Even so, it would be great to see them again.

"Please bring them all, if you can. The wedding's at 12.30..."

At the end of the conversation, Brendan put the phone down and turned to Carol. "That's another five for the wedding," he said. Then he told Carol all about the Yimits.

★ ★ ★

Louisa had cooked up what she thought was a Fantastic Idea. It came to her one night, as she sat in bed. "Ben, you know how Dad doesn't want a limo for his wedding?"

"Huh?" grunted Ben. It'd been a long day.

"Well, how are we all going to get there?"

"Haven't got a clue," said Ben. "I expect I'll drive our car, with Jack, Brendan and Carol in, and Ruth and Paul will go in their car, with you and Matthew."

"But it'd be good if we all arrived at once, wouldn't it?"

---

[77] Alimjan Yimit, a former food retailer, was sentenced in October 2009 to 15 years in prison for "divulging state secrets", a trumped-up charge which hid the fact that he'd been targeted because he'd converted from Islam to Christianity and was the leader of a house church. This real-life character features in my second work of fiction. In Brendan's second journey, he expresses the wish to visit Alimjan's wife, Gulnur, in their home in Kaxgar, a remote town in Xinjiang province in Western China, in order to draw attention to the plight of the Persecuted Church. In "Brendan and the Great Omission", page 254, when Brendan arrives at the house, he discovers that the Chinese authorities had just released Alimjan as a result of the bad publicity. Sadly, though, the reality is that Alimjan is, at the time of writing, still in prison, with ever-deteriorating health.

"Well, we'll be behind one another, I expect, so it's as good as."

Louisa sighed. Men – they just didn't have a clue. "Well, I've been thinking about afterwards. How is everyone going to get to the Grand?"

"The same way they get to Church. Anyway, there's only a few of us, aren't there?"

"Are you kidding? I've told them there'll be at least 30 of us in the restaurant. When you add up all these extra guests and folk from the Circuit, it'll be at least that. And no-one will want to drive, so that they can have a drink."

Ben took a big breath. "Are you sure, love? They did say that they wanted no fuss..."

"Don't be daft, Ben. We've got to show that we're doing our best for them. How about hiring a coach?"

"Well, OK, love. I suppose so. I'll have a look on the Internet tomorrow, see what I can arrange."

"No, I'll do it," said Louisa, a smile on her lips, "Leave it with me."

Chapter 60

Thursday May 16th dawned bright and fair, if a little cold. But the sun soon burnt off the early chill, and by 11 o'clock the North Tyneside coast was at its most glorious, with a full, buttery sun blurring through light clouds. Longsands was its usual golden strand of dog-walkers, joggers and squealing children impervious to the temperature, running and splashing in the long spreading wavelets.

But above the sand, on the grass opposite Brendan's house further towards Cullercoats Bay, the people were already gathering, flags ready to wave, cameras ready to capture anything that smacked of The Wedding. At 11.30, bang on time, the big red partly-open-top bus arrived with "City Discovery Newcastle" emblazoned on its bodywork. It was usually to be seen taking tourists round the sights of the riverside in Newcastle, but Louisa had hired it for the day. The back half of its upstairs was open, making it brilliant on a good day, and OK on a rainy one.

But today was a good day. By noon, the crowds were ten-deep, lining the pavements, anxious for the first sight of anyone who looked significant. And then, on cue at 12.05, the eight chief characters came out, to a great roar from the crowd. Brendan looked completely taken aback, both by the crowds and the bus, but allowed himself to be led slowly down the path by his beautiful bride. Carol had chosen a long flowery maxi dress in a deep cherry red colour, with a stylishly-cut jacket and a small fascinator in her hair. Brendan had referred to it as a pill-box hat, which produced a snort of contempt from Carol.

"Where have you been, Grandad? It hasn't been called *that* since Jackie Kennedy." But she gave him a kiss to show that she was only joking.

They got on the bus, and all eight of them climbed to the top deck – Brendan taking it nice and slow because he felt a bit wobbly, Carol taking it nice and slow because steep stairs weren't easy in the dress, and Ruth taking it nice and slow because she was carrying Matthew. Paul, Ben, Louisa and Jack bounced up the stairs as if they were Olympians receiving their medals. On the open deck they sat waving to the crowds.

With a honk of the horn, the bus set off, past the crowds lining the road, then turning up towards the Metro bridge and on towards the Broadway roundabout. The whole way there were people – cheering, waving, jumping up and down, running round the back of the onlookers trying to keep up with the bus, hanging out of their bedroom windows to get a good view. Cars tooted, dogs barked, seagulls swooped. They turned right past Cullercoats Methodist Church, where people had gathered on the steps to get a better view, and on along Broadway, both sides of the road lined with bystanders.

Brendan was amazed. Where had they all come from? What was happening? It wasn't meant to be like this. Yet he was thrilled too. Fancy all these people coming to wish him and Carol well. How wonderful was that! He felt his wobbliness subside, and a surge of strength coursed through him. He grinned and waved like a footballer showing off the trophy. Past Marden Bridge they rolled, up Hillheads towards the Ice Rink – and still there were crowds and crowds of people, just like when Whitley Bay won the FA Vase so many times in a row – but even more people, even more noise, even more flags waving and even more dads lifting their kids above their heads so that they could see.

On to Foxhunters, and the traffic was stopped on the roundabout to let the bus through, tooting horns and waving out of the windows. It was wall-to-wall people again all the way up past the hospital, and up to the top of Rake Lane, past Jacksons Farm and onto Jact Lane before New York village. So many people! The lane was narrow, but it had accommodated some strange vehicles over the previous months of Ben's Challenges. The bus was wide, and slowed as it edged past the single line of people squeezed up against the hedgerow, then they were round the corner, coming down into the village itself – more open spaces, more crowds of people, more cheering.

So much for a quiet wedding.

When the bus finally pulled up outside the Methodist Church, which was strewn with bunting, the crowds were massing, taking up every bit of grass in front of the church, with children stood on the wall balancing against their mother's shoulders. When the wedding party descended, a narrow gap was made for them to get to the front door, to reveal a church packed with people, a beaming Superintendent and a highly emotional Esther Blanchett.

"Oh my God!" she shouted, rushing past the Super to give Brendan a massive hug, unaware that it probably wasn't the best exclamation to use at the church door. "It's so good to see you, Brendan!"

Then she turned to a rather star-struck Carol. "And you, my dear, are one lucky lady. Congratulations!"

She swept Carol up in a massive hug too, crushing the flowers Carol had brought with her. The crowd roared, most of them seeing Esther for the first time, because she'd swept up in her limousine a few minutes earlier and been rushed inside by several "minders".

The film crew, of course, got it all. "Thought we weren't having a video," whispered Brendan as they got themselves ready for walking in.

"That ain't a video," said Carol. "It's Esther Blanchett, courtesy of Oracle Productions, from the mighty fine U.S. of A."

Then she whispered in his ear, "Just keep smiling, Brendan. This'll probably be seen by over a quarter of the entire world population..."

If he'd retained any vestige of nerves, that would have floored him. But Brendan had strength for the day, and led Carol slowly into the church, which was full of people, resplendent with more flowers than he'd ever seen in one place apart from the crem.

The worship band, Dead to the World, opened their version of Geraint Williams' classic "Happy Day"[78]. Brendan instantly recognised it as soon as the familiar beat opened on the honky-tonk piano. How did they know it was one of his all-time favourite songs? First, only the honky-tonk piano, then the guitars and drums came in, and a sax picked a high descant before the grinning pianist growled the words into the microphone like Satchmo himself:

"I just can't keep the smile off my face, I belong to the human race, it's my happy day; I just take one big look in your eyes, and I've lost myself in Paradise, it's my happy day; So I'm so happy, sitting on top of the world; Dreams come true, I'm telling you – she's a beautiful, beautiful, beautiful girl; Stars in my eyes, dreams in my pocket, my heart's beating, I just can't stop it, it's my happy day.

Everybody was swaying to the beat, as the musicians took over, in a wonderful jazz style, with the sax swooping high over the steady beat of

---

[78] From Williams' 1997 album "Watkins Bold as Love", transcribed from www.youtube.com/watch?v=GDjxs4Ykq6A.

the drum and the piano, the guitarists keeping the rhythm going throughout. Then the pianist leaned into the microphone again.

"It's been a long time a-coming, I'm gonna make the most of it; I'm well wrecked but like a brand new habit I just can't quit; Stars in my eyes, dreams in my pocket, my heart's beating, I just can't stop it, it's my happy day. I'm so happy! It's my happy day! Oh yes it's mine! Happy, happy day!"

The whole place erupted in massive applause and whistles. Brendan beamed at Carol, who had tears running down her face. Everyone was smiling.

The Super came to the front. "Ladies and gentlemen, can I remind you that Brendan wanted a quiet wedding..." Everybody roared with laughter, and cheering could be heard from outside. "...So we'll give him one, won't we?"

"Nooooo!" came the response.

"But seriously, my friends, we know that this is a very special day for Brendan and Carol, a very poignant, proud and wonderful celebration of God's love, and we'll reflect that in our short time together. I call upon the best man, Revd. Jack Turner, to read the lesson."

Jack read it slowly, pausing at "Love never ends", and again at the penultimate verse: "Now we see but a poor reflection; then we shall see face to face. Now I know in part; then I shall know fully, even as I am fully known." It was a passage about love continuing into and beyond death, and held a special significance in the light of Brendan's illness – and everyone understood.

The Super announced that he wouldn't be preaching a sermon – to which the congregation roared their approval, but then proceeded to talk for a couple of minutes about St. Brendan's Day, commemorating Brendan's bold, trusting journey out into the stormy sea, obeying God's call. He left it at that – again, everyone understood its poignancy.

Then, the vows, clearly spoken, from the heart. When the Super announced that they were "husband and wife", everyone roared once again.

Carol leaned across to Brendan and whispered, "He's forgotten the "You may now kiss the bride"!"

Brendan whispered back, "That only happens in America and in soap operas!" – but he gave her a quick peck anyway.

"Now," said the Super, "My original instructions were that there wouldn't be enough of us to sing... (more cheers) ...but the band have been practising hard a familiar wedding hymn, which I think would be very suitable before we sign the registers. Please stand."

The band played a simple introduction to Love Divine, before letting rip when the singing began. Nobody had the words, but everybody seemed to know them. The band were great, with a funky little interlude between verses, and when they came to the final verse, and its final stanza (Changed from glory into glory / till in heaven we take our place / Till we cast our crowns before thee / Lost in wonder, love and praise), there wasn't a dry eye in the village.

It was only while they were signing the registers that Brendan spotted Eric and the Yimits in the second row on the other side of the aisle, sitting behind Paul and Ruth, and just along from Melanie and a stocky fellow looking uncomfortable in his suit and tie. That must be her Alan, he assumed, but thought no more about it, because he wanted to greet the Yimits. He got up from his seat, even though it was in the middle of the signing, and crossed the church to give Alimjan a huge embrace – chatting excitedly with them and Eric, until Eric pointed him back to the table.

After the signing was completed, the band struck up with a "soft reggae" version of the Wedding March, which contained yet more incredible musicianship but was more a wedding bop than a march. Esther particularly appeared to be enjoying it, and grabbing hold of Arnold Joseph's arm, followed the wedding party, the bemused Yimits, and various others out of the church and straight onto the bus, standing with them on the open deck waving to the crowds. The empty limousine followed as the bus set off to the Grand Hotel, with its elegant facade overlooking the best view in England.

The Grand hadn't seen anything like it since Laurel and Hardy stayed there. The restaurant was packed, not just with the thirty places on the long table but every other table taken up by those smart enough to anticipate the possibility of gate-crashing the reception, for the original idea of having the normal lunchtime menu had never been revoked, despite everything else being changed, and the restaurant was still open to the public. So a further eighteen tables were taken, and the poor staff were running round like mad fools trying to take orders from everyone whilst smiling at the film crew who'd also taken up their positions.

It was gone 4pm by the time some of them were served their main course, but no-one seemed to mind. By that point, Brendan had gone upstairs for a rest, but no-one minded that, either. Esther tapped her spoon on the table and called for a toast to the bride and groom, "wherever he's sloped off to", and then announced that she would be happy to pay the restaurant bill. No-one minded that either.

In fact, no-one minded anything. It was just a happy, happy day.

Chapter 61

Brendan sat in bed at 3am the next morning, wide awake, contentedly watching Carol's chest gently going up and down as she slept next to him, her arm draped across his leg, a tendril of her hair softly wafting with her breath. Life's good, he thought to himself.

Yesterday had been exhausting, but exhilarating. His original thought – about slipping into church for a quiet wedding – had been silly, and what had happened had been so much better. To see all his friends again had been amazing – especially the Yimits. Eric had put the family up in the Grand overnight, with Esther (as ever) offering to pay the bill, so Eric stayed there too. It'd been great to meet them again, eighteen months after being hauled out of their house by the Chinese police and imagining that he'd never see them again. Now he knew that he wouldn't – but that was OK...

Everything was OK.

He looked down at his scrawny body, with its peculiar pot-belly which made him look like a thin Buddha. I might not have hypochondria any more, he smiled to himself, but I've got everything else. His throat now hurt constantly, despite the morphine patches. His gums ached; his earache made his jaw hurt; his lungs laboured to breathe; he felt like he had an alien eating away at him from the inside, getting bigger and bigger like a slimy octopus wriggling its tentacles along his internal pathways.

Yet everything was still OK.

Carol mumbled in her sleep, and he fondly stroked her hair. She smiled as she slept, and snuggled in closer to his leg. Yes, everything was OK.

He reached across for a handful of cards that he'd piled on his bedside table, with boxes of others by the side of the bed, according to his request. He spent a happy hour skimming through them, smiling at some of the names, puzzled by others which meant nothing to him. One was from his first wife Jenna and her husband. He smiled as he mouthed this new status for Jenna – first wife, not ex-wife, for now he had a new wife, and he looked down at Carol proudly. They were wishing him and Carol every happiness – which seemed to bring an extra little dollop of healing to his memories. He sat back, reminiscing. He and Jenna had had a good few years together, and had been good for each other, but somehow after the girls were at school they'd just drifted apart without realising it until it was too late. Still, it'd been a good divorce, if that were possible – no animosity or bitterness, and he'd genuinely wished her all the best when she got together with Homer. Yes, everything was OK...

He opened a card from Melanie and Alan, and smiled when he saw that she'd wished them "successfully saggy coccyxes" on their wedding night. He wasn't quite sure what that meant, but didn't really care. Melanie had done him proud, retrieving his power of speech so that he could say his vows and tell Carol how happy he felt – and nothing else mattered. He tried to remember what Alan looked like, imagining some vague resemblance to someone he'd once known, but the thought fluttered away as he read more cards.

★ ★ ★

Later that day, Melanie popped in to see how he was and tell him that she thought there was no more she could do for him. "You've been one of my best patients and one of my most successful outcomes," she announced. "And it was lovely for me to have a day off yesterday so I could come to the wedding."

"It was good to see what your fiancé looked like," said Brendan. "I'm sure I've seen him somewhere before."

"His Mam and Dad live in Jact, so maybe you saw him when you worked there."

"Did he say that he'd seen me before?" asked Brendan.

"Only on the telly," said Melanie.

Brendan urged her to keep popping in to see him, even though professionally she was writing him off.

"When's the wedding? Can I come?"

"July 13th, and of course you can. I'd love you to come." she answered.

"A good day for it," Brendan declared. "That's Albert Ayler's birthday."

"Who?"

"Albert Ayler, the great American sax player. You know – "Spiritual Unity"[79]? "Ghosts"?"

Melanie shook her head. "Never heard of him."

Brendan sighed. Perhaps it was him who was a bit out of touch, not Melanie. "Albert Ayler was the best sax player ever, apart from maybe Charlie Parker. He was the king of improvisation. Let me play you "Ghosts"..."

He ferreted around for the CD he wanted, then sat back as the harsh tone of the tenor sax filled the room. After a simple tune, the percussion and bass came in and Melanie wrinkled her nose. "Bit weird and random, isn't it? I prefer something I can hum to."

Brendan smiled. "It's known as free jazz, but I know what you mean. It's an acquired taste, I suppose. Try this one..." He plucked another CD from his jazz collection and got the right track. "You'll recognise this." Light piano music tinkled into the room. Brendan said, "It's called "Goin' Home"[80] and it's my favourite bit of music ever, I think."

They settled back, then suddenly a wonderfully mellow, rich-vibrato tenor sax burst out the melody. They listened to the whole piece, then Brendan sighed with pleasure.

"I like that," said Melanie, brightly. "He's good, isn't he? What's he called again?"

---

[79] Spiritual Unity is the title of an album by the Albert Ayler Trio, recorded in 1964. It features two versions of "Ghosts", the track which the critics described as "shockingly different" and which brought him to international attention.

[80] "Goin' Home" is the first track on the album of the same name, also recorded in 1964, comprising a jazz duet version of a well-known Negro Spiritual, with Call Cobbs on piano. An upload is at www.youtube.com/watch?v=en-kFaxgg3Q

Chapter 62

During the first week of their marriage, Brendan failed to shake off his exhaustion. He was thankful that he'd been strong on the day, but recognised that the excitement and extra effort had taken it out of him. He slept most afternoons when Carol was awake, but then struggled to sleep at night when Carol was asleep.

Towards the end of the following week, Brendan could sense that his throat was getting tighter, and it was harder work to take each breath. Sometimes, he heard a soft whistle as he breathed, like air escaping from a balloon, but he didn't mention it to anyone. At night he'd had a few episodes where the breath seemed to snag in his throat, and not quite get down to his lungs. After an initial panic each time, he'd managed to catch his breath without disturbing Carol, but it didn't augur well.

Then one night, he suddenly found that he couldn't breathe at all, and shook Carol awake, pointing to his throat as he turned pink, then red, then purple, before collapsing on the pillow. Carol shrieked and shouted for Louisa, who came in and tried to revive him, but couldn't get any air in. Frantically, she tried to unblock his airway, but there didn't seem to be a blockage as far down as her fingers would reach.

"Phone the ambulance! Quick!" she shouted, to a shocked Carol, who rushed out of the room.

Louisa calmed herself. She knew what she had to do. She'd seen it done a few times, and had asked Dr. Aggarwal a few weeks ago what to do if the need arose. He'd given her what she needed, but warned her that she should only do it in a dire emergency – the best option would be to rush her Dad into hospital before an emergency occurred. But it was too late for that now. She ran to the bathroom where she'd stashed what she needed, washed her hands, knelt astride her Dad's unconscious body, and set to work quickly.

Carol came in as Louisa was about to make the incision. "What are you doing?" she screamed.

"Putting a tube in," she answered. "It's our only hope. Can you help me?"

At least she knew where to go in, because the scar from his previous tracheostomies was still pinky-white, just underneath his Adam's Apple. Louisa ripped the sterile bag with the tube in and handed it to Carol, then took a deep breath and made the cut with the scalpel across the scar, trying to gauge the half-inch depth which Dr. Aggarwal had advised. There was surprisingly little blood, but Carol dabbed it away so that Louisa could see what she was doing. Louisa grabbed the small tube and pushed it into the incision to a depth of about an inch, and breathed into the tube with two short breaths. She waited a few seconds, then gave another short breath, and was rewarded with a strange noise and the sight of her Dad's chest going up, then down, then up, then down. He moved, as if uncomfortable, and Louisa got off the bed and talked gently to him as he regained consciousness, aware that she was shaking with the release of adrenalin after the event. Carol was sobbing next to her and stroked Brendan's face as his eyes fluttered and opened.

The door-bell rang and suddenly there were paramedics in the room, who stopped as they saw the tube sticking out of Brendan's throat.

"Have you just done that?" said the paramedic, seeing the blood on Brendan's pyjamas. Louisa nodded.

The paramedic looked intently at the tube, checked Brendan's breathing, and looked up. "Bloody 'ell," he said. "Some job, that! Well done, hinny. Let's get him to hospital."

Alan's Story: September 1ˢᵗ 2004

Alan and Pauline were driving home after seeing Spider-Man 2 at the UCI cinema at Silverlink. It'd been released earlier that summer[81], but was still running at one of the smaller screens. Today was their 36ᵗʰ wedding anniversary, and they'd been out for an early meal at Frankie and Benny's too. Alan was a bit annoyed when he realised that there wasn't a Happy Hour before 6.30pm, so it had cost him a bit more than he'd budgeted for, but they'd had a pleasant evening, and Alan had particularly enjoyed the film.

Pauline and Alan had been living in the same house again for three years now, after a two-year partial separation while Alan (Junior) was failing all his GCSEs and then dossing around for a year before he decided what he wanted to do in life. He and his Mam had lived at his grandparents in Jact, while Alan stayed on his own in Murton Close at the other end of Jact. After a few months completely separated, however, Pauline had sought some negotiated reconciliation – not because she particularly harboured any thoughts of intimacy again with Alan, but because she felt sorry for him and wanted him not to fall apart completely.

Alan (Senior) had reacted badly to the big bust-up, refusing to apologise or make the first move towards any reconciliation. Alan (Junior) had been glad to be shot of the animosity, as had Pauline, and living with her parents turned out to be helpful for them too as they were getting on a bit now and Pauline's help was very welcome. Outwardly, though, Alan and Pauline had agreed to "keep up appearances", so no-one knew any different at the Methodist Church or in the village. This was achievable mainly because they'd never particularly had much to do with anyone in Jact. Well, Alan hadn't, anyway.

When Alan (Junior) left school and started kipping on his mates' floors and appearing less and less at his grandparents' home, Pauline spent more time around at her marital home, tidying, washing and

---

[81] Its UK release was July 15ᵗʰ, and crowds packed the cinemas to watch it at the start of the school holidays.

ironing, but sleeping back at her parents. When Alan (Junior) came back to his grandparents' house one night and announced that he was joining the Army, Pauline saw it as the right time to start negotiations about her re-entry to 12 Murton Close on a permanent basis.

So they'd resumed their marriage on roughly the same basis as before, but with Alan fully aware that he'd got to put more into the relationship or Pauline would be gone for good. She didn't feel any loyalty to Alan beyond what he could earn from now on. His continued estrangement from Alan (Junior) was pretty much the unforgivable sin in her book, and neither father nor son seemed able or willing to contemplate peacemaking. So she demanded that Alan gave more help around the house, spent more time with her doing things together, and paid less attention to the Methodist Church.

And that's what he'd done. The spark had definitely gone out in many respects, and he'd become a sullen, passive old man, even though he was only just in his sixties. He began to feel old. Over the last three years his spirits had slowly settled into a rut of domestic routine, more pettiness and occasional petulance at the church, and an antisocial surliness which brought further isolation.

Alan had not been going out to the church so much in the evenings, because the number of meetings had greatly reduced due to the age of most of the members and the corresponding lack of church midweek activities. Brendan, the Minister, had pushed for the introduction of something called the Alpha Course, which apparently was all the rage, but he and Sarah had managed to get it voted out at Church Council, on the grounds that they'd tried something like that before and it hadn't worked. Sarah found out that it was headed up by some ex-barrister in a plush part of London[82], who talked a lot about the squash club and his posh friends and, delivering what she believed to be the most telling blow in her argument, she concluded with a flourish that "he speaks in a posh London accent". Alpha didn't really stand a chance in Jact.

Alan was quietly impressed that Brendan had taken his defeat manfully and carried on regardless, doing what he was supposed to do, which, of course was to service the needs of the church community: visiting, preaching, leading the Bible Study, talking at the Women's Fellowship etc. And things had trundled on without too many hiccups

---

[82] The Alpha Course is indeed headed up by Nicky Gumbel, but the impact of his talks seems to have been felt across all parts of British society, including North Tyneside.

– and without too many meetings, which kept Pauline happy.

Yes, life was OK, really.

The film they'd just seen, Spider-Man 2, curiously and unexpectedly moved Alan. At the start of the film, Peter Parker found himself in a mess, with which Alan instantly empathised, recognising that his own life had been in a bit of a mess until they'd sorted it out again three years ago. Peter was estranged from his heartthrob Mary Jane and his best friend Harry, and Spider-Man was getting a bad press and everything was falling apart. So he gave up his super-hero role as Spider-Man and devoted himself to his own selfish agenda, only to rediscover his calling when he rescued a little girl from a fire.

It dawned on Alan with an unprecedented flash of revelation that this was a commentary on his own struggles, and particularly that he was being tested by all that had happened to him, for a bigger purpose. He too, like Peter in the film, had somehow managed to keep hold of who he was meant to be. This was not found in his puny job at the Ministry. Nor was it even his relationship with Pauline, though he was heartened that when Mary Jane saw Peter/Spider-Man as he truly was she'd decided to take the risk of staying with him at the end, no matter what. His true identity, Alan knew, was to be found in his public responsibility and duties as Church Steward. This was his vocation, his destiny, his reason for being..

At the end of the film there was a touching scene where Mary Jane promised that she would wait at home for Peter as he went off as Spider-Man to save the world, and Alan found himself, to his great embarrassment, having to wipe away a tear. Pauline thankfully didn't seem to have noticed.

Yes, Alan reflected as he drove home, he'd made a mess of a lot of things, but in his role as Church Steward, if nowhere else, he felt that he was doing something useful.

June 2013

Chapter 63

The Famous Five had, indeed, achieved considerable notoriety through the six "See Esther" shows broadcast so far. Some had been taken to the hearts of the viewers, like Darren, Eric (who'd been getting noticeably weaker show by show) and, of course – more than any of them – "Sharon from Shields". Dawn had her fans as well as her critics, but there was a near-unanimous dislike of Alan who, even though he was obviously getting worse, received no public sympathy whatsoever.

He didn't seem to care, and Lilian wondered if, in fact, he had any idea how badly he was coming across to people. He'd had to have more strings of lumps removed from his nose and forehead, and looked more and more like people in the old seat-belt adverts who'd gone through the windscreen. Lilian asked him at the start of his last burst of treatment about the skin cancer.

"I've had over forty operations so far. My back's where it started, then my neck, my chest, my head. All over, really."

"What do you think, Alan – are you just unlucky?"

"No, not really," said an unusually reflective Alan. "It's my own fault, I suppose – not that they told you about it at the time."

"What do you mean?"

"Sunbathing all the time, and we were one of the first families in the North East to get a sun-bed. Cost me hundreds. I was always proud of my tan." He sighed, then snarled. "Bloody sun-bed people, I should sue them for all they've got."

★ ★ ★

On June 3rd, Eric died.

Lilian and the film crew went to see the widow, who sat there in her beautiful sitting room, twisting her hankie as she spoke to Lilian.

"I suppose it just wasn't meant to be," Doreen said. "He'd had a kidney out last year, but they thought that they'd caught it in time. Then it re-appeared on his neck, and that's why he was put on the trials, but it was obviously too late."

They filmed a brief scene at the funeral, but it wasn't really the sort of footage Esther wanted for her show, so it never appeared.

★ ★ ★

Brendan had returned from the hospital with a now-permanent tube in his neck. The tumour in his throat was now extending down and around his gullet with some rapidity and the oncologist said that it was too risky to take the tube out.

He'd gone a bit yellow, which they said was a sign that there might be a problem with his liver. He was having pain in his back too, which indicated kidney trouble, they said. It was almost like Berlin in the final months of the Second World War – which enemy would get there first?

Carol remained unswervingly chirpy, always taking trouble with her appearance so that she'd look her best for him, always chatting to him about anything and everything that she'd done, about the news, about Paul in Gulu, about the latest little milestone Matthew had just achieved, about the weather...

Brendan was unable now to eat through his mouth, so he was once again on the Jevity gruel, and was getting dramatically thinner day by day. He looked awful, but everyone kept up the facade that life was normal.

It became more and more difficult for Brendan to pee normally, and he got in great pain one evening, so the doctor catheterised him. This relieved the immediate problem, but the pain persisted, and the next doctor to call put him on a morphine drip and warned them that the time was close when Brendan ought, for everyone's sake, to consider going into a hospice.

★ ★ ★

Jack visited, and spent an intense hour talking with Brendan about spiritual matters.

"Are you scared, Brendan?" he asked.

Brendan smiled. "I've spent my whole ministry telling people near to death that they shouldn't be afraid, without ever knowing whether I'd be afraid or not. Now I know. There's nothing to fear about being dead, it's the process of getting from here to there that worries me a bit. I'm not very good at pain."

Jack grimaced. "Nor am I. I suppose that what I hope for is that it'll be somehow dignified, and that I won't die feeling that I'd let the side down."

"Yes," said Brendan. "You've got it. Exactly that."

"Are you still pleased that you and Carol got married?"

"Yes," said Brendan without needing to think about it. But then he paused. "I'm disappointed that she'll have to go through more grief, after everything else that she's been through. But I'm not worried about her. She's tough, is Carol. And she's really taken to the rest of the family, so I hope she'll want to stay."

"It's rather a wonderful story – the decision to stand up for love, no matter what."

"I feel myself very blessed. It's all through God's grace – every chapter of the story."

Jack wondered if he understood fully what Brendan meant. "Do you mean the two of you finding each other again?"

Brendan shook his head. "No, not just that – though that was amazing, even if it was in the midst of such tragedy. I mean the whole thing: the way my ministry has gone; the doldrums which led to the call to do the journeys; the risks I took and the dangers I got myself into, only for me somehow to escape; and now the cancer; the chance to help Carol in her time of need, and her to help me in mine; and this interesting thing called dying."

Jack looked askance at him. Interesting?

Brendan continued, thinking as he went. "The Bible story all the way through is about grace, isn't it? From Adam and Eve not being slaughtered after their rejection of God, through Moses' call after murdering an Egyptian, David's kingship even after his adultery and murder, Israel's rehabilitation after exile, then in the New Testament Peter's commission after his denial, Paul's ministry after persecuting the church."

Jack nodded. "God's always there to rescue people, even if they think he's abandoned them."

"But why does He do it?" asked Brendan.

Jack thought, and got his Bible out. "I'm looking at Amos 4, the bit where Amos lists all the punishments God brought on the rebellious Israelites. And there's a constant refrain: "..."Yet you have not returned to me," declares the Lord." Maybe that's the underlying purpose of it all."

Brendan nodded. "And God will do anything which will point people to their need to return to Him. Like giving me such a high profile, so that I could speak about Jesus' call to follow God's agenda. Like this cancer, which has brought so much generosity from people, and may even bring some progress in the fight against cancer. Just as the Cross seemed like a defeat, but wasn't, so my dying won't be a defeat either.

"There's grace even in the loss of everything precious, such as the love I've found with Carol. Even that, a wonderful gift from God, is not God. Sometimes people think it is, and then when their loved one dies, they don't have any sense of God any more. So even the loss of love is a gift of grace, to point us to the one certain truth, which is that it is God who rescues us, who gives us meaning, who is eternal."

"What about your regrets, Brendan?" asked Jack. "Do you have any?"

"Course I have. I regret not meeting Carol sooner. I regret not being more faithful in my ministry, not taking enough risks, not spending more time with my children."

"So where's the grace in our regrets?"

"In showing us how much we're in need of God's rescue."

"And now, as you get weaker?" asked Jack, gently.

"Grace again, for so often people, especially blokes, think that they're invincible and self-sufficient. It's good to be dependent on others, to help us to realise our need of God. I always liked reading Deuteronomy 8 to the folk at Jact: "You may say to yourself, "My power and the strength of my hands have produced this wealth for me." But remember the Lord your God, for it is He who gives you the ability to produce wealth and so confirms his covenant.""

"Yes," said Jack. "I've used that passage a few times too. What about dying?"

"Full of grace. Physical stuff is transient, shot through with temporariness and decay. Dying confirms that, and points us to the spiritual stuff that's eternal, beyond, yet interwoven into the physical so we can trace it, follow it, pursue it, grasp at it, and finally realise it for what it is."

"So it's all about us seeing, isn't it?" asked Jack.

"Yes," Brendan agreed, sinking back into his pillow. "That's the biggest grace-gift of all: seeing. "Now we see but a poor reflection but then we shall see face to face..."[83]

---

[83] 1 Corinthians 13:12

Chapter 64

Louisa went to see Dr. Aggarwal again to catch up with the latest feedback. She knew about Eric's death, and wondered whether this was a significant set-back.

"It's very sad, obviously," said Dr. Aggarwal. "But it doesn't really tell us that much, except that DMC isn't in itself a magic cure for cancer. But we knew that anyway. Eric's previous history meant that he was always less likely to achieve a beneficial outcome from the trials, so what's happened isn't a huge surprise."

"What about the rest of them?"

"Well, seven of them seem to be responding positively to the chemoradiotherapy, in the sense that they're not struggling with toxic side-effects. If they'd been on cisplatin without the DMC, we'd expect a higher vulnerability to nausea. We won't be able to make any definitive conclusions, though, until we get the scan results back at the start of July, when we can compare and analyse the results from the other trials around the world."

"So Eric, of course, and Alan are two of the three who are not responding so well, is that right?"

"Yes, those two plus one of the other five who didn't want to be on television. We're a bit worried about Alan, because his skin cancer seems to be advancing rapidly, and it's probably affecting the outcome of the trial in his case too. His skin cancer is SCCA of the skin, so there are all kinds of links, but the onset of so many keratoacanthomas is not a good sign."

"Are they the lumps?"

"Yes, but they're actually carcinoma mounds with a central crater. They spread quickly and need excising as soon as they appear."

"So what's the prognosis?"

"Impossible to say, though probably not very good. But we won't know quite how he'll die, or when, as these keratoacanthomas won't kill him off even though they're quite disfiguring. It's pretty rare for someone to have Stage 4, or *spreading* SCCA from skin cancer, but sadly, that's what Alan seems to have got."

"What's the latest on the other centres?"

"Well, without getting too excited, we're still getting a complete absence of toxicity with all fifty patients on one of the multi-agent regimens. The way the trial was organised was to split the four different regimens between the twenty centres, with all ten patients in five centres sharing the same regimen. So it's easier to see and compare results, because each centre makes reports at the end of each three-week burst of treatment. One of the other multi-agent regimens is showing good toxicity results too, so at least those patients' quality of life is better than it would have been without the trials. Let's hope that the scan results give us some benefits on quantity as well as quality of life."

★ ★ ★

Lilian was revelling in her new-found fame. She was still doing an odd shift at the Freeman, but was finding it more difficult to concentrate because most of the patients kept asking her about Esther and the show. She'd had a letter from Oracle asking if she'd be prepared to come to America at the end of her present contract with them, as there were "a few other on-camera possibilities we're considering." She'd been completely overwhelmed with the idea of being a TV star, and went around telling everybody that she was about to go off to Hollywood. She was not only 2,000 miles out, but hadn't quite appreciated that film and TV were two entirely separate entities. And it was only a tentative approach by Oracle, not an ironclad promise, but she believed nonetheless that that was now her destiny.

It didn't affect her on-screen performance, though. The penultimate interviews were at the end of their treatments, quizzing the four survivors on how they thought they'd done as if they were students at the end of their finals. It was potentially pretty final, of course, but that was the only similarity. There was no skill or knowledge involved – that was part of the awfulness of cancer. It was all so dreadfully random. Even the trials were random – their selection for it, the arbitrary choice of the drug regimen, the timing of it in the development of their cancer, etc. But Lilian breezed through these difficulties with the panache of a seasoned operator, with the peculiar but compelling combination of the physical appearance of a human fridge-freezer and the warm devotion of a mother labrador brooding over her puppies.

She didn't beat about the bush, asking the hard questions of staff and patients alike, but kept whispering to the camera in a way which conveyed how deeply she felt every rise or fall in their fortunes. She'd found something which gave her a sense of fulfilment, just like when she'd first started nursing thirty years ago. But she also knew that there were thousands of nurses, but very few TV presenters. God really had been good to her, and she couldn't stop thanking Him for rescuing her from herself.

★ ★ ★

Everything settled down at the 10.08 Church surprisingly quickly after The Wedding. Jack was back ten days later, leading worship with Ben. He told people what Brendan had said about grace, and about God saving us from ourselves. He didn't say it quite as fluently as Brendan, but he thought that it'd gone rather well. The band produced a funky version of Amazing Grace at the start of worship, then at the end did a reprise which was the Chris Tomlin version with the chorus "My Chains Are Gone". It was magnificent, and dozens of people stayed for prayer and ministry afterwards.

★ ★ ★

Melanie finally met her future father-in-law. She'd been chatting with Alan about the wedding and they decided to go to Murton Close to confirm some of the arrangements. Melanie's parents were easy-going about everything, but Alan was less confident about his Dad in particular.

"He's a miserable git. He threw me out when I was 15 and I haven't looked back since."

"What had you done to make him so mad?" she asked.

"Nothing much. Just normal teenage stuff, like staying over at me mates' and wagging school, being late for dinner, stuff like that. Then one day he hit me so I hit him back, and that was that."

"And you haven't seen him since?"

"I've seen him, but I've never spoken to him, nor him to me. I've always got on well with me Mam though."

"So what do you think your Dad's going to say if we go round there?"

"Dunno. Don't really care either. He can come to the wedding if he wants, but I wouldn't be upset if he didn't."

When, a few days later, they did go round, Alan (Senior) was just about to go to Outpatients for his 41st excision. He'd got a massive keratoacanthoma along his lower lip, at which Melanie found it impossible not to stare, as it went right across his face like a speed bump.

"Nice to meet you," she said, shaking hands with him but fascinated by the scars and the new additional feature. Alan (Junior) stayed back. Alan (Senior) grunted, got in the car, and drove off.

Chapter 65

Alan's latest keratoacanthoma was one of the biggest the doctors had ever seen, and necessitated a major operation and a skin graft from his backside to fill the gaping hole left where his lip had been. Later, they said, he'd have to have plastic surgery to rebuild another lip.

When he heard, Alan (Junior) thought it was hilarious. "He's always talked through his backside, so this shouldn't be any different for him."

Melanie told him off, even though she appreciated his wit.

It meant that all the wedding arrangements could be discussed only with Pauline, who was quite happy with everything and looking forward to the day. "It's about time we had something good to look forward to," she declared. "I do hope your Dad's well enough to go, but I'll be worried that he might say the wrong thing or draw attention away from you two – now that he's been on the telly."

"Don't worry. Mam," said Alan. "Everybody hates him, so no-one'll take any notice of him."

Melanie told him off again, because Pauline had been obviously hurt by what he'd said, even though it was true. Melanie got Pauline smiling when she fixed a day to go off with her to search for an outfit, and invited her to her hen party.

"Oh my," said Pauline. "I've never been to one of them. Won't everybody be much younger than me?"

"My Mam's going, so you won't be the oldest. She'll look after you. Or, more likely, you'll have to look after her – she gets drunk after a couple of Babychams."

They had a good girly giggle and everything seemed to be going rather well – as long as Alan (Senior) didn't find a way of wrecking everything.

★ ★ ★

On June 17th Brendan felt a burning pain in his throat and his already scratchy voice suddenly disappeared. It didn't gradually peter out. One minute it was there; the next, it had gone. And it never came back.

The following day, back at the oncologist, he was poked, prodded and scoped, then sent for his umpteenth scan, which revealed that the tumour had reached and eaten its way through the recurrent laryngeal nerve, one of the functions of which was to supply nerves to the muscles controlling the vocal cords. One side must have been severed recently to produce Brendan's huskiness, but when the whole nerve collapsed, that was the end of Brendan's voice altogether. There was nothing they could do.

The oncologist gently explained that this was a bad sign. "The recurrent laryngeal nerve is part of the vagus nerve which is one of the super-highways running from the brain to the major organs. As and when the tumour attacks the vagus nerve, you'd still survive, but it passes very close to both the carotid and subclavian arteries and to the aortic arch, and as and when the tumour ruptures any of those, I'm afraid death will be very quick."

Brendan looked him straight in the eye. "And how long do you think that will be?"

The oncologist paused, but didn't duck the question. "The cancer seems to be advancing aggressively, so I think we're probably talking weeks rather than months, maybe not many weeks. Or any time. I really don't know. I'm very sorry."

* * *

Brendan was taken home by Carol, speechless, both physiologically and psychologically. It had really hit him hard – never to speak again. Him, a preacher, unable to utter a word...

"Ah well, Brendan," sighed Carol, as she recognised his distress, and interpreted it correctly. "What was it St. Francis said: "Tell others about Jesus at all times – and, if necessary, use words."[84]? "Well, you can't use words now except by writing them down, so you'll have to carry on doing it in other ways. Deal?"

Brendan nodded, smiled and shook hands on the deal.

He found, over the next few days, that the pain got sharper, and his morphine dose was strengthened, but it only seemed to dull the edge of

---

[84] This quotation is frequently attributed to St. Francis, but its provenance is uncertain.

the pain rather than eradicate it. He was producing no urine at all, even with the catheter, and his breathing grew even more laboured.

On June 21st the doctor recommended that Brendan should go into the hospice, as his pain management needed constant attention, which couldn't happen at home. There were many tears that night, but Brendan settled quickly into a small two-bed room at the Marie Curie Hospice in Elswick. The other bed was empty, which meant that Carol could stay with him until he finally fell asleep in the early hours. She crept out, crying, and drove home in floods of tears. But she was back first thing the following morning.

★ ★ ★

Ruth was struggling now with what was happening. Knowing that her Dad wouldn't be coming back home was a frightening thought. Knowing that he was being cared for by Carol and the hospice staff rather than her was a relief but also a sadness. She'd enjoyed being able to care for him, even though it was pretty exhausting because of Matthew.

She reflected on the last few hectic months. Carol had suddenly sprung into their lives – and it had been wonderful, once Carol had got through the initial horror of what happened back in Texas. She'd not only been able to give her Dad such joy at the end of his life – she'd also become a real help around the house: cooking; cleaning; looking after Matthew; shopping. As and when she lost Brendan as well, it'd be really tough, but at least she now had a family around her once again. There was no question about her not staying – she was part of the family.

She shared some of her feelings with Paul that night, who'd just come back from Gulu, where he was working hard with plans for a goat farm (of all things).

"I'm really proud to be leading the Trust with you," she said. "It's great what we've been able to do. I know that Dad was really embarrassed when Watoto set up the Brendan Priest Trust to receive and deploy the money he raised from his second journey, but I know he's really proud of it now. It's just such a shame that he'll never see any of the projects again, or see what you and I are achieving for the people of Gulu."

Paul agreed. "But at least he'll leave behind something which will keep making the Gospel come true. That's what your Dad's about, and not many people can say that they've made as much of a difference as he has."

Ruth sniffed. She knew that Paul was right, but it still seemed so *unfair.*

★ ★ ★

Louisa too was struggling. She knew the answer to her difficulty, but she didn't want to recognise it. The problem she had was trying to motivate herself to continue to administer and plan the strategy for the Cancer Care Trust, when her Dad, after whom it was named, was dying of cancer before her very eyes. Nothing she could do was able to help him, no matter how many millions they'd raised, no matter how many clever doctors were able now to pursue their valuable research.

She knew that she was being unreasonable and ridiculous. It wasn't just about her Dad. It was about trying to make life better for millions of cancer sufferers. And the indications were really promising, if the toxicity results were matched by the scan results. Brendan was really proud of the Trust and what it was achieving. It was just such a shame that it couldn't do anything for him.

Ben perked her up when he came back home from Jact to report that two of the people at the previous Sunday's service had reported that they'd become Christians.

"It was all because we mentioned your Dad. That guy can preach even when he isn't there."

Chapter 66

On the last morning of June, Melanie came round unexpectedly to Beverley Terrace, unaware that Brendan had moved into the hospice, and also unaware that the tumour had got to his vocal cords, and that he'd never speak again. Carol happened to be in – she'd not yet gone into the hospice that day because she needed to do some washing and catch up on her emails.

Melanie was really upset, so Carol sat her down and made her a coffee.

"It's not because all my work has been ruined," Melanie insisted. "I gave him his voice back when he really needed it for his time with you and the wedding and everything – and nothing can take away the satisfaction that that gave me. I'm sad for me, if I'm honest, because I don't like the thought that he's dying and he won't be around for very much longer."

She sobbed at that point, and blew her nose loudly. "I'm sorry," she said, standing up to go. "You don't need this, but I do hope that you both can still come to my wedding."

That jolted her into remembering why she'd called, and she sat down again. "Carol, I'm ever so sorry. You may think it's a bit insensitive of me to talk about my own wedding, but when we were checking the replies we'd had back, we double-checked and discovered that somehow you and Brendan hadn't been sent your invitation to the wedding in the first place, so I came round to pop it in. I won't stop, because you need to go in to see Brendan, but I just wanted you to know that you're definitely invited!"

★ ★ ★

It was the last round of filming for Lilian, split over three or four days. First, there were the all-important scans, with Lilian taking them through the process – not that any of them were there for the first time. It was being filmed for the sake of the viewers, because it was all new to most of them. The thinking was that the more familiar everybody was with medical procedures and places, the less mystery and the less fear might ensue. That was the theory anyway.

Lilian reckoned that most British people got their expectations of hospitals from watching Casualty on the telly, where many more people died, were attacked, poisoned, blown up, treated shabbily, (mis)treated by charlatan doctors or swept up in disasters than ever happened in real life. The problem often was that people expected hospital to be more exciting than it actually was, and felt let down that it wasn't like Holby City.

The scans were not very exciting, except that it was the first sight the viewers had of Alan's cross-stitched torso. It made him look even sicker than ever, and he'd lost an awful lot of weight and seemed very frail. The skin graft on his lip hadn't taken properly, and there was some infection round his chin which looked particularly gruesome. He had to be assisted up onto the bed of the scanner, and groaned as he laid out flat, as if his body was protesting at being put through yet more punishment. His breathing was ragged, and his concave chest seemed to shudder before each breath.

In sharp contrast, the other three – Darren, Dawn and Sharon – breezed in and out like it was a routine check-up at the dentists.

"See you in six months," was what the technician said to those three – but kept significantly quiet when parting company with Alan. It might have been Alan's record of rudeness and unpleasantness – or it might have been out of an awareness that his condition was so serious.

★ ★ ★

Carol sorted herself out and packed a bag for the hospice. She missed not being with Brendan, but knew that he was in the best place, really. It had been a blow when the doctor initiated the move to Marie Curie, but she knew that it would help her and the girls as well as Brendan. It was one layer of protective distance away from the foreboding reality of death, taking its presence out of Beverley Terrace, helping them to cope when the inevitable eventually happened.

She popped the wedding invitation from Melanie into the bag. It would give her something to talk about with Brendan, even if he couldn't join in the conversation.

★ ★ ★

The penny dropped for Brendan when he read the wedding invitation. He'd not really paid much attention to the publicity surrounding the "See Esther" shows about the clinical trials, and hadn't followed up on the little detail which Melanie had mentioned several weeks ago. But the invitation made it all suddenly fall into place.

George and Doreen Hopkinson request the pleasure
of your company at the marriage of their daughter
Melanie Alice

to Mr. Alan Smoulders

at North Shields Registry Office

on Saturday 13th July 2013 at 10.30am

and afterwards at the Park Hotel, Tynemouth.

49 Astley Gardens
Seaton Sluice
NE26 4JN
RSVP

That's who Melanie's fiancé had reminded Brendan of – Alan Smoulders, the Church Steward at Jact who'd made life so difficult for Brendan during his ministry there, always opposing any changes and wanting everything to stay as it was. Fancy that... This must be his son.

Brendan smiled as he put together all the pieces: Melanie's comments that Alan Junior hadn't got on with his Dad and that he'd been in the Army; a vague memory that one of the clinical trials patients came from Jact but that everybody disliked him on the programmes because of his surliness. It all suddenly made sense...

Alan's Story: November 6th 2009

It was the worst day of Alan's life, he thought, as he lay in his bed at 11am on that overcast Friday. The weather matched his mood. What was there to get up for?

He'd finally retired from the Civil Service a few years ago, and realised that he had no real interests. His job had been a way of hiding this unpalatable truth from him and everyone else, and he'd found it really difficult to fill his days. Church, of course had been a lifeline, and he'd done more and more down there. Pauline had initially argued that he should spend more time with her, but then she realised that it was actually better all round if he disappeared off to the church, as he was so miserable and grumpy sitting at home making the place look untidy.

But now he'd been forced out at Jact Methodist Church. What would he do now?

It was all Brendan Priest's fault. He'd let it be known that he was fed up of Jact and wanted to go off travelling round the world. It was all right for some. But before he went, Brendan had duped the General Church Meeting into agreeing to doing away with the pews and installing chairs. Thankfully he and Sarah had been able to veto that by arguing over the summer that it wasn't the GCM's role to make such decisions, so nothing had got done and Brendan had left. The trouble was that he'd left Jact in the lurch, and they hadn't been able to find a proper Minister to replace him. The Circuit had pulled a fast one and installed a Cuban Minister who'd quickly wrecked everything.

First of all, this Dago Minister, or whatever he was called[85], wanted his family to run things at Jact. His wife and his many children all seemed to take over. Mostly, this was fine, but then they started running different activities and changing the ethos of the church, ignoring Jact's traditions.

---

[85] The story of Brendan's departure from Jact, and of Caridad Diego and his family, is told in "Thule for Christ's Sake". Alan continually calls them the Dagos, initially to the hilarity but then the embarrassment of the people of Jact. It is never clear whether Alan deliberately realises that he's got their name wrong and the offensiveness of the name he uses, and doesn't care – or whether it is a genuine mistake...

Dago had immediately made it clear that he wanted everyone to come to a daily early-morning prayer meeting. Well, stuff that for a game of soldiers, some people had jobs to do – but then Alan remembered that he didn't have that excuse any more. He still didn't go.

Then Dago had the cheek to rebuke him and Sarah for not running the church properly, for not coming to the prayer meetings, and set up a Church Council to ditch the pews. He'd gone about it completely unconstitutionally, but had deflected his and Sarah's attention by the devious trick of praying over them for twenty minutes till they were too bamboozled to know what was happening[86]. It was like hypnotism, and there was probably a rule against it somewhere, but Alan didn't seem to be functioning properly. Sarah had been hypnotised even worse than he had, and seemed to be in a daze for weeks. She wasn't herself at all.

The wretched man then calmly announced that the pews were going to be burnt on a public bonfire! How appalling was that! He'd spent all the church's money on fancy chairs, got his family and others to pull the pews out of church and stack them up on a bonfire, to be lit as part of the celebrations on Bonfire Night.

That was the last straw. The silly man was ruining everything, and Alan had gone down early to take the pews off the bonfire out of respect for those who'd installed the pews over 80 years ago – and those whose worship had come from those same pews over those 80 years. But Dago had tried to stop him and then got into a fight with him[87], calling on his heavies to throw Alan out! Him, thrown out of his own church – just for trying to bring a bit of respect back into things!

It was shameful. What would he do now?

And it was at that precise moment that he winced. He'd suddenly got a burning pain on his back. He jumped up to have a look at his back

---

[86] Caridad had laid hands on the two of them and prayed in tongues. It was a hugely important moment for Sarah, who subsequently entered into a new and vibrant spiritual experience of God's presence and love.

[87] The story is told from Alan's point of view. "Thule for Christ's Sake" tells it rather differently. Alan was the one who got violent when Caridad intervened to stop him from getting hurt pulling the pews down on himself. It was Alan who hit Caridad, and no-one threw him out. He was restrained from hitting Caridad, and dragged away when he wanted to continue the fight. Alan then left of his own accord. One of the sad truths about Alan is his lack of self-awareness, and his inability to see anything from anyone else's viewpoint.

in the mirror. There was a big volcano of a zit in the middle of his back that he'd never noticed before, and it was that that seemed to be the source of his discomfort.

July 2013

Chapter 68

In her many years as a nurse, Lilian had sat in on all kinds of conversations in which doctors had to impart bad news. Most were useless at it – either impersonal, avoiding eye contact and retreating into medical jargon, or alternatively beating about the bush, using imprecise language that caused confusion, or getting emotionally involved. She wasn't sure that she'd developed the art any better, but she'd certainly had lots of experience. She was surprised, therefore, that she found herself nervous about going in with the patients to get their scan results. As a nurse, she'd always found it relatively easy to have a professional detachment, but as the TV presenter/ interviewer she'd got involved with them and couldn't step back from the importance of this next moment.

Alan went first, accompanied by Pauline, his wife.

"Ah yes, Mr. Smoulders, said the oncologist, nervous himself, for he'd never appeared on television before. "How are you today?"

It was a silly question, really, given that the man in front of him looked like a cross between a human jigsaw, an Auschwitz survivor and a cadaver after a post-mortem.

Alan gave a little, painful cough. "I'm fine, can't you see?" he growled.

"Er, right," said the oncologist, aware that he hadn't started too well. "OK. I can now reveal that all our Newcastle patients were on the single agent chemo, and got the same dose of radiation, but you were chosen randomly to have a middle dose of 400 mg of the DMC drug. I'm afraid to say, though, that the treatment has not, in your case, been able to stabilise or reduce the size of the tumour, which has in fact extended into your lymphatic system and seems to have spread nodules in most of the vital organs. I'm very sorry, but there's nothing more that we can do."

Pauline burst into tears. Alan clutched his fists as if by doing so he was holding onto life itself.

But the oncologist hadn't finished.

"I'm afraid there's worse news. The scans reveal that there's an enlarged tumour in your pancreas which could bring things to a head much more quickly, I'm afraid. You've obviously lost a lot of weight, which is probably due to your pancreas malfunctioning. It is the pancreas which is normally responsible for helping you to digest food, by releasing enzymes into your intestines. But if your pancreas is unable to release these enzymes because of the tumour, then your body will find it harder to digest food, particularly high-fat foods, and you'll become seriously malnourished. I suspect that this is what's happening with you. Have you got pain in your tummy which spreads to your back, especially when you're lying down or eating?"

Alan nodded. Pauline sniffed.

"Then it makes it even more probable that it's the pancreas which is the most serious problem. Unfortunately this cancer is notoriously quick, so I recommend that you prepare for going into a hospice where your pain management can be properly managed and the best palliative care be given. And, once again, I'm very sorry."

Lilian and the film crew accompanied Alan and Pauline out of the office.

"That's that, then," said Alan, to Lilian and the worldwide audience. "How lovely that he knows so much about it now. Just a crying shame that he can do bugger all about it."

★ ★ ★

With the other three, however, the news was much better. All three were told that their tumours had shrunk considerably. Darren had been on the maximum dosage and his tumour had reduced by 75%, but so had Sharon's and her dosage was 500mg. Dawn had a 60% reduction but had been on the lowest dosage, 200mg. The results were similar in four of the five other patients on the Newcastle trials, indicating that the optimum dosage was 500mg. All of these seven patients would now be given DMC orally at that dosage twice-daily for a year, but there would be no further radiotherapy. The other patient, unfortunately, had had a bad stroke as a result of a probably-unrelated brain haemorrhage, and the DMC had been withdrawn.

Lilian felt like the junior reporter who'd been sent round to interview students opening their A Level results, but it was great to see the faces of Darren, Sharon and Dawn as they received their news, and to follow them up the next day and re-create the moment when they told their families. Darren's Mum cried. Dawn's colleagues, now aware of her illness, presented her with a big cake and flowers. Sharon's daughters weren't there. They were off to Ibiza again with the bairns.

★ ★ ★

A few days later, Louisa met with Dr. Aggarwal for further analysis of the Newcastle results.

"We've established that the DMC optimum dosage is 500mg, and that early indications from across the other four centres running with the same single-agent regimen concur with this judgement. The shrinking of tumours is more pronounced in Newcastle than the other four, but only marginally. In all five centres the average shrinkage is 40 – 50%. There are two instances of the tumour disappearing altogether. It really has been a very successful outcome. DMC seems to be a very powerful drug against SCCA in this particular combination of chemoradiotherapy. But the results elsewhere are even more exciting." He paused, milking the announcement he was about to make.

"Go on," said Louisa, laughing. "Don't keep me in suspense."

"OK, here we go. The initial analysis from the five centres offering DMC with the combined cisplatin and paclitaxel regimen had really good results too, similar to your own. The control group, of DMC plus fluorouracil and hydroxyurea – with no cisplatin at all, had results that were no different from what we'd expect at the moment with cisplatin, including some high toxic side-effects. But the fourth regimen, which was DMC plus the combined cisplatin with fluorouracil has produced some remarkable results.

"This is the group which had no toxicity whatsoever, even with high-risk patients with poor kidney function. But the tumour shrinkage rate has been averaging at between 80 and 95%. And this has been evident in every one of the five centres running with that particular combination. It's pretty remarkable, to say the least! The dosage variation doesn't seem to be significant, suggesting that the minimum dosage of 200mg DMC is just as effective as the more expensive 600 mg dosage."

"Wow!" whispered Louisa. "That *is* remarkable! So what happens now?"

"I don't know," said Dr. Aggarwal. "That's up to the managers of the trials and the Medical Research Council. But I would have thought that they'll monitor the patients' outcomes at six-monthly intervals, and if it were down to me I'd authorise further biological analysis and clinical trials of the DMC-cisplatin-fluorouracil combination."

Louisa nodded. That's what she was thinking too. It was a very promising start.

★ ★ ★

Brendan was getting weaker. He could feel it. Carol could see it, even though she was there all the time. The girls could see it even more clearly, for they only came in every other day and the deterioration was more obvious. He was now stick-thin, still being pumped with the disgusting Jevity, but it was just passing straight through.

The pain was still there, but the staff had managed to dull it considerably. The flip-side of that, though, was that he was fuzzy-minded and constantly tired. Better that than the pain, though.

Chapter 69

On the morning of May 10th, the manager came in and told Brendan and Carol that she needed to put "another gentleman" into the other bed in the room, and hoped that they wouldn't mind. They looked at each other, smiled and shook their heads. They'd had what amounted to a private room for the last three weeks, so they couldn't really complain.

And in came Alan.

He was pushed along in a wheelchair, and grimaced when he saw Brendan in the chair at the opposite end of the room. It could have been a smile – with Alan's patched-up face and lack of a bottom lip it was hard to tell. "Well, that's all I need," he growled.

The manager stopped instantly. "Do you two know each other?" she asked. "Is there a problem?"

Brendan shrugged and shook his head.

Alan sat slumped in his wheelchair, but then heaved himself up and said, "He used to be my Minister."

"Is that good or bad?" asked the manager.

Alan cracked his grimace/smile once again. "At least it'll give me someone to argue with," he said.

The manager took that as a thumbs-up and wheeled him over to his bed. "Now you stay there for a moment while I go back up to Reception and help your wife fill out the paperwork. OK?"

Carol was looking on bemusedly, glancing at Brendan's face and seeing his amusement. She eventually cottoned on as to who this new roommate was.

"Are you the guy whose son's marrying Melanie?" she asked.

Alan looked up, surprised. "Yes, that's right. On Saturday, in fact."

He paused. "If you know that, you probably know that I don't get on with my son that well. But I *was* going to go to the wedding. They did invite me. But I won't be able to go now..."

"Surely they can take you just for the morning, can't they?"

"Maybe," said Alan. "But I don't want to spoil it for them, so I'm going to stay here. I've made my decision. It's best for everyone."

"What a shame," said Carol. "If it were my son..." Then she stopped, and gulped hard.

Alan hadn't noticed. "At least it's given my wife something to smile about," he continued.

Brendan grabbed Carol's hand and squeezed it, sympathetically. Then he scribbled a note on his pad and handed it to her, gesturing for her to give it to Alan. It read, "Bet you a bunch of grapes that I can make you smile."

Alan took it, read it, and sneered. "Bet you can't. You couldn't make me smile for ten years when you were my Minister, so how are you going to do it now?"

Brendan scribbled away on his pad for a couple of minutes or more, then handed the pad to Carol. She took it over without reading it.

Alan took it, read it – and laughed.

"Very good, Brendan," he said. "You win. That's the second time you've got the better of me now." He showed Carol what was written on the pad.

"Robin Hood lay dying, and all the faithful gathered round. With his weak and fading breath, Robin asked Marion to bring him the best arrow from the quiver beside his bed, and then asked Little John to bring him his bow. He put the arrow to the bow and aimed through the open window into the generous green back-drop of Sherwood Forest beyond, which he loved so much. He asked Friar Tuck, "Promise me that wherever the arrow falls, there you will bury me." And when Tuck had promised, Robin demanded the same of the others. Then with his last strength he drew on the bow and let the arrow fly. And then he died, smiling. And next day, they did as they had promised, and buried Robin Hood on top of his wardrobe."

Carol smiled too. To be able to keep cracking jokes in a hospice showed what an amazing husband she had. She turned to Alan.

"What did you mean when you said it was the second time Brendan had got the better of you?"

"Oh yes, I forgot. You're new, aren't you? Well, all through your husband's ministry I managed to suppress his daft ideas until just before he left, when he tricked the church into deciding to get rid of the pews and buy a load of chairs. Total waste of money, and the place went downhill quickly after that."

Carol decided that there was no point arguing on Brendan's behalf. Did it matter?

Brendan was smiling, as he listened. He scribbled a short note on his pad.

Alan read the message quickly when Carol carried it over, and smiled/grimaced.

"Nah," he said. "Probably not."

Carol looked on the pad. She read what Brendan had written: "It doesn't seem very important now, does it?"

Alan's wife, Pauline, came bustling in at that point. "Sorry I'm a bit late. I had to fill in a load of papers upstairs at Reception. Oh, hello, Brendan..." she said, noticing for the first time with whom her husband was sharing the room.

Then she thought about it. "Er, is everything OK?"

"Yes," snapped Alan. "We're getting on fine. Now, have you got all my stuff from the car..."

★ ★ ★

Brendan and Carol were thrilled to see Melanie enter the room with her fiancé Alan the following day.

"We heard from Pauline that you two were roommates. How nice that you can reminisce with each other."

She broke off, realising that she'd probably jumped to a conclusion that might not be accurate. "I mean, you've got a lot to talk about. Oh, sorry, Brendan... I forgot..."

She turned bright red, having remembered that Brendan couldn't talk, then burst into tears and rushed out of the room. Alan went with her, so did Carol.

Alan (Senior) piped up. "It must be hard for them, having to come in to visit the dying. At least they've got a whole day tomorrow to recover from seeing our ugly faces – before their happy day."

Brendan sat there, mute and without his messenger. He still wrote the note though: "Maybe it's not just a matter of duty, but have you ever considered the possibility that they might care, might realise that neither of us can be at their wedding but they still want us to be included. Do you ever think of anybody but yourself?"

When Carol and the two visitors came back, Brendan shoved the pad into her hand and made it clear that she should give it to Alan immediately.

Melanie was talking. "I'm so sorry, Brendan. I just didn't think, as usual. I didn't mean to upset you."

She paused, and Brendan smiled and held his hands up in a greeting, asking for a hug. All was well.

Alan was quiet.

"Hello, Dad. How are you doing?" asked Alan (Junior), suddenly.

All eyes turned to the two of them.

"Not so good, son. But better for seeing you. Thanks for coming in to see me."

★ ★ ★

Alan and Melanie didn't stop long.

"We've got to pick up the favours from a shop in Eldon Square," Melanie explained.

It meant nothing to Brendan. What were favours? But they only left after sharing a lot of hugs, and both men (and Carol) wishing them a very happy day on Saturday.

Carol, Brendan and Alan were just settling again, when Melanie hurtled back into the room. "I'd forget my head if it wasn't screwed on," she said, as she handed a small present over to Brendan. "I got this for you, to cheer you up a bit on Saturday even though you can't come to the wedding." With that, she gave Brendan another kiss, and rushed off.

Brendan fumbled with the paper, so Carol helped him unwrap it. Brendan looked at it a long time before passing it to Carol.

It was a CD: "Goin' Home" – by Albert Ayler.

Brendan scribbled on his pad: "It's his birthday on Saturday." When Carol looked puzzled, he pointed at the picture of Albert on the front of the CD. He wrote another sentence, then fell back in his chair, exhausted.

Carol read "It'll be a happy, happy day", and smiled. She held Brendan's hand, but he'd already fallen asleep, smiling.

Chapter 70

On Saturday July 13th, Louisa and Ruth toyed with the idea of going to Melanie's wedding to represent their Dad, but decided that they'd go in and spend the morning with him and Carol instead. Paul had gone back to Uganda a few days before. Ben got the job of looking after Matthew, and was planning to take him onto the beach and introduce him to the ancient art of building sandcastles.

In the hospice, Alan and Brendan watched the clock tick round. At 10.15am, the three visitors arrived in Ruth's car, embraced Brendan, and settled into their chairs, having said Hello to Alan.

Ruth said, "I've brought a candle, Dad – hope that's OK. I thought we could light it at 10.30 and pray for Melanie and Alan." Brendan nodded his approval.

Carol suddenly remembered the Albert Ayler CD and fussed around the corridors trying to locate a CD player. They lit the candle while she was gone.

Brendan scribbled a message on his pad, then passed it to Louisa, nodding in Alan's direction. She understood what he was asking, and took the note across to Alan. She looked at the note, thinking that her Dad's writing was more spidery and jerky than ever.

Alan took it with a smirk, or what passed for it when you only had half your face left. Louisa didn't notice any difference. He read: "Luke 23: 32-43."

"Silly bugger thinks I know the Bible off by heart," he said. "Can someone get me a Bible and tell me what it says?"

Louisa got the Gideon Bible from the locker, and read, out loud: "Two other men, both criminals, were also led out with Jesus to be executed..." She continued the account of the thief who repented, right down to Jesus' answer: "Today you will be with me in paradise."

Alan squirmed. "I don't believe it! Now the pompous fool's making himself out to be the Messiah!"

Louisa furrowed her brow. That wasn't very nice, or very

appropriate, but Carol at that point rushed back in, CD player in hand.

"I'll just get it set up over here," she declared.

Brendan was busy writing another note, as the light piano introduction to the first track tinkled into the room.

Brendan finished the note, quivering a little as something pulsed inside him, and gestured for Carol to take it across to Alan, who opened it, and read: "Oh no I'm not. I'm on one cross, you're on another, and He's on the big one in the middle of us. I'm the thief who asks for forgiveness – and you can do the same. It's up to you, as always…"

Then he sat back, exhausted, holding Carol's hand, just as the wonderful, mellow tenor sax burst in with the melody. Brendan closed his eyes, and instantly saw the garden, and the gate. He was right next to the gate, and inside was something he couldn't see because of its brightness, but he wasn't frightened.

In fact, he stepped straight through the gate.

"It's true!" were his final, earthly thoughts. He was goin' home.